A *Christmas* To Remember

KANDY SHEPHERD **CARA COLTER** **MICHELE RENAE**

MILLS & BOON

Published by
Mills & Boon
An imprint of Harlequin Enterprises (Australia) Pty Limited (ABN 47 001 180 918), a subsidiary of HarperCollins Publishers Australia Pty Limited (ABN 36 009 913 517)
Level 19, 201 Elizabeth Street
SYDNEY NSW 2000
AUSTRALIA

MIX
Paper | Supporting responsible forestry
FSC
www.fsc.org   FSC® C001695

Printed and bound in Australia by McPherson's Printing Group

CONTENTS

The Tycoon's Christmas Dating Deal

Kandy Shepherd

Kandy Shepherd swapped a career as a magazine editor for a life writing romance. She lives on a small farm in the Blue Mountains near Sydney, Australia, with her husband, daughter and lots of pets. She believes in love at first sight and real-life romance—they worked for her! Kandy loves to hear from her readers. Visit her at kandyshepherd.com.

Visit the Author Profile page
at millsandboon.com.au for more titles.

Dear Reader,

Do you believe in love at first sight? Does it seem possible? I can vouch for love at first sight. I remember the very first time I met my husband. A friend introduced us, and it was instant attraction. Three days later we decided to spend our lives together. Ten months later we married. We recently celebrated our thirty-fifth anniversary. Love at first sight worked!

What about Marissa and Oliver, the heroine and hero of *The Tycoon's Christmas Dating Deal*? There's instant, powerful attraction between the lovely event planner and the movie-star handsome hotel tycoon. Both have heartbreak in their pasts, and I loved bringing these wonderful people together. But there are complications...not the least of which is the secret Marissa is keeping from Oliver.

The Tycoon's Christmas Dating Deal is a Christmas story set in a fabulous country house hotel—Oliver's ancestral home. Marissa's brief is to create the best Christmas celebrations ever at Longfield Manor. Think luxury, beautiful rooms, gorgeous gardens, Christmas trees and snow—lots of glorious snow.

I hope you enjoy following Marissa and Oliver's journey to a once-in-a-lifetime forever love.

Warm regards,

Kandy

To my longtime friend and fellow author
Cathleen Ross, for being my first reader.
Thank you!

Praise for
Kandy Shepherd

CHAPTER ONE

Marissa Gracey hated Christmas. As she strode along Kensington High Street in London, two weeks before December the twenty-fifth, she felt assaulted by Christmas cheer. Everything that could possibly be festooned with lights twinkled garishly in the evening gloom—trees, lampposts, storefronts, even a bus stop shelter, which should surely be illegal. Alcoves and shop windows were stuffed with overdecorated Christmas trees. Clashing Christmas carols, loud and shmaltzy, blared out from doorways.

Fa-la-la-la-la, la-la-la-la, indeed, she thought with a deep scowl.

Every step she took she was exhorted to feel merry, happy and jolly. But she didn't feel any of that. Not even a glimmering of merriment. Not anymore.

Marissa knew that behind her back she was called a Scrooge and a Grinch. That hurt. But she couldn't share the details of why she no longer celebrated the season. Because she couldn't bear to be reminded of the heartbreak and pain. Bad things had happened to her at Christmas. The car crash five years ago that had killed her parents. Her brother's departure to the other side of the world. The out-of-the-blue firing from her dream job on Christmas Eve. And the most recent—the betrayal of her boyfriend, whom she'd last year caught kissing another woman under the mistletoe. Disasters that had rocked her world at Christmastime. She'd begun to believe she was jinxed. If she allowed herself to enjoy Christmas, who knew what other horrible thing might happen?

There was excited chatter among her fellow pedestrians when a scattering of fat snowflakes drifted down from the sky. She looked up but resisted the temptation to try to catch a snowflake on her tongue, like she'd done when she was a child. Back then, Christmas had seemed magical.

A man started to sing, very off-key, that he was dreaming of a white Christmas.

Huh, Marissa thought, *a sleety, slippery Christmas more likely.*

London rarely had decent snow in December. Thankfully, she would be out of here in five days, flying to a small island off the east coast of Bali, where Christmas wasn't part of the culture. By the time she got back, the decorations and all the painful reminders they brought with them would be taken down.

She detoured into the supermarket—more detestable carols were piped through the store—in search of a ready meal for her dinner. She lived alone in her flat in West Kensington and often couldn't be bothered to cook for herself. She studiously avoided the displays of mince pies. Her father had loved the small, sweet, spiced fruit pastries, traditionally only available at Christmastime. His Christmas Eve ritual had been to eat an entire packet of six mince pies—with lashings of custard and ice cream—in one sitting, egged on by a laughing Marissa and her brother while her mother pretended to be shocked. Until that Christmas Eve five years ago when the mince pies had remained uneaten in the kitchen while her dad lay still on a hospital bed, attached to tubes and monitors that hadn't saved his life. It still hurt to see mince pies and remember his joy in them.

When her friend Caity Johnston called on her mobile phone, Marissa had to swallow hard against the lump of remembered grief that threatened to choke her.

'Everything okay?' she asked, when she was in control of her voice. Caity was expecting twins, due in the middle of January.

'Actually, no,' Caity said. Her friend's voice sounded anxious, frayed at the edges.

Terror for her friend shot through Marissa. 'The babies?'

'Okay.'

Marissa breathed a sigh of relief.

'But I have to go to hospital and stay in bed until the due date. Or whenever the consultant decides it's time for the babies to be born.' Caity's voice rose.

'Oh, Caity. What can I do to help?'

'Could you... Could you get over here now?'

'On my way,' Marissa said as she hailed a black cab.

Mentally, she urged the driver to hurry. It seemed the longest trip ever to the west London suburb of Ealing. She'd normally go by the Underground, it was nearly as fast and a tenth of the cab fare, but there was an edge of fear to Caity's voice that had truly scared Marissa. Two years ago, her friend had miscarried at twenty weeks. Marissa would do anything she could to help her carry her twins to term.

When she arrived at Caity's house twenty minutes later, a terrace in a street of terraces that she and her husband, Tom, had painstakingly remodelled, her friend was waiting for her. Her face was pale, and she was anxiously wringing her hands. Caity was tiny and slight except for her enormous bump. Marissa noticed a bulging overnight bag in the hallway.

She hugged her friend gently. 'What's happened?'

'I'm sure I mentioned before that the twins share the same placenta. That can be dangerous so the doctors want me under observation. My bump and I will be hooked up to monitors for the next few weeks.'

'Oh, no!' Marissa exclaimed, and then immediately backpedalled. She didn't want her alarmed reaction to add further to Caity's obvious fears. 'I mean, that's good they're being vigilant.'

'It's unlikely I'll leave hospital until the babies are born.'

'You'll be in good hands. Do you want me to go with you to the hospital, to get you settled?'

Caity shook her head. 'No. Tom's taken time off work. He's out getting the car from where it's parked. But there is something you could do to help me.'

'Anything,' Marissa said.

She and Caity had started work as interns in a public relations firm back when they'd been fresh out of uni. They'd both specialised in event planning until there was a big downturn in business and they were both let go from the jobs they'd loved—just before Christmas. Caity had bounced back quickly and started her own company, while Marissa freelanced for her and other marketing companies in the city, trying to find the place where she best fit. Now, at age thirty, Marissa wasn't sure about what direction she wanted her career to take. She only knew that she didn't want to tie herself down to the one employer. Not yet. Experience had taught her that it was too dangerous to put her fate in someone else's hands.

'I hate to ask you this, as I know you're not a fan of Christmas…' Caity began, tentatively, not meeting Marissa's eyes.

Marissa's heart sank. Caity was one of the few people who understood her aversion to the festive season. So why was she bringing it up now?

She narrowed her eyes. 'Er, yes?' she said.

Caity's words spilled out. 'There's this Christmas event I've been working on. Longfield Manor is a beautiful country house hotel in Dorset. Family run. Christmas is a huge deal for them. People come from around the country—even the world—year after year to celebrate the holiday season there, and this year is the first time the family has brought in an event planner to organise the festivities. And now, two weeks out from the most important commission of my career, I have to go into hospital.'

To save her babies' lives.

The words were unspoken but Marissa heard them.

'And you want me to step in?' she said, trying to keep the dismay from her voice. 'Caity, you know how I feel—'

'About Christmas? I know. And I wouldn't ask you if I had any choice. The grandson of the hotel owners, Oliver Pierce, is the CEO of The Pierce Group of hotels.'

'The most exclusive, fashionable hotels in London. I know of them.' Although as she'd need to take out a mortgage to buy a cocktail there, Marissa had never been to one.

'I've done some work for him in the past and it went really well, and I *need* to keep The Pierce Group as a client. Oliver Pierce himself asked me to help with the Longfield Manor Christmas. Marissa, this job could change the entire trajectory for my company. It's my big break. I can't risk losing his business.'

'Couldn't someone else—?'

'He's a very discerning man,' Caity said, cutting her off. 'I couldn't trust anyone else but you to take over this particular job.'

'Surely there must be another planner who—?'

'You're the only person who is good enough and I know you would never let me down,' Caity said. 'Or try to steal my client.'

That was Caity all right. A shrewd businesswoman whose boutique event planning business was very successful, yet not established enough to be able to risk losing an important client. Marissa knew how vital the personal relationship between client and planner could be. And satisfied clients led to recommendations and further business. If Caity couldn't trust anyone else but her—her best friend—to run this job, Marissa could put up no further resistance.

'Please,' Caity pleaded. 'I… I'm begging you. You know

how much I want these babies.' Her voice caught. 'And I can't do the job from a hospital bed.'

Marissa took a deep breath. 'Of course not. Nor should you. All your energies should be going to keeping your babies safe and getting ready to welcome them.' She had read up about the risks for identical twins who shared a placenta and knew how dangerous it would be for her best friend not to follow her doctors' advice to the letter.

She had a momentary vision of warm aquamarine waters, golden sands, palm trees—her tropical holiday far, far away from the commercial frenzy of Christmas in London. It had been booked and paid for months ago and she had been eagerly anticipating the escape. But as she focussed on her friend's wan face, the vision faded away. She needed to be here, and she needed to do this for Caity. She only hoped she'd be able to get at least a partial refund.

'Of course I'm happy to do the job for you,' she said. She injected as much enthusiasm as she could into her voice. And was rewarded by the relief in her friend's eyes.

'I knew you wouldn't let me down,' Caity said. She took a deep breath. 'I'll quickly brief you. Longfield Manor is in Dorset, near the coast. Very traditional. Nothing like the ultra-contemporary Pierce Group hotels. It was owned by my client's grandparents. But the grandfather died this year, so Oliver Pierce stepped in to help his grandmother run it. There's a story there but I didn't get a chance to dig into it. You might have more luck. Christmas has always been a big deal, and they want it even bigger and better this year.'

Marissa was determined not to let her friend see how she dreaded the thought of working on Christmas for an entire week. 'Understood,' she said.

'Everything that can be ordered has been ordered. Local staff have been briefed. You'll find all the files waiting in your inbox so you can hit the ground running. I sent them as soon as I knew you were on your way over.'

Marissa smiled. 'You were very sure I'd say yes.'

'I trusted you'd help me,' Caity said simply.

Marissa gently hugged her friend. 'You know you won't have to worry about a thing.'

'I know. I trust you implicitly. But you can get in touch with me any time.'

'I promise I'll try not to bother you.'

It had been heartbreaking when Caity had lost her first baby, and Marissa feared what state her friend might sink into if something were to go wrong with the twins. She had to step up for her. Even though immersing herself in Christmas at some staid country house hotel was the last thing she wanted to do.

At the sound of a key turning in the door, Caity stepped back. 'Here's Tom to take me to hospital.'

Marissa greeted her friend's husband, then picked up her handbag and the shopping bag containing her solitary dinner. 'Go. The sooner you're in that hospital bed, the better.'

'Just one thing before you go. Oliver Pierce is expecting you to stay on site at Longfield Manor for the seven days before Christmas.'

'On site? For a week?'

'It's a hotel. Why would you stay elsewhere?'

Marissa would prefer to keep a distance from a client. But this was Caity's client so she really had no choice. 'Done. Can't say I like it. But done.'

'And…there's one more thing.'

A sneaky smile played around her friend's lips. Marissa knew that smile could spell trouble. 'Yes?' she said warily.

'Oliver Pierce is hot. Really hot. Movie-star hot.' She put up her hand to stop Marissa from protesting. 'I know you're on a break from dating. An overly long break in my opinion. But I respect that. I just thought you should know how gorgeous your new client is. And I believe he's single. Single, sexy and solvent.'

Marissa rolled her eyes. 'No, thank you. I won't ever get mixed up with a client again. Totally not interested. Besides, you know I'm immune to gorgeous men. Next time—if there is ever a next time—I'll be going for ordinary, average and safe.'

Caity laughed. 'I wouldn't call Oliver Pierce safe. Not in a million years would I call him safe.'

Could this be his last Christmas at Longfield Manor? The thought troubled Oliver. If there was one thing he didn't care for, it was uncertainty. And the future of the beautiful old manor house, which had been in his family for five generations, was shrouded in uncertainty.

He stamped his feet against the cold and rubbed his gloved hands together as he observed the familiar front elevation of the house. It was lit by the soft, early-morning sun that shone from a cloudless winter sky. He never tired of admiring the building that dated back to the sixteen hundreds, its ancient walls made of the local limestone, the peaked roofs and mullioned windows, the perfection of its proportions. The surrounding gardens were stark in their winter beauty, the only splashes of colour coming from large urns overflowing with lush purple pansies, the pride and joy of his grandmother.

Oliver hadn't lived there for years, but he considered Longfield Manor his home; his grandparents, Charles and Edith, were more his parents than his parents ever had been. He had spent so much of his childhood here, an only child caught in the to-and-fro that had been his parents' disastrous marriage. And it was the refuge to which he'd fled after his mother had abandoned him when he was fifteen years old. If he honoured his late grandfather's dying wish, he would have to put Longfield Manor on the market. And there lay the uncertainty.

Just days before he took his last laboured breath at the age of eighty-seven, his grandfather had taken Oliver aside for a private, heartbreaking conversation. His grandpa had known he was dying and he'd told Oliver he feared for his beloved wife, five years his junior at eighty-two. He had shared his concern that Edith could be displaying signs of dementia. It seemed she'd had memory lapses, misplaced things, sometimes seemed confused about long-standing everyday routines, and her devoted husband was worried how she would cope after he'd gone.

It had been gut wrenching for Oliver to listen to that, but he'd owed it to the grandfather he'd adored not to show his own anguish. Grandpa had also worried that with the pending retirement of a longtime trusted manager, overseeing the running of the hotel would be too much for Edith. He'd believed the best option would be to sell, then find Edith a home, perhaps in London so she could be closer to Oliver, somewhere she could easily access the round-the-clock care she might soon need.

Oliver had been shocked, not just by the news about Granny, but also because he had never imagined Longfield Manor would be sold. He had long expected that it would pass down to him—his mother had been disinherited—and in due course to his children. Not that so far, at the age of thirty-two, he had ever met a woman who inspired thoughts of marriage and parenthood. He made very sure his girlfriends knew the score—he wasn't ready to commit.

He had immediately reassured his grandfather he would take over the hotel alongside his grandmother. Hotels were his business. He had got his love of hospitality from growing up here, absorbing what worked and what didn't from the way his grandparents ran the place. Longfield Manor was a successful and profitable business, as well as a cherished private home.

But his grandfather had asked him to think long and hard before declaring an intention to add Longfield Manor to his portfolio. Not to make that offer out of sentimentality or obligation. Charles hadn't wanted the hotel to become a burden on his grandson. Oliver's life was in the city with his ultra-contemporary boutique hotels. And didn't he want to expand into New York? Where did a traditional hotel in the country fit into that plan? A hotel that needed hands-on management with buildings that required ongoing repair.

Oliver had acknowledged all that, and yet he fought against

the idea of losing Longfield Manor. His grandfather had repeatedly asked him to agree to selling the hotel after he died. Oliver prided himself on being a hard-headed negotiator yet finally, to put Grandpa's mind at ease, he had acquiesced and said he would 'look into' selling. Now Oliver felt duty bound to honour that deathbed promise. Even if he'd had his fingers crossed behind his back at the time.

Since Grandpa's passing in August, Oliver had observed some out-of-character behaviour from his grandmother but nothing overly untoward. Many of those quirks could be, he thought, attributed to her intense grief at losing her husband of so many years. Granny was grieving, as was he, although he knew he had to keep it together for her sake. The only thing that sparked her back into her old self was discussing plans for Christmas.

His grandparents had put their hearts and souls into Christmas every year. Guests came from around the country—even the world—to share in the hotel's fabled Christmas celebrations. And Oliver was determined their first Christmas without Charles would be extra special so that his absence hopefully wouldn't be felt quite so keenly.

To that end, he had engaged an event planner with whom he had worked very successfully at his London hotels. Caity Johnston was a small, blonde dynamo who was totally on his wavelength. She had reacted to the brief on the Longfield Manor Christmas with enthusiasm, and he had been pleased she had accepted the job. However, complications with her pregnancy meant Caity had had to be hospitalised. 'Never fear,' Caity had rushed to reassure him. She had secured someone wonderful to take over from her. Marissa Gracey was the absolute best, she'd assured him.

There had been no opportunity to interview Marissa Gracey. He'd had to accept her sight unseen—and that didn't sit well with Oliver. Marissa Gracey had become yet another uncertainty. He hoped Caity hadn't overdone the enthusiasm for her

substitute. This Christmas was important. A successful celebration would not only lift his granny's spirits, it would also reassure the guests that the hotel could go on successfully without
Charles. In his experience, fans of a hotel liked things to stay
the same. He needed to prove to both himself and others that
the future of Longfield Manor would be safe in his hands—
one way or another.

But planning a traditional Christmas celebration on a grand
scale was outside his area of expertise. He needed help. There
were seven days to Christmas and as the celebrations went
into full swing on Christmas Eve, the countdown was on. He
glanced at his watch. Marissa Gracey was due to arrive in half
an hour for a midmorning start. He hoped her work would be
up to scratch.

Marissa swung her vintage Citroen van through the ornate
iron gates that were set between high stone walls and led up to
a sweeping gravel driveway lined with well-kept gardens. Even
in winter the grounds of the hotel showed a certain stark grandeur. If she was here for anything other than Christmas, she'd
be feeling stirrings of excitement.

Marissa had looked up the hotel's impressive website and
read with interest the high-rating reviews on impartial travel
sites. The reviews from guests had raved about the beauty of
the buildings, the comfort of the rooms, the excellence of the
food. It was clear that the hotel's guests came back again and
again and one regular had described it as a 'home away from
home—a very posh home, that is.'

If only she were coming here to work in summer. Or autumn.
Really anytime but Christmas. The thought of the extravaganza
to come made her feel queasy, but for Caity's sake she had to
overcome her aversion to the job. She could do this. The back
of her van was filled with bespoke Christmas ornaments from
a famous London designer and all other manner of expensive
and stylish decorations that would give an 'old with a new twist'
feel to the festive decorations here. Apparently, the grandson

of the family, Oliver Pierce, wanted to put his own stamp on the family traditions. She wondered why he would mess with a formula that clearly worked.

As the house came into view, Marissa caught her breath. It was stately and magnificent, yet not so large as to dominate the landscape. Framed by two enormous winter-bare oak trees, the hotel sat nestled into the landscape like it belonged—as it had been standing in that very spot for hundreds of years.

She thought of Oliver Pierce with a stab of...not envy—not exactly—more like curiosity, at how it must feel to be born to a place like this. To take the immense wealth that this house and the grounds that surrounded it stood for, as his due. She had grown up in a middle-class family, comfortable but not wealthy. This was a different realm altogether. And that, she had realised from reading the reviews of the hotel, was its charm. A place like this gave the guests the chance to imagine for the length of their stay that they were taking part in an exclusive house party. That was the key to Christmas at Longfield Manor, to create welcoming, intimate but extravagant festivities. A posh home away from home, where the Christmas holiday was utterly splendid and utterly without worry or stress or hours in the kitchen.

She confidently swung the van—its quirky exterior finished in a rich brown and chrome as befit its former life as a coffee van—into the circular drive that led up to the house. The discreet signage at the entrance of the hotel maintained the illusion of arriving at your own house in the country. Marissa knew there was parking around the back, but she'd been asked to check in with reception when she arrived, so she pulled the van into the closest space out front.

Once inside, she caught her breath at the splendour of the entrance hall. Ornate high ceilings, wood-panelled walls, a magnificent staircase, wooden floors laid in a centuries-old herringbone pattern, paintings in heavy gilded frames. A large arrangement of artistically styled winter-bare stems and brightly coloured berries sat in a marble urn on a tall plinth. It was all perfect, but not too perfect, which befit a house of such venerable years. She'd read that the house had been sympathetically remodelled to become a hotel, but on first glance it still retained both the grandeur and the intimacy of a private home to the privileged.

Inside, she was greeted by a charming young woman behind the reception desk. Marissa put down her small suitcase and wondered when she'd meet with the client, Oliver Pierce. She didn't have to wonder for long.

Almost immediately, the grandson of the house strode into the foyer. Suddenly, the room seemed smaller, as if he took up more space than one man should. He was taller than she'd thought he'd be, and broad shouldered in an immaculately cut dark suit. Black hair framed a handsome—a very handsome—face. Caity was right. He was hot. So hot Marissa could not help but stare. And then, when he got closer, stare some more.

'Marissa Gracey?' he said in a deep, well-spoken voice that managed to be just as attractive as his looks. 'Oliver Pierce.'

All Marissa could do was nod before he continued.

'You're right on time. That's good.'

It was as well he hadn't expected a reply because she was suddenly without a voice. She felt the colour flush hot on her cheeks then rush back to pale as a realisation struck her.

She knew this man.

Only he'd called himself Oliver Hughes back then. Back when they'd both been teenagers and she'd thought him the most insufferable, arrogant, rude person she had ever met. When he offered his hand for her to shake, she didn't know what to do.

CHAPTER TWO

MARISSA'S THOUGHTS FLASHED back to when she'd been fourteen years old and deeply, desperately and very secretly in love with a sixteen-year-old boy she'd known as Oliver Hughes.

This couldn't be the same guy.

It just couldn't be.

Yet, he looked like him, spoke like him. Did he have a twin? If so, wouldn't they have the same surname? And why the same first name?

Oliver Hughes had been the friend of her schoolfriend Samantha's brother, Toby. Toby had been at boarding school with Oliver and brought him home to stay for a midterm break. Marissa had immediately crushed on tall, quietly spoken Oliver like only a totally inexperienced girl could. She'd jumped at any chance she could to be at Samantha's house.

But that crush had come crashing down the day she'd overheard Toby and Oliver discussing her and Samantha. Toby had asked Oliver what he thought of Sam's friend Marissa. Oliver had made a rude comment about Marissa's appearance, then both boys had sniggered in a mean, hurtful and entitled way. Marissa had been shocked, horrified and deeply hurt. It had been a first lesson painfully learned—men weren't always what they appeared to be.

Now she realised she couldn't hesitate any longer before taking Oliver Pierce's hand in a short, businesslike grasp. She'd never got even handshake-close to Oliver Hughes. It had been purely a crush from a distance. She looked up at Oliver Pierce and caught her breath. The black hair. The green eyes. His height. It had to be the same guy. Super-attractive as a teenager, devastatingly handsome as an adult. Why hadn't she researched him when she'd agreed to take on this job? She'd only looked up Longfield Manor and had trusted Caity's notes for the details of the Christmas plans.

I'm immune to gorgeous men, she'd boasted to her best friend.

She'd had no interest whatsoever in the hotness levels of her client.

'Welcome,' he said. 'Thank you for taking Caity's place.'

His voice was deep and resonant. More mature than at age sixteen, but somehow it sounded the same to her. Oliver Hughes had had the beginnings of a man's voice even then. *The fantasies she had had over him.* She almost gasped at the memory of the feelings he had aroused in her.

'I'm…er…glad I was able to help out, Mr Pierce,' she said. *Not.*

As if having to fake a love of Christmas was bad enough, now she would be trapped for a week with a man she'd never forgotten. She remembered him not because of his extraordinary good looks that back then had set her teenage heart thumping, but because of how deeply he had wounded her. It had taken a long time to restore the confidence his mocking words had caused to her fragile teenage ego.

'Oliver, please,' he said.

'Sure,' she said. 'Oliver.' She felt like she was choking on his name.

He smiled. Yep, same toothpaste-commercial white teeth. Almost too perfect to be true. 'There's a lot to do,' he said. 'I'm sure Caity briefed you about how I want this year's Christmas to be better than ever?'

As he spoke, Marissa realised there was not even the merest spark of recognition in his eyes. He had no idea that they'd met before.

If indeed they had.

Perhaps it was an insane coincidence that this Oliver was so like teenage crush Oliver. But she didn't think so. It had to be him. But she couldn't really be sure until she investigated his surname. In the meantime, as he had not recognised her—which added further insult to his insults of sixteen years ago—she wouldn't say a thing. That would only revive the humiliation.

'Caity briefed me very thoroughly,' Marissa said, in a cool, businesslike tone, totally at odds with her inner turmoil. 'I'm looking forward to going through the timetable of events with you and meeting the local staff and suppliers Caity engaged. There are, however, questions I need to ask you, to fill in the gaps.'

'Of course. How about we set up a meeting in half an hour at my grandfather's study.' He paused and she was surprised at the flash of pain across his face. 'I mean *my* study.' He sighed. 'Grandpa died in August. I forget sometimes that he isn't here.'

'I understand,' she said, fighting the sudden empathy she felt towards this man. She knew only too well about loss in various heartbreaking ways. 'It does get better with time. Although I don't believe you ever completely get over losing someone you love.'

He looked down into her eyes—she was tall but he was taller—and she saw the pain in his eyes. 'You...?' he said.

Marissa met his gaze as she swallowed against the lump in her throat. 'My parents. Five years ago. A car accident.'

On Christmas Eve.

'I'm sorry.'

'I'm sorry about your grandfather.'

An awkward silence fell between them. How did that business conversation suddenly swerve to something so personal?

Oliver Pierce cleared his throat. 'Did you drive directly from London?' he said, very obviously changing the subject.

Marissa jumped at the opportunity to do so. 'Yes,' she said. 'The traffic wasn't too bad.'

Traffic was always a safe topic of conversation between strangers. It had taken three hours in her van, which wasn't as fast on the road as more modern vehicles. But she loved her van; it was different and quirky but very practical.

'I'll show you to your room.' Oliver Pierce picked up the small suitcase she had brought in with her. She had another with more clothes in the van.

'Where should I park my van?'

'If you leave the keys at the desk, someone will take your van to the garage at the back of the hotel.'

'Is it secure? There are boxes of valuable things in there.'

The moment she uttered the query she chastised herself. They were in the middle of nowhere, up a long driveway behind secure gates on a private property. Who was going to break into her van and steal Christmas decorations? She was too used to living in central London.

'Very secure,' he said. 'But I'll arrange for someone to transfer them to a storeroom, if that would make you feel better?'

'Thank you,' she said, nodding.

She followed Oliver Pierce up the magnificent carved wooden staircase. As she trailed her hand over the top of the balustrade, she thought about how many other hands must have trailed along it over hundreds of years, what stories these wood-panelled walls could tell. She also couldn't stop wondering about Oliver Pierce, possibly Hughes. How would she deal with him?

'There are ten bedrooms on this floor, all en suite, and a further ten on the next floor,' he said when they reached the first floor. 'A further twelve bedrooms are located in a converted barn. Our family lives in a separate wing.'

'It's such an amazing building,' she said, still disconcerted by the thought that this Oliver must be *that* Oliver. She felt she had to weigh up every word she said to him.

'Longfield Manor has been in my family for a long time,' he said. 'My grandparents turned it into a hotel thirty years ago.'

Oliver strode ahead of her with athletic grace. Marissa couldn't help but admire the view as she followed him. Broad shoulders, long, strong legs. He was one of those men who looked really good in a business suit.

He stopped at a door at the farther end of the corridor. 'This is your room,' he said, opening the door. 'It makes sense for you to stay here as a guest rather than stay in the village, where the rest of the staff lives or stays, and have to drive in every day.'

'Of course. I appreciate it,' she said. He would have had to pay for her to stay elsewhere so why not have her on site? It made good business sense.

But it was immediately evident that he hadn't stinted on her accommodation. Her room was spacious and elegant, with antique-style furnishing, curtains and upholstery. It had been brought into this century with a light hand that allowed its historical charm to shine through. There was nothing stuffy about the decor, no heavy dark colours or cumbersome furniture. Rather, muted colours and lush, pale carpets gave it a feel of contemporary luxury that was not at odds with the building's history. A top interior designer had obviously been employed to find the perfect balance. 'What a beautiful room,' she said, looking around her. 'Timeless and elegant.'

'My grandmother always likes to hear that kind of feedback,' he said. 'She was an interior designer when she was younger and has put her heart and soul into this place.'

'She's done a wonderful job.' Marissa paused. 'About your grandmother. It's my understanding she and your grandfather organised the Christmas festivities themselves. Will I be treading on her toes?'

'Good question,' he said.

Marissa didn't like it when people said, *good question*. It usually served to stall an answer or was a condescending response to a question they didn't think was good at all.

But Oliver Pierce spoke the words as if he meant them. 'I asked her about that before I got Caity on board. Granny said she was relieved that she didn't have to do all the work by herself. That even with my grandfather organising it with her, the Christmas festivities were beginning to become too much.'

'That's good to hear. I know you want to make changes and I wondered how she felt about that.'

'Granny is eighty-two years young, as she likes to say. She's not resistant to change, but she'll certainly let you know what she thinks if she disagrees with anything.'

Marissa smiled, in spite of her resolve to stay distant. His words were underscored with affection and she liked that. She respected people who were close to their families—she who had been left without family and ached for their loss.

'Granny and Grandpa were partners in every sense of the word. She's struggling without him, but grateful that I can take over some of what he did. She will be sure to want to meet you as soon as possible. I'll ask her to attend our meeting.'

'I'll look forward to meeting her.' Caity had told her she'd liked Edith Pierce very much and had enjoyed working with her.

'I'll leave you to unpack. See you in half an hour.'

The second he shut the door behind him, Marissa threw her coat on the bed and reached for her phone. An internet search might help clear up the mystery of the two Olivers.

Thankfully, it was a mystery quickly solved. Oliver Pierce, according to the gossip columnists, was notoriously private. But that didn't stop stories about the handsome hotelier finding their way into the news. Oliver had changed his name from his father's name, Hughes, to his mother's name, Pierce, when he'd been about twenty-four. A bold move to make. His mother, an only child, had been a famous model and, according to well-documented gossip, it seemed her marriage to Oliver's father had been tumultuous. But to change his name? As Caity had said, there was a story there. Perhaps it was a sad one. But it was none of Marissa's business. What she'd discovered didn't make her change her mind about Oliver.

Odious Oliver, she'd called him in her secret thoughts for so long.

Today's Oliver seemed very personable. Charming even. She'd found herself warming to him when there was still a doubt he might not be the Oliver from her past. But now she knew the truth. She shuddered. His mean words were indelibly carved into her memory. However, that would not stop her from treating a client—Caity's client—with professional courtesy. Aside from that, she intended to avoid him as much as possible.

Marissa Gracey was gorgeous. Oliver didn't know why the fact that Caity's replacement was so attractive should come as such a shock. Perhaps because Caity had gone overboard on stressing how smart and efficient and capable her friend Marissa was. He hadn't given a thought to what the paragon might look like.

Not that the appearance of his new event planner mattered in the slightest. Of course it didn't. He never dated staff—even those on a short-term contract. An early disaster dating an assistant manager had made sure he steered clear of such ill-advised liaisons. He just wanted the event planner to have all the attributes Caity had promised that would ensure Christmas at Longfield Manor this year was outstanding.

Still, he found it disconcerting that Marissa was such a classic beauty, tall and willowy with dark hair that tumbled over her shoulders, deep blue eyes, a generous mouth, cheeks flushed pink from the cold outside. Oliver had found it hard not to stare earlier when he'd seen her waiting for him at the reception desk, elegant in narrow black trousers, high-heeled black boots and a striking purple wool coat. He'd also found himself taking surreptitious side glances at her as he showed her to her room, where she'd slipped off her coat to reveal a long-sleeved silk shirt in an abstract black-and-white pattern. While discreetly professional, the snug-fitting shirt made no secret of her curves. She really was a stunner.

She was punctual, too. He was pleased to see that Marissa arrived at his office for their meeting five minutes early. Punctuality and order were important to him, among the tools with which he'd tried to ward off the craziness of his early years. His mother had fallen pregnant with him 'accidentally' when she was at the peak of her modelling career and married his father because it was the done thing at the time. He didn't know if it had ever been a happy marriage. His earliest memories were of them arguing—noisy and angry, and worse when they'd been drinking. Every time he'd been dumped off with Granny and Grandpa, their house had been a haven of peace and unconditional love.

Had his mother loved him? She'd told him she loved him, but it was difficult for him to believe her when she'd left him so often. Every time, he'd felt abandoned. 'Mummy's working, models have to travel,' Granny used to explain as she'd wiped away his tears. His father had been in a never-quite-made-it rock band and was also away on tour a lot of the time. However, the truth was obvious to him now—a child got in the way of their complicated lives, and they took the easy route of foisting him onto others so that they didn't have to worry themselves with his care. He sometimes wondered if they had ever considered what it was like for a child to be constantly referred to—to their face—as *an accident*.

They'd shunted him into boarding school at the age of eight. His parents had then separated and reconciled several times before divorcing when he'd been thirteen. When he was fifteen, his mother had met a man who lived in New Zealand. She'd gone to visit him and hadn't come back since, except for occasional fleeting visits to England. Oliver had expected to go with her but his mother hadn't thought it appropriate for him to change schools at that stage of his studies. So she'd left him behind. Like a piece of unwanted baggage. Again.

Marissa sat down in the visitor's chair opposite from him. She put a large folder and a tablet on the desk in front of her and outlined an agenda. Professional. He liked that, too.

'Caity's already done all the hard work,' she said. 'She's organised suppliers, discussed the menus with your chefs, engaged musicians, briefed the florist, hired decorating staff and so on. As per your instruction, she's used local people wherever possible. Now it's up to me to make it happen flawlessly so your guests have the best Christmas ever.'

'Sounds like everything is on track to me,' he said.

She paused and a frown pleated her forehead. 'One thing I'm not quite sure of is the gift-giving ceremony after lunch on Christmas Day presided over by Santa Claus and Mrs Claus. I understand all the guests receive a gift from the jolly couple?'

'Oh, yes,' he said, unable to stop himself from smiling. The mention of the tradition had sparked so many happy memories from over the years. 'It's a family tradition that morphed into a hotel tradition.'

'How so?' she said, her head tilted to one side.

'When I was a child, Grandpa and Granny dressed up as Santa and his wife on Christmas morning. Apparently, they'd done that for my mother when she was a child. I loved it. When they started the hotel, it turned out the guests loved Santa and Mrs Claus, too. The hotel ceremony takes place after the long Christmas lunch.'

'I see,' she said.

Oliver wondered why a shadow passed over Marissa's face as he explained the tradition. That could mean she had happy memories of Christmas or, on the other hand, memories that were less than happy. People who spent Christmas at a hotel often included those who were escaping unhappy family situations, those with no families, people who were far away from home at Christmas, as well as the people who wanted a traditional Christmas with all the trimmings without all the work. Marissa had agreed to work Christmas Day at Longfield Manor without hesitation or demands for extra remuneration. Where would she be on Christmas Day otherwise? Or with whom?

'That sounds fun,' she said at last. 'I find it endearing that the owners of a hotel would celebrate like that with their guests. I'm wondering, though...how will it happen this year?' she said, as though carefully choosing her words.

'Without Grandpa, you mean?' he said, with a painful wrench to his gut.

She nodded.

Oliver felt overwhelmed by sadness that Grandpa wouldn't be here to play Santa. It was just another reminder that Christmas wouldn't be the same ever again. Marissa's sympathy for his loss was there in her expressive blue eyes. He looked away, unable to bear it. 'It will be me stepping into Santa's big black boots. I can do a *ho-ho-ho* with the best of them,' he said, forcing positivity into his voice.

'And your grandmother?'

'She'll be Mrs Claus as usual.' He put up his hand to stop any possible objection. 'I know I should be Grandson Claus. But the white curly hair and beard of the Santa outfit will disguise the age difference. It's all in the Christmas spirit.'

'Of course it is,' she said.

Damn. He suspected she could tell how upsetting he found this conversation. Oliver knew he was good at masking his feelings—he'd learned that from a very early age—so how could this woman he barely knew see through his mask?

There was a loud knock on the door, accompanied by the door opening. Granny. She never waited for a *come in* invitation before she entered the room.

He was pleased she'd chosen to join them. It must come as a shock to her every time she saw her grandson seated behind her husband's big antique desk. It was still a shock to him, too. He'd known his grandfather wouldn't live forever, but he'd wanted more years with him than what he'd been given.

He rose and came around his desk to greet her. 'Talking of

my grandmother. Here she is,' he said to Marissa. She got up from her chair, too, so they stood side by side.

His grandmother swept into the room with her usual aplomb. She paused as she took in Marissa, then smiled. He hadn't seen her smile like that since Grandpa's death.

'Granny, this is Marissa Gracey. Marissa, my grandmother, Edith Pierce. Marissa is here to help us with Christmas.'

His grandmother positively beamed as she turned to Marissa. 'I know why Marissa is here. It's very good of you, my dear, to come down to us from London to help.'

'I'm glad I was able to make it,' Marissa said politely.

Granny turned back to him with a puzzled frown. 'But Oliver darling, why did you put Marissa in Room eight?'

'It's a lovely room,' he said. 'I want her to be comfortable while she's here working with us.' Did Granny think it more appropriate for Marissa to be in the staff quarters?

'It's a very nice room,' Marissa said.

'But surely she should be in your room with you, Oliver?'

Marissa gasped. Oliver stared at his grandmother in disbelief.

'I might be old but I'm broad minded, you know. There's no need for you and your girlfriend to scurry around behind my back playing musical beds. I suggest you move her into your room right now.'

CHAPTER THREE

MARISSA STARED AT Edith Pierce, speechless with shock. Why would the older woman say such a thing? She glanced at Oliver, but he seemed equally shocked.

Mrs Pierce looked from her grandson to Marissa and back to Oliver again. She was an elegant older woman, beautifully groomed with silver hair cut in a short bob and discreet jewellery of the very expensive kind. A smile danced around her perfectly lipsticked mouth.

'Do I shock you? Your generation didn't invent sex, you know.'

Oliver looked mortified. He glanced at Marissa, as if beseeching her for help. But what could she do? This was his grandmother, a stranger to her.

The thought of having sex with Oliver Pierce in his bedroom sent a flush to Marissa's cheeks, those fervent teenage fantasies she'd had about him rushing back.

'I know that, Granny, but—' Oliver finally said.

Marissa found her voice. 'I'm not his—'

'Marissa is our new event planner, Granny. Remember Caity, who you liked so much, had to go into hospital to have her pregnancy monitored?'

'Of course I remember that,' Mrs Pierce said, sounding annoyed. 'My memory might fail me a little these days, but not about important things like our Christmas celebrations.'

'Marissa is her replacement. She's a very experienced event planner and comes with glowing references.'

Mrs Pierce smiled. 'You don't have to hide from me the fact she's also your girlfriend. She's lovely and—'

'She is that,' said Oliver. 'Very lovely, I mean.'

That's not what he said about me when he was sixteen.

'But she's not my—'

Mrs Pierce spoke over him. 'I know you like to keep your private life private, Oliver. But I'm delighted Marissa is able to spend Christmas with you, and that I get the chance to get to know her. It makes me so very happy to see you with such a beautiful girl. Smart, too, as you say.' Her words were gushing, but to Marissa they seemed sincere—if completely misguided.

The older lady paused. To gather her emotions or for dramatic effect? Marissa couldn't be sure. This was so awkward she could scarcely breathe. Oliver had to say something. It was up to him to stop this nonsense. She, Marissa, was a stranger and a contracted employee to boot. She couldn't get into an argument with the owner of Longfield Manor.

But before either of them could say anything, his grandmother continued. 'You know, Oliver, how sad I've been since my beloved Charles's death. So miserable I... I've sometimes wondered if it's worth living.' Her voice wavered as she bowed her head. Oliver looked alarmed. He stepped towards her, put a hand on her arm. Mrs Pierce looked up at her grandson. 'There seemed...nothing to look forward to.'

'Granny. You can't say that.' There was an edge of anguish to his voice.

'I just did, though, didn't I? I'm sorry. I know you're grieving him, too. But the loss of a husband is something else. Soulmates. That's a term we didn't use when we were young. But that's what we were—soulmates.'

'I know,' Oliver said. 'You were so happy with Grandpa.' It was his turn to sound bereft.

Marissa shifted from foot to foot, uncomfortable at being witness to his family's pain and loss. She was an outsider who shouldn't really be there. If she could back out of the room without them noticing her, she would.

However, the older woman seemed intent on involving her. 'But this. Marissa. I'm not jumping the gun or anything, but perhaps... Well, the prospect of seeing my grandson settled, that makes me happier than I'd imagined I'd ever be again. You know, new life and all that.'

'Granny,' said Oliver, obviously through gritted teeth. 'It's not like that. It really isn't.' He didn't look at Marissa. *Couldn't* look at her, more likely.

This was awkward. To see this tall, powerful man at a loss of what to say to this petite older woman, whom he obviously loved and respected. Did Edith Pierce really believe her to be Oliver's girlfriend? Or was it...old age speaking? She didn't know her so couldn't make a judgement. Her own grandmother had become decidedly odd in her final years.

Mrs Pierce sighed, a sound Marissa found heart wrenching. With that sigh, the older lady seemed somehow to diminish, and even her beautiful, smooth skin and expertly applied make-up couldn't hide the fact that she was frail. Marissa noticed that her cashmere cardigan hung loosely on her and that her tailored tweed skirt seemed loose at the waist.

'My first Christmas without my beloved Charles in more than sixty years. I... I don't know how I'll manage.'

Oliver put his arm around her. She was tiny, and only came up to his elbow. 'Granny, I'm here. You're not on your own.' His voice was kind and gentle.

'I know. And neither are you. You have Marissa.'

He spoke through gritted teeth. 'Granny, you really have got the wrong idea about—'

Edith Pierce aimed a sweet smile at Marissa. 'You've made

an old lady very happy, my dear,' she said. 'Thank you for coming here with Oliver. He's never had a girlfriend visit Longfield Manor before, so you must be very special. I'm looking forward to getting to know you.'

Marissa had to say something in response. She cast a quick glance at Oliver but got no help from him. He seemed as stunned as she was. 'Er, me, too,' she managed to choke out. 'Getting to know you, I mean.'

Oliver Pierce had never brought a girlfriend home before? What did that say about him? Marissa was so disconcerted she couldn't utter another word.

'Now, shall we go through our plans for Christmas?' said Mrs Pierce in a matter-of-fact tone.

Oliver shot Marissa a glance and gave the slightest shrug of his shoulders. Marissa nodded in reply.

He indicated for her and his grandmother to take seats at a round conference table in the corner of the spacious study. Feeling more ill at ease than she could ever remember, Marissa picked up her folder and tablet and followed him. Initially, she found it an effort to act normal and businesslike with the owner of Longfield Manor. Especially after Mrs Pierce had expressed so firmly her belief that she was her grandson's girlfriend. Why hadn't Oliver denied it more vehemently?

But once seated at the table, Oliver's grandmother became pure businesswoman, alert and savvy when it came to finalising the plans for the hotel's Christmas. She was totally on top of things, including the financials. She referred to her meetings with Caity and expressed her pleasure at the way the traditional Christmas celebrations were to be enlivened with some more contemporary twists. She also liked the idea of the new designer ornaments and decorations. And was in full agreement with the innovative vegetarian and vegan additions to the menu, as more guests were requesting those alternatives to the traditional fare.

'Well done, Marissa,' she said, as she viewed the final presentation on Marissa's tablet. She seemed very much the competent, well-established owner of the hotel. Perhaps the girlfriend confusion had been an aberration.

'I'm glad you approve,' Marissa said, feeling as though she'd passed an exam.

Edith—she'd asked Marissa to call her by her first name—turned to Oliver. 'Where did you say you first met Marissa?' she asked.

'I didn't say,' he said. He looked to Marissa and back again to his grandmother. 'But...it was through a mutual friend.'

Caity. That was what he believed and it was true. Their mutual friend Caity had indeed organised their meeting for Marissa to take over from her while she was in hospital. But it was also true in another context, given he'd actually first met her through his friend Toby, brother to her friend Samantha, when they were teenagers. Oliver appeared to have no memory of that first meeting all those years ago, but she wasn't about to remind him of it. Did he still see Toby? She and Toby's sister had lost touch after Samantha had moved to a different school.

'The best way to meet your life partner,' his grandmother said approvingly. 'I don't like the idea of these dating apps.'

Oliver spluttered an indecipherable reply.

Life partner?

Marissa was so astounded she had to stop her mouth from gaping open. Yet, secretly, she found it amusing to see this hot, super-successful tycoon, who had been so vile to her years ago, shocked speechless by his grandmother. How the tables had turned.

Despite that, she was beyond relieved when the meeting concluded and Edith left the room. She waited with Oliver, near the door, until she could be sure the older woman had definitely gone and wouldn't overhear her. She swung around to face Oliver. 'What was that about? Why did you allow your grandmother to believe I was your girlfriend?' She wasn't speaking as contractor to client; his grandmother's absurd assumptions had swung them beyond that.

'I did not. I explained who you were.' He appeared very sure of himself, yet she could tell he was shaken by the encounter with his grandmother.

'You didn't outright deny it. And I didn't know her well enough to contradict her. Although I did try. You noticed I did try. It was so awkward for me.'

He gestured with his hands. 'I'm sorry, Marissa. Granny took me by surprise. You are here to do a job, we have no personal connection and it was…unprofessional of me not to try harder to stop her. I can only say in my defence that I was stunned almost speechless.'

Marissa had been just about to accuse him of being unprofessional, so that somehow took the wind out of her sails. What family drama had she found herself caught up in here?

'I was so embarrassed. Where on earth did your grandmother get the idea I was your girlfriend? What did you tell her about me that would have made her think that?'

Oliver shrugged broad shoulders. He had discarded his suit jacket during the course of their meeting and his tailored linen shirt did nothing to hide the ripple of muscle beneath. Gone was the gangly teenager she remembered. Oliver Pierce was built.

But she was immune to gorgeous guys.

Wasn't she?

'Nothing. I told her you were replacing Caity to work with us on Christmas.'

'That's all?'

'That's all,' he said emphatically. 'She's very old and has recently had some memory issues, but nothing like this level of confusion.'

Marissa took a moment to answer. 'I see.' She took another moment. 'I can tell you care very much for your grandmother,' she said carefully.

'I do. She was more a mother to me than my own mother, her daughter.'

Really? She would love to ask for more details. But the way

his face closed up and his green eyes shadowed, stopped her from asking. It was none of her business.

But his grandmother mistaking her for her grandson's *life partner*-status girlfriend was very much her business. She realised he felt uncomfortable about the situation. But not as uncomfortable as she did. She had to work here for the next week.

'Can you please clear up the misunderstanding with her as soon as you can?' she said. 'I'll feel awkward dealing with her until you do.'

'I understand that. Thank you for your patience and kindness towards her,' he said. He took a deep breath and paced the space in front of his desk before coming to a halt to face her. 'But here's the thing. I haven't seen Granny smile like that since before Grandpa got ill.'

'What do you mean?'

'The way she smiled at you. The look on her face when she said how happy the thought of us—' he cleared his throat '—uh, of us being together, how happy that made her feel.'

'But she got it wrong, didn't she?'

'Very wrong.' He looked down at her, his eyes narrowed, his expression intent. 'But what if she got it right?'

Marissa took a step back from him. 'What are you saying?'

'Would it be asking too much for you to pretend to be my girlfriend for the week you are here?'

'What?' She was too stupefied to say anything more.

'I want you to pretend to be my girlfriend to make my grandmother happy and give her a wonderful Christmas—her first since she lost my grandfather.'

She shook her head in disbelief. 'You can't be serious.' She realised she had crossed her arms over her chest, and she had to force herself to uncross them.

'I know it's out there, but you can see how frail she is, and how unhappy. She really took to you, although I have no idea why she thinks you're my girlfriend.'

'My own grandmother got a bit, well, eccentric is the kind

way to put it, when she got older. Is Edith...?' This conversation was getting surreal.

'Before he died, my grandfather told me he was worried Granny might be displaying signs of dementia. You know, memory loss, forgetting things. I haven't seen serious signs of it myself, apart from some minor lapses that I could put down to the loss of her husband, and possible fears about her future. But this. This has shocked me and, to tell the truth, the extent of her delusion frightened me.'

Marissa frowned. 'She seemed very *compos mentis* to me when we were going over the Christmas plans.'

'She did. As sharp as she's always been. Which makes this girlfriend thing hard to understand. Unless it is a sign of...of mental deterioration.'

'Or wishful thinking, perhaps?'

'What do you mean?' he said.

'Your granny seemed so happy about the idea of us being a couple. Perhaps she's become aware of her own mortality and wants her grandson to be settled. You know, ready to produce the next generation of your family. The walls of the downstairs corridor are lined with portraits of your ancestors. There are more in here.' She indicated the panelled walls, the bronze bust of some revered past Pierce on the bookshelf. 'She might be clutching at straws. Are you the oldest son?'

She couldn't meet him in the eye, especially as the fantasies she'd had about them being a couple when they were teenagers flashed again through her mind. Although her brain might dismiss those feelings, her body knew only too well that the attraction still simmered, no matter how deeply she tried to stomp on it. Pretending to be the girlfriend of this excitingly handsome man would be madness.

'I'm an only child,' he said. 'And the only grandchild, in fact.'

'There you have it.'

'You could be right,' he said slowly. 'Although I thought

Granny had long given up trying to matchmake me with her friends' granddaughters.'

'Perhaps she's muddled me up with one of them.'

'I doubt it. None of them are as beautiful as you are,' he said dismissively. Had he really said that so casually?

'Oh,' she said, unable to meet his eye. He certainly hadn't found her beautiful when he'd first met her. Still, it was hard not to feel flattered.

He paused, tugged at the collar of his shirt. 'I know this is an off-the-wall plan. Not something I could ever have imagined I would propose. But I'm worried about Granny, and it seems nothing could make her happier than the belief that you and I are together.'

Marissa was still reeling at the thought of it. 'I suppose there's the chance that she might have forgotten about this girlfriend notion already?'

'Unlikely, with you around to remind her of it.'

'I could leave. It would be difficult to find you another event planner at this stage but I—'

'No,' he said with a dismissive gesture. 'You going could make her worse.'

'Or we could continue to deny it. Any relationship, I mean.'

'It would be more unsettling for her if we have to continuously deny it. Pretend to be together and we can all get on with the job of making this a memorable Christmas.'

She frowned. 'You're serious about this?'

'I am.'

'I... I don't know what to say.'

'*Yes* would be a start.' A hint of a smile lurked around the grim set of his mouth.

Slowly, she shook her head. 'I really don't know that this would be a good idea.'

'Name your price.'

'Excuse me? I'm not for sale!' He seemed different. But it

appeared he hadn't changed at all since he was sixteen. He was still arrogant and overbearing. No. He was worse.

'Aargh,' he said, pushing his fingers through his hair. 'That came out wrong. Of course I don't think you're for sale. I meant we could make the pretence an extension of your role as our event planner. Pretend to be my girlfriend and I could add a substantial bonus to your fee.'

'Not interested,' she said, shaking her head.

Exchanging personal services for money? Not happening. Never happening. And she had vowed never, ever again to get involved with a client. That was how she'd met the Christmas mistletoe disaster boyfriend.

'In fact, I think I should leave,' she said. 'Now. Your grandmother has a good handle on what to do for Christmas, as our meeting showed, and that will solve the girlfriend problem.'

'I fear it wouldn't.' He looked up to the ornately patterned ceiling and back to her. His black hair stuck up in ruffles, which had the effect of making him look more vulnerable. Vulnerable? Oliver Pierce? *Huh.*

She frowned. 'Why is that?'

'I'm worried how she might react to you leaving so abruptly. What if she blamed herself? I couldn't bear it if she reacted badly.' He looked somewhere over her shoulder, not meeting her eyes. 'It's difficult for me to talk about personal stuff. Especially to a stranger. But given you've suffered your own loss, you might understand.' He swallowed hard. 'Granny is all I've got. She and Grandpa pretty much raised me. My parents... Well, they weren't that interested in their son.'

Marissa thought about the gossip pages she'd read. The supermodel mother. The rock-musician father. The way Oliver had felt the need to change his surname. His upbringing had been so different from her happy, secure childhood.

'Your parents. Where are they now?'

'My mother lives in New Zealand. I haven't seen her for

years. My father took off a long time ago. He has another family now, somewhere in Cornwall.'

'I'm sorry,' she said. They felt like such inadequate words in the face of his loss, but she couldn't think of anything better to say.

'Don't be,' he said with a bitter twist to his mouth. 'They're no great loss. It's my grandparents who suffered when their daughter left. And now that Grandpa is gone—'

'You're all she has,' she said softly. 'In terms of family, I mean.'

He nodded. 'She's eighty-two and I want to hold on to her for as long as I can. I want to keep her happy. I want to do whatever I can to help her stave off possible dementia. And if that means pretending a woman I've only just met is my girlfriend—how did she put it?'

'Your *life-partner* girlfriend.'

'Yes. That. If I have to pretend to be in a relationship that doesn't exist with a beautiful stranger to make Granny happy for her first Christmas without Grandpa, then I will. If that stranger is willing.'

Not quite a stranger, but he didn't know that. Should she tell him? What would be the point? Their first meeting was so long ago, it wasn't surprising that he didn't remember her. She didn't remember other boys she'd met at that time. Only Oliver had lodged himself in her memory.

'I'm here for seven days,' she said. 'What would happen after that?'

He shrugged. 'I'd tell her we'd broken up. That wouldn't surprise her. I don't have long relationships.' His mouth twisted. 'Much as Granny would like to see me married, I'm not interested in being tied down.'

Why did that not surprise her? He had ranked high in a gossip page's list of elusive, eligible bachelors.

But he'd made her think. She empathised only too well with his fierce love for his grandmother. She'd lost her parents she'd adored in the accident. The only grandmother she'd known, her mother's mother, had died of a stroke just weeks afterwards brought on, the doctors said, by shock. Of her immediate family, her brother Kevin was all she had left. But Kevin hadn't been able to bear the thought of a Christmas without his mother and father and had escaped to Australia for the Christmas after the accident. He'd met a wonderful girl while in Sydney and had settled there. He and his lovely wife, Danni, meant everything to her but distance made things difficult.

She turned away from him, took a few paces forward and then turned back. 'If—and I said *if*—I were to agree to be your pretend girlfriend, how would it work?'

'I don't know. We'd have to work it out together. Figure out something you were comfortable with, but that seemed genuine. Does that seem reasonable to you?'

Oliver waited for her reply. He was so tall, so powerful, so very handsome, but she sensed again that surprising vulnerability. Awareness of him as a man shot through her like a sizzling electric current. He had been a teenage crush, but her attraction had been intense and no less real because of her age. Although long dormant, it might not take much to revive that attraction. She might want to be of help, that was her nature, but her own emotional safety needed to be considered, too.

Be careful, Marissa.

'I suppose so,' she said slowly. 'It's a lot to take on.'

'Understood,' he said.

But she saw hope flicker in his eyes and it chipped away at her resolve to walk away and drive her van back to London. He'd shown her a different side to him, one she hadn't imagined he possessed. He loved his grandmother, and she would be doing a good turn for a woman who had lost not only her soulmate husband but also, it seemed, her daughter. And acting as this man's pretend girlfriend could be, she had to admit, a fun distraction at a time of year she found distinctly depressing.

Fun, yes, but dangerous too, her common sense warned her.

It was dangerous that she found this man just as hot as she had when she'd been a teenager. But she was thirty years old now, and no stranger to heartbreak and disillusion when it came to men. As long as she stayed aware of that danger, kept her guard up, there should be no risk to her emotions.

'Reasonable would not mean sharing your bedroom,' she said firmly. 'Let's get that straight up front.'

'Of course not. I'd tell Granny we...uh...weren't ready to be that public about our relationship.' The lie slipped out so easily it gave her a shiver of concern.

'And there would be no payment, no bonus, required,' she added. 'It would be purely an act of compassion on my part to help a lonely, bereaved old lady over the Christmas period.' That would ensure she kept the upper hand. She would be doing him a favour rather than being beholden to him.

'If that's the way you want it.'

She sighed. 'I have to say up front that I don't like lies and dishonesty—and the fake-girlfriend thing would be one big fat lie.'

His face tightened. 'I don't like lies, either. If there's one way to get on my wrong side, it's to lie to me. But for Granny's sake, I'd think of it as a kind of charade.'

'An extension of the Christmas celebration?'

'Something like that, I guess.' He raked his fingers through his hair again. 'Hell, Marissa. I've never done anything like this before. I don't know how it might work. But when I saw how happy she was at the idea of us together...'

He seemed so genuine. So committed. She wanted to help. 'I'll do it,' Marissa said. 'I'll pretend to be your girlfriend for seven days.'

CHAPTER FOUR

OLIVER LOOKED DOWN at Marissa, searching her lovely face. Had she really accepted his proposition without requiring financial recompense? Or any other reward? Purely from the goodness of her heart?

For his grandmother's sake he wanted to believe that. Needed to believe that. Yet, his parents' treatment of him had made him cynical and distrustful, even as a child. Had he made a huge mistake in trusting this stranger with his off-the-wall idea? What was in it for her?

His life in London as a successful hotelier had only deepened that early cynicism. In business, but also when it came to dating. He'd become used to dealing with women with ulterior motives. For some people, money seemed to be the most attractive thing about another person. The wealthier he'd got, the more appealing he—or his bank balance—seemed to become to women.

But he wasn't looking for long-term relationships—a short-term affair with a negotiated use-by date was more his style. An affair where both partners knew the score, and nobody got hurt. Pleasure, fun and a pain-free goodbye. Not that he had a rotating list of lovers—in fact, he lived a large part of his life alone and celibate. Relationships were difficult. Love was a goal that had always remained out of his reach.

There'd been one woman who had tempted him to break his self-imposed rules on commitment. Sonya was a journalist, covering the opening of the Pierce Haymarket. She'd been vibrant, clever, gorgeous. He'd been enthralled by her, let himself dream of a future with her. Then had been shocked to the core when she'd told him she was polyamorous, he was one of several lovers and that was how she wanted it to stay. Oliver had respected her life choice—but he'd wanted a one-on-one exclusive relationship. The breakup had left him lonely, miserable and plagued by feelings he hadn't been enough for her. As he hadn't been enough for his parents to want to keep him.

Marissa looked up at him, a challenge in her clear blue eyes, a slight smile curving her lips. For a moment he felt mesmerised by that unexpected smile, and the way it brought into play a very cute dimple in her right cheek. 'Now that I've accepted, please don't tell me you're having second thoughts?' she said. 'Because I'm looking forward to starting the charade.'

How did she guess the doubt that had slithered its way into his certainty?

'Of course I haven't changed my mind,' he said firmly, to convince himself as well as her. 'Making sure my grandmother enjoys this first Christmas without Grandpa is important to me. I appreciate you agreeing to help. I can't thank you enough.' He couldn't say to anyone that it might be the last Christmas at Longfield Manor if selling became the most realistic option.

'So we're really going to do this?' she said.

'Yes,' he said. 'Yes, and yes.'

On reflection, he couldn't see why she would have an ulterior motive, or where it could lead. Caity had stressed her friend's honesty and integrity. Perhaps Marissa was exactly what she seemed to be—a kind person who had let herself get talked into his scheme because it would make an old woman happy for the holidays. 'And the timing is good,' he said.

'Why so?' she asked, again with that appealing tilt of her head.

'You're not known to anyone here and I'll need to introduce you to the hotel staff anyway as the person who is here to help us with Christmas.'

'And at the same time, you can introduce me as your girl-friend?'

'Who happens to be a professional event planner.'

'Who also knows Caity, and so it seemed logical I would come to help you.'

'On both a personal and professional basis.'

She raised her dark eyebrows on the word *personal* and he wondered if she was wavering. But she nodded.

'And if anyone asks why you hired Caity instead of me in the first place?' she queried.

'I'll say we didn't want to mix business and pleasure but with Caity out of commission it seemed only natural for you to step in, as you were going to be coming here to celebrate Christmas with me anyway,' he offered.

'That makes a lot of sense,' she said approvingly. 'Straight away, we need to formulate a strategy and get it clear in our heads.' Caity had said her friend was formidably efficient. Why would she be any different when formulating a plan for a mock-relationship?

'Understood,' he said. 'But we'll have to create that strategy on the fly. There are no rules to follow. No precedent to guide us.'

'If there are, I don't know of them. I guess The Complete Book of Faking a Relationship doesn't exist.'

She laughed, a warm, delightful laugh at their complicity. For a flash of a moment he thought the way she laughed sounded familiar. But that couldn't be. He met so many people in the hospitality business, and he had no specific memory of ever having met her. Perhaps she'd momentarily reminded him of some passing acquaintance.

'That book certainly isn't in our library here,' he said, taking his turn to laugh, a laugh that felt a little rusty. There hadn't been much opportunity for jollity since his grandfather's death. Besides, he wasn't known as a jovial, laugh-out-loud kind of guy. 'Serious with a tendency to brood,' was how his old friend Toby often described him. Oliver didn't mind the serious label, but that didn't mean he was humourless.

'Strategy one, we don't tell any other person about what we're doing,' he said. 'Not even Caity.'

Marissa nodded. 'I was about to suggest the very same thing. Safer that way.'

'We don't want leaks.'

'We also need to get our stories straight about how we met. It could be disastrous if we contradicted each other.'

'True. Shall we say we met at an event at the Pierce Soho hotel that Caity had organised?' he said.

'Inspired idea,' she said. 'When did we meet? Why not first week of November?'

'We're a relatively new couple?' he said. That would be believable. He wasn't known for lengthy relationships.

'Yes, that could be a good cover if we make any errors in our knowledge of each other.'

'Quick quiz,' he said. He tried to think of the things people got to know about each other in the first weeks of a new relationship. 'Your birthday?'

'Twenty-seventh of February. Yours?'

'August twentieth.'

'Favourite food?'

'Chocolate,' she said with a wicked grin. 'Okay, maybe not. I'll go for Italian.'

'You?'

'I'll go with Italian, too.'

She laughed. 'One thing at least we have in common.'

'Where did you grow up?' he asked.

'Putney, mostly. You?'

'Between London and Dorset. Whatever best suited my parents' peripatetic lifestyle. My grandparents used to have a London townhouse until they had to sell it.'

'Oh?' she said, the one word a question.

He turned to look at a painting of Longfield's famous walled garden that his grandfather had commissioned not long before he passed. 'They were very wealthy until they lost most of their money in an unwise investment of a big insurance company. That's why they turned Longfield Manor into a hotel.'

'I didn't know that.'

'But you would be expected to if you were my girlfriend.'

'Agreed,' she said, but he could see she was shocked. 'How awful for them.'

'Grandpa and Granny are canny with money. They managed to claw back much of their fortune.'

'Good to know,' she said. He wouldn't mention that his grandparents had been early investors in The Pierce Group and had done very well out of that investment.

'Where do you live now?' she said.

'In the penthouse apartment at the top of Pierce Soho.'

'Nice,' she said. 'I live in a mansion block apartment in West Kensington.'

'A good part of London. That must be very nice, too,' he said.

'I inherited it from my godmother,' she said. 'She was my mother's best friend.' He could hear the sadness that tinged her voice. If she'd inherited, that meant her godmother must have passed. Another loss.

'I'm sorry,' he said. 'For the loss of your godmother.'

'She was very special,' was all she said. She paused. 'Back to the get fake agenda.'

He laughed again. 'That's one way of putting it,' he said.

'We have to take it seriously, but not too seriously. If you know what I mean.'

'I think I do,' he said slowly. 'Otherwise, the relationship might not seem believable. Granny is quite astute. When she's not inventing girlfriends for me, that is.'

'I can see that,' Marissa said with another smile. 'With that in mind, we should try to be discreet. A private couple. No exaggerated public displays of affection, for example, to try and signal we're together. I'm not that kind of person and I suspect—judging by the very short time we've known each other—you're not, either.'

'Quite right,' he said, again amazed at her perception.

He did not like his private life exposed to the world. His very beautiful mother had been a magnet for the press and unfortunately, it had not been uncommon for drunken incidents outside nightclubs to be splashed across the tabloid newspapers. Too often, there had been a finger-wagging mention that she was the mother of a young son. His father, as handsome as his mother was beautiful, had got off more lightly. It seemed to be an expectation that a rock musician would be hedonistic, a suspected consumer of illegal drugs, a bad father.

'That said, to be convincing, there will have to be some outward signs of a supposed inner…uh…passion,' she said, not meeting his gaze. She flushed high on her cheekbones, which served to make her blue eyes even bluer and emphasise the creaminess of her skin. 'But again, not too exaggerated.'

Passion. Marissa. He had to force his mind away from such arousing thoughts.

She was out of bounds.

He cleared his throat. 'What would be on the list of approved hinting-at-passion behaviour? Holding hands?'

She nodded. 'Definitely. But not while we're in a business situation. If we were really boyfriend and girlfriend, we wouldn't be flaunting our relationship in front of the staff. Especially when I'm working for the hotel on behalf of Caity.'

'Flaunting only allowed in front of my grandmother.'

'Quite right. But again, a discreet flaunting. Nothing that would embarrass her.'

'After what Granny has said today, I doubt that we could embarrass her. It might be more the other way around.'

Marissa laughed again. Her laughter seemed to lighten the atmosphere of this traditional room, to invite mischief into a place that might never have witnessed it.

'I know exactly what you mean,' she said. 'I really didn't know what to say or where to look when she told us that our generation didn't invent sex.'

'Me, too. All the while fighting off any images from entering my brain of my ancient grandparents indulging in what we didn't invent.'

'Please,' she said, her eyes dancing. 'I'm going to try and forget you ever said that.'

He found himself laughing, too. 'So we're agreed, just enough flaunting to make us seem believable.'

'Yes. Perhaps a discreet brushing of a hand across an arm. A low-voiced exchange of what could be perceived to be private talk between lovers. Enough to make it believable.'

She paused, looking thoughtful. 'Actually, I think that might be the secret of making this work. We try to behave as though we really are in a relationship. When we're not sure what's appropriate behaviour, we conjure up thoughts of what we would do if we really were together and act on that.'

He looked down at her. Her dark hair was pulled back in a high ponytail, which drew attention to the perfect oval of her face. Her eyes were the deep, rich blue of the delphiniums his grandfather had so prized in his spring garden. He could not keep his eyes from her lush mouth with its Cupid's bow top lip, defined with glossy pink lipstick.

He cleared his throat. 'What would we do if I—behaving as though us being a couple were real—felt the urge to kiss you?'

'What?'

'If we were in a relationship, I would want to kiss you.'

He wanted to kiss her now. And the urge had nothing to do with pretending. She was so beautiful, and every minute he spent with her his attraction to her grew. Had it only been a few hours? Lust at first sight? But he couldn't let himself think this way, couldn't let her know how appealing he found her. The endgame was to help Granny. And finish the charade after seven days. 'And you might want to kiss me. If we were for real, I mean.'

Her dark eyelashes fluttered and she looked away from him and back. 'I…er… I guess. A light, affectionate kiss in front of others when appropriate would be on the cards.'

'We probably wouldn't want our first kiss in front of others to look like our first kiss ever. That might give the game away.'

'What do you mean?'

'I mean a practice kiss might be in order.'

Her eyes widened. 'Here? Now?'

'Now is as good a time as any.' He glanced down at his watch. 'Time is marching on. I need to introduce you to the staff. They'll soon be arriving to help decorate the Christmas trees and whatever else you want them to do.'

'The five fully decorated Christmas trees, each of which would normally take me an entire day to complete and which we need to get up ASAP? I'll try not to panic at the prospect of that.' She nodded thoughtfully as if kissing him was something to be checked off the list of pretend intimacies. 'Seriously. Yes. If we need to practise a kiss, now might be the time to do it.'

She took a step closer. Her eyes were wide with more than a hint of nervousness—a feeling he reciprocated. She bit her lower lip with her top teeth, which drew his eyes again to her mouth—so eminently kissable. She lifted her chin to bring her face closer to his. An atmosphere that had been amicable and warmed by laughter suddenly seemed fraught with tension. Her shoulders hunched up around her neck. She didn't seem to want him to kiss her. He wouldn't touch her without consent. He froze. What had he started?

Then she laughed, her delightful laugh that seemed already familiar. 'This is seriously weird, isn't it? Both of us holding back. I've been kissed before and I'm sure as heck you have been, too. If we need to practise, let's go for it.'

Before he could formulate his strategy for the kiss, she kissed him. She put her hands on his shoulders and planted a kiss on his mouth. Her mouth was firm and warm and fit his as if it was meant to be. But before he could relax into the kiss, it was over. She laughed again, but this time her laughter was high-pitched and tremulous. She flushed high on her cheeks. 'So, ice broken, we've kissed. Okay?'

'That's not much of a kiss,' he said, his voice husky. 'I think we could do better.'

Her eyes widened and her mouth parted. 'Er, okay,' she murmured.

He dipped his head to kiss her gently at first then, questing, exploring, her kiss in return tentative. When she responded, he deepened the kiss. She gave a little moan, which sent his arousal levels soaring. When she wound her arms around his neck to bring him closer, his arms circled her waist to pull her tighter. '*This* is a kiss,' she murmured against his mouth before returning to the kiss with increasing enthusiasm.

For practise purposes that was probably as far as they needed to go. But she felt so good in his arms. He didn't want to stop. Her scent was intoxicating, roses and vanilla and something indefinably hers. He traced the seam of her lips with the tip of his tongue, and she responded with her tongue. The kiss deepened into something hungry and passionate and totally unexpected. He wanted this kiss to be for real.

He wanted more than this kiss.

He scarcely registered the knock on the door when it came. He just wanted to keep on kissing Marissa. Then there was another knock. And his grandmother's familiar voice. 'Oliver, I wanted to ask—'

Marissa sprung back from his embrace. He caught a glimpse of flushed cheeks, her mouth swollen from his kisses, a flash of panic in her eyes, before he turned to face his grandmother.

'Granny,' he managed to choke out from a constricted voice. He tried not to make it obvious that his breath was coming in short gasps. He probably had Marissa's lipstick on his face and he swiped his mouth with the back of his hand.

'Edith,' Marissa said, smoothing down her top where it had come untucked from her trousers, pushing back her hair from her face. He noticed her hands weren't steady.

'You two,' said Granny with a fond smile, as she looked from him to Marissa and back again. 'I don't know why you tried to hide it from me. I knew you were together the second I saw you. And I couldn't be happier about it.'

Their first test. And they'd passed.

'We realised it was pointless to deny our relationship any longer,' Oliver said. 'Especially when you're so perceptive.'

His grandmother beamed in response. The plan was already working if she could look that happy from simply observing their kiss. Still, he found it difficult to look at Marissa—so delightfully sensuous in his arms just seconds before. Could she tell that kiss had been suddenly, urgently *real*?

'We're happy to have your blessing,' said Marissa.

Was she overdoing it? *Blessing?* But it seemed she knew exactly the right thing to say.

'You have my blessing indeed,' Granny said with another big smile. 'I'm looking forward to being a grandmother-in-law.'

Marissa was unable to stifle her shocked gasp.

But Oliver knew they had a plan, and he was going to work within the constraints. He wasn't exactly sure whether his grandmother was serious or teasing them.

'Granny, that's going too far. Marissa and I only started dating last month. Our relationship is still new. I don't want you to scare her off by getting ahead of yourself.'

Granny looked contrite. Again, he wasn't sure if she was playing them. 'Of course, darling. I won't say a word about marriage or even great-grandchildren.' Oliver protested but she put up her hand to stop him. 'I'll leave you two alone.'

'Wasn't there something you wanted to ask me?' Oliver said.

Granny gave a dismissive wave of her hand and a smug smile. 'That can wait,' she said as she closed the study door behind her.

Oliver turned to Marissa. She was shaking with the effort of suppressing a fit of the giggles. 'Flaunting it to Granny went well,' she choked out. 'Maybe too well.'

Oliver groaned and put his hand to his forehead. 'Sorry about the great-grandchildren thing.'

'I hope I hid my shock.'

'You hid it well, better than I did. In fact, you performed perfectly. Especially when we were caught by surprise. Thank you.'

'Edith's reaction proved we're believable in our roles,' she said. 'It's a good start.'

That kiss had been only too believable—and only too enjoyable. He had not intended for the kiss to go that far. He couldn't let it happen again. That surge of passion had been a lapse of judgement.

But she had seemed to enjoy the kiss as much as he did.

And that would make it difficult for him to hold back on kissing her again.

CHAPTER FIVE

WHAT HAD SHE DONE?

Marissa turned away from Oliver, desperately trying to conceal how shaken she'd been by his kiss. Not a practice kiss. Not a pretend kiss. A passionate kiss that teased and aroused. She had responded as if she hadn't been kissed for a year. Which, in truth, she hadn't. But it had been more than banked-up carnal hunger. Not just any kiss but a kiss with *him*. She was reeling with the realisation of how much she'd liked it, how his kiss had made her dizzy with desire.

How she wanted more kisses.

If the kiss had been with anyone else but Oliver Pierce, who knows where she might have wanted to take it?

That wasn't how it was meant to be. This game of pretend couldn't work if real feelings and real desires entered into it. That could lead to disaster.

She made a further fuss of tidying her hair. Then turned back to pick up her folder and tablet. 'The practice kiss served its purpose. But I don't think we need to...to go that far again.'

'You're right,' he said, his voice gruff.

'We know we can be convincing and that's all that was required.'

'Yes,' he said. He was looking somewhere over his shoulder.

Did he feel, like she did, that the kiss had got out of hand? She didn't know him well enough to ask.

'We're agreed on that, then?'

He nodded.

She looked down at her watch, staged a gasp of surprise. 'Look at the time. There's so much to do today.'

He looked back at her. To her relief, his glance said *business as usual*. 'First step, introduce you to the staff, as we agreed.'

'Then I'll need to get my van unloaded and be directed to the storeroom where all the rest of the Christmas decorations are kept.'

'Granny can help with that,' he said.

'About that.' She looked directly up at him. 'Oliver, I can't do my best work if Edith is interrogating me about our *relationship*. Would you mind if I politely say to her that it's all still too new and...er...precious for me to be discussing it? Pretty much what you said to her just then?'

'I'll back you up by saying the same thing when she inevitably starts to grill me.'

'Good. That's what we'd do if it was a real relationship.'

He frowned. 'There's something I didn't think to ask you. Is there a *real relationship* waiting for you back in London?'

'No. I broke up with someone about this time last year.'

She'd caught awful Aaron kissing his work colleague under the mistletoe at his company Christmas party—a serious kiss that made her instantly aware he must be sleeping with her. He hadn't even tried to deny it, and the woman concerned had sent her a glance of gloating triumph. It had been a sickening, heartbreaking moment as she had really liked Aaron and thought they were exclusive.

'There hasn't been anyone serious since. To be honest, I haven't wanted there to be. What about you?' she said.

'No one serious. I can't afford to let anything get in the way of growing my business. A new London hotel is in the planning stage. That's confidential, of course.'

She noted he said *anything* not *anyone*, which was telling.

'So, no one is going to come barging down here to Dorset to protest if anything slips out about us. As a *couple* I mean.'

'Not from my side. No.'

'Okay, then, it seems like two resolutely single people have found each other,' she said, forcing a light-hearted tone. 'Or that's our story, anyway.'

'You're good at improvising,' he said. 'Very good.'

'A lot of marketing is about selling a story, so I suppose you could say that. What I have to be careful of is that I don't over-embellish our story. I have a tendency to do that.'

He smiled. 'Just stick to the facts, ma'am.'

She smiled back. 'You mean our made-up facts?'

'If in doubt, leave it out.'

'A suggestion that I'll try to stick to.' She paused. 'Nothing like a cliché or two to sort things out.'

He laughed. 'Clichés developed for a reason. They might be overused but we know exactly what they mean.'

Oliver was transformed when he laughed; his green eyes, warmed, the somewhat grim set of his mouth curved upwards, even his rigid posture seemed to relax. Caity had been right. He was hot. And he had never looked hotter than at this moment.

And her reaction to that kiss warned her not to give in to the attraction that time had not dimmed.

Even more of a problem was that, contrary to anything she could have imagined, she was beginning to like him. And that was seriously disconcerting, considering for how long she had nurtured her dislike.

Oliver introduced her to the hotel manager, Cecil Bates, a grey-haired man whom Oliver told her was on the point of retirement. He seemed warm and kind, but she could also see him being tough when necessary, and she began to see why this hotel had such a five-star reputation for comfort and good service.

'Cecil truly was Grandpa's right-hand man and will be sorely missed. Granny doesn't know that he's handed in his resignation,' Oliver explained in an undertone, after they'd left Cecil's office. 'Grandpa's death and the changes that brought with it are enough for her to deal with right now.'

She frowned. 'Edith will have to know soon, though, won't she? It seems a bit unfair to keep her in the shadows simply because she's elderly.'

He shook his head. 'It's not that at all. There might be other changes happening next year. I just want her to enjoy her Christmas without unnecessary worry.'

Marissa shrugged. She had the distinct impression Edith might not appreciate being kept out of the loop. Was Oliver being thoughtful or controlling? But it was none of her business. Nor were those mysteriously hinted at *changes*. On Christmas Day she'd be out of here and heading back to London, free of Christmas and Oliver Pierce and his family. In the meantime, she had to make sure everything between her and Oliver stayed on an even keel.

No more passionate kissing.

And certainly no more thinking about how exciting and arousing that kissing had been.

She immediately liked the assistant manager, Priya Singh. Priya was the lovely woman who had greeted her when she'd arrived at the hotel. Priya seemed around her age, and Marissa straight away knew she would enjoy working with her. Priya's smile was warm when Oliver introduced her as his girlfriend and explained she was stepping in for Caity.

'I liked Caity so much. Fingers crossed all goes well for her. If you need help with anything, just let me know,' she said to Marissa. 'Christmas at Longfield Manor is so special. The extra work involved is worth it to make it the best ever Christmas this year.'

Oliver thanked Priya before he steered Marissa away. 'Granny just texted me. She's waiting for you in the storeroom where all the existing Christmas stuff is, as well as the boxes you brought down with you. She's keen to get started.'

'So am I.' Anything to keep her mind off her growing awareness of Oliver.

But a room full of Christmas? How would she cope without giving away the game that she was in fact a bah-humbug Scrooge? *Stick to the script*, she reminded herself. *And step into the role of someone who loves everything about Christmas*. She needed to pretend to be the person she'd been before the night of that fatal car crash.

She took a step nearer to Oliver. It brought her whispering-distance close. She was again dizzyingly aware of his warm, spicy and very male scent. It was a mix of some undoubtedly expensive aftershave with a hint of something uniquely him.

'Wish me luck with Edith,' she murmured. 'I'll make very sure I don't say anything controversial about my beloved boyfriend.' She knew there were people in the foyer watching them, some of them most likely guests. She turned up the volume. 'Shall I see you later?' she said as she leaned up to press a kiss on his cheek, then trailed a finger down it in a proprietorially girlfriend manner.

'Of course,' he said. He caught her hand in his and pressed a kiss on it, playing his role to perfection. 'I won't be there for lunch. We'll meet for dinner.' Even that light kiss on her hand felt good.

Too good.

Dinner? Of course it would be expected that they'd have dinner together. Would that happen every night? If she was really his girlfriend, of course it would. Breakfast, too. She'd be seeking any moment to be alone with her hot, gorgeous boyfriend, whose very closeness sent tremors of awareness coursing through her.

'Text me if anything untoward comes up I should know

about,' he said. 'We may need script amendments as we go along.'

A script. It was a good reminder of this crazy scheme she'd got caught up in. Both she and Oliver were essentially playing roles in a Christmas play. That kiss, however, had not felt like play-acting. Unless Oliver was a *very* good actor. She realised how very little she knew about him apart from the personal memory of a boy from sixteen years ago. A boy she'd never been able to forget. And she realised she wanted to know a lot more.

He took her to meet Edith in a storeroom behind the kitchens in the back end of the hotel, in the staff-only areas where guests were not permitted, so she could seriously start work. He had things to do, places to go, Oliver said with a grin before making his escape. Marissa watched his retreating back and felt suddenly alone and unprepared to deal with his grandmother.

The room smelled faintly of Christmas: the lingering scent of pine leaves and pine cones, a hint of dusty potpourri, the leftover waxy trace of perfumed candles. Marissa had to swallow against a sudden rush of nausea at the thought of the terrors of Christmas past and her fear for Christmas future. She took a deep, steadying breath and pasted on a smile for Edith's benefit.

Again, she wondered what on earth she'd got herself into. Yet, to be able to help Caity at a time of great need for her friend made it worth it. And, she could not deny it, there was a bonus in the totally unexpected chance to see again that man she'd had such a huge crush on when she'd been a teenager.

Edith greeted Marissa with delight but, thank heaven, no risqué references to her love life with Oliver. She asked after Caity and was pleased with Marissa's report on her friend's continued good health while on hospital bed rest.

'Caity didn't mention to me that Oliver was dating a friend of hers,' Edith said with narrowed eyes.

When it came to clichés, 'thinking on her feet' now came to mind. 'That's because we didn't tell her,' Marissa said. 'The Pierce Group is her client. We didn't want to make things awkward for her. Besides, you know how private Oliver is. I'm the same. Our relationship is too new and too precious for us to want to go public with it.' The words tripped quite happily off her tongue, much as she'd rehearsed them with Oliver.

'I guessed as soon as I saw you. Your chemistry is so obvious,' Edith said.

Chemistry? Is that what had fuelled that incredible kiss? Was it chemistry that had fired the intensity of her teenage crush on the same man? Marissa was too taken aback to reply to the woman who fancied herself as her future grandmother-in-law. 'Er...yes,' was all she could manage in reply. This conversation was suddenly heading way off script.

The older woman continued. 'You know how pleased I am about you being together and I respect your need for privacy. It's just that Oliver hasn't had an easy life and I do want him to be happy. As happy with the right person as I was with Charles. We had our ups and downs, of course we did, but we were always there for each other. That's a great comfort through life.'

All Marissa could manage to choke out was, 'That's lovely.'

She couldn't do this.

How could she possibly do her job properly when all Oliver's grandmother seemed to want to talk about was Marissa's *relationship* with her grandson?

Edith chuckled. 'That's *lovely*, you say. But you've already told me you don't want to talk about you and Oliver. And as I want to keep on your right side, I'll butt out.'

Please do!

But Edith was relentless. 'I just want to be sure, my dear, that you know where I stand.'

'I most certainly do,' said Marissa, stifling the urge to laugh.

It was clear that Edith loved her grandson just as much as

he loved her, and each was working in their own way to make the other happy. Marissa appreciated that. If she wasn't stuck in the middle of it, she would appreciate it even more. Still, she could do this job standing on her head, and the intrigue of the fake dating made it entertaining and edgy.

Edith showed her where the containers of heirloom tree ornaments, lights, staircase swags, buntings and Christmas linens had been placed, all brought down from the attics from where they spent the rest of the year.

'Some of the glass tree decorations go right back to when Charles was a little boy, living here with his parents, long before we turned the house into a hotel. We don't always put them up and, when we do, they're on a small tree in our private residence.' She sighed. 'I don't think I'll bother this year. Not on my own. The five hotel trees in the guest areas will be enough.'

'Are you sure?' Marissa said. 'I'm here to help with everything Christmas.'

Edith patted her on the hand. 'Thank you for your kind offer, my dear. But I'll pass. For this year anyway.'

Marissa thought about where she herself would be next Christmas. On that Balinese island, for sure. On her own and loving it.

The Christmas trees were to be placed in the guest areas, including the foyer, the living room, dining room, reading room and in the living room of the converted barn.

Edith pointed out that the decorations for each room had been packed together and put in clearly marked boxes and wooden packing crates. Marissa knew that from Caity's detailed handover document, but she had to check for herself to be sure. Attention to detail was all important.

Some of the ornaments and decorations were packed in very old suitcases that harked back to the golden age of sea travel to Europe, America and far-flung destinations of the Commonwealth before air travel took over. The suitcases were plastered with overlapping labels emblazoned with the names of grand ocean liners and stamped 'First Class.' Port labels told of voyages to destinations such as Marseille, Naples and Athens; transatlantic crossings to New York; further afield to exotic destinations like Bombay and Sydney, and back home to Dover.

She found the labels fascinating, telling a story of a glamorous era long gone for Oliver's wealthy family. She'd love to know more about their history. But now wasn't the time to delve into that. Perhaps it might be a good conversation starter over dinner with Oliver.

There were also the boxes of new product she'd brought with her in the van—including custom-made Christmas crackers. She cut open the box closest to her, using a utility knife with a retractable blade from the table nearby. She had, of course, inspected all the products at the designer's London headquarters to ensure the quality was up to scratch for her discerning clients. But she'd inspect them again for any possible damage sustained in transit.

She referred to her tablet. 'Soon, the team of contract staff will arrive,' she said. 'And the trees are due to be delivered from the Christmas tree farm later today. We have five trees of varying sizes for each of the five main public rooms. The trees will be stored outside in the barn and then brought inside when required.'

'We have the same helpers most years, so they know what to do,' Edith said.

Marissa had also engaged a professional interior designer with expertise in Christmas trees. Andy Gable had made a lucrative career out of decorating Christmas trees for private homes and hotels, department stores in both London and New York, along with many different magazines and catalogues. Marissa marvelled at how he made each tree so unique to that job. His job—his vocation, he called it—allowed him to take summers off to travel the world. Marissa had called him to ask for tree-decorating advice. To her delight, an unexpected cancellation had given him a free four days to help her out at Longfield Manor. He'd be arriving first thing the next day.

Caity had recruited fresh blood, too—a team of local university students on their Christmas break.

Strong young people who will be safe on ladders, unlike some of the regular elderly helpers.

That was what Caity had written in her notes.

Marissa smiled to herself as she read the notes but didn't read them out loud. She wasn't in any way ageist; in fact, she respected the knowledge and wisdom older people brought with them. But the fact remained that decorating a hotel of this size, with massive rooms and high ceilings, would be hard, physical work. Especially within this tight time frame.

She turned to Edith. 'I'm going to say goodbye and pop up to my room and change into jeans.' She'd dressed in business clothes for her first meeting with the clients, but now she needed to dress for hard work.

There was a guest lift, but she enjoyed climbing that magnificent staircase. For a moment, she imagined how it would be to be holding up voluminous long skirts of a bygone age as she manoeuvred the steps. Once in her room, she changed into jeans, a long-sleeved T-shirt and sturdy sneakers. Nothing scruffy, all designer, in keeping with the high-end hotel. Her role as event planner was a supervisory one. However, she had never been one to stand back if hands-on help was needed.

She pulled her hair back tighter into the ponytail; she hadn't realised stray wisps had come free during her enthusiastic kiss with Oliver. It was a battle to keep the luxuriant waves sleek. She looked in the mirror to check her make-up and touched up her lipstick where it had been kissed off. A shiver of pleasure ran through her as she remembered how good his kiss had felt.

How was that possible when it had been with the man who had been so awful to her as a teenager?

Today Oliver Pierce had called her lovely. He had called her beautiful. And he'd sounded like he'd meant it. A stark departure from what had happened in the past. Back when he was sixteen and named Oliver Hughes, her friend Samantha's brother Toby had asked Oliver what he thought about his sister's friend. The boys were sitting on a sofa in Samantha's family's living room, where they'd been playing games on their consoles. They didn't know she could overhear them from the other side of the open door into the room.

Eavesdroppers rarely hear good things about themselves, her mother had told her. How true that had been back then.

Oliver certainly hadn't had anything flattering to say about her infatuated, self-conscious fourteen-year-old self. Neither had Toby, whom she had always liked up until then.

That day Toby had kicked off the critique by pointing out how flat-chested she was—true, she hadn't developed significant curves for another two years—how gawky—she hadn't grown into her long limbs yet then, either—and how she giggled too much—also unfortunately true, especially in the company of boys other than her brother.

It was such a cruel summing-up for a girl who was just beginning to find her place in a world where she had believed she might have something to offer. Where boys had become interesting rather than nuisances. Her heart had shattered when Oliver had agreed with Toby's assessments. Before that, she had never thought she was ugly, but when she'd seen herself through his eyes...she'd felt it.

Then Oliver had asked Toby, 'What's with those caterpillars crawling across the top of her face?'

Toby had sniggered. 'Marissa's monobrow, you mean.'

Toby had laughed and Oliver had joined in, too. Laughing at *her*.

She had been super-self-conscious about her eyebrows. Hearing the boys' laughter, she'd thought she would die of shame and embarrassment. But she couldn't crawl away, or they would have known she'd been there listening to them on the other side of the door. And for them to know she'd heard their mocking laughter would have made her feel even worse.

Thankfully, the boys had then headed off to the kitchen in search of food, and she'd crept away and gone home, even though she'd been expected to stay for lunch with the family and Toby's friend. There had still been two days left of their half-term break but she'd made excuses not to go back to Samantha's house again. Not until obnoxious Toby and his equally obnoxious friend had gone back to their boarding school. Oliver had thankfully never visited again, and she had avoided Toby every holiday he'd been home.

After the pain and rejection she'd felt from that overheard conversation, that cruel laughter, she'd been determined to do something about her bothersome eyebrows.

Back then, her eyebrows had been bushy and black, and stray hairs had met in the middle above her nose. She'd hated those eyebrows but her mother had forbidden her to do anything about them, apart from the most gentle plucking. 'You can ruin your eyebrows for life if you pluck too much,' she'd warned.

So she'd saved up her pocket money and her babysitting money. Then she'd defied her mother by taking the bus to Knightsbridge to visit an eyebrow clinic reputed to be the best in London. Those errant eyebrows had been plucked, threaded and waxed into the elegant arches that today framed her eyes. She was still absolutely vigilant about keeping them that way.

Was that why Oliver hadn't recognised her? There was a curious satisfaction in knowing that he now found that skinny, gawky, monobrowed girl beautiful. That his kiss indicated he was attracted to her. But now her relationship with the client had veered into the personal, should she remind him that they'd met before? She still wasn't sure there would be any point to such a revelation.

CHAPTER SIX

BUSINESS HAD KEPT Oliver confined to his office for most of the day. It was Christmas in his London hotels, with no vacancies across the three properties, which meant there were a lot of calls on staff. There were guests who'd come to London for shopping, London people who wanted to spend Christmas being pampered at a hotel, travellers from other countries wanting to enjoy a legendary English Christmas. He should really be in London himself, but he had excellent managers and for the moment he was putting Granny and Longfield Manor first. Thankfully, much of what he needed to do could be done remotely.

However, busy as he was, he found his thoughts straying often to Marissa. He was looking forward to having dinner with her. Not in his private residence—to be alone with her would be a test of his endurance as he definitely wanted to kiss her again—but rather at the hotel dining room. He wanted to get to know her better.

He'd had time to think about the fake-girlfriend scenario he had proposed. Where had that idea come from? Making quick decisions and taking risks in business had certainly paid off for him. But when it came to his personal life, he didn't do rash, impulsive things like asking a stranger to pretend to be his girlfriend. Or to suggest they practise kissing because all he'd been able to think about since meeting her was kissing her.

Yet, the scene in his office that morning had seemed so right. He recalled his fears for his grandmother, so caught up in her delusion. Marissa, an acquaintance of—what had it been then? An hour?—unwittingly caught up in it, unaware of the sad back-story of his family, so willing to be kind and thoughtful about Granny. This empathic woman seemed aware of his pain at his loss because she had suffered loss, too.

And it was working. Granny had a definite spring to her step that had been missing for a long time, even before Grandpa had died. Simply because she believed he had a girlfriend. No. Not just any girlfriend. Marissa. A girl she thought he must be in love with if he'd brought her home for Christmas.

He was so grateful to Marissa. He would find some accept-able way to reward her when this was all over. After he had gracefully 'broken up' with her. For the first time since coming up with his scheme, he felt a twinge of concern. If Granny was so obsessed with Marissa, how would she feel about having to say goodbye to her? Yet, no one would be surprised. Oliver did not do long-term relationships, and everyone knew that.

There wasn't much daylight left given that at this time of year sunset was at 4 p.m. and, as Oliver liked to take a walk around the gardens while it was still light, he decided to take a break. He pulled on his coat, hat and gloves as he headed out-side. The sky was clear and blue and the air distinctly chilly. A heavy frost was predicted. But it was so good to be outside. He headed past the walled garden, enclosed within high walls of the same stone as the main buildings, a suntrap where spring came earlier than for the rest of the garden.

As he walked past, heading for the wild garden area, he saw that the iron gate was pushed open. For a moment he didn't recognise Marissa, in jeans, a puffer coat and scarf wrapped high to her chin. 'You startled me,' she said. 'I was taking the chance to get some fresh air.' She indicated the garden behind her. 'What a wonderful private garden.'

'Granny's pride and joy,' he said. 'It was originally the kitchen garden to supply vegetables and fruit to the house. In the old days, they also grew herbs for medicinal purposes. We still grow herbs there for the restaurant. And although it's now mainly a flower garden, you might have noticed fruit trees espaliered onto the walls.'

She laughed. 'I don't know much at all about gardening. Or what *espaliered* means. But I sensed a feeling of peace and fulfilment in there. In winter it has a certain bare beauty. It must be awesome covered in snow. But in summer, it must be delightful to sit on one of those stone benches and contemplate.'

'Granny grows lavender and roses and other scented plants there, because she thinks that way, too. She chooses plants with texture and others that attract butterflies. There's a fountain, too, emptied now so it doesn't freeze. She calls it her sensory garden.'

'Not that you get much time for sitting in there contemplating, I should imagine. Not with your hotel empire.'

'You're right. I don't.' But as a young boy he'd liked to hide in there behind the walls at the end of the school holidays, hoping they wouldn't be able to find him to take him back to boarding school. 'I'm walking down through the lawns to the wild garden if you'd like to join me.'

'Wild garden?' she said as she fell into step beside him. He didn't feel he had to hold her hand as there wasn't anyone to see them. Strangely enough, though, an inner compulsion made him want to reach out for her hand. Instead, he kept his hands firmly shoved into his coat pockets.

'An area that's been sown as a natural meadow. It attracts butterflies and wildlife like hedgehogs. It was my grandfather's idea. The Manor gardens are…were…his passion. He told me it was difficult for him to deal with strangers living in his home when they first opened it as a hotel. So the gardens became his domain.'

'How did you feel?'

'I don't remember it any other way,' he said. 'Guests tended to be nice to a little boy, so I was fine with it. Sometimes I got to play with children staying here and I liked that.'

'Liked it enough to become a hotel tycoon yourself when you grew up?'

'There's that,' he said, not wishing to be drawn in to further conversation about his childhood. Or the years spent relentlessly proving himself as a success in his own right.

'It must have been an amazing place to grow up in,' she said, looking around her at the formal gardens and the lawn that ran down to a rise from where the sea was visible.

'It was,' Oliver said. Which was why he would do everything in his power to keep Longfield Manor in the family. 'I hear you're doing brilliantly with the Christmas decorations.'

Marissa smiled. 'A report from Edith, no doubt? She's been great. No interrogation about possible birth dates of the great-grandchildren.'

Oliver laughed. 'I'm glad to hear that.'

'Seriously, she's just letting me get on with my job supervising the crew while she does her own thing with the family heirlooms.'

'I love Christmas at Longfield Manor,' Oliver said, looking around him. 'The happiest memories of my life are here and the happiest of all are from Christmas. I hope you're enjoying taking part in it.'

'About that.' Marissa came to a halt next to him. 'Before you go any further, there's something you need to know about me.'

Oliver frowned. What could possibly have brought that serious expression to her face? 'Fire away,' he said.

'I don't celebrate Christmas,' she said bluntly. 'In answer to your question, while I'm enjoying the job and liking the people I'm working with, Christmas itself leaves me cold.'

Oliver was so taken aback, he struggled for the right words. 'Is it your religion?'

She shook her head. 'Nothing to do with that. You spoke about memories... Well, my memories of Christmas aren't that great. My most recent ones, anyway.'

'But...but everyone loves Christmas,' he said.

'Many people don't celebrate Christmas,' she said. 'And there are people who find it stressful, or feel lonely and left out at this time of year.'

'Point taken. But you...?' Did she have an unhappy child-hood? Abusive parents? He realised how very little he knew about her.

'I have my reasons, and I don't want to talk about them,' she said, looking at the ground. 'But I thought you needed to know why I don't wax enthusiastic about Christmas. That doesn't stop me appreciating the beauty of the decorations we're putting up or the deliciousness of the menu. This Scrooge will do as good a job for you as any Christmas fan, I promise.'

'I appreciate that,' he said. 'But why did a self-professed Scrooge take on the job?'

'To help out Caity. She's my best friend.'

'Does she know how you feel about Christmas?'

'Yes.'

'So why did she choose you to replace her?'

'Because she trusts me to do every bit as good a job as she would to make this Christmas special for Longfield Manor.'

'Did you resent coming here and immersing yourself in Christmas?' He didn't like that thought at all.

'Not for a minute,' she said. 'And I'm enjoying being here.' She looked up at him and her eyes danced. 'Including pretend-ing to be your girlfriend. That adds an edge to the job to make it even more enjoyable. Everyone is very interested in us, by the way. I've had to field lots of questions.' She put up her hand. 'Don't worry, I've stuck to the script.'

'I've been in my office for most of the day and have managed to avoid any questioning. Although both Cecil and Priya made a few less than subtle hints that they were interested in our story.'

'I think the staff might feel it would be out of place to question you about your personal life. You can seem…forbidding.'

He bristled. 'I'm the boss. It comes with the role.'

'Of course. But remember you're meant to be madly in love. At the mention of your lover's name, you might want to soften a tad. Maybe show a hint of a goofy grin.'

He drew himself up to his full height. 'Me? A goofy grin? I don't do goofy.'

'You could try.' A mischievous smile tilted her lips and exposed that delightful dimple.

Oliver gave an exaggerated grin and he rolled his eyes at the ridiculousness of it.

She laughed. 'That's terrible and you know it. If you can't do goofy you need to try at least a gentling of your expression. You have resting stern face.'

She took a step closer to him and walked the fingers of her right hand up his arm to his shoulder. He was hyperaware of her touch, of her rose-and-vanilla scent.

'Now, look down at me with the dazed and besotted expression of a man in love. A man so in love he has brought a woman to his childhood home for the very first time.'

Oliver tried. And tried again. But he knew he was only achieving a grimace. He shrugged.

'Okay, call that a fail,' said Marissa. 'Why not try to picture someone who you were in love with and recall how you felt when you looked into her face.'

Oliver swallowed hard. 'I… I can't do that,' he said. He shook his head. 'I just can't do it.'

'Because you're not good at imagining?' Marissa paused. 'Or…or because you've never been in love?'

'Right the second time,' he managed to choke out. He saw from her expression that perhaps this wasn't an answer that reflected well on a thirty-two-year-old man.

'You've never been in love?' She sounded incredulous.

'Never. Attracted. Infatuated. Interested. But no, not in love.'

'Oh,' she said with a frown. 'But you're handsome, rich, nice. Women must be falling over themselves to date you.'

She called him *nice*? That wasn't a word often used to describe him. Oddly enough, he liked it. 'True,' he said without arrogance. After all, it was the truth. 'But that doesn't mean I've fallen in love with any of them.'

'I see,' she said. 'I wasn't expecting that. No wonder you can't fake it, then.'

'What about you?'

'Have I ever been in love?' Her perfectly shaped eyebrows rose.

'Yes.' He found himself holding his breath for her answer.

'Well, yes. A couple of times. But it didn't work out either time. Then there was—' She stopped.

'There was…' he prompted.

She didn't meet his eyes. 'Another time. When I was a young teenager I fell wildly, irrationally in love with a boy who… who didn't even notice me. I…guess I could put that down to infatuation. Kid stuff.' Her mouth set into a tight line at what seemed to be a painful memory. She opened her mouth as if to say something else but evidently decided against it.

'Infatuation can come easily,' he said, for want of saying anything more meaningful.

Had he consciously resisted love? He'd been so rejected by his parents he could see how that could have put a lock on his feelings. Or had his determination to succeed as a hotelier blocked anything and anyone that could get in the way? Could he have grown to love Sonya if given the chance? Or had what he'd felt for her been classified as infatuation?

He started to walk again and Marissa walked beside him. It was getting colder by the minute and her breath fogged in the sharp, late-afternoon air.

'What about someone else you loved?' she asked. 'We've got

quite an audience back at the Manor. Can you manage to conjure up feelings to give authenticity to our mock-relationship?'

He realised the only people who had loved him unconditionally and whom he had loved in return were his grandparents. But that was a very different kind of love. And it was that love for them that was behind his determination to ensure the happiest of Christmases for his grandmother. Marissa was talking about romantic love, something entirely foreign and unfamiliar to him.

She stopped walking and he came to a halt near her. 'What about a pet? A dog or cat or horse? I adored my cat. She was old when I inherited her along with my flat from my godmother, so I didn't have her for long. But I loved her so much. If I think about her, I think love would show in my eyes.'

He stared at her. 'What? You think it would work if I called up the love I had for my dog?' He laughed. 'Seriously? You want me to fake a goofy grin with memories of my dog? Who I did love a lot, by the way. He was actually Grandpa's dog, but he was mine when I was here.'

'Er, it's a thought,' she said.

He turned her around to face him. 'So to evoke the required emotion, I look into your face and imagine you're Rufus, my black Labrador?'

Her eyes widened, she bit her lip and she laughed—an awkward, half-speed kind of laugh. 'Not one of my best ideas. Sorry. Scratch that one.'

She was obviously embarrassed, and he didn't want her to feel worse by saying anything else. Although the memory of the best-ever dog Rufus, who'd lived a good long life before succumbing to old age, did warm his heart. Grandpa had been feeling his years at the time, and they'd decided as a family not to get another puppy. But one day, if he ever settled down, he knew he'd want a black Labrador.

He and Marissa turned and walked back to the house. He was disconcerted to find that when he looked into her face, he couldn't conjure up images of past infatuations or even women he'd liked. Because the only face he was remotely interested in seeing was Marissa's own.

He also realised that with her talk of goofy grins and love and infatuation and dogs, she had diverted the conversation quite away from herself and her loathing of Christmas. What had happened there?

CHAPTER SEVEN

OLIVER SAT AT his personal table in the hotel dining room. The staff knew it was his exclusively for the times he chose not to dine in his private quarters. Some of the guests gave him discreet nods, but most of them would have no idea he was the grandson of the owners of Longfield Manor and owner of the most fashionable hotels in London.

That gave him the opportunity to check on service. Every night he'd sat here, he'd seen exemplary service and high levels of guest satisfaction. His table, laid with the same fine but not fussy linen and china as the other tables, was in a secluded corner of the large, welcoming room. A fire blazed in the massive medieval fireplace at one end, emanating warmth and cosiness.

Oliver was dining here tonight with Marissa. He was early and she was spot on time. As she stepped tentatively into the room, looking around her—looking for *him*—he caught his breath. She looked sensational in a black dress that hugged her curves and ended above her knees. Her jeans and trousers had hinted at long, shapely legs, and his guess was now confirmed by the dress and sky-high black stilettos. Yet, her look was subtle, in keeping with her role as a consultant. If she hadn't been pretending to be his girlfriend, might she have kept her hair tied back from her face? Instead, she'd let it tumble below her shoulders, thick and luxuriant, glinting with highlights from the chandeliers. How would it feel to run his hands through it?

She spoke a few words to the maître d' who, with a flourish, led her towards Oliver's table. As she approached, Oliver got up to greet her. The maître d' made a fuss of her, pushing in her chair, making sure she was comfortable, shaking out her table napkin onto her lap. The older man had been with the hotel for years, and Oliver recognised the gleam of speculation as he sat his *girlfriend* opposite him.

Her blue eyes looked even bluer, outlined with dark make-up, and her lips were defined with deep red lipstick. He was often in proximity to beautiful, glamorous and famous women as The Pierce Group hotels were the current cool places to be seen in London. But not one of those women could hold a candle to Marissa. His heart started to thud. He couldn't let her know how attracted he was to her. That wasn't part of the charade.

'You look very beautiful,' he said slowly, his gaze taking in every detail of her appearance. The neckline of her dress revealed the swell of her breasts, an amethyst pendant nestling between them.

Lucky necklace.

As her boyfriend it would be *expected* of him to compliment her. But just being him, Oliver Pierce single guy, he found he *wanted* to tell her how beautiful she was.

'Thank you.' She smiled. That cute dimple was a well-placed punctuation mark to her lovely face. 'I thought I'd better up my game if I'm to pass muster as your girlfriend.'

'You have no cause for concern in that regard,' he said hoarsely.

She was super-hot.

'As long as you approve.'

'I approve,' he said wholeheartedly.

Her eyes widened. 'Well done!'

He frowned. 'Well done?'

'That look. I see emotion. I see affection. I see everything we discussed earlier. You've got it.' Her eyes narrowed. 'Are you channelling your feelings towards your dog Rufus? Is it because I'm wearing black?'

Oliver laughed. 'Of course not. I'm just acting. Playing a role.' What had she seen in his eyes? What had he revealed about how he felt seeing her so sexy and vivacious?

'Well, Academy award for you,' she said. 'There should be no trouble convincing people we're in a real relationship.'

He didn't like to say that his reaction to her had nothing to do with love but everything to do with lust. There could be no doubt he liked her more with every minute he spent with her. But liking someone plus being attracted to her did not equate to love—even the stirrings of love. Not that he and love and Marissa had anything to do with it. Would ever have anything to do with it. This was all pretend.

He indicated the menus on the table. 'Shall we start with a cocktail?'

'A mocktail for me, please. I never drink alcohol while I'm working.'

'You're not working now.'

'Aren't I?' She leaned across the table close to him and lowered her voice to a murmur. 'I'm on girlfriend duty, remember.'

'Point taken.'

She was doing the extra job for which she'd refused payment. And so far, she was doing it brilliantly. But even though he'd devised the whole scheme, something started to rankle with him. This gorgeous woman—more than one head in the restaurant had turned to admire her as she'd made her way across the room to his table—equated spending time with him as a chore. Perhaps he was the one who needed to lift his game.

He ordered mocktails for them both.

Marissa held the folder in her hand without looking at the carefully curated menu, which highlighted local produce. 'What a treat,' she said. 'This room is amazing. And the food sounds fabulous. I'm going to have a hard time deciding what to eat.'

'The food is excellent, even if I say so myself,' he said. 'But you haven't read the menu yet.'

'I don't need to. I had a quick meeting with the head chef today about the Christmas menus. He ran me through the menu choices for tonight. My mouth was watering by the time he'd got through the appetisers.'

The good-looking French chef was a notorious flirt, and Oliver was surprised at the sudden flare of jealousy that seared through him at the thought of Jean Paul turning on the charm for Marissa. He dismissed it immediately as foolishness. Besides, he knew Jean Paul was devoted to his wife and two young sons.

'Jean Paul is an excellent chef. We are fortunate to have him with us.'

'He told me how much he loves the lifestyle here for his family.'

Good. No flirting with Oliver's *girlfriend*, then. Jean Paul's job was safe. Oliver gritted his teeth. He couldn't believe he'd entertained that thought for even a second. He wasn't a jealous guy. And Marissa wasn't really his girlfriend. As a hotelier, if he had to choose between a highly regarded and sought-after chef and a woman, the woman wouldn't even get a look-in.

But if that woman was Marissa?

He couldn't go there, and was shocked at the direction his thoughts had taken him.

Marissa looked across to Oliver, darkly handsome in a charcoal-grey shirt. He'd obviously shaved to keep the stubble on his chin at bay. He must be a twice-a-day shave man. She'd read somewhere that meant high levels of testosterone. A shiver of awareness ran through her at the thought.

Why did he have to be so darn handsome? And such good company. Keeping up the fake-girlfriend thing in front of other people was stressful; there was no doubt about that. She had to be on the alert not to let the mask slip with an inadvertent comment or response that would reveal they were lying—there was no other word for it—about their relationship. Yet, when she was alone with him, she felt relaxed and enjoyed their conversations. Not to mention she was still wildly attracted to him. Good looks aside, he seemed so different from when he'd been sixteen. Did her concept of him, forged in teenage angst, no longer fit the man he was now? Twice today she'd started to tell him about their past acquaintanceship but twice couldn't find the courage to continue. But did it matter?

They ordered from the menu. For a starter, she chose the wild mushroom tart followed by the trout with almond butter. Oliver ordered the lime-cured salmon and the herbed fillet of beef. She'd been very impressed with Jean Paul, the chef, and wanted to see if the meals tasted as good as they sounded. Caity had, of course, already done a tasting of the proposed Christmas menus along with Edith, so that was one less thing to worry about.

Oliver sat back in his chair. 'I have to keep reminding myself that I only met you for the first time this morning.'

Not quite the first time.

'I feel as though I've known you for longer. As if we've put a week's worth of getting to know you into one day.'

'Funny, I was thinking the same thing. I guess it's because we had to accelerate the process to make it believable that we're a couple.'

'That must be it,' he said, not sounding totally convinced.

'It makes our relationship seem more authentic and that's all that counts, isn't it?'

She wondered if there was any chance of a continuing friendship or acquaintanceship of any kind between her and Oliver, or even with Edith whom, despite her outrageous comments, she had already become quite fond of. But that was unlikely, she thought. Although if she did a good job of this—of Christmas, of faking it—she could at least ensure Caity's ongoing business with The Pierce Group. And that was the sole reason she was here, wasn't it?

No, after pretend kissing that had seemed only too real, it would be impossible to see Oliver again after this was over and act normally. She would probably never see him again. And she wasn't sure how she felt about that.

'You have very good online reviews for Longfield Manor,' she said.

'You looked them up?'

'Before I got here.'

'There are many other letters and testimonials, too, from guests who aren't into the internet,' he said.

'That must be very gratifying.'

'It is, especially for Granny. A lot of guests feel a personal connection to this place.'

'My favourite review was one that said the hotel was like a home away from home, only a very posh home.'

Oliver laughed. 'I like that. It's just what we want them to think. The home-away-from-home bit, I mean.'

'Posh without being intimidating,' she said.

Again, she thought about what it must be like to grow up in surroundings like this. And how clever his grandparents had been to turn around their fortunes by transforming their home into a hotel.

'Of course it's posh but I don't think of it that way. It's home.'

An exceedingly posh home. 'How long have your family lived here?'

'Since the early nineteenth century. Going back to then, my ancestors were industrialists who cashed in on the railway boom. No blue blood but plenty of money and quick to seize an opportunity. They had good taste in real estate. I don't remember it but, by all accounts, the London townhouse was also very grand. I know my mother was devastated when it was sold.'

'And now there are your hotels in London. It must be in the blood.'

'Perhaps,' he said with a slight smile.

'Talking of posh, I loved the old suitcases that store some of the decorations. Your ancestors were very well travelled.'

'They're amazing relics, aren't they? From an era where travel was leisurely, not just trying to get from A to B as quickly as possible.'

'In those days it would have taken weeks to get to India or Australia.'

'I would be too impatient for that,' he said.

'Me, too,' she said. 'Have you travelled much?'

'Not as much as I'd have liked to. Establishing my business has always been my priority. Travel has mostly involved staying in other company's hotels to see how they worked and to size up the competition.'

'So you're a workaholic?'

'And proud of it.'

She would be proud, too, looking at what he had achieved. She wondered what motivated him to be so driven. His childhood, perhaps? She didn't dare ask.

Their meals arrived and the food lived up to its descriptions and more. It was so delicious she wanted to savour the taste, rather than chat. Jean Paul was a genius. Living at Longfield Manor for another six days was not going to be a hardship.

'Pudding?' asked Oliver.

'Not tonight, thank you, tempting as that menu is,' she said. 'I had an early start followed by a big day. And my Christmas tree designer will be arriving early in the morning tomorrow so I should turn in soon.'

'A Christmas tree designer. Is that a thing?'

'It is for Andy. He's made a career of it and he's in great demand. I was only able to book him as he had a last-minute cancellation because of a fire on the site where he was scheduled to be working.'

'Lucky us,' said Oliver.

'Do I detect a note of sarcasm there?'

'Certainly not. I respect any designer. My hotels wouldn't be the successes they are without the talented designers who work with me. They excel at Christmas trees and make sure everything they do fits with the overall design vision for the interiors.'

'Whereas here there's a wonderful mishmash of old and new, family heirlooms and the new decorations Caity commissioned to be unique to Longfield Manor.'

'You're okay working with them? The Christmas decorations, I mean.'

She felt her expression shut down as it did when Christmas was mentioned. 'Of course,' she said.

Oliver paused before speaking as if he was carefully choosing his words. 'Is there a reason you don't celebrate Christmas?'

'Not one I care to discuss,' she said, aware of the chill that had crept into her voice.

Why had he ruined such a thoroughly pleasant evening by bringing up her aversion to Christmas? Did he expect that she'd happily spill some answers? She could predict what would come next if she did so. Inevitably, the person she'd confided in would try to change her mind. Why would Oliver be any different? This whole place, him included, was happy-clappy about Christmas.

She got up from the table. 'Thank you for a marvellous dinner. But I really need to be getting up to my room.'

Oliver rose from his chair. 'Let me escort you.'

'I can manage on my own, thank you,' she said.

He came around to her side of the table. 'I'm your boyfriend, remember?' he said in a low voice.

'Sorry. How could I forget?' she murmured as she put her hand mock-possessively on his arm.

Just don't forget even for a second that this—he—isn't real.

Marissa wasn't sure what to say as Oliver walked beside her up that magnificent staircase to her room on the first floor. There was a small guest elevator, but she was determined not to ever take it and miss out on an opportunity to take the stairs and think about the grand past of the manor house.

In silence he walked down the corridor beside her, until they reached her room. Marissa pulled the old-fashioned brass key to the room out of her purse. 'Here I am,' she said, her voice coming out as an awkward croak. Why had he asked her about Christmas? They'd been getting on so well.

'Room eight,' Oliver said. 'That sounds so mundane, doesn't it? When my grandparents started the hotel, Granny had the idea she'd name each room after a Dorset wildflower.'

'A lovely idea.'

'She thought so, too. She started off with Honeysuckle, Snowdrop and Primrose. But when it came to Butterwort and Bogbean she decided to pass on the idea.'

'Seriously?'

'That's how she tells it.'

'The Bogbean Room wouldn't have quite the same cachet, would it?' Marissa laughed. But Oliver just smiled.

'You have a delightful laugh,' he said.

'Do I?' she said.

'Your face lights up. And your eyes, well, they dance. I never knew what that expression meant until I saw you laugh.'

'Oh,' she said, flushing, not sure what else to say.

She looked up to him—even in her high heels he was taller— seeking words for an answer that never came. His expression was serious; his green eyes darkened. She was conscious of her own breathing, the accelerated beat of her heart, his stillness. 'Marissa,' he finally said, her name hanging in the air of the silent, empty corridor. 'I appreciate so much what you're doing for me, for my family. Especially since you don't celebrate Christmas. If I get it right, you don't actually *like* Christmas.'

She put up her hand to stop him. 'Oliver, I—'

'The whys and wherefores of that are totally your own business. I'm sorry I brought it up over dinner and I won't ask you again.'

She didn't drop her gaze from his face, sensed his genuine remorse.

'Thank you,' she said.

She couldn't stop looking up at him, drawn to him as if mesmerised. Her breath came faster at the intensity of his gaze. He traced a finger down the side of her face, a simple gesture that felt like an intimate caress. She reached up to take his hand, not sure whether she meant to run her tongue along his finger or push it away. Instead, she laid her own fingers across his, keeping him close.

Then his mouth was on hers and he was kissing her. There was no need for him to kiss her, no witnesses in that corridor who could attest that their relationship was genuine. There was nothing pretend or fake about this kiss and she should push him away. But she didn't want to stop. She wanted to kiss him, to kiss him hard.

To kiss him for real.

She returned the pressure of his mouth with hers and wound her arms around his neck. He pulled her closer and deepened the kiss. Desire pulsed through her. She wanted him. He wanted her, too, she could tell.

She wanted more than kisses. When she thought of it, she'd always wanted him—right back to when she'd been fourteen years old. Back then her longing for him had gone no further than the hope of exciting, sweet kisses and cuddles. Her virginal imagination had taken her no further. Now her thoughts so easily took her to what would happen if she pushed her door open and they stumbled, kissing and caressing, into her room with the door slammed shut behind them.

There would be no going back.

Everything would change.

The game would be for real—and she would not come out the winner.

She broke away from the kiss, pushed him away, took a deep, steadying breath, felt her cheeks flushed. 'If we continue kissing like this we both know where it will lead us. And I don't want to go there. That's not part of the deal. To work with you after that would be so awkward.' She wanted him too much to play with the flickering flames of intense desire.

'We could make it work,' he said hoarsely.

'No,' she said, and he immediately let her go. 'I'm attracted to you. I think you know that. But I don't do one-night stands or casual flings.'

'Understood,' he said as he took a step back. She noted he didn't say he didn't do casual, either. But then that didn't surprise her. He'd made his stance on relationships very clear.

She wrapped her arms around her middle as if barricading herself. 'So far, we're doing well with the fake relationship for the sake of your grandmother. I'm happy to continue that. But now I want to say good-night, and when I see you tomorrow it should be as if this had never happened. Please.'

CHAPTER EIGHT

AFTER A RESTLESS NIGHT, when sleep had proved elusive, Marissa was glad of the distraction provided by her friend Andy, the Christmas tree designer, and his visit to Longfield Manor. She and Andy had first worked together years ago when they were on staff at the same company.

Andy's full-on personality wouldn't allow time for regretful thoughts about Oliver. She was so drawn to him, the attraction so magnetic. Should she have invited him to her bed and taken the chance on something wonderful but ephemeral? Was she being overprotective of her feelings? On balance, she decided she'd made the right decision last night. It was hard enough to keep on an even keel surrounded by Christmas let alone being immersed in emotional angst if she went too far with Oliver. He had an immense power to hurt her. Even his thoughtless insults as a teenager had caused long-lasting pain.

She stood patiently by while Andy chastised her for not letting him go out to the Christmas tree farm to choose and cut the trees himself.

'I know you're Mr Perfectionist, and like total control over the tree,' she said. 'But this has all been a bit last-minute. I'm standing in for Caity,' she explained.

'I get it, you had to help Caity out,' Andy replied. 'And the bonus is the hot boss.' He made a lascivious face. 'How does he identify?'

'He. Him. Heterosexual.'

'You go, girl,' Andy said.

Marissa was about to totally deny any interest in the CEO of The Pierce Group. But she quickly pulled herself up. *No slips.* She was meant to be Oliver's girlfriend.

She smiled the fakest of smiles. 'We're together, actually.'

'Together as in *together*?'

'Yes. I'm dating him. Have been since early November. We met at—' There she went, overembellishing. 'Never mind where we met.'

'Congratulations.'

Marissa couldn't resist adding something vaguely truthful. 'I'm keeping quiet about it as Oliver isn't...isn't into long-term relationships.'

'And you are?'

'One day, yes,' she said, surprising herself. She hadn't thought she was ready.

'And you don't want to put pressure on him?'

'No. It's not like that. I don't want to be embarrassed when it ends.'

'You pessimist! Is it good to anticipate the end when you've barely started?'

'Less painful that way when it doesn't work out,' she said.

It would end and end soon. *Because it wasn't real.* And already she knew she would be sad when she had to say goodbye to her fake boyfriend. In spite of her longtime grudge, she liked him.

'If you say so,' he said, not seeming convinced. 'Now, take me to the Christmas trees.'

Marissa was on her own in the reading room, a drawing room also called the quiet room. It was one of the smaller public rooms where guests were encouraged to take time out to read, listen to music through headphones, or even nap in the comfortable sofas and easy chairs. The beautifully proportioned room was decorated, as everywhere in Longfield Manor, with impeccable taste in traditional English country house style with Edith's unique twist on it.

Marissa stood on the jewel-toned Persian carpet, just her and a Christmas tree, the smallest of the five trees to be placed around the hotel. Andy had started the decoration and had left strict instructions on the precise order in which to place each bauble, bead and star in exact colour combinations, a measured distance from the end of the branch.

It wasn't she who was meant to be actually dressing the tree with such precision. She wouldn't volunteer for the task in a million years. In fact, she'd only been in this room to introduce two of the temporary student staff to Andy and leave them to it. However, Andy had been so impressed with the students' design skills and willingness to learn, he'd spirited them away to assist him in dressing the tallest of the trees. That giant fir would tower in festive grandeur over the living room and be the star of the Christmas celebrations. He'd asked Marissa to watch the room and keep guests out until he returned with another team.

She was wearing black jeans and a smart textured jacket and she began to feel uncomfortable. The room was very warm, stuffy even, with a wood fire burning in the fireplace. Marissa hated the smell of pine needles. The scent from the tree pervaded the room, no matter how far she stood away from it. There was no escape from it. She put her hands to her head as it began to overwhelm her.

The sharp acrid smell of pine permeated her lungs, making her feel dizzy and disoriented. Her breath came in short gasps. She clutched on to the back of a high-backed chair. Nausea rose in her throat and she swallowed against it.

On Christmas Eve her parents had been transporting the Christmas tree home on the top of the car when the accident had happened. The pine needles had scattered all over the car, all over them. Afterwards, she and her brother, stricken by grief and disbelief, had wanted to see where it had happened. Pine needles and broken glass had been all over the ground where the car had left the road and smashed into a fence. When she collected her parents' possessions from the hospital, her mother's handbag had been full of the needles and they'd been scattered over her father's favourite tweed jacket.

Marissa started to tremble and shake. She had to get out of this room. As she pushed herself away from the chair she stumbled and tripped. But strong arms were there to stop her from falling, to hold her tight.

'Marissa, what happened? Are you okay?'

Oliver.

Oliver had thought Marissa was about to faint and hurt herself on the way down. Thank heaven he had come into the room, looking for her, when he did. As he held her tight in the circle of his arms, he felt a powerful urge to protect and comfort her. In this moment, she seemed so vulnerable, she who presented as formidably efficient and self-contained. She clung to him not just, he thought, for physical balance, but also for emotional support. What had happened here?

'Let it out,' he said. 'If you need to cry, do so.'

'I'm not crying,' she said, her voice muffled against his shoulder. 'I'm really not.'

He held her in silence, aware of her softness, her rose-and-vanilla scent, how much he liked having her there so close to him. He resisted the urge to drop a kiss on the top of her head. That would be too intimate, too personal, for a woman who had set very clear boundaries.

Finally, her breathing became more even. Marissa pulled away and looked up at him. She was very pale, in spite of the warmth of the room. There was no evidence of tears, but her make-up was smudged around her eyes and, without thinking, he reached down to tenderly wipe away the mascara smear with his finger.

'Thank you,' she said. 'And…and I'm sorry.'

He frowned. 'Sorry? Sorry for what?'

'For having you see my panic attack.'

'Panic attack? Is that what was happening? There's no need to apologise. I thought you were going to faint and fall, possibly get injured. I'm so glad I came into the room at the right time.'

'Thank you,' she said. Those unshed tears made her eyes seem even bluer. 'I'm glad you were here, too.'

'Are you feeling okay now?' he said, reluctant to step back from her. They were still close. At the same time, he was wary of treading where she didn't want him to be. 'Did you get bad news?'

'Not really. Not…not new bad news. It…it's the smell of the Christmas tree. The pine needles. They bother me.'

'An allergy?'

'In a way.'

'It's stuffy in here and the smell of the pine needles is very strong. We could open a window, but it would quickly get icy cold. It's bitter out there. They're predicting snow for Christmas. Besides, you wouldn't want wind coming through the window when you're decorating a tree in here.'

'It's not me dressing the tree, it's Andy.'

'So why are you in here by yourself?'

'Long story. But Andy asked me to keep the room free of guests and to keep an eye on these fragile, valuable decorations. I can't leave here until he gets back.'

'Why don't I ask Priya to send someone in here to take over guard duty, while I take you off for a cool drink or a coffee?'

'I don't want anyone to see me like this,' she said shakily.

'Let me take you to my apartment, where you can have all the privacy you want. If you feel like telling me why the scent of pine needles bothers you so much, you can. If not, you can take some time to get yourself back together and get on with your day.'

Her shoulders went back, and she stiffened. 'Are you worried this…this incident might affect the quality of my work? I assure you it won't. I'm on call twenty-four hours while I'm here.'

'I know how committed you are. I'm certainly not concerned about that. But I am worried about you.'

'Like a good fake boyfriend should,' she said with a curve of her lips that wasn't quite a smile, her dimple the merest indentation.

'I wouldn't be much of a fake boyfriend if I didn't look after you, would I? But just as one human being to another, you're distressed and in need of a break and perhaps something to eat.'

'Ugh, I couldn't eat a thing,' she said, shaking her head. 'But I like the idea of going somewhere out of sight. And, to be honest, I'm curious to see the private areas of the building. I feel I owe you an explanation for why I collapsed all over you. And I'm very grateful to you for catching me.'

Within minutes of Oliver's calling Priya, she was there. Priya looked curiously at the somewhat dishevelled Marissa but, being a perfectly trained hotel manager, she didn't say anything except to reassure them that the room would be guarded until Andy returned with a new team of decorators.

Oliver kept his arm around her as he escorted Marissa to the private wing of the Manor at the east end. His grandmother still lived in the large house-sized residence fitted out for her and Grandpa when they'd converted their country house into a hotel. They'd sold off the farmland that had still been part of the estate to fund the conversion. As a child, he had lived there with them on his frequent extended visits, then permanently when his mother had left the country. When he'd turned twenty-one, his grandparents had given him his own spacious apartment in their private wing. They'd been so good to him. Paid for the law degree studies he'd dropped out of, as he'd found hotels to be so much more interesting. Helped bankroll the startup of his business. He could never repay them for what they'd done for him. Everything he'd ever been able to do for them had been worth it. Even pretending that Marissa was his girlfriend.

He showed Marissa to the oversized, squashy sofa—big enough for a tall man to stretch out on. Marissa sat tentatively on the edge, obviously ill at ease.

'Granny will be delighted I've dragged you to my lair so we can be on our own,' he said, sitting down next to her.

'Do you really believe Edith thinks that?'

'Of course she does. She'll be disappointed when you return to Room eight.'

'Which I now can't help thinking of as the Bogbean Room.' He was pleased to see her tentative smile—more of the dimple this time.

'Don't let Granny hear you say that. She would be horrified.'

'You think so?'

'I know so.'

Marissa looked around her. 'Your apartment is amazing. I could fit three of my apartment into it. Impeccably created by Edith, I suppose?'

'I was twenty-one when I moved in. I had no say in how it looked. Granny kept in mind what she thought I'd like when she chose the furnishing and decoration. It was done in a simpler style than the rest of the private wing, more contemporary but still with a nod to the building's ancient bones. Fortunately, it turned out she was right. In fact, I incorporated some of her design ideas into my penthouse at Pierce Soho they suited me so well.'

'What if you hadn't liked what she did here?'

'I wouldn't have told her. No way would I have wanted to hurt her feelings.'

'You would have pretended to like it?'

'Yes.'

She paused for a beat. 'You're good at pretending.'

'So are you. We wouldn't be getting away with the fake-relationship thing if we weren't equally good at pretending.'

'True,' she said.

But he wasn't pretending about how attractive he found her, how compelling. He couldn't remember feeling like this about a woman, certainly not over the space of a few days. It surprised him.

'Coffee? Or something stronger?' he asked, getting up from the sofa.

'A big glass of water, please.'

As Oliver poured the water in the kitchen, he remembered their discussion on favourite foods. He took a block of dark Belgian chocolate from the pantry, broke it into pieces and presented it to her on a plate. 'This might also help,' he added.

'How can I resist a man who gives me chocolate?' she said, but her voice was still shaky, and her smile didn't light her eyes.

'You did tell me it was your favourite food,' he said.

Oliver watched as she nibbled on the chocolate. She savoured every bite with exaggerated pleasure. It made him wonder if there was anyone back in London to look after her when she needed a boost to low spirits. Not to look after her in a patriarchal male way; he suspected she'd run a mile from that. Not in a warm, family way, either, as he knew her parents were dead and so was her godmother. But in the way of someone who cared about her and had her best interests at heart. Someone to be her wingman—or wingwoman. Perhaps that was Caity, but her friend ran a thriving business and would soon be mothering twins. Not that it was likely Marissa would ask for her friend's help. He got the impression she was so fiercely independent, she would tell him she didn't need anyone to look after her, thank you very much. Not a commitment-phobe like him, that was for sure.

But as he thought about Marissa, he realised he didn't have anyone, either. He had staff at his beck and call at his own hotels and here at Longfield Manor. Call room service from his penthouse and anything he wanted would be delivered within minutes. And his grandmother jumped at any opportunity to dote on him. He still saw his schoolfriend Toby on occasion, but Toby was married with young children and his family was his focus. Marissa had an air of aloofness about her that might very well be, he thought, loneliness. Was he lonely? He was surrounded by people and his business took up every second of every day. He didn't have time to be lonely.

Marissa downed the water as if she hadn't drunk for a week, then put her glass down on the coffee table. 'Do you mind if I sit back on your sofa?' she said. 'It seems too perfect to use with all those cushions so precisely arranged. I don't dare disturb them.'

'Toss the cushions on the floor if you want to. I do. But, again, don't tell Granny. She's a cushion fanatic. Wait until you see my bedroom. There are a million cushions on the bed.'

What had he said?

An awkward silence hung between them at the impact of his words. Inwardly, he cursed himself. 'I didn't mean—'

'I don't think—'

'You're not interested in seeing my bedroom? Point taken. But I won't pretend I don't want to see you in my bedroom.' He paused. 'In my bed.'

She flushed high on her cheekbones. 'And I won't pretend that I wouldn't like to be there. In your bed.' She met his gaze directly. 'With you.'

His breath seemed to stop, and his heart hammered at the sensual thoughts she conjured. Knowing she could match him made him want her even more.

She shifted away from him on the sofa as she continued. 'But I don't do flings and you told me you don't have long relationships. I've decided I want commitment and everything that comes with that. What you might find boring. Security. Marriage. Even kids. Not now. Maybe not for a long time. But it's what I ultimately want. Whereas you're not interested in being tied down. We're looking for different things.'

'That's true,' he said, thinking how crass his words sounded being quoted back at him. Had he really said that to her? Yes, he had. Because he always made it clear to a woman that short-term was all he wanted and that he would pull the plug if awkward emotions developed or demands were made.

'Truth is, I want you, but I also like you,' she said. 'Having a fling with you would most likely not end well. And I don't want that. Besides, I don't want to jeopardise this good thing we're doing for Edith by making things awkward and uncomfortable between us. So can we not mention your bedroom again?'

Oliver nodded. He would be respectful and not try to argue. Even as at the same time he regretted the lost opportunity to see where that mutual attraction might take them.

'And I'll take you at your word that there are lots of cushions in there,' she added.

CHAPTER NINE

IN TRUTH, Marissa ached to count the cushions on Oliver's bed. To throw them one by one onto the floor followed by every stitch of Oliver's clothing—and then her own.

What had Caity said about Oliver? *Movie-star handsome.*

With his black hair and green eyes he was that all right—but he was so much more than his good looks. She was drawn to him like she'd never been drawn to a man—except, that is, his sixteen-year-old self. Who could have predicted that arrogant boy would grow up to be so thoughtful? But she'd meant every word about keeping her distance from him.

She was so attracted to this man it would be easy to let her senses take over. To share glorious sex—and she was convinced it would be glorious—with him with no thought of tomorrow. And then where would she be? Exactly what she would appear to be at the end of this seven days—another discarded girlfriend. Only she wouldn't have been a real girlfriend, rather a pretend girlfriend with benefits.

Aargh! She felt her head was spinning, not from the pine needles but by the realisation that she could fall for Oliver in a big way. Actually fall in love with him—and that would be disastrous. All those danger signs that had been beeping at her from the moment she'd realised who he was and what he'd been to her as a teenager were now urgently flashing a warning.

Protect your heart.

He was keeping a respectable distance from her on the sofa. How ironic. If there was anyone there to see them, they would have to keep up the pretence of their fake relationship and he would quite probably have his arm around her. But when there was no one there, they could be what they really were to each other—he the boss, she the contract employee. A possibility of something else he could be crept into her mind—*a friend.* They were halfway there; she enjoyed his company so much. If they kept out of that bed with its multiple cushions, could she and Oliver end up friends? Before the thought had a chance to lodge in her brain she dismissed it. For her, it would have to be all or nothing with Oliver. Because of the reasons she'd give him, *all* was never going to happen. Just these remaining five days.

'Thank you for the chocolate, for looking after me,' she said. 'I feel so much better now. In fact, I feel a little foolish. I probably would have been fine without—'

'Me catching you when you fell? I don't think so.'

He moved closer to her on the sofa. She was acutely aware of his warmth, his strength, the spicy scent of him, how grateful she was that he was there.

'You'd had a shock of some kind. Are you ready to tell me about it?'

Marissa angled her knees so it was easier to face him and took a deep, steadying breath. His expression invited confidence; his eyes were kind and non-judgemental. No matter, she still hated sharing her story—it never got easier. 'You deserve an explanation,' she said. 'You were right about it being linked to why I don't like Christmas. Why I'm reputed to be a Scrooge and a Grinch.'

He frowned. 'Surely not? Do people really call you that?'

'Sadly, yes. And it's true. Though only a very few people know why.'

She gripped her hands tightly together in front of her and looked ahead, rather than at Oliver. She couldn't, after all, face the pity she knew she would see in his eyes. He had a stark, black modern clock on the wall opposite that suited the room perfectly as its metallic hand ticked relentlessly around the clock face. She was shocked to note the time—there was so much to be done—but this needed to be said.

'Christmas used to be a big deal in our family. There were just my parents and me, my brother Kevin and my grandmother. Nana used to join us for Christmas, too. But my parents being the warm, hospitable people they were, our house was also open to waifs and strays who didn't have family to go to or were away from home. The house would be decorated to the max, and my parents cooked for days to have the full-on traditional feast with all the trimmings. If you'd asked me then, you would have heard me say I adored Christmas.'

She turned back to look at Oliver. Noticed that he swallowed hard. She'd told him her parents had died, but not how they'd died. He must have guessed she was about to recount something awful. She forced herself to continue. It was always difficult for her to tell someone what had happened. 'Five years ago on Christmas Eve, my mother and father were returning home with the Christmas tree when they were killed in a car crash. My mother went instantly, my father died later in hospital, early on Christmas Day.'

Oliver gasped. He moved closer, reached out, untwisted her hands and enfolded them in his much larger ones. 'I'm sorry, Marissa.'

She felt comforted by his touch, understood how difficult it was to utter more than platitudes at times like these. 'It was an accident, a horrible accident.' She would never, ever forget the shock, disbelief and deep, wrenching pain she'd felt when she'd been notified.

'The police couldn't be sure exactly what happened, as my parents were on a back road with no cameras. It was raining.

The narrow road was slippery. They were running late with their decorating because of work commitments. Did they swerve to avoid an animal on the road? Did the tree slip free of its moorings and slide off the car? Perhaps they were rushing, driving too fast, but whatever the reason, the car went off the road and crashed head-on into a very solid fence.'

Oliver's grip on her hands tightened. 'I have no words. I can't imagine how you must have felt.'

'Because it happened at Christmastime, I can never forget it. Christmas is the anniversary of my parents' deaths. There were pine needles everywhere. All through the wreckage of the car, through…through my parents' clothes. My dad still had a few pine needles in his hair when he was in hospital. The smell… I hate it. It brings back so many bad memories. Back there, in the reading room, the scent was so strong I felt overwhelmed.'

'No wonder. There are pine Christmas trees everywhere you look at this time of year.'

'Which is why I try to avoid them. I wish more people used artificial trees, although nothing looks as good as a real pine. But even a fake tree symbolises everything I lost that Christmas.' She paused. 'You know, both Kevin and I had offered to pick up a tree for them, but Mum and Dad insisted it was something they liked to do themselves. They'd made collecting the tree a ritual since their first year of marriage.'

'So you and Kevin tormented yourselves with endless *if-onlys*. If only you'd gone instead…if only—'

'We tormented ourselves with many regrets and recriminations. As you can imagine, Christmas that year was hell. Organising funerals instead of festivities. The paperwork, the legalities, the pleasantries while accepting condolences, when all I wanted to do was crawl into a dark hole and howl.'

He squeezed her hand. 'My grandpa's death wasn't a tragic one like your parents'—'

'Every death is tragic when you lose someone you love.'

'But at least it was expected. Grandpa was eighty-seven with inoperable cancer. We knew we were going to lose him but that didn't make his loss any easier.' He paused. 'Granny was too distraught to handle the formalities, so I had to do it. Who knew how much time and effort was involved?'

'Every time I had to write down their details it was another blow, another reminder they were gone and I would never see them again. I was never that sure of the year of my father's birth when I was younger. I sure knew it after filling out all those forms. Then, just weeks after the accident, our grandmother died of a stroke brought on, the doctors said, by the shock of her daughter's death. My mother was her only child. As next of kin, I had to go through it all again for Nana.'

'Loss upon loss,' Oliver said hoarsely, his grip tightening over her hands. 'How did you bear it?'

'We didn't cope well. When it was all over, we were left with nothing—no family except distant cousins in Norfolk we barely know, and friends who didn't know what to say so stayed away. My brother is two years younger than me. He took it very hard. The next year he couldn't deal with the prospect of Christmas without Mum and Dad. He took off on a trip to Australia and never came back.'

'What do you mean, *never came back*?'

'He met a wonderful girl, Danni, and they got married. He lives in Sydney permanently now.'

'That seems like a happy ending, though.'

'For them, not for me. It meant I lost my brother, too. I know that makes me sound selfish, and I don't mean it to. I'm really happy for them, and she's awesome. But they're just so far away.'

'Have you been to see them in Australia?'

She felt like she should get up and walk around the room, instead of sitting there, static. But she didn't want to lose the comfort of Oliver's hands cradling hers.

'The second Christmas after my parents' deaths, I flew down to Australia, glad to get away from London and the memories. Sydney is an amazing city. We celebrated Christmas with Danni's family. Although everyone was very kind and welcoming, I felt like an outsider, an interloper. As well, a traditional northern hemisphere Christmas celebration in a hot Australian summer just didn't seem right. And it wasn't different enough for me to forget my memories of that terrible Christmas.'

'I thought Aussies had barbecues on the beach for Christmas?'

'Some might. But I was told many prefer the traditional turkey, plum pudding, brandy custard, mince pies, Brussels sprouts, the lot. I felt so sorry for Danni and her family slaving away in a hot kitchen. I might not like Christmas but to me it means winter, fires roaring in the fireplace, frost and the possibility of snow. Like here, in this beautiful place. No wonder guests flock here at this time of year.'

'Sydney gave you another bad Christmas experience? I hope that was the end of it.'

'There's more to come. Are you sure you want to hear?'

'I do,' he said. 'I want to understand you, Marissa. I'm beginning to appreciate what an effort it must have been for you to come here as a Christmas event planner.'

'I did it for Caity. I'd do anything to help her.' She didn't go into detail; that was Caity's business.

'I see that now. I appreciate your help even more.'

'And I…well… I'm really glad I came.'

And got the chance to meet you.

'Dare I ask what happened the next Christmas?'

'The next year I decided to lock myself away in my flat for Christmas and come out when it was all over. Then out of the blue, I got fired from my job on Christmas Eve. The marketing company I worked for decided to close its event planning division. My position was made redundant.'

'That sounds grim. Can they do that on Christmas Eve?'

'It's heartless but legal, apparently. My Grinchiness really set in then.'

He slowly shook his head. 'A series of awful things that just happened to occur at Christmas. I mean, it's not really the fault of Christmas, is it? More like coincidence.'

'It's jinxed. Christmas is jinxed for me.'

'You can't seriously mean that.'

'Then how do you explain that the next year—last Christmas—I caught my boyfriend kissing another woman under the mistletoe at his office party. Passionate kissing. Complete with spiteful triumph from his so-called *just a friend* colleague.'

'Awful. Was the boyfriend a serious relationship?'

'I was gutted. I really liked him. He was a client and initially I knocked him back when he started asking me out. But he persevered. When he was no longer my client, I finally said yes. I fell hard for him. We were talking about moving in together.'

'That's serious.'

'As serious as I've ever got. And another regret. Up until then I had a strict *no dating a client* policy. That's been put in place again, I can assure you.' Not that anyone had tempted her with thoughts of breaking it again. Until now.

'Me being the exception,' he said with a smile.

'My policy didn't cover fake dating.' There it was, under all the angst, an easiness between them she felt very comfortable with.

He let go of her hands and got up. 'Would you like that coffee now?'

'Yes, please,' she said, also getting up to follow him to his kitchen, which was at the end of the open-plan living room.

'Where would you have spent Christmas if you hadn't come here?' he asked, as his impressive espresso machine steamed and hissed.

'I had flights booked to Nusa Lembongan, a small island off the east coast of Bali. Christmas isn't part of the culture there, so I figured I wouldn't be immersed in festive cheer like I would be in London. The tourist hotels cater for Christmas, but I don't think it would have been difficult for me to avoid any festivities.'

'Instead, you're here, working for me, immersed in our Christmas events.'

'And loving every minute of it.' She looked up at him. 'I mean that. Working here has been a revelation.'

'Except for incidents when you're confined to a stuffy room with a Christmas tree.'

'There's that,' she agreed. 'But look how chivalrously I was rescued.'

He laughed. 'And not just because I'm your fake boyfriend. Let's get that clear.'

She smiled. 'That's another problem with this job.'

'And what's that?'

'I can't include my stint as pretend girlfriend to the CEO on my résumé.'

'We might have to keep that one to ourselves.'

'I wholeheartedly agree,' she said. 'Also, I'd appreciate it if you didn't share what I've just told you with anyone else. You know, my history regarding Christmas and why I'm a Christmas-phobe.' It was a relief to have told him, but she didn't want other people to hear her story, including his grandmother, Edith.

'That's understood. It's entirely your business. But thank you for opening up to me about the tragedy in your past. You've suffered quite the litany of grief, too much for one person. Tell me about your godmother. Did she pass at Christmas, too?'

'No, she died before my parents did. My mother took her loss badly. They'd been friends since primary school. And, before you ask, my cat didn't die at Christmas, either.'

'That's something,' he said cautiously.

She couldn't help but laugh at his comment, which lightened the atmosphere.

Oliver opened his pantry to pull out a packet of Italian almond biscotti. 'I keep stocked up on snacks. Needless to say, this kitchen isn't used much. Not when I live in a hotel.'

'Lucky you. I'd never use my kitchen if I could eat Jean Paul's food rather than cooking it myself.' What a difference her meal last night had been to her rotation of ready meals warmed up in the microwave, or hastily constructed salads.

'One night we could have dinner sent up here rather than eat in the restaurant,' he suggested.

'Do you think that's wise?' she asked, thinking how very unwise it would be for her to be alone with him—particularly near his bed or the inviting sofa.

'Probably not if you want to continue resisting my attempts to seduce you,' he said with a wry twist to his mouth.

Marissa's heart skipped a beat at the thought of a full-on seduction by Oliver, but she managed an appropriate response. 'Restaurant it is, then.'

She sat on a high stool at the kitchen counter to drink her coffee and he stood opposite her. 'Oliver, now that I've done so much soul baring, can you tell me some more about yourself? If it's not too painful, that is.'

He bridled and that easy moment of repartee evaporated immediately. 'Why would it be painful?' He shrugged. 'My parents weren't around a lot of the time, but I didn't lack for anything.'

She didn't reply, just let a silence fall between them, and waited for him to speak.

'Okay, except for parental love,' he said finally in a self-mocking tone.

Heartbreaking, she thought. 'A lack of love from your parents is kind of serious,' she said.

'Fact is, my parents weren't ready to have a kid. They hadn't known each other for long when my mother fell pregnant. I believe my father had doubts I was his, until I turned out looking very like him. A baby hardly fitted with their lifestyle—a model and a rock musician. They'd go away for months at a time and leave me with my grandparents. My schooling could only be described as erratic.'

She hadn't expected that, not when he came from wealth,

his mother a well-known model and socialite—this place their ancestral home.

What was that old saying? *It's better to be born lucky than rich.*

'That doesn't sound great,' she said, not sure what else she could say. How grateful she was for her stable upbringing with parents who loved each other and their children, whereas Oliver seemed to have had terrible luck in that area.

'When I was eight, they put me in boarding school.' She knew he'd been in boarding school when he was sixteen but not as young as that. He'd put down his coffee and she noticed his fists were tightly clenched by his sides.

'Eight? You were a baby. How was that?'

'By being sent away, I felt I was being punished, I didn't know what for. There was no actual abuse, but my years at boarding school didn't rate highly on the scale of my youthful experience,' he said.

The tight set of his jaw, the shadow that darkened his green eyes, told her not to probe any further. But she couldn't help shuddering. 'I can't imagine it would,' she said. She'd heard some traumatic stories about boys' private boarding schools; bullying, cruelty.

'The marriage was on and off with screaming fights then dramatic reconciliations. They finally divorced when I was thirteen. When I was fifteen my mother chased after a man to New Zealand and settled there.'

'She didn't take you with her?'

'I wasn't wanted,' he said baldly. 'Her excuse was that it was a bad time to interrupt my private schooling by moving to a different system.'

'I'm sorry, but that's out and out cruelty,' Marissa said fiercely.

'I suspect my mother lied about her age, and it didn't suit her to have people know she had a child my age. I was…inconvenient.'

'Of course you weren't inconvenient. Don't say that. It couldn't possibly be true.'

He sighed a weary sigh. 'Marissa, you weren't there.' His voice dripped with cynicism. 'All I can say is thank heaven for my wonderful grandparents.'

'No wonder you want to do everything you can to help Edith.'

'They were my real family. The reason I love Christmas at Longfield Manor was that my grandparents always made it special for me when I was a child, and even my self-centred parents made an effort to be here. Although one year neither of them showed up, without explanation. I waited all day for them.'

She wondered, as she had several times, about their conversation at dinner the night before. Oliver's confession that he had never been in love had surprised her. But if he hadn't received love from the people who were supposed to love him most, was he capable of giving love?

She slid off her stool and walked around to where he stood. 'You need a hug. For that sweet little boy. For that betrayed teenager. For the wonderful man you are now.'

She put her arms around him in a big hug. He hugged her back, powerful arms circling her. They stood there, close together for a long moment. Body to body. Arms wrapped around each other. He pulled back from the hug, their arms still around each other to look down into her face. 'Thank you,' he said.

'I'm sorry I made you dredge up uncomfortable memories,' she said.

'All in the past,' he said brusquely, with a *conversation over* stamp to his voice.

He looked down into her face, and she met his gaze unblinkingly. Her heart started to beat faster at his closeness. His face was already so familiar, those green eyes, his nose slightly crooked, his smooth olive skin, already at 11 a.m. darkly shadowed, his beautifully sculpted mouth. A mouth she knew felt so good against hers. A mouth she wanted to feel again for a dizzyingly pleasurable kiss. As she swayed towards him, her lips parted in anticipation. Nothing had ever felt better than being with this man.

Oliver's arms tightened around Marissa as he bent his head to kiss her. Her mouth yielded to his as she pressed herself close to him and kissed him back with passion and enthusiasm that matched his.

This wasn't pretend. It was as real as a kiss could be. Her kiss was as exciting, as arousing, as their other kisses, but this also soared to a somehow different level. He knew it was because of the emotional connection he now felt for her. He understood her so much better after her confessions of heartbreak and loss. And she seemed to understand him, too. After revisiting his painful memories of abandonment, her spontaneous hug had been just what he'd needed but he would never be able to ask for. Somehow, she had known that.

He didn't want to let her go.

Yet, he would have to. He didn't have what it took to make a woman like Marissa happy. And her happiness now seemed somehow his concern. There should be no further kisses, no talk of seduction. She'd been honest about what she wanted for her future. He couldn't even commit to having a dog in his life, let alone a wife and a child. His focus was on a relentless drive to succeed. Riding the wave of the popularity of The Pierce Group hotels made him strive for more. He was looking for sites to expand into New York. Romantic relationships had never been part of his life plan.

One former girlfriend had accused him of being damaged. Not that she'd known of the tumultuous on-and-off relationship with his parents, particularly his mother. The way Mummy would arrive laden with presents, swoop down on him and cover him with kisses. Until boredom—with motherhood, with him?—had set in. Then she'd depart on a modelling shoot or on an extended holiday to heaven knew where, and he wouldn't know when he'd next see her. It was the same story with his father, although truth be told his father had never been effusive with affection. If it hadn't been for the love and stability given by his grandparents, maybe he would indeed be damaged. Although it was true that he didn't trust easily and was wary of commitment. And that sometimes he felt an emptiness that no amount of work and casual dating could make go away. But was that so uncommon in men of his age?

Marissa broke the kiss. Reluctantly, he let her go. She stepped back. 'I…er…have to get back to work,' she said, her voice not quite steady.

He looked down into her face. She was flushed and breathless and so beautiful his heart contracted. Not only was she the most gorgeous, sexy woman he'd ever had the privilege of kissing, she was also a thoroughly lovely person. Kind. Fun. Loyal. He really liked her. He'd only known her for two days, yet his gut instinct was telling him—screaming at him—that this woman was different from any other woman he had met, that she could be special. His gut instinct had never let him down. He'd made good business decisions about people on less acquaintance than two days, by listening to it. Yet, this wasn't just about him, and the last thing he wanted to do was hurt her.

'Are you sure you're feeling okay now?' he asked.

'Quite sure,' she said. 'Again, thank you for getting me out of that room and looking after me. How did you know I was there?'

'Granny said you might be in the reading room. I needed to talk to you.'

That wasn't strictly why he had sought her out in the reading room. Truth was, he'd missed her. He had simply wanted to see her and reassure himself that this amazing woman was still there under the same roof as him. He'd spent a restless night thinking about her. Wondering why he'd become so obsessed with her so quickly. She'd made her position clear that she wanted something more from a man than a fling with a short use-by date.

But what if he wanted more than that with her, too?

'I was looking for you to tell you I have to go to London for a few days.'

'Oh,' she said. 'That's a shame.' Disappointment flashed in her eyes before she blinked hard to dispel it.

'Something urgent has come up that requires me to be at my hotel in person.'

He'd been putting the visit off, but the way things were developing between him and Marissa meant now might be a good time for him to get away to London for a bit. The way that kiss, still warm on his lips, had made him feel was disconcerting. He needed to think through this mad attraction, these unsettling feelings, away from her. He didn't want sexual attraction to be mistaken for something deeper. He caught his breath. Was he really thinking about something deeper? He didn't like uncertainty. He needed to deal with this—and he could only do so away from the distraction of her beautiful face and body.

Out of sight, out of mind. Yet another useful cliché.

'I'll have to leave now,' he said.

'I understand,' she said. 'What will this mean for our fake relationship? How will I explain your absence to Edith?'

'She'll probably suggest I take you with me.'

'I couldn't do that,' she said hastily.

Why not? he immediately thought. But wasn't her not being with him what he wanted, so he could think things through without distraction?

'I'm needed here,' she said. 'I'm here to organise your Christmas and there are things to do, teams to coordinate.'

'Tell Granny that's why you can't go with me. She won't be surprised I have to go. A hotel is a twenty-four-hour business. After all her years here, she'll be aware that emergencies arise. And it's not always something a manager can sort, no matter how good they might be. There are so many variables, not the least of which is the people—including staff and guests.'

'I bet you have some interesting stories to tell,' she said.

The smile, that enchanting dimple, was back and suddenly

he wished he wasn't going to London at all. This was confusing. And Oliver did not allow himself to get confused.

'There might be a few tales I could tell—with names blacked out of course.'

'I'll look forward to that,' she said. 'But…in the meantime, I…er… I'll miss you.' She was obviously having difficulty in meeting his gaze, her eyes cast down to her feet.

He tilted her chin back up with a finger, so he looked right into her eyes. 'Me, too. Miss you, I mean. It doesn't seem like we've only known each other for such a short time, does it?'

'Sometimes friendships work like that,' she said with a slow smile.

Friendship? Did she only see him as a friend? He wasn't sure he liked that idea. But surely she wouldn't kiss someone who was just a friend the way she'd just kissed him?

'Reassure Granny that we'll be in touch the entire time I'm away,' he said.

'I've got so much to do,' she said. 'We'll make Christmas super-special for you and Edith this year, I promise.'

'While you'll loathe every minute of it?'

'I won't lie and say I love Christmas, and now you know why. But it's so very different here from any other place I've experienced Christmas. I'll be okay. I can deal with it.'

'Will you be all right in the evenings?' Without him, he meant, but didn't like to say.

'Of course,' she said. 'Andy and I might go to the pub in the village for dinner tonight. It's been ages since we caught up.'

Jealousy sparked through him. Maybe it wasn't such a good idea to leave her. 'You're old friends?'

'We used to work together. I went to his wedding last year. It was such fun.'

'He's married?' he said, hoping the relief he felt didn't sound in his voice.

'His husband, Craig, is a wonderful guy. They're very happy.

They travel the world together when Andy isn't working on Christmas trees.'

'That's good to hear,' he said.

'And I expect I'll have dinner with Edith tomorrow night. I think she'd like that,' she said. 'If I let her do most of the talking and am very careful with my responses, I should be okay.'

'Nice idea,' he said. He couldn't possibly be jealous of his grandmother enjoying Marissa's company for an evening, could he? He wasn't used to feeling this possessive about a woman. He wanted her with him.

He didn't know how to deal with these unfamiliar feelings.

'I think so,' she said. 'I really like Edith, despite her odd vehemence that you and I are a couple.'

'Right. Back to the fray, then,' he said, turning towards the door.

'Onwards and upwards,' she said. She looked sideways at him with a mischievous smile. 'You do realise everyone will think we sneaked up to your apartment for a quickie?'

He could only wish they had.

CHAPTER TEN

TWO NIGHTS OF Oliver being away from Longfield Manor turned to three, then four. Marissa missed him. She might pretend to herself that she didn't care—after all, how could she ache so badly for a man she'd known for such a short time? But she knew she was kidding herself.

She cared.

As he'd promised, although he seemed as flat out as she was, he kept in regular touch with brief businesslike texts and calls, even a video call. It was more contact than she might have normally expected between hotelier and contract event planner. And his cute emojis that accompanied the texts made her believe they were friends. Friends with the potential for more? Who knew?

When he returned in the morning of the day before Christmas Eve, she planned to be friendly but not over the top. Cool. Businesslike. A kiss on the cheek in greeting, as befit a pretend girlfriend who'd decided with him against public displays of affection.

That plan disintegrated the second she saw him. He'd asked her to meet him in the foyer of the hotel, near the recently placed, superbly decorated Christmas tree. She dressed carefully in a body-conscious deep purple knit dress and heels.

She had her hair up in a messy bun and subtle make-up. She planned to be there before him and walked calmly down the staircase. Only to see him already there. Oliver. Tall and imposing in black trousers and cashmere sweater, and a very stylish charcoal-grey coat that spoke of Italian tailoring. He was talking to Priya behind the desk.

Movie-star handsome? *Oh, yes!* He was so handsome her heart accelerated into a flurry of excitement, her breath came short and she felt her cheeks flush.

For a moment she froze before she stepped down to the bottom step. Did he sense her closeness? He turned. For a very long moment they stared at each other across the distance of the foyer. Time seemed to stand still. There was just him and her and the ticking of the large antique clock. Then he smiled and she smiled back at what she saw in his expression. She broke into a run towards him, to be swung up into his arms.

'I missed you,' she said, her voice breaking with a sudden swell of emotion, breathing in his heady, familiar scent. She almost didn't even notice the pungent smell of pine from the Christmas tree.

'I missed you,' he said at the same time.

'It's been awful without you,' she said. She'd counted every minute he'd been away.

'I cursed the problems that kept me in London longer than I wanted to be.'

'Video calls were not the same.'

'You can't hug a screen,' he said.

He kissed her, briefly but passionately. Oh, the joy of being back in his arms! She felt like she belonged there.

How could something pretend seem so real?

At the sound of clapping, Marissa broke away from Oliver's kiss to find Priya and one of the young admin staff smiling and applauding their reunion. All Marissa could do was smile back. It was impossible not to keep on smiling. Oliver was here.

'Thank you,' said Oliver with a slight bow and a grin to the hotel staff.

'We'll take this to my office,' he said to her. 'You can fill me in with what's been happening with the Christmas plans.'

He kept his arm around her, holding her close to him, as they walked the short distance to his office. Again, she had that feeling that she belonged there with him. That no other man would ever do.

Once they were inside the room, he closed the door behind them. Marissa looked up to him. It killed her to say the words, but they had to be said. 'You did that very well. The fake-girl-friend greeting, I mean.'

His face clouded over and he frowned. 'You think I was faking it?'

'I...assumed you were. That...that was our dating deal.' It was difficult to find the right tone. She hadn't realised just how badly she'd missed him until she'd seen him again, so familiar but still very much a stranger. Yet, he'd given her no indication that he felt anywhere near the same.

He put his hands on her shoulders. 'Marissa, not a word of what I said was fake. I genuinely missed you. In fact, I couldn't stop thinking about you and resented the time I spent away from you. Usually business occupies my every thought when I'm in London. Not so this time. Thoughts of you kept intruding.'

'Really?' she said, happiness and relief flooding her.

'What about you?' he said. 'Fake or real?'

She didn't have to think about her answer. 'Real all the way.' Her gaze took in every detail of his handsome, handsome face. 'I missed you and thought about you all the time.'

'Good,' he said, pulling her closer for a brief kiss before releasing her.

'I mustn't have done a good job of hiding how I was feeling, because I was constantly teased by Andy that I was pining for you, my boyfriend, the boss.'

'In reality, Granny is the boss.'

'Everyone here thinks of you as the boss, the new boss. They like and respect you. And some of them fear for the future of Longfield Manor. They're worried about Cecil retiring soon.' She paused a beat. 'Of course you probably know that.'

'Yes. He's worked for the family since my grandparents started the hotel. He'll be sorely missed and difficult to replace. Granny relies on Cecil so much and I'm worried about how she's going to take the news.'

Marissa laughed, but it came out as a kind of snort. 'You still think Edith doesn't know? Of course she knows Cecil is retiring. I sometimes wonder if you underestimate your granny, with her business acumen and people skills. Cecil and his wife are moving to Portugal. As he won't be on hand to advise his replacement, your grandmother is hoping you'll be here to keep your hand on the wheel as the hotel transitions to a new era, but she knows your Pierce Group hotels are your passion. I think she worries about the future of the hotel as she gets older.'

He nodded. 'You kept your ears to the ground while I was away.'

'Who else would the staff confide in than the boss's girlfriend?'

'And the fact that they all like you.'

'Perhaps. I like them, that's for sure.'

'They sing your praises. Anyone I spoke to while I was in London mentioned what a good job you were doing.'

'That's gratifying to hear,' she said. 'I don't know what you intend Longfield Manor's future to be. But you don't have to look far for someone to step into Cecil's shoes. Priya is excellent. A real gem. She knows everything about this place, how it ticks, peoples' strengths and weaknesses. She has some interesting thoughts about how certain things that have been done one way forever, could be done another, better way. She knows how to graciously interact with your grandmother, too.'

Oliver slowly nodded. 'I like Priya. I'll have to get to know her better. Perhaps put her through an interview process.'

'She'd be more than willing. And Cecil would approve of her taking over from him. I think he's been pretty much training her for the role.'

'I learn so much about what's been happening in my own home in my absence,' he said, but he smiled, and his words were in no way a reprimand.

'My priority is Christmas, of course, but it's been interesting to learn more about Longfield Manor.' She dreaded the prospect of saying goodbye to the hotel—and to Oliver—on Christmas Day evening.

'Back to our game of pretend,' he said. 'I was most certainly not pretending. My reactions were very real. In fact, when I saw you on the staircase, your hand on the railing, in that dress, not only did I think you looked hot, I thought you looked like you belonged there.'

'At Longfield Manor? I have come to love the place. Are you thinking of offering me a job?'

'Not at all. But come to think of it…'

She turned her head away, unable to meet his gaze. 'I don't want a job here. I… I would find it hard to work with you, after our charade ends.'

Not when she ached to be his girlfriend for real. Anything else would be untenable. Imagine having to smile and be pleasant when he brought other women here, maybe even a wife. The thought of him with someone else was like the sharpest of stilettos stabbing into her heart.

However, practically, she could see a real role for her here, taking over some of the duties that had always been Edith's but were obviously becoming too much for her. A job as an inhouse event planner. The hotel already hosted weddings and other functions but she could see further scope to capitalise on the location. A paid role for something Edith had always done for love and pride in her hotel. Such a job could be an answer to Marissa's dissatisfaction with her current freelance career.

But it couldn't be. Not when she was on the edge of falling in love with the boss.

'Which brings us back to where we started,' he said. 'The line between real and pretend has totally blurred for me.'

Marissa stared at him, stunned speechless. 'Me…me, too,' she said breathlessly. 'I can no longer think about you in a pretend kind of way.'

He cradled her face in his hands and looked down into her face. 'I really like you, Marissa. I can't believe we've known each other for such a short time.'

'I… I really like you, too. So much.'

'I missed you so badly yesterday I nearly got in the car and headed down here to Dorset, leaving my business unfinished.'

'A trip to London to knock on your door entered my mind after the first two nights without you. Only…only I wasn't sure I'd be welcome and—'

He stopped her words with a swift, hard kiss. His voice when he spoke was hoarse. 'Can you, will you, stop looking at your role as pretend girlfriend as something irksome and—?'

'I never saw it as irksome.' It had started as fun, a game, a distraction from the reality of impending Christmas. A quiet poke back at that mean sixteen-year-old boy whom she now rarely gave a thought to.

'What I mean is could you see yourself transitioning into the role for real?' he said. 'As in…a real relationship?'

'To actually date you? To…to be your girlfriend?' She held her breath for his answer.

'Yes,' he said. 'That's exactly what I mean. What I want.'

This was so much more than she'd hoped for in those long nights he'd been away, and she'd realised how much she'd grown to care for him.

She let out her breath on a sigh. 'I would like that,' she said, a tremble in her voice.

He took her in his arms for a long, deep kiss, a kiss of affirmation of those unbelievable words.

She was Oliver Pierce's girlfriend.

'That felt more like a proper girlfriend kiss,' she murmured against his mouth, her entire body tingling with pleasure.

'I'm sorry, I should warn you that I can't promise you anything. I'm not good at making relationships last.'

'When you think about it, neither am I,' she said. 'Perhaps we should just take it day by day.' She couldn't worry about how long this thing with Oliver might last, if there was any future to it. She just wanted to be with him. Here. Now.

'I've never felt this way before,' he said, sounding bemused. 'So sudden. So quick.'

'Me neither. Your grandmother calls it a *coup de foudre*.'

His brow furrowed. 'A bolt of lightning?'

'Sudden, fast, powerful, from out of nowhere.'

Love at first sight.

That was what Edith said the French phrase meant. But Marissa wasn't going to share that particular translation with Oliver. Moving from fake to real girlfriend was enough for her to absorb, without progressing to contemplating actual *love*.

'That works,' he said.

'She said it was like that for her and Charles. That the power of that initial attraction kept their marriage strong through all those years—especially when things got tough.'

Oliver smiled. 'Grandpa used to look at her like he still couldn't believe she was his.' He paused. 'How come you were talking to Granny about *coup de foudre*?'

'She wanted to talk about us, of course. I had to tread carefully with her, as you know, so I didn't trip myself up. But I told her we liked each other straight away when we met.'

'Which was true.'

'It was, wasn't it?' She'd fought it because of a brief shared past he didn't even remember, but the attraction was too powerful.

He drew her to him for another, deeper kiss. She wound her arms around his neck to pull him closer as she kissed him back.

There was a substantial vintage leather Chesterfield sofa in front of the fireplace. She started to edge him towards it.

As she neared her goal, she heard a sharp knock then the door open. She stilled. Oliver had told her his granny never waited to be invited in, a leftover from when this had been his grandfather's study. Oliver pulled away from the kiss.

'Good morning, you two.' Edith practically trilled the words. By now, Marissa knew just how very much Edith wanted her grandson to be happy in a committed relationship.

'So glad you're back, grandson of mine. You were missed. Your lovely girlfriend missed you the most. She was moping around the place, quite lovesick, wishing you were here.'

'Edith!' said Marissa, laughing. She was getting quite used to Oliver's grandmother's outrageous assumptions and exaggerations. And yet...had the older woman been on to something, seen a spark of real attraction between her grandson and the event planner?

Oliver smiled. 'I missed Marissa, too.' He looked down at her. 'I've got used to having her nearby.'

Edith nodded approvingly. 'It was true Marissa did do some moping, but she was very, very busy, too. I've never seen the Christmas preparations carried out so efficiently. The decorations are superb. The heirloom accessories have been used in different ways and the new ones are stunning. And I think you'll really like the creative new ideas for the Christmas table settings.'

'We're ahead of schedule,' Marissa said. 'All the trees are up, and Andy will put the final touches on them today. Edith tells me that Christmas Eve is a big day and, as that's tomorrow, everything is on track for Christmas to start at Longfield Manor.'

'The trees look the best they've ever looked, thanks to your charming friend Andy,' said Edith. 'What a find he is. I've already booked him for next year's Christmas trees.'

'Smart move,' said Marissa. 'He gets booked up very quickly.'

'As it's Andy's last day with us, I've invited him to have dinner with me tonight,' Edith said. 'It would be great fun if you could both join us.'

Marissa looked up at Oliver. They shared raised eyebrows and a glance that told her he was looking forward to having dinner with just the two of them. But that it would be churlish not to accept Edith's invitation.

'Thank you, Granny, we'd like that,' Oliver said.

Marissa was disappointed not to be with Oliver, just the two of them, in his apartment for dinner. But she knew she would enjoy the meal with Edith and Andy and be able to relax now she and Oliver were officially dating. There'd be no need to be on edge guarding against slip-ups in a fake-relationship performance in front of her perceptive friend Andy—not to mention Edith's eagle eye.

Marissa had enjoyed her dinner alone with Edith on the second night Oliver had been away. Back on that night, she hadn't intended to pry into Oliver's past, but everything about him had become intensely interesting to her and she couldn't resist encouraging Edith's reminiscences. Edith had been only too happy to talk about her beloved grandson. She had told Marissa that, while she would never stop loving the daughter she rarely saw, she would also never forgive her for neglecting her child the way she had neglected Oliver.

'Little Olly was the dearest, brightest, most energetic little boy,' she'd said. 'We adored him, but grandparents can't fully make up for absent parents. Our daughter disappointed him so many times. Now he has no interest in her whatsoever, and I don't blame him—it's self-protection. He's done so well with his hotels and has big plans for expansion. But my husband and I were always concerned about the barriers he put up against letting people get close to him. Emotional barriers, that is. He always puts work before relationships. I mean, look at him now. He's up in London and you're here. That isn't right, especially just before Christmas.'

Marissa had reassured Edith that she totally understood why

he'd had to go to London, because she was somewhat of a work-aholic herself. Edith had seemed satisfied. Marissa's heart had swelled with compassion towards Oliver for what he had gone through as a child. All that wealth and yet he'd been starved of love from the people who should have loved him the most. But she had been left wondering if he would ever let her get closer.

She didn't see much of Oliver for the rest of the day, but Marissa didn't mind too much. It was like starting over with him, after the fake relationship had morphed into something genu-ine. Affectionate gestures that had been staged for maximum effect on an observer, now naturally sprung from genuine feel-ing and a desire to be together. The hunger for him was still there. But it was as if they'd given each other permission to take it slowly, to get to know each other better before they started tossing cushions off his bed.

Marissa felt energised by the shift in her relationship with Oliver. Reassured. *Happy.* There was still work to be done, the finishing touches put to the trees and decorations on this, the final day with the team of temporary staff. But they were near-ing the finish line. As was customary, Edith hosted a lunch in one of the function rooms to thank the temporary crew for their work. Marissa was delighted to see that Edith's established peo-ple and the new crew recruited by Caity got on so well, work-ing as a team. New friendships had been made. They hoped Edith and Oliver would have them back the next year. 'All in the spirit of Christmas,' Edith said.

Oliver disappeared for the afternoon with some of the crew, saying he had business in the village he needed to attend to. As he kissed Marissa goodbye, he said he'd see her at dinner. He didn't say what that business was, and she didn't ask him. She now knew him well enough to believe he was a man of his word. Still, she was intrigued. Curiously, Edith could not be drawn on his whereabouts.

That evening, as she made her way up the staircase to her

room to get changed for dinner, she looked out the ancient mullion windows on the landing to the garden below. Andy had strung the large fir trees with the tiniest of twinkling lights. As she admired the spectacle, a lone deer made its way across the frost-rimed grass, stood in front of one of the sparkling firs and looked up at the building. For a long moment it was as if its gaze met Marissa's and she held her breath. At such a sight, even the most entrenched of Scrooges could not help feeling just a touch of Christmas magic.

CHAPTER ELEVEN

LONGFIELD MANOR WAS completely booked out for the Christmas period and on Christmas Eve a high level of festive excitement thrummed through the high-ceilinged old rooms. It was that time of year when people didn't say hello to people they encountered, but rather, Merry Christmas. Oliver was kept busy with his grandmother greeting guests, many of whom were regulars returning for Christmas like they did every year. His grandfather's loss was felt, with guests offering condolences as well as greetings. Oliver was very aware that people saw him as stepping into his grandfather's shoes—but his grandfather's shoes didn't fit him, as Grandpa had known only too well.

The future of Longfield Manor was beginning to look very clear to him.

'Is all this making you too sad?' he quietly asked his grandmother. 'Are you sure you're okay with it? You don't have to greet everyone.'

'Absolutely I'm okay,' she said. 'Charles would expect it of me. Of course I miss him terribly. But you were wise to make changes to the way we celebrated Christmas this year. Things aren't quite the same, are they? Changes here and there, some more subtle than others? In a good way, I mean, an updated way, which shows we're moving forward. That makes it somehow easier to cope with. Thank heaven for Marissa.' She looked up at him. 'In many ways, thank heaven for Marissa.'

'I'll second that,' he said, not even trying to disguise the longing in his voice. 'She's wonderful in every way and I'm so grateful she's here with us.'

'She is special,' Granny said. 'And if I were you, I would think about getting a ring on her finger.'

'Granny,' he protested half-heartedly.

'Think about it,' Granny said. 'There is some magnificent heirloom jewellery in the safe, just waiting to be worn by a new generation.'

Oliver was getting used to having Marissa by his side. Where was she now? He was concerned that this immersive Christmas might be upsetting her, bringing back her painful memories of this time of year. Again, he marvelled at her loyalty to her friend Caity that had brought her down here, knowing she would be facing so much of what she hated and feared. He'd been calling her for the last half hour, but she must have her phone turned to silent. Had she locked herself away in her room?

'Granny, I've got to go find Marissa. Do you know where she is?'

'She's been flitting around checking everything she's organised is perfect for our guests. Right now, she's in the dining room with the head waiter, checking on the place settings with the new Christmas table linen. We're launching it tonight for the Christmas Eve carols dinner.'

'Thanks.' He turned to go.

'Wait,' said Edith. 'I said I'm okay. But I don't think I can deal with being Mrs Claus tomorrow.'

'I understand that might be difficult for you. Don't worry. I'll be Santa on my own.' He wasn't listening as hard as he should, keen to get back to Marissa. If he could, he would spend every minute of the day and night with her. Yet, he was taking it slow in their new, official relationship. They had time. He was thinking of taking her away somewhere after Christmas where they could be alone and private, away from interested observers.

'That won't work,' Granny said firmly. 'There must be a Mrs Claus. This tradition goes back a very long way, too long to break it.'

'I'll ask Priya if she can step in for you. Maybe next year you'll be feeling up to being Mrs Claus again.'

'Priya is a fine manager, but Mrs Claus has to be family. How do you feel about Marissa taking my place as Mrs Claus?'

He looked at Granny, aghast. 'Marissa isn't family, Granny.' *Not yet, anyway.*

'Are you sure about that?' his grandmother said with narrowed, speculative eyes.

'I can't ask her to be Mrs Claus.'

He had honoured his promise to Marissa and not told anyone about her feelings about Christmas. So he couldn't tell Granny just why he couldn't ask this of Marissa. How it could traumatise her. She'd done enough for his family. Acting as Mrs Claus would be torture for a Christmas-phobe. And he didn't want anything to hurt or upset his lovely girlfriend. Not after what she'd been through. Not when she was beginning to mean so much to him.

'I couldn't ask that of her, Granny. And please don't *you* ask her. Promise me?'

He didn't quite trust Granny not to seek Marissa out and ask her herself. He had to find Marissa first. He looked around. 'There are Mr and Mrs Lee. They look like they want to speak with you.'

He headed to the dining room to find Marissa heading out. How she could walk around in those sky-high heels he didn't know, but he liked the sexy sway they gave her. Her face lit up as she saw him, and his heart turned over. How had this woman become so special so quickly? He kissed her in greeting. 'I've come to find you before Granny does.'

Her brow furrowed. 'Why? Is there something she wants to ask me to do?'

'Yes. Well, I've told her not to ask you, but you know what she can be like.'

'I'm intrigued. You'll have to tell me now.'

He led her away to a quiet end of the corridor. 'Granny has decided she can't face being Mrs Claus this year. It would be too hard for her without Grandpa as her Santa Claus.'

Her face softened. 'That's a pity. Poor Edith. I can see it would be very difficult for her. You told me they started being Santa and Mrs Claus long ago when your mother was a baby. Of course she wouldn't want to do it without her soulmate.'

'That's right,' he said. 'It's just too sad.'

'Perhaps you should put the idea in mothballs for this year?'

'Or I could play Santa Claus by myself.'

'Bachelor Santa,' she said. 'That could work.' She reached for his hands and pulled him towards her. 'Handsome Bachelor Santa.' She kissed him. 'You'll drive the lady guests crazy. Better steer clear of the mistletoe.'

He snorted. 'In the red Santa suit with a pillow down my front and a fake beard? I don't think so.'

'You could still be cute.'

'I could and I would. But Granny wants a Mrs Claus and she wants it to be you.'

Marissa dropped his hands and took a step back. *'What?'*

He put his hands out to placate her. 'I know. I told her I would not ask you. Of course I didn't tell her why.'

'To dress up as Mrs Claus and hand out presents, what torture that would be for a Scrooge like me?'

'You don't need to make light of it,' he said. 'I know Christmas holds painful memories for you and I totally understand.'

'And don't forget Christmas is jinxed, too.'

He wasn't so sure about that. 'It will have to just be me as Bachelor Santa, whether Granny likes it or not. I'll tell her that.'

'Wait. Not so fast. Perhaps I... I should try it.' She bit down on her bottom lip. 'Being Mrs Claus, I mean.'

'You don't have to do that. Really.'

'I know I don't have to, but what if I want to? A Longfield Manor Christmas is somehow different. Quite out of my experience. It's like a different world. Also, despite my Christmas phobia, I've helped to create these celebrations.'

'You have. Everyone is delighted with the way things have turned out.'

She looked up at him. 'Maybe I need to face up to my fears. Being Mrs Claus wouldn't be desperately difficult. It's only for an hour or so, isn't it? Handing out gifts to the guests. Could it be any worse than helping to decorate a tree?'

'Perhaps not.'

'Does Mrs Claus go *ho-ho-ho*, too?'

'I don't think Granny ever did. It was Grandpa that liked to ham it up.'

'Was Edith a quiet, submissive type of Mrs Claus?'

'You could say that. She put talcum powder in her hair to be old Mrs Claus even when she was much younger.'

'So, a Mrs Claus with traditional values of what a wife should be? Defer to Santa?'

'I wouldn't like you to be like that,' he said. 'I want my Mrs Claus to be right up there with me sharing the spotlight.' Was he actually talking about Mrs Claus here or something altogether deeper? He just might be getting carried away.

'Equal rights for Mrs Claus?' she said.

'Something like that,' he said. 'But seriously, Marissa, you don't have to do it.'

'I know...'

'You really want to do it?'

She took a deep breath. 'Perhaps I need to challenge myself,' she said thoughtfully. 'Seeing everyone so happy and excited makes me remember what it was like before my parents died.

What I'm missing out on. Do I want to run away from Christmas forever?'

'Only you can answer that,' he said. He hoped not. Christmas was important to him and he was beginning to hope that Marissa would be part of his life for Christmases to come.

Her brow furrowed. 'Only problem is the Christmas couple costumes. We brought them out of the attic to air. They're definitely old-style Claus family. Not to mention they wouldn't fit either of us. But it's Christmas Eve, there's no time to get new costumes or even alter the old ones.'

'Granny has thought of that, of course,' he said. 'Which makes me wonder for how long she's been planning the Mrs Claus switch.'

'I have long stopped wondering about your granny's motives,' she said. 'What do you mean?'

'She had a parcel delivered to me in London and asked me to bring it with me when I came back down here. When I asked, she said it was new Santa and Mrs Claus costumes. I put the box in the storeroom.'

'Let's go get it,' she said.

Marissa tore at the wrapping in her haste to get at the costumes. She pulled out the Santa one. 'Much nicer than the old one,' she said. She held the red outfit up against him. 'More streamlined, and the white beard is not so outrageous, either.' Her eyes narrowed and she pouted suggestively.

Did she have any idea of what that did to him?

'You'll look quite the sexy Santa in this.'

'If there weren't so many people around, I might have to try it on and show you what a sexy Santa can do.'

To his surprise she blushed. 'I'd like that,' she said. She looked up at him, eyes wide and doing the dancing thing. 'Can I take a rain check on that?'

'There's a chimney in your room. Perhaps Sexy Santa can pay you a visit tonight?'

She laughed. 'I'll keep an eye on that chimney. Now, let's see what Mrs Santa's costume looks like.' She pulled a red garment out of the box and held it up. 'This is cute. I've said it before and I'll say it again, your granny has excellent taste.'

The outfit comprised a long-sleeved red velvet dress with a short, flared skater skirt, all trimmed with white fake fur. Marissa burrowed further in the box and pulled out red-and-white-striped tights, black ankle boots and a black belt with a big buckle that matched the belt for the Santa suit. Plus, the requisite Santa hat with a white pompom at the end that also matched Santa's.

'There are even Christmas earrings in the shape of reindeer.'

'I don't know about the earrings, but you'll look hot in that dress, Mrs Claus.' He waggled his eyebrows and attempted to leer.

'As hot as a woman could look in red-and-white-striped tights,' she said with a delightful little giggle. Had she giggled like that before? He wasn't sure, yet it seemed familiar and very much her.

'What makes me think this outfit was purchased by Granny with precisely Marissa Gracey in mind?' he said drily.

'Everything about it,' she said. 'And it's the right size, too.' She looked up at him. 'I can't not wear it, can I?' Delight and mischief shone in her eyes and it made him smile to see her like that. Again, he felt that urge to protect her and care for her, to want her life to be secure and happy after all the loss she had endured. Like his grandfather had cared for his grandmother. Maybe he was more old-fashioned than he considered himself to be.

'So you'll be my Mrs Claus?' he said.

'I will,' she said.

He helped her pack the outfits back into the box. 'I'll take the box up to my apartment to keep it safe. We'll make our appearances after Christmas lunch tomorrow.'

'It will be a big day tomorrow.'

'Are you sure you'll be okay about it all? No panic attacks?'

'I'll try very hard not to have a panic attack but it's not something over which I have much control. But really, I'm determined not to let any jinx master ruin my time here with you in this truly wondrous place.'

'We're going to find ourselves without a second to spare tomorrow. Anything that's going to go wrong invariably goes wrong on Christmas Day. But after Boxing Day, things will settle down. There'll be more time for us to spend together then.'

She cleared her throat. 'You realise I'm meant to finish up tomorrow afternoon and head back up to London?'

Fear gripped him with icy claws. 'You wouldn't do that, would you?' He couldn't be without her.

'Not if you don't want me to.'

He put his hand on her arm. 'Marissa, I want you to stay.' If she went, he would follow her. Even if it meant leaving Longfield Manor in the middle of its busiest season.

'I'd like to stay here with you. I don't have any other work on, as I was meant to be on holiday in Indonesia.'

'Do you regret cancelling that trip and coming down to Dorset?'

'Not one bit. If I hadn't, I would never have met you. What a shame that would have been.' She paused. 'That didn't come out quite right, did it? I mean, we wouldn't have known we'd like each other if I hadn't agreed to the job and met you.' She smiled. 'Never mind, I think you know what I mean.'

'I know exactly what you mean,' he said, thinking how adorable she was.

There were so many things he badly wanted to say to her, but he'd never said them before and the words didn't come easily. It was too soon, anyway. After all he'd only known her for a week.

Marissa knew the Christmas Eve dinner at Longfield Manor was a very special occasion—the prelude to Christmas Day, which would be the pinnacle of Christmas excitement. For some of the European guests, Christmas Eve was the more important of the two days. The highlights of the evening were to be a special menu from Jean Paul and carols performed by the village choir. It comprised all ages and apparently was no ordinary choir—but a prize winner at national choral competitions. The choir was very much part of the community and led the door-to-door carolling in the village, too. That afternoon, Oliver had invited her to go to the village with him for the carolling, but she'd decided that might be a Christmas overload. Making a good show of being Mrs Claus the next day was more important.

Now she was at dinner with Edith and Oliver—back from the carols—at his private table in the dining room. She looked around her, quietly pleased at how fabulous the festive decorations looked, right down to the table settings. Thanks to Andy, the Longfield Christmas trees had become gasp-worthy in their splendour. People had got up from their tables to admire the dining room tree. Fortunately, it was set up some distance from Oliver's private table so she wasn't bothered by the scent.

The string quartet played background classical music as she, Oliver and Edith enjoyed the first two courses together. But then Oliver excused himself. 'I need to help out with the choir,' he said.

'If they need help, surely that's my job,' Marissa protested.

'You're off duty now,' he said. 'Stay and enjoy the music.'

Edith put her hand on Marissa's arm. 'Oliver has friends in the choir,' she said. 'You'll see.'

Marissa couldn't help but feel a little left out. Crazy really, when Oliver had done so much to make her part of Longfield Manor and Edith had made her so welcome. But everything between her and Oliver had happened so quickly, she still felt she was on shaky ground.

The string quartet started to play a medley of Christmas carols as the choir of twenty-five people trooped into the room, wearing the traditional chorister's white surplice over a red cassock and red Santa hats with a pompom on the end. The look was perfect for the occasion and the room. Marissa was stunned to see the last chorister to take his place was Oliver. He looked over to her and smiled, obviously aware she would be shocked. She smiled back, shaking her head in wonder.

'I had no idea Oliver was in the choir,' she whispered to Edith.

'He wanted to surprise you,' Edith whispered back. 'He used to sing with this choir and asked if he could join them again for tonight.'

'That's amazing. I never would have guessed,' Marissa whispered back. She couldn't keep her eyes off him.

The choir launched into 'The Twelve Days of Christmas' and continued with a medley of favourite carols.

Marissa realised straight away that the singers were superb—as indeed was Oliver, who sang in a deep baritone voice. When he sang solo in 'The First Noel' she was spellbound. She couldn't sing in tune herself, and deeply admired those who could. He was so talented and she was so proud of him.

'Wow…just wow,' she whispered to Edith.

She saw the same pride and love shining from his granny's eyes as she must see in hers.

She pulled herself up. *Love?*

Marissa could deny it to herself no longer. Of course she was in love with Oliver. But that didn't seem as disastrous a realisation as it might have been just a few days ago—because, with a secret fluttering thrill to her heart, she was beginning to sense he might be feeling the same way towards her.

That thought was confirmed when the choir moved to singing contemporary Christmas songs. As they started on 'All I Want For Christmas Is You,' Oliver broke away from the choir and danced towards her table. She caught her breath.

The man could dance, too.

He serenaded her with the song before lifting her out of her chair to swing her around in his arms. Laughing, she blushed bright red with embarrassment, enchanted by his gesture. His romantic move was met with clapping and applause and good-natured catcalls. When he dropped a quick kiss on her mouth the other diners cheered. After he guided her back to the table, she dropped back into her seat feeling bemused, elated and very happy. She had never met a man like Oliver Pierce—and she wanted him so much it hurt.

He had introduced her to a Christmas like she had never before experienced. She realised that listening to the Christmas carols hadn't left her feeling nauseated or panic stricken. When the choir sang 'Silent Night' she thought about her mother, who had loved that carol and although her eyes pricked with tears, all she felt was peace.

'When did Oliver start singing with a choir?' she asked Edith, keeping her voice low.

'When he was a young child living here with us, he sang in the church choir. Then he sang in choirs at his boarding school—I think it made the place more bearable for him. His father is a musician. He obviously inherited his musicality and voice from him.'

When the choir finished, to rapturous applause, Oliver joined Marissa and his grandmother at the table. She stood up to greet him.

'I can't believe you did that,' she said, smiling.

'You didn't like it?' he said with a grin.

'I loved it. You're a man of many surprises,' she said. Marissa couldn't stop looking at him, wondering what other hidden talents he might have. She realised how little she really knew about him.

She knew enough to allow herself to fall in love.

'I don't want you to think I'm predictable,' he said.

'You were amazing. Such a talent. I'm in awe.'

'With that beautiful voice, he could have made a career of his singing, if he'd wanted to,' Edith said, ever the proud granny.

'I never wanted to make a career of it. No way would I ever

follow in my father's footsteps. Singing for me is about relaxation and fun. So is playing my guitar.'

Oliver played guitar? He just got better and better. Not just movie-star good looks, but rock-star good looks, not to mention wealthy-tycoon good looks—and the talent and business savvy that took his appeal beyond his handsome face. She had a feeling that life would never get a chance to be boring around Oliver. And she longed to be part of his life. She realised with a painful jolt to her heart how empty her life would be if, her job here over, she went back to London and never saw him again.

'Is that where you went yesterday, when you disappeared?' she asked.

He nodded. 'Choir practice.'

'I'm glad you didn't tell me. Seeing you in the choir was a real surprise.'

'I was surprised at how much I enjoyed singing with them again. Unfortunately, my life in London doesn't allow time for a choir. So I'm making the most of being in this one. Part of the deal that the choir took me back was that I sang with them for the midnight church service in the village tonight. Would you like to come with me?'

One part of her wanted to go, another feared that might be too much Christmas overload. 'Thank you, but no. Mrs Claus needs her beauty sleep.'

'Mrs Claus is beautiful just the way she is.'

'But her looks are not enhanced by dark circles under her eyes.'

'I could debate that.' He paused. 'Do you have surprises in store for me?'

His question surprised her. She shrugged. 'Me? You'd roll around laughing if you heard me sing. What you see is what you get.'

'Sounds good to me,' he said.

'Can I tell you something?'

'Any time.'

She looked up at him, hoping he would understand that her words weren't spoken in jest. 'I can't sing it, but I can say it. All I want for Christmas is you. And I'm very glad you want me for Christmas, too.' When she kissed him, it was to gentle applause from the tables nearby.

CHAPTER TWELVE

IT WAS CHRISTMAS MORNING, her clock had ticked over past midnight more than an hour ago, but Marissa was still restlessly awake in what she took delight in calling The Bogbean Room rather than the somewhat pedestrian Room eight. She'd looked up the Dorset wildflower to find it was a plant that grew in damp soil with clusters of white star-shaped flowers. Not such a bad name for a room after all. That was if the mundane name was accompanied by an image of the pretty flowers. On the door.

Aaargh! Why was she letting irrelevant thoughts like that churn around her mind and keep her awake?

Then there was the song the choir had sung that urged 'Santa baby' to hurry down the chimney. It was going relentlessly around and around in her head. Oliver had teased her by saying he was going to do just that.

There's a chimney in your room. Perhaps Sexy Santa can pay you a visit tonight?

Would he? Could he? *Did he really want to?*

A quiet knock sounded at her door. She smiled a slow, secret smile to herself as she got out of bed to answer it. Through the security peephole, she confirmed it was Oliver.

'You came by the door,' she said, pouting, pretending to be

disappointed as she let him into the room and shut the door behind him.

'I didn't dare risk the chimney tonight. It's started to snow, so not such a good move to be clambering over an ancient, slippery roof in an effort to find the correct chimney.'

'Wise move,' she said. She wound her arms around his neck to pull him close. 'If you were covered in black chimney soot, I might not want to do this.' She pressed a kiss to the curve of his jaw, loving the roughness of his stubble against her skin.

'I don't think I'd care if you were covered in soot, I want you so much,' he said hoarsely, his hands around her waist.

'I want you, too, so much,' she said with a hitch to her voice. 'But if soot was a concern, I might have to strip off your clothes and take you into the shower with me.'

'Forget the soot, feel free to strip me anyway and drag me into the shower. If you strip, too, I'd go willingly.'

'I'd prefer it if you strip me first,' she said. 'And the bed might be more comfortable than the cold tiles of the shower cubicle.'

She reached up to claim his mouth in an urgent, hungry kiss that went on and on.

The man could kiss.

The time was way past for saying no to more than kisses. She wanted to make it clear she was saying yes to wherever he wanted to lead her.

She pressed her body against his, intoxicated by his now familiar scent, instantly aware of his desire for her and she shuddered with the answering desire that flooded her. She was wearing boxer shorts and a tank top. When he slid his hands up inside the top to caress her breasts, she gasped her arousal. 'Take it off,' she said. 'Now.'

'With pleasure,' he said hoarsely, sliding her top over her head and tossing it on the floor.

When his hand moved lower under the boxers, she moaned her pleasure and arousal. He knew just what to do to ignite her pleasure zones.

'My turn,' she said, pulling his cashmere sweater up over his head, followed by his T-shirt. That left him in only his black jeans. 'Oh my...' Marissa breathed, feeling light-headed as she feasted her eyes on his powerful chest, his six-pack.

She caressed his chest with the flat of her hands, revelling in the feel of smooth skin over hard muscle, the right amount of dark body hair. She fumbled with his belt, but her fingers were awkward with nerves and the more impatient she was, the less luck she had in undoing it.

'Let me,' he said. Soon, she was sliding his jeans down his thighs, her excitement levels soaring.

'Darn!' He was still wearing his boots and the jeans were going nowhere. He laughed. 'Again, let me,' he said, as he kicked off his boots and socks.

Then he was there in just his boxers. He kissed her again and she pressed herself close, warm bare skin against bare skin. There was a mirror behind him, and she looked up to see his back view reflected in it. Broad shoulders tapered down to the best butt a man could ever have. She almost swooned at the erotic vision of their nearly nude bodies entwined, her pale skin against his olive. She kept in shape, and clearly so did he, and she thought they looked beautiful together. It was another level of turn-on.

'Bed or bathroom?' he said.

'Bed,' she choked out. They could shower together some other time.

He picked her up and effortlessly carried her to the bed, an experience she found thrilling. He laid her on the mattress and lay down beside her, resting on his elbow as he looked down at her with those amazing green eyes. He traced her mouth with one finger. 'You are so beautiful.' His gaze roamed over her body and she felt it like a caress. 'Perfect, in fact.'

'I'm glad you think so,' she said huskily. 'You're utterly wonderful and perfect and I'm so very glad you're here, even if you didn't come via the chimney.'

'I couldn't have stayed away. I didn't want you to wake up alone on Christmas morning.' He paused. 'And I couldn't stop thinking about how much I wanted to make love to you.'

'What a magnificent man you are.'

'Says she, in the first flush of attraction,' he said, laughing. *Not quite the first.*

She knew she should remind him of their first meeting but again, it didn't feel like the right time.

His hands slid below her waist and divested her of her boxer shorts. She did the same to him, taking time to explore and caress him while she did so.

He kissed his way down her bare skin to take her nipples in his mouth, one after the other, teasing them with his tongue until she ached for release. Then he explored her body with his hands and mouth until she bucked against him. 'Please, I want you inside me. Now.'

He took a condom from the thoughtfully provided amenity pack in the bedside drawer, and she helped him put it on. Then he entered her and she welcomed him into her body. He fell into just the right rhythm for her and she orgasmed before he did and then again after, melting in ecstasy. The man sure knew how to please her. 'I have to say again how wonderful you are,' she murmured sleepily. 'When I said all I wanted for Christmas was you, I knew what I was talking about.'

She fell asleep in his arms, feeling happier than she could remember feeling for a very long time.

They awoke early in the morning, to the sound of church bells pealing out a joyous Christmas message and made love again. This time their lovemaking was tender and unhurried, building to a powerful, mutual climax before they sank back into sleep.

Marissa woke later to find Oliver sleeping beside her, his arm slung across her. She admired him for a long minute, his face even more handsome in repose, his body strong and sleekly muscled. How lucky she was to have found him. She slid out from under his arm, so as not to disturb him. The room seemed oddly quiet, with no noises coming from outside, just the steady sound of his breathing from inside.

She shrugged on the ink-coloured velour hotel robe she'd left on the chair and padded barefoot over the lush carpet to the window. She drew back the heavy curtains. Snow. She watched, entranced, as a flurry of fluffy snowflakes drifted past the window-panes. The gardens below had been transformed by a heavy coverage of snow. The lights Andy had strung up on the fir trees struggled valiantly to twinkle through the layer of white that now frosted their branches. She might have to get some help to shake some—but not all—of the snow off.

Oliver came up from behind her and slipped his arms around her. She leaned back against him, rejoicing in their closeness, the warmth and strength of his body clad in the matching robe to hers he'd taken from the closet.

'It's unbelievably beautiful, isn't it?' he said softly. 'All the familiar landmarks transformed into something magical. Form becomes more important than colour or scent or anything else but this purity. A white Christmas. We'll have some very happy guests, especially those from Australia and South Africa.'

'It's utter magic,' she murmured. But the real magic was being here with Oliver, in the security of his arms around her, her body aching pleasantly from the sensual aftermath of intensely satisfying lovemaking.

'Thank you for letting me stay with you,' he said. 'As I said, I didn't want you to wake up alone on Christmas Day.'

'I'm so glad you stayed.'

'Now I don't know whether to wish you a Merry Christmas or not.'

'Please do. I think being here with you, becoming so involved with the Longfield Manor festivities have helped me. Perhaps, just perhaps, the jinx has been lifted. Maybe I can allow myself to enjoy Christmas this year without the fear that something terrible will happen.'

'I sincerely hope so. Do you think you'll ever be able to re-member your parents without connecting their loss to Christ-mas?'

'I'm beginning to believe I will. Maybe one Christmas I'll even be able to eat a mince pie again without breaking down. They were my dad's favourite, you see.'

'Grandpa loved them, too. Can't say I care for them myself. Jean Paul's fruit pastries are far superior in my opinion.'

'I'll try them and I'm sure I'll enjoy them.'

'Maybe that's what Christmas will mean to you this year. Laying down new memories. Not banishing the old ones, but letting happy new memories override them.'

'What a lovely idea,' she said, hoping fervently that it could be so, thinking how perceptive he was.

Oliver turned her to face him, searched her face. 'Perhaps some of those happy new memories could be made with me, Marissa?'

Her heart leapt. This was something she hadn't dared to let herself imagine. 'Perhaps...'

'I know we haven't known each other for long but, as I've said before, it seems like you're meant to be part of my life. Not just for Christmas but into the New Year, too, and beyond. Maybe next year we could be enjoying Christmas together again at Longfield Manor?'

Exultation at his words fought with caution. 'That's a beau-tiful thought.' Could she trust this man who'd made it so clear he didn't want commitment? How she wanted to believe in a future together. But it was a big step forward.

'You're thinking that's perhaps too great a leap?' he said, ob-viously sensing her doubt. 'Maybe we could go away by our-selves in the New Year to talk about how we could make our relationship work? Paris maybe? Or anywhere you would like.'

'Paris would be perfect.' She could think of nothing better. Just him and her.

He cradled her chin in his hands, in the way she had come to love. It made her feel cherished, special, safe. 'I really like you, Marissa,' he said. He could not seem more sincere.

'I like you a lot, too. Being here with you means so much. I… I would like to look into the future with you.'

'So, I can wish you Merry Christmas?'

This Christmas was so different. 'Please do. Although I'll wish you a Happy Christmas.'

'Is there a difference?'

'You wouldn't think so, would you? My father had this eccentric old aunt who used to spend Christmas with us. She was a sweetie, but she very primly used to say that *merry* meant drunken, and that to wish someone a Merry Christmas meant you were wishing them a Drunken Christmas and that was simply not on. You can imagine the fun my brother and I had with that one. We thought it hilarious and, for a while there in our lives, it was probably true.'

'But you say Happy Christmas now?'

'I just got to like happy better than merry. Happy is the best thing you could wish a person to be, isn't it?'

He laughed. 'I think it's kinda cute that you do.'

He let her go and headed over to pick up his jeans from where Marissa had tossed them the night before. She was disappointed that he was going to cover up his gorgeous body that had given her so much pleasure. But no. He didn't put on the jeans but rather dug into a pocket and pulled out a small, professionally wrapped parcel. 'Merry Christmas, Marissa,' he said, handing it to her.

'A gift for me? Really?'

'It's Christmas morning, Marissa. Gift-giving time.'

Of course it was.

She tore off the wrapping—she was never very good at decorously opening a present or reading the card first—to find a small box embossed with the name of a famous London jeweller. With trembling fingers, she opened it to find a bracelet of finely linked platinum studded with diamonds. She looked up at him. 'Oh, this is lovely,' she said. 'But it's too much, I—'

'I wanted to get you something special,' he said.

'This is special, all right,' she said. 'But—'

'Let me help you put it on,' he said. He fastened it to her right wrist. 'It fits perfectly. I bought it when I was in London and had to guess the size.'

She held up her hand to admire it. 'It's a lovely bracelet,' she said. 'But it's very extravagant of you.'

'You deserve something lovely,' he said. 'If this is prevarication because you don't like it—'

'No, I love it, I really do,' she said. 'It's just I wasn't expecting...' She kissed him on the cheek. 'Thank you very much. I shall treasure it.'

She went to the drawer under the desk and, in turn, pulled out a parcel of her own.

'Happy Christmas, Oliver,' she said, handing it to him.

'Me? You bought me a gift?'

'Why would you be surprised?' At the time she'd been unsure whether or not it would be appropriate, but she'd gone ahead anyway. She'd bought his gift from a shop in the village, and something for Edith, too, the afternoon she'd gone in with Andy. Then wrapped it in some exquisite paper she'd found in the same shop.

Would he like it? Oliver pulled out the soft, charcoal-grey Italian designer cashmere scarf in a muted windowpane check with an exclamation of pleasure. 'Thank you,' he said, holding it up. 'It's my favourite colour and perfect for this weather. How very thoughtful of you.'

'Are you sure? I wanted to buy you a book, but I felt I didn't know you well enough to know what you like to read.'

'The scarf is better. I confess, I don't get much time to read.'

'Let me,' she said, taking the scarf from him to put around his neck. She stood back to admire how it looked, somewhat incongruous in the neck of a hotel dressing gown. 'Yes, the colour is great on you.'

Truth be told, he would look good in any colour. Oliver dressed with a natural flair and style that befit a man of his position as CEO of London's most fashionable hotels, and heir to this awesome ancestral home.

But she liked him best wearing nothing at all.

CHAPTER THIRTEEN

OLIVER HAD NEVER imagined the day would come when his grandparents wouldn't be playing Santa Claus and Mrs Claus on Christmas Day. The fond memories stretched right back to when he was a toddler.

And now he was Santa Claus and Marissa had stepped in as Mrs Claus. He wasn't sure Mrs Claus was meant to be so beautiful and sexy. Maybe Granny's interpretation of Santa's wife with a lacy white cap on grey hair pulled back into a bun, and wire-framed spectacles was more customary. But then he was only a thirty-two-year-old Santa, despite the white curly wig and ill-fitting beard. He wouldn't fool a kid that he was the real deal for a minute, that was for sure.

Marissa looked sensational in the new Mrs Claus outfit, her luxuriant dark hair waving from under her Santa hat to around her shoulders, her lipstick a rich, kissable red, the short skirt and striped tights showing off slender legs that went on forever. She'd replaced the plastic boots that came with the outfit with her own high-heeled black boots, which also added to the hot new Mrs Claus look. He didn't want her to take that outfit off after the gift-giving ceremony. He'd like to slowly strip it from her and make love to her. If he'd thought he'd been obsessed with Marissa before they'd spent the night together, it was nothing on how he felt about her now.

The Christmas feast was over. The guests who chose to take part in the gift-giving had gathered around the spectacular towering Christmas tree in the spacious guest living room. It was time for Santa and Mrs Claus to give out the presents, one for each adult guest. There were also age-appropriate gifts for the few children who accompanied their parents.

Christmas here was more an occasion for well-heeled adults than lots of kids tearing around the place. But Oliver liked their presence—Christmas didn't seem like Christmas without children. For the first time, he let himself imagine what it might be like to have *his* children spending Christmas at Longfield Manor. Little dark-haired children, because surely he and Marissa would have dark-haired babies—

Stop! He couldn't let his thoughts stray in that direction. Not now. Not yet. Maybe never, depending on what she thought of the idea.

This year the adult's gift was a handblown glass frosted bauble tree decoration with a resin miniature of the hotel inside it and the words *Longfield Manor* and the year hand-painted in silver script on the outside. It was an exquisite keepsake, the brainchild of Caity. He had a lot to thank Caity for—not the least of which was bringing Marissa into his home and his heart. Marissa reported her friend was doing very well in hospital, which pleased him.

Granny introduced the new Claus family, with a heartfelt homage to Grandpa, announced her retirement as Mrs Claus and then the ceremony commenced.

Who knew this could be so much fun?

Marissa was a brilliant sidekick and they traded banter and laughter with each other as they handed out gifts and well wishes to the guests. She was lovely with the children, squatting down to their level, giving hugs where appropriate. You would never guess Marissa was a Christmas-hating Scrooge.

But might that be because she was that no longer? Thanks in part, he liked to think, to him?

When the gift-giving was over, one of the guests pointed out that Mr and Mrs Claus were standing right under a strategically placed bunch of mistletoe. Wasn't it time for Santa to give his wife her Christmas kiss? He looked to Marissa and she smiled back. Santa obliged with a passionate kiss and a backwards swoop of Mrs Claus. By now everyone knew they were a real-life couple.

'Are you two going to be naughty or nice tonight, Santa?' a longtime guest, who had known Oliver as a child, called out.

Marissa looked up at Oliver with wide eyes and a lascivious smile. Then she looked back to her audience and gave an exaggerated wink. 'Both naughty *and* nice,' she said in a slow and sexy voice.

To the guests' laughter and applause, Granny took the spotlight to thank everyone for choosing Longfield Manor to spend Christmas. She reminded them to book now if they planned to return next year, as returning guests had priority.

'I'll finish by thanking Marissa and Oliver for being such a brilliant Mr and Mrs Santa Claus.' She made a dramatic pause. 'And to express my opinion that they'd make a brilliant Mr and Mrs Pierce, too.'

'Granny,' groaned Oliver. 'That's going too far.'

But people were laughing and applauding, and Marissa didn't look embarrassed or upset; in fact, she was laughing, too.

And, really, was the Mr and Mrs Pierce thing completely out of the ballpark? He had never, ever felt for a woman what he felt for Marissa. He might need to think about securing her.

'Sorry about Granny,' he whispered to Marissa. 'She really got carried away this time.'

'Water off a duck's back,' she said. 'Nothing Edith says shocks me anymore. She means well. Remember, everything she says is motivated by love for you and her desire for you to be happy.'

Marissa was beautiful both inside and out. He hugged her, so grateful for the way she was unfailingly good to Granny. And the fact was, that since Marissa had been here, Granny had had very few forgetful or disoriented episodes. She was her old self more often than not.

The gift-giving over, waiters brought around trays with flutes of champagne and plates of exquisitely decorated festive cookies. 'These beat a mince pie, hands down,' Oliver said to Marissa.

She took a cookie shaped like a Christmas bell off the tray and nibbled. 'You're right. It's delicious. In fact, I might have to have another one. A Christmas stocking one.'

Oliver stepped away to call the waiter back with the tray, when Granny came over. She took his arm. 'Look who just got here. Such a lovely surprise. Toby and Annabel.'

Oliver was pleased to see his old friend. He greeted him with a hug. Then unhooked his Santa beard to better kiss his wife, Annabel, on the cheek—an awkward procedure with the Santa beard. 'Where are the kids?'

'Annabel's parents have a house down here so we're spending Christmas with them,' said Toby. 'They're minding the children to give us some grown-up time. You've always said I've got a standing invitation to visit, so here we are.'

'Great to see you. I must introduce you to my girlfriend.'

Toby's eyebrows rose. 'You? A girlfriend? One that lasts more than a week?'

Marissa had her back turned to them, chatting animatedly to a guest. Oliver tapped her on the shoulder and excused himself to the guest. 'May I borrow Mrs Claus? There's someone I really want her to meet.'

'Who?' Marissa said, turning to face him.

With a hand on her elbow, he guided her towards his friends. 'My old friend Toby,' he said. 'We go back a long time.'

He felt her stiffen. Perhaps it was too soon to be introducing her as his girlfriend.

'Toby and Annabel, let me introduce—'

'Marissa,' said Toby. 'So you two finally got together after all.'

The colour drained from Marissa's face.

This couldn't be happening.

Marissa was so shocked she couldn't speak, just looked from Toby to Oliver and back again. She barely registered Toby's blonde wife, who was looking curiously on.

'Do you remember me?' Toby said.

'Samantha's brother,' she said. 'How is she? We lost touch a long time ago.'

Toby wouldn't be diverted. 'Sam's fine. But how about you two? This is a surprise. Olly, you sly dog. I thought you didn't see Marissa again after that summer we first met her. So long ago. How old were we? Sixteen?'

Marissa could see recognition slowly dawn on Oliver's face. Recognition and a tight, contained anger. 'Yes,' he said, tight-lipped, not looking at Marissa.

'And you were fourteen, right, Marissa?' Toby said. He looked her up and down. 'You sure have changed.'

'One tends to in sixteen years,' Marissa said through gritted teeth.

'You wanted to ask her out then, didn't you, Olly? But Sam told us her parents wouldn't allow it. She was too young to date.'

'I don't remember that,' Marissa said, trying to force a smile.

'Nah. I reckon Samantha only said that because she fancied Olly for herself,' Toby said. 'She was right peed off that he only had eyes for sweet Marissa.'

Sweet Marissa?

How about Monobrow Marissa? Gawky and giggly? Now she remembered she hadn't liked Toby very much back then, though she'd been forced into his company in the school holidays. And after that overheard conversation, she'd completely avoided him.

'Sounds like something Samantha would do,' Annabel said, shooting a sympathetic glance to Marissa.

'So when did you and Marissa hook up again?'

Hook up? Was Toby being purposely offensive?

'Quite recently,' said Oliver, still not looking at Marissa. 'We met at a function at The Pierce Soho.'

'Did you recognise her straight away? Bet you didn't.' He ran his fingers across his eyebrows. 'The eyebrows, right?'

'I think you've said enough, Toby,' his wife interjected.

'She was just as lovely,' Oliver said, without actually answering Toby's question.

'I didn't recognise him,' Marissa said, not daring to look at him. 'He was Oliver Hughes then, if you remember. I had no idea he was the same person.'

For a while, that is.

It wasn't excuse enough for not reminding Oliver they'd met before, and Marissa knew it. She'd had several chances to tell him. Now she'd blown it.

She tried to change the subject by asking Annabel about the children, but their conversation was stilted.

'I'm sorry, it's been lovely to meet you, but I'm helping Edith with something, and have to go find her,' she said after one too many awkward silences. 'Catch up later?' she said, knowing full well she wouldn't.

'I look forward to seeing you again,' said Annabel.

'Me, too,' said Toby, homing in for a kiss that Marissa adroitly avoided. He reeked of alcohol.

'*Merry* Christmas,' she said.

'I'll be back,' Oliver said to his friends. 'Grab some champagne.'

He followed Marissa out of the room and into a deserted part of the corridor, not giving her a chance to gather her thoughts, let alone to plan any kind of strategy. A grim-faced Pierce male ancestor with mutton-chop whiskers from the Victorian era peered down at her from the wood-panelled wall.

His equally grim-faced descendent took her by the arm, forcing her to look up at him. 'Why did you lie to me?' he said, his eyes cold and accusing.

'I didn't actually lie. It was more of a...a...lie of omission.'

'A lie is a lie. I don't tolerate liars, Marissa. In any shape or form.'

'Understood,' she said. She wanted to say she didn't, either, but that might seem more than a tad hypocritical.

'Did you recognise me straight away?' he said.

'You looked like Oliver Hughes, but you were Oliver Pierce. I had no idea there was a connection when I agreed to work here. Oliver isn't an uncommon name.'

'A misconception easily cleared up, I should imagine.' He let go of her arm.

'Yes, the first morning I was here. All it took was an internet search.'

'Why didn't you remind me straight away that we'd met?'

'Because you had no idea who I was, and I decided to leave it that way. I was only going to be working here a week. I didn't know you were going to ask me to be your fake girlfriend.'

'And you still didn't tell me.' His eyes narrowed. 'You know, I thought there was something about you that was familiar, an expression, a giggle, but I meet so many people.'

'What you don't realise is that I loathed you.'

'What?'

'Back then, I actually had a huge crush on you. Huge. Then I overheard you talking to Toby. Shredding my appearance to pieces. There wasn't anything about me that you both didn't snigger and sneer over. I was gawky, flat-chested, giggled too much and boy, did my eyebrows come in for ridicule. I was devastated. I slunk off to lick my wounds. Avoided you for the rest of your visit. My fragile teenage confidence was shattered. Can you imagine my shock when it turned out I was going to have to work with you for a week? Worse, stay under the same roof.'

'Did I really say all that about you?'

'You absolutely did. You were not a pleasant young man. And Toby was even worse.' She wanted to say that she'd forgiven him. That he'd grown into a wonderful man. That we all said stupid things when we were teenagers. But she doubted he was in a mood to be receptive.

'So you were looking for revenge?'

'The thought crossed my mind. But then…'

'Then what?'

'I very quicky got to like you.'

'But you still didn't tell me. You slept with me, and you still didn't tell me.'

'That's right, because by then I didn't think it mattered,' she said, which was a fib in itself. She knew she should have told him. She didn't actually have a leg to stand on.

'This changes everything, Marissa. You're not who I thought you were.'

Her chin rose. 'Perhaps I'm not,' she said.

'I've never felt more humiliated than when Toby outed you back there.'

'I actually don't think Toby saw it that way. He bought our story that we'd recently connected.'

'He's drunk. When he sobers up he'll realise I didn't recognise you as that girl we'd met sixteen years ago. He'll also realise you'd recognised me and wonder about that.'

'Does it matter what Toby thinks?'

'It matters that you made a fool out of me.'

'I think you're wrong, but if that's what you want to think, feel free.' She glared at him. He was right. Everything had changed. She'd been kidding herself there was something special between them. Besides, did she want to be with a man so rigid and judgemental?

'If you'll excuse me, I need to go up to my room.' She indicated what she was wearing. 'I need to get rid of Mrs Claus.'

'Go,' he said.

For a moment she almost laughed, a hysterical, non-funny

kind of laugh, at the thought of them in this corridor, arguing in their Santa costumes. Thank heaven no one had seen them. It must have looked ludicrous.

As she headed for the stairs, she encountered Priya.

'That went so well,' Priya said. 'You were brilliant as Mrs Claus.'

'Thank you,' she said, barely able to string the words together.

Priya frowned. 'Are you okay?'

'Fine. But I finish up here today. I need to pack up my room and head back to London.'

'Haven't you heard? The roads are closed. We're snowed in.'

'You're joking.'

'We had some very heavy falls.'

'So I'll have to hope I can get out tomorrow.'

'Oh,' said Priya. 'We'd rather hoped you'd be staying.'

Marissa forced her voice to sound calm, businesslike. 'I'm sure I'll be back. It's been marvellous working with you. I have all fingers and toes crossed for you that you'll be taking over from Cecil when he retires.'

'I think I've got a chance,' Priya said with a smile.

'Look, I'm going to head up to my room to change. Then I need to get outside for some fresh air, before it gets dark.'

'Be quick,' Priya said.

Marissa couldn't bear to linger in Room eight for any longer than she had to. Too many memories of her and Oliver making love. She had never been happier than she had been twelve hours ago. Now she couldn't look at the bed for fear of a heart-wrenching vision of their sensuously entwined limbs.

How stupid she'd been to think she could escape the Christmas jinx—that it could have turned out any other way. What had Oliver said?

Anything that's going to go wrong invariably goes wrong on Christmas Day.

Another horrid thing had happened to her at Christmas. What

could be worse than breaking up with him when they'd only just begun? He'd appeared so kind, so understanding. But it seemed that underneath that gentlemanly facade beat the heart of that mean-spirited, arrogant teenage boy. She'd look on this in years to come as a lucky escape. But it didn't feel like that now and she was desperately fighting tears.

She cringed at her remembered jollity. At the way she had dressed up as Mrs Claus, for heaven's sake, when she should have been Scrooge. Flirting with Oliver's Santa as Mrs Claus, letting her feelings for him show in her eyes, making no secret of where her heart lay. How could she have let her barriers down like that?

She put on jeans, a sweater, her warm puffer jacket, boots and headed back down the stairs, carrying her hat, scarf and gloves. If she didn't get outside soon, away from the central heating and the ever-present scent of pine needles, she feared another panic attack.

Thankfully, there was no wind, but it was bitterly cold outside and light snow was drifting down. Long afternoon shadows were falling across the snow-blanketed garden. It was beautiful and peaceful and being out in nature should be good for her battered soul. She stepped out onto the snow that covered the driveway and onto the grass. The snow was deep but not impossible and she set out towards the walled garden, the occasional snowflake landing lightly on her eyelashes. She would miss Longfield Manor, she would miss Edith, but most of all she'd miss Oliver.

She refused to let her thoughts go there. She'd only really known him for a week—she would as easily forget him; of course she would. Truth was, she'd first met him a lot longer than a week ago, and that teenage attraction had been like smouldering coals ready to ignite into fierce flames when she'd seen him again. She wondered if the reason she'd never had much luck with men was because she'd compared them unfavourably with her teenage heartthrob. But what about now?

Would she compare every new man she met in the future to Oliver Pierce and find them lacking?

As she neared the iron gate to the walled garden, the snow started falling more heavily, until suddenly she could hardly see ahead of her. When she got to the gate, she turned back to see her footsteps had already been covered. She didn't have the world's best sense of direction, and she wasn't quite sure which was the way to turn back to the Manor. She hadn't thought to bring her phone to use the compass app, either. Don't be silly, she told herself. The walled garden is in a direct line to the house; it's still light, you'll be fine. She pushed the gate open and gasped at the beauty of the garden covered in snow. She'd just take a few moments here to contemplate her future and then go back.

How could he have spoken to Marissa the way he had? Oliver berated himself. It had been such a shock to discover that they'd met before. That this Marissa was *that* Marissa. Why on earth hadn't she reminded him? Was it because she was too nervous to, because he'd been so critical of her then? He shouldn't have called her a liar.

He'd gone back to Toby to ask him what exactly had happened when they were sixteen, only for his old friend to confirm that they had indeed picked Marissa's appearance apart and had a good laugh. When Annabel had gone off to the bathroom, Toby had confessed he'd liked Marissa for himself and had wanted to put Oliver off her by enumerating her 'faults.' It had backfired on him, though, as Marissa had never again come around to her friend Samantha's house when her brother was in residence. Toby reminded him that they'd been private schoolboys at an all-boys school, desperate for female company and ignorant of what to do when they found a girl they liked. That was no excuse, Oliver knew. He had been keeping up with Toby, saying what he felt he was meant to say, as good friends had been few and far between in the hierarchical structure of his boarding school.

He had hurt Marissa, back then and just now. He had to apologise, grovel if required. Because he knew if he didn't, he wouldn't get her back. And he desperately wanted her back.

Priya told him that Marissa had gone outside.

'In the snow?' he said. 'When it will be dark soon?'

'She insisted,' Priya said. 'I'm sure she's okay.'

But what if she wasn't?

Fear sliced through him. What if she got lost in the snow?

What if he'd lost her?

Not because of the snow, but because of the way he'd treated her?

He couldn't bear it if, having found her again, he was once more without her. Because he had liked her back then, really liked her. He remembered now he'd told Granny he'd met a beautiful, friendly girl named Marissa in the midterm break when he'd visited Toby. But he'd been too shy and uncertain around girls to follow up with her. Had that name *Marissa* lodged in Granny's mind and that was why she'd made those extraordinary statements about her when Marissa had arrived at Longfield Manor. Who knew? But he did know he had to find her now, before she had time to hate him again.

There had been a light fall of snow since Marissa had set out, but not enough to completely obliterate her footsteps. He wasn't surprised to see she'd headed for the walled garden; she loved that place, felt a special bond to it.

But her footsteps were more obscured by snow when he got closer. 'Marissa!' he called. The word was loud in the silent garden blanketed by snow. He called her name again.

Then she was there at the open gate of the garden. 'Oliver. I'm here.'

He ran in the snow to the gate where she waited, all bundled up against the cold. 'Are you okay? I was worried.'

'Of course I'm okay,' she said. 'I just needed some fresh

air, to clear my head after...after what happened back there.'
There was a distinct chill to her voice that had nothing to do
with the snow.

'Marissa, I'm sorry, so sorry for speaking to you like that. I
was wrong. I was so shocked by the fact you remembered me
and didn't say. But that's no excuse.'

'I was in the wrong, too,' she said. 'I should have let you
vent. I had so many chances to remind you we'd met sixteen
years ago but I didn't.'

'I was awful back then. Toby confirmed that we did say those
horrible things you overheard. I have no excuse. I really liked
you but was too shy and ignorant to know what to do about it.
I wanted to keep up with Toby because he was one of the few
friends I had at boarding school. My life was pretty awful in
the aftermath of my parents' divorce. So even though I was uncomfortable with what he was saying, I let him egg me on. And
he's stayed a good friend. Obnoxious when he's drunk, but still
a loyal friend. And Annabel is a darling. He's lucky to have her.'

'You liked me then? Really?' Her eyes were huge.

'I had a funny way of showing it, didn't I?'

He explained then his theory of why the name Marissa might
have triggered Granny's odd behaviour.

'It's an interesting thought,' Marissa said. 'She was right,
though, wasn't she? About us being together.'

'Are we together still?'

'If you want us to be,' she said tentatively.

'Will you forgive me for my crass sixteen-year-old behaviour? Teenagers can say such stupid things, behave so badly.'

'I already have forgiven you.'

'That wasn't us back then. Fourteen-year-old you and sixteen-year-old me. They were immature, semi-formed versions
of ourselves.'

'And yet, I think that's when I was struck by the *coup de
foudre*. Not a week ago. Sixteen years ago.'

'You think so?'

'I know so. I have a strong feeling you have always been the man for me. We just had to find each other again.'

'And will I always be the man for you?' he said hoarsely. He held his breath for her answer.

'You always will be,' she said.

'I love you, Marissa,' he said. He had never told a woman he loved her and he was struck by how...*wonderful* it felt. 'I really love you.'

She smiled a slow, sensual smile. 'And I love you, darling Oliver.'

He kissed her and their kiss told them everything they needed to know.

'I've had a thought,' he said. 'I liked having you as my Mrs Claus and calling you my wife. How would you feel about becoming Mrs Pierce?'

'Are you proposing to me, Oliver?'

'You mean sixteen years after I first met you, I still can't find the right words to say to you?'

'Think about it. I think the right words are probably on the tip of your tongue.'

He laughed. 'Marissa Gracey, will you marry me?'

She smiled. 'I would love to marry you, Oliver Pierce, so the answer is yes.'

They kissed again, long and sweet and full of hope for their shared future.

'There are things we need to talk about,' he said. 'The future of Longfield Manor being one.'

'Is it in doubt?'

'Grandpa wanted me to sell it.'

'No! You couldn't.'

'That's the conclusion I've come to as well.'

'Good,' she said vehemently.

'I'd want you to be involved with The Pierce Group. You bring something to the table when it comes to the Manor's future as a hotel.'

'I could be the events manager. And help Edith. She'd like Priya to take over from Cecil, by the way.'

'Can we schedule in us having a family here, too?' he asked.

She smiled her delight. 'Absolutely. It'll be our top priority.'

'The women have it sorted.'

'We're good at that,' she said.

'You're good at lots of things,' he said. 'Including making me the happiest man in the world.'

'You're very good at making me the happiest woman.'

She looked up at him, her beautiful face glowing with love. 'You know you said you wanted to help me make new, happy memories of Christmas?'

'I remember.'

'I think we've just made the most wonderful memories of Christmas, of Longfield Manor and of you. Something tells me my Grinch days are over.'

He kissed her again.

EPILOGUE

April the following year

COULD THERE BE a more beautiful place for her wedding to Oliver than the Longfield Manor walled garden? Marissa didn't think so. The day was perfect, a blue sky with just a few wisps of white cloud trailing across the horizon. She stood outside the iron gate to the garden, looking in to the scene so perfectly set for the ceremony.

The fruit trees espaliered on the stone walls were blossoming in frothy bunches of white and pink, and tulips and other spring flowering bulbs lined the stone pathways. A heady, sweet scent from lily of the valley wafted through the air. Water trickled from a central fountain, at the base of which, Marissa was tickled to discover, bloomed the starry white flowers of the bogbean. The string quartet—the same one as they'd had for Christmas—played romantic, classical music.

They both wanted a simple wedding, with a celebrant from the village and an elegant lunch in one of the private rooms in the hotel. The celebrant stood at the far end of the garden, with Oliver and his best man Toby waiting for her to walk down the central pathway so they could start the ceremony. There were thirty guests, a mix of friends and family, including her brother

Kevin and his wife, Danni, who had flown in from Sydney, standing and sitting around the garden. Kevin kept a firm hold on Oliver and Marissa's black Labrador puppy, Rufus Two, who was being a very good boy.

Marissa took a deep breath. She would walk down that pathway in her lovely, long white dress, her dark hair up under an exquisite veil, as Marissa Gracey, and walk back up it married to the man she adored. She could hardly wait to be his wife.

She held on tight to her bouquet and got ready to walk—she'd been told she should glide—up the pathway to where Oliver waited. First up the pathway ahead of her, in an elegant violet lace dress, was her special attendant, Edith, beaming her joy that her dream for her grandson was about to come true. Marissa had a quiet, reflective moment that her parents couldn't be here. Her mother had always wanted to see her as a bride.

Her bridesmaid Caity stepped close to her long enough to whisper with a smirk, 'I thought you were immune to gorgeous men,' before making her own way down the pathway in her slinky orchid-coloured silk satin dress. Caity's healthy, perfect twin girls were with her husband, Tom.

The quartet struck up Mendelssohn's 'Wedding March.' Then Marissa stepped onto the pathway, seeing only Oliver waiting for her, his love shining from his eyes, as she walked towards her husband-to-be and her new life with him.

To love, honour and cherish.

* * * * *

The Billionaire's Festive Reunion

Cara Colter

Cara Colter shares her home in beautiful British Columbia, Canada, with her husband of more than thirty years, an ancient crabby cat and several horses. She has three grown children and two grandsons.

Books by Cara Colter

Blossom and Bliss Weddings

Second Chance Hawaiian Honeymoon
Hawaiian Nights with the Best Man

Matchmaker and the Manhattan Millionaire
His Cinderella Next Door
The Wedding Planner's Christmas Wish
Snowbound with the Prince
Bahamas Escape with the Best Man
Snowed In with the Billionaire
Winning Over the Brooding Billionaire
Accidentally Engaged to the Billionaire

Visit the Author Profile page
at millsandboon.com.au for more titles.

Dear Reader,

This story is set at Whistler Blackcomb, a British Columbia resort that encompasses two mountains and is consistently ranked the number one ski destination in the world.

There is no Cobalt Lake Resort. This upscale boutique lodge was invented almost entirely by Michele Renae, my coconspirator on this duet.

Michele did such a brilliant job and got it so right that I found myself wishing it did exist, just so I could go to the s'more station by the lake and maybe catch a glimpse of a celebrity or two!

There is also no Feeney Pass and no secluded hot springs, though both these places are based on the kind of secrets small towns fiercely guard.

It was a pleasure to create this winter wonderland and this cast of characters with Michele. In book one, billionaire dad and widower Brad Daniels is given a second chance with his high school sweetheart. And in book two, his strong-willed, independent daughter, Cassandra, meets her match in a wounded champion ski hopeful, Rayce Ryan.

Michele and I invite you to join us for this partly truth and partly fiction—and wholly magical—White Christmas in Whistler.

Warmest wishes for the holidays!

Cara Colter

For the gifts of strength and hope

Kai 'Ehitu

Oh, yeah!

Praise for
Cara Colter

"Ms. Colter's writing style is one you will want to
continue to read. Her descriptions place you there....
This story does have a HEA but leaves
you wanting more."

—*Harlequin Junkie* on *His Convenient Royal Bride*

CHAPTER ONE

"CASSIE," BRAD DANIELS said to his daughter, "it's the third day of November. You just got the Halloween things put away. It's a little early to be working on details for Christmas, isn't it?"

His daughter—he was the only one allowed to call Cassandra "Cassie"—gave him the raised-eyebrow look. It was so like her mother, Cynthia—in charge, would not suffer fools lightly, a need for perfection—that he felt a shiver go up and down his spine.

He used to call the pair of them his dream team.

"Dad! We're actually *behind* where we should be. The tree for the front lobby needs to be a blue spruce and it has to be twenty-eight feet tall."

"One foot for each year of your life?" he asked dryly. "By the time you're my age we'll have to raise the ceiling."

He was treated to *the* look again.

"The height of the tree has nothing to do with my age, as you well know."

He grinned at her, just to assure her that, yes, he did well know.

She sighed. "Do you think you just go to the Boy Scout Christmas tree lot and get one of those the day before you need it?"

His daughter was beautiful, as her mother had been. Willowy, fine-featured, blue-eyed. She had done something with her hair that turned the natural blonde to an unearthly shade of platinum that was extraordinarily striking, even as he wondered, *What is this generation's rush to gray? It would come soon enough.*

As gorgeous as she was, Brad found her intensity—a kind of earnestness—to be the most compelling thing about Cassie. He felt a rush of tenderness for her.

The last two years there had been only the most desultory efforts at making Christmas the spectacular event that was expected of the Cobalt Lake Resort, the ski and accommodation destination in Whistler their family owned.

Christmas had been one of the things they were best known for before the loss of Cynthia in a horrible accident had left Brad and Cassie reeling.

This year, from the almost feverish look of determination sparking in those blue eyes, it was clear that Cassie was planning to make up for it, with the best Christmas ever.

"You're right," he conceded. "Bring on Christmas. I'm sorry. I won't be much help. I don't have any idea where the Christmas stuff is."

"Oh, Dad, it's all in the main storage room, on shelves Mom labeled!" She looked at him indulgently. "Go back to running your empire, and I'll look after the resort. But remember, Christmas isn't a season, it's a feeling."

It was her favorite Christmas quote.

Brad groaned. "I have a *feeling* I'm going to be hearing that a lot over the next two months."

"It's not even two months."

"You're making my head hurt."

Cassie smiled at him then, and regarded him thoughtfully.

"Hey! Are you thinking I look old?"

"Not at all. You're only fifty-six. I was actually thinking how great gray hair looks on you."

His hair, salt-and-pepper when Cynthia died, had turned completely gray over the ensuing two years.

"Not every guy can say that," Cassie said affectionately, "but you look very distinguished, like Gregor Watson."

Watson, an actor, had just departed. He was one of many celebrities who had become a regular at Cobalt Lake, enjoying the upscale boutique nature of it, and that the resort was small enough they could go to great lengths to protect the privacy of their guests.

Security had had their work cut out for them this time, though. A couple of very determined members of the paparazzi had camped just outside the private property line, somehow having gotten wind of Watson's stay.

Security had nicknamed the most persistent of them "Gopher" because he kept popping out of various hiding places looking for the money shot.

He had not succeeded, however, in getting his prize—a photo of Watson, who had been named World's Sexiest Man about a million times.

"World's Sexiest Senior, here I come," Brad said dryly.

Cassie laughed.

As always, it was like the light had come on in his world. From the day Cassie had been born, it had been a source of amazement to him that two people as different as he and Cynthia could somehow create such a miracle.

It had been an accidental pregnancy. He remembered, clearly, on their twelfth anniversary, Cassie standing in front of them, hands on hips, doing the math.

"But I'm twelve! Did you get married because of *me*?"

"Oh, darling," Cynthia had said so smoothly. "We found out I was pregnant the very same day we had our engagement party. Which made it just about the best day of my whole life."

It was the tiniest of white lies, but what was important was that Cassie had been completely satisfied with the answer, and as far as Brad knew, it had never been mentioned again.

Brad sometimes wondered if that accidental pregnancy was part of what had sent his wife's need to be in control into overdrive. And now, he found himself wondering something else.

He felt he and Cynthia had enjoyed a good relationship, based on mutual respect for each other and love for their daughter.

Cynthia had loved Cobalt Lake, and as his parents aged, she had basically taken over the daily operations of the resort. By the time his parents had passed, she had been shifting the place to fit her vision.

Brad had always pursued other business interests, thinking of Cobalt Lake, even though it was a substantial holding, as more of a family hobby than a viable business venture.

Cynthia had proven him wrong on that front. She had taken the property from what had essentially been—despite the delusions of grandeur of his mother, Deirdre Daniels—a quaint little mom-and-pop ski hill to one of the most sought-after vacation destinations in Canada.

And Cassie seemed intent on taking it to the next level.

Had Cynthia been as happy with the marriage as he had been?

He had thought so. And then, two weeks ago, in search of a paperclip, he had looked through the desk his wife had always used. He had come across an envelope. It looked as if maybe it had been taped underneath the lip of the drawer, and the tape had dried over time, so that letter had whispered out of its hiding place, maybe even from him opening the drawer that had been closed for so long.

"You know, Dad," Cassie said carefully, drawing him back to the present, "maybe you're ready to meet some—"

"No," he said firmly, "I'm not."

The last thing he needed was his type A daughter thinking he needed to get back in the game. Much as he loved Cassie, Brad couldn't imagine anything worse than becoming one of her projects and having her devote her considerable energy to finding him a new partner.

He hoped his tone would be enough to make her back off, but, of course, that was not Cassie.

"Why not?" she pressed.

"I don't have the energy for it. If you think Christmas gives me a headache, you can't even imagine how I would feel sitting across a restaurant table with a perfect stranger, trying to think of things to say."

"It doesn't have to be like that. Traditional dating can be kind of lame. People need to think outside the box. Think how much you'd find out about someone if your first date was in a panic room!"

"I don't even know what that is." But he wasn't sure it could sound more awful than that.

"It's like a puzzle, only in real time. You get locked in this room, and you have clues and you find your way—"

He pressed his temples. "Here comes the headache."

She laughed. "Okay, okay, backing off. But if you did decide you were ready, you could tell me, and I could help you."

By locking him in a room with a stranger?

Really? At least the name was apt. Panic.

"I'm just letting you know," she said softly, "that I wouldn't be mad, or resentful that you weren't going to mourn Mom forever. I'd be behind you one hundred per cent if you decided it was time to move on. It has been two years."

He knew that Cassie's grief for her mother was still raw, and so, while misplaced, it was such a generous offer.

Under all that drive, there it was—a loveliness of spirit that she tried to hide from the world, as if it was a weakness.

"Thanks, sweetie. You'll be the first to know if I need a captain for Team Brad."

Not that it will ever happen.

"Go find your Christmas decorations," he told her gently.

She waved a hand at him, and left in her typical flurry of energy.

After she was gone, Brad got up from his desk and reached

for the jacket, which was hanging on the back of his office door. Time for a run. He'd always been a runner, and since Cynthia died, it brought him comfort he no longer got from the ski slopes. He called it his physical therapy.

It was cold and crisp today, the ice starting to form on the lake. He warmed up with a few stretches, but even when he started to run, his mind didn't clear.

He hated it that he had never questioned the strength of his and Cynthia's relationship while she'd been alive, or even after she died.

But that envelope, yellow with age, addressed in her firm hand...

Beloved

She had called him *dear* sometimes, and *darling* on occasion, but *beloved*? Never. So who was that letter for?

He had not opened it, or even decided if he would, but the questions it had stirred up were upsetting.

Was there someone she had loved before him? Had she married him only because of the pregnancy, because she thought she had to?

And an even worse thought: had the pregnancy been an accident at all? Or had his being a rising star in business—achieving billionaire status before he was thirty—been something that Cynthia, from a working-class background, wanted?

His mother had alluded to that possibility once or twice, until Brad had made it clear it would not be acceptable to him for his mother to air her habitual harsh judgments on the newest member of their family.

Cynthia had shown her mettle in very short order. She had left those humble beginnings behind her without a backward glance, sliding effortlessly into the world of prosperity that his business interests, more than the resort, at least at first, had provided.

She had been a perfect fit for that world, classy and refined. Okay, occasionally she'd overdone it, like using French words to sound chic. And when things reached her standard of perfection, she was fond of pronouncing them *marvelous*.

Still, any kind of accident, never mind pregnancy, was so out of her nature.

And yet, an accident had also killed her.

If she was happy, why had she loved those midnight skis by herself so much? Why had she taken a chance that night and gone into the avalanche zone?

Had she addressed a letter to *Beloved* before or after their marriage? Why had she kept it?

Should he open it, or respect the fact she had kept it secret? What if it blew apart everything he had believed about their marriage?

Brad shook off his thoughts, irritated with himself.

He had Cassie. And none of the rest of it mattered. At least not now.

It was colder out than he had thought it would be. His breath came out in icy puffs. He took the wide sidewalk that led him to the boardwalk that surrounded Cobalt Lake. He drank in the amazing view of Mount Sproatt. As always, the crisp air was a balm to his soul.

He caught sight of Gopher, hiding out in a group of trees just off the property line. He nodded to him, not letting on how annoying he found him, and thought to himself, *At least if he's here, unaware Gregor departed this morning, he's leaving someone else alone.*

He began to ramp up his speed, sprinting by one of the hot-chocolate-and-s'more stations provided by Cobalt Lake Resort. It was empty right now, but tonight the pathway would be lit up and people would be sipping hot drinks and taking—just as Cassie had planned—selfies against a magical backdrop that just happened to include the resort's logo.

It wasn't quite ski season, so there wouldn't be throngs yet. Christmas was the busiest time of year.

Brad noted the lake had formed quite a thick crust of ice around the edges. The water at the center was still open, though, and was the exact shade of dark blue that had earned the lake its name. If it stayed this cold, the lake would completely freeze over, and they'd be skating soon.

The ski portion of Cobalt Lake Resort was sandwiched between the two giants, Whistler Mountain and Blackcomb Peak, both of which he could see from here. Like their more well-known neighbors, Cobalt Lake was scheduled to open at the end of the month, snow conditions permitting.

They had a new ski pro, Rayce Ryan, arriving. He had been an Olympic gold contender before a skiing accident had shattered his leg.

Cynthia had always looked after hiring resort staff in the past, so this was Brad's first venture into it at Cobalt Lake. He hoped the new hire wouldn't come with the bitterness of dreams as shattered as his leg.

Skiing accidents had a way of changing how people felt. Brad lifted his eyes to the majesty of the mountains around him. All his life he had loved the mountains and the slopes so much. Cassie had been raised on skis.

Now, his daughter wouldn't ski at all.

And neither would he.

After Cynthia's death the resort had implemented a GPS tagging system for all their guests who ventured onto the slopes. It had already helped them find several skiers who had gone out of bounds and gotten lost.

But still, in the shadow of these mountains, Brad was aware how puny his defenses really were.

No matter what anyone thought, he was aware that the idea you could protect others was largely an illusion.

Again, he needed to shake off the shadows that threatened the beauty of the day. The sky was clear and blue, an osprey

screeching and spreading its wings over the lake, the peaks of
the mountains—Blackcomb, Whistler, Sproatt—shimmering
with snow that had fallen at the higher altitude, but not down
here.

Then, as if confirming Brad's thoughts about man's illu-
sions about control, the perfection of the day was completely
fractured. Suddenly, screams pierced the pristine mountain air.

CHAPTER TWO

THE SCREAMS HELD the pure and unmistakable—almost animalistic—sound of panic, the kind of terror of someone facing a threat to their very life.

It seemed to be coming from the area near the covered dock, which was located about halfway around the lake. Brad had already been running fast, but now he put on the jets, thankful that he was in great shape.

When he got to the dock, he pieced together what had happened in an instant. Out beyond the dock, on the ice toward that blue-black open water, a dog had broken through.

It looked as if a child—a girl, if the bright pink toque was any indication—was out there in the icy water with the dog.

The girl was screaming and scrabbling hard to get back on the ice, but every time she grabbed for it, the shelf broke away from her, like shattering glass. It didn't help her efforts that she wouldn't let go of the dog's collar.

A woman—the mother?—was racing back and forth on shore, dog leash in hand, screaming hysterically.

"Call 911," Brad called to her firmly She stopped, her mouth frozen open, and stared at him blankly, tears streaming down a face distorted by pure terror.

"Call 911," he ordered her. "Do it now."

He was thankful for the hours and hours of relentless training as a volunteer with the search-and-rescue team.

When he was satisfied the woman was following his order,
he looked around for something he could use as a reaching assist on the icy lake.

Search-and-rescue trained for this situation precisely, and
so Brad found himself extraordinarily calm as he raced toward
the flagpole at the end of the dock, pulled it from its holder and
dropped down off the wooden platform onto the frozen surface
of the lake, two feet below it.

He threw off his jacket. At first, where the ice was thick
enough to support him, he ran flat out. But at the initial, barely
discernable hint of the ice sagging under his weight, Brad
dropped onto his belly. He tiger-crawled, using his elbows. He
placed the pole well in front of him, horizontally, trying to dis-
tribute its weight across the ice as much as he could.

He inched closer and closer to the open water, to the flail-
ing child and the frantic dog. The child was losing energy fast.
The splashing was not so frenzied as it had been even moments
ago, and the screaming had given way to a desperate gasping.

And still, she would not let go of the dog!

The ice creaked and groaned menacingly under Brad's
weight.

And then, there was a giant crack.

It was sound like a gun going off and Brad braced himself
to be plunged into the frigid water. He held his breath, but the
ice, shockingly, held.

He inched forward again. Finally, he was nearly at the crumbling edge. Despite the fact that both the girl and the dog were
tiny, Brad felt the surprise of how wrong he had been. This was
no child in the water.

She was a mature woman, maybe his age, though the pink
toque, with its huge pom-pom now completely bedraggled,
looked like something a child might wear. Her soaked dark
hair curled out from underneath it, and was plastered onto a

face as white as the snow on the peaks that surrounded them. Her lips were already blue.

Her brown eyes, against all that white, looked huge, and filled with terror. The lashes were outlined in ice.

"You're going to be okay," he said firmly, deliberately keeping his voice calm and even. "Grab the pole."

He would not allow desperation to show in his voice, and he would not allow himself to get closer to the edge of the ice, even though he wanted to. There was no sense in all three of them ending up in the water. In fact, that was the possibility that Brad had to guard against most.

So, not daring to go any closer to that fragile edge where ice met water, he shifted the position of the pole, skidded it across the ice and felt an exquisite sense of relief that it was long enough. She could reach it.

Crazy to notice, right now, that she was cute, rather than beautiful. There was something elfin in her features, even as contorted as they were by fear and shock.

"Let go of the dog," he ordered her.

Even freezing, even in this perilous situation, he could see a certain raw determination residing side by side with her terror.

"I'll get you first," he promised, "then I'll get the dog."

Only with that promise did she loosen her hold on the dog's collar and make saving herself a priority.

She grabbed the pole with soaked woolen mittens. He could see her strength was nearly gone. That realization made his own power, adrenaline-fueled, ramp up a notch.

Inch by careful inch, Brad pulled her, but the ice just kept breaking as the weight of her body hit it. Still, he stuck to his plan. He kept backing up, kept keeping himself from the point where the ice would give way. He held his position and the ice didn't break underneath him, though it groaned threateningly.

Finally, they reached a place where the ice was strong enough for him to yank her onto the surface and out of the cold black water.

She lay there, exhausted, like a beached seal. He heard a little sob of relief escape her.

The dog had stayed close to her, and was paddling furiously in water and chunks of broken ice.

"Stay on your belly. Spread out your weight and crawl to me."

Finally, she was right in front of him, her face down, crying, her breath coming in great heaves.

"The dog," she gasped through chattering teeth.

He had a decision to make. Rescuing the dog did not feel as if it should be a priority. She was already very close to hypothermic, though her chattering teeth told him she wasn't quite there, astonishingly.

Brad decided to make one attempt. If that did not work, he had to make saving the human life his primary goal.

"Do not move," he ordered her, and made his painstaking way back to the edge of the crumbling ice.

Knowing he had given himself one chance at this, he focused intensely. He managed to get the pole, lengthwise, underneath the dog. It took every bit of his strength to use the pole as a fulcrum point to lift the dog out of the water. The ice held under the pressure. The dog, thankfully, was one of those ridiculously tiny things, maybe a Pomeranian.

Brad brought his full weight down on his end of the pole. It acted like a teeter-totter and flipped the dog into the air and onto the ice.

The canine looked like a drowned rat when it dropped in front of him. It deftly evaded his effort to grab it, and gave him a few half-hearted challenging barks, the ungrateful beast. It shook itself indignantly. And then, all four paws going in separate directions, the dog took off running, slipping and sliding toward the shore.

Brad crawled back to the woman. She had not moved, her coat rising and falling with her huge intakes of breath.

"Thank you," she said, her voice a hoarse whisper.

He was pretty sure she meant for the rescue of the dog, not her.

They weren't off the ice yet, but he didn't let her know they were still in danger.

"We're good," he said, deliberately using the same soothing tone he might have once used on Cassie for a scraped knee. "Just listen very carefully to what I tell you."

She nodded.

"We're going to go together. We're not going to stand up. Not yet."

"I don't think I can move," she whispered.

"That's okay. I can. That's what I'm here for."

And suddenly it felt as if that was about the truest thing he had ever said. That he'd been put in this place, at this time, to do this.

He slid his arm under her soaked jacket. It was candy-floss-pink, like the toque. He got a good grip on her. He was immediately aware that he was pumping heat, from exertion and adrenaline, but that she was dangerously cold.

He pushed, pulled and cajoled her, both of them crawling back across the ice, one painful inch at a time. It probably took minutes, but it felt like hours.

Finally, the surface beneath them felt thick enough to take a chance. He got to his feet and crouched. He got his arms under her knees and around her shoulders and scooped her up.

Her wetness soaked into his pants and shirt—it was about the coldest thing he had ever felt, like picking up a block of ice.

Despite the fact that she was soaked, and maybe because his adrenaline was running so high, she felt as light as a feather.

She was limp, and yet with her cradled body against him, it felt as if the bottom was falling out of his world.

Because he saw pure strength there.

There was the vaguest tickle along his spine, of knowing her. Deeply.

Maybe that's just how adrenaline made a person feel after sharing this kind of dramatic life event with a stranger.

As if you knew every single thing about a person.

Their heart.

Their soul.

"Thank you," she said again, but this time her voice was stronger.

It was when he heard her voice, for this second time, not whispering, not a croak of desperation, that he knew.

"Faith," he said, not quite knowing if he was speaking her name, or if that's what she—and this incident—was restoring him to, in a world where he had walked without that particular quality for a long, long time.

CHAPTER THREE

"FAITH CAMERON?"

It had been so long since anyone had called her that, that Faith felt faintly puzzled. Or maybe it was shock.

Who was she, again?

"Saint-John," she said, correcting her rescuer.

Her voice felt like it was far, far away, detached from her, coming from outside of herself. She was so cold. She had never been this cold in her entire life. She wondered, foggily, if maybe it went deeper than being cold.

Maybe she was dead.

There had been a moment out there in that icy water when she had resigned herself to fate. *This is it.* She had fully expected to die out there, the price to be paid for that foolish decision to go after the dog.

Not that it had felt like a decision.

She'd felt compelled, and had been out on the ice in an instant. It was as if her brain had turned off, and instinct had kicked in.

Though she would have thought instinct might weigh a little more heavily on the self-preservation side. Faith mused that she could have spared a thought to her poor family. Hadn't they suffered enough?

She mulled over the possibility that she might be dead. She had read stories—scoffed at the time—of people who had died and been unaware of it.

Maybe all the rest of it—that man coming on his belly across the ice—had been a fabrication of hope.

And Faith, of all people, should know the dangers that lay in hoping.

So, possibly, she was dead. Somehow, it seemed totally unfair, that on death she would be greeted not by the husband she had spent thirty years with, Felix Saint-John, but by her first love.

But just as with hope, Faith Saint-John, should know life was unfair.

She squinted at her rescuer. Real? Or was her shocked mind fabricating? Or was he a greeter on the other side?

The other side had very sexy greeters if that was the case. Brad Daniels had changed, of course. Who didn't, thirty-plus years later?

His hair was completely gray, but the varying shades were exquisite, like storm clouds with the sun behind them. That same shade was in the faint stubble that speckled his flawlessly masculine cheeks and ever so slightly cleft chin. He had lines on his forehead, and crinkles around his eyes, but if anything, maturity had taken the raw handsomeness of his youth and refined it.

The lines around his eyes made him look as if he had laughed a lot. Once. Though laughter was the furthest thing from the intensity of his features at the moment.

His strength seemed unchanged, though. She remembered that about Brad Daniels. Strong, athletic, comfortable in his own body in a way so few people of that age were.

But those eyes! The same dark brown eyes that held a soul-deep calm that called to the very thing she thought she might have lost forever.

Some essential part of herself, gone.

Of course, she hadn't told her daughter that part. Only that she was returning to Whistler to fulfill the final wish of her father, Max—Maggie's grandfather—and have his ashes spread in his favorite place.

"Maybe you should wait until I can go with you," Maggie had said, but her daughter was a busy lawyer with two young children, which meant the right timing for her was a long way away. And Felix's illness had already delayed the granting of Max's request by far too long.

"Or maybe Sean could take some time off work."

Maggie was forever volunteering her good-natured firefighter husband for the Mom-needs-help projects, so much so that Faith referred to Sean as her saint-in-law rather than her son-in-law.

"How about Michael?" Maggie had suggested her brother.

For all her good intentions, there had been something mildly insulting about her daughter's insinuation that Faith wasn't up to making the journey on her own, so much so that Michael could be called home from his studies in Scotland.

Michael. Would he come home, if she asked? Of course. But would he come out of duty, or love?

Their poor family, so damaged.

No, asking Michael was complicated and out of the question.

"I'm going by myself," she had told her daughter firmly, shutting the door on further discussion even though she knew Maggie was only sensing what Faith was feeling. She was lost. Her name seemed to mock her, because that's what she had the least of after six years of giving everything she had to Felix. After six years of watching the man who had given her her whole life, and whom she had given her whole life to, morph into a stranger before her eyes.

And not a very nice stranger, at that.

"Unbelievable," Brad Daniels said gruffly, sternly, drawing Faith back, "that you would risk your life for your dog."

Faith frowned. If she was dead, that would mean Brad, greeting her at heaven's door, was dead, too. It seemed that the odds of her being welcomed to heaven by a lecture about dogs from an old boyfriend were ridiculously slim. On the other hand, what were the odds of being rescued from the cold jaws of death by her first love?

She managed to smile weakly. She couldn't take her eyes off his face. She wanted to touch it, to determine if he was real, but she couldn't move. Her hands were so cold that she doubted she would be able to feel his skin—what she thought would be the delightful texture of those rough whiskers—anyway.

"You know what's even more unbelievable?" she asked, finally managing to answer him. "It's not my dog."

Was he taking her clothes off? It seemed he was, dispensing with her sopping jacket, and then, quickly, the sodden blouse underneath.

She couldn't be dead! Would she care that he left her bra in place, left her some semblance of modesty, if she was dead?

In a flash, his own jacket was around her. That scent could be described as heavenly, so maybe… Then his hands were rubbing the outside of that jacket, firmly, relentlessly.

It was a good thing she couldn't feel anything, because she was pretty sure if she could, her every resolve would be weakening under his firm touch. At least his physical touch made her very aware that yes, she was definitely alive!

"The ambulance is coming," Brad said, cocking his head. "Almost here."

And sure enough, Faith could hear sirens getting louder and louder.

There was a woman hovering around Brad's shoulder, clutching the wet dog and sobbing. "Thank you. Thank you. I don't know how to thank you."

And then Brad was not at her side. Peripherally, Faith was aware of him putting his body squarely between her and someone else. A man, with a very bulky camera. Brad seemed highly annoyed. He blocked the man from taking a picture, and she could hear the sharpness of his tone, if not the actual words he was saying.

The ambulance was here. So much commotion! People asking her questions, more sirens in the distance, the dog giving sharp, bossy little barks. Then, she was being lifted onto a stretcher.

And Brad was beside her again, holding her hand, and the world felt quite, quite still.

"Why?" he asked her, with a kind of urgency, as if he might never see her again. "Why did you risk your life to save a stranger's dog?"

"Its name was Felix," she said, and then she was suddenly aware of the fresh pain she could have brought her family with that impulsive decision. She was crying, aware the tears felt unbearably hot on her cold face.

He let go of her hand and the first responders took his place.

"I'll come with you," Brad said as they moved the stretcher toward the waiting ambulance.

"No," she said firmly. So firmly it stopped him in his tracks. She tried for a softer tone. "It's okay. Really."

The stretcher was being loaded, the doors were shutting and the only warm part of her was where the tears had tracked down her cheeks. And the part she least wanted to be warm was the part around her heart, which she had resolved must be kept frozen.

So that it could never be hurt again.

That's why she had said no to Brad coming with her in the ambulance. She didn't want to see him again for the exact reason that she wanted to see him again.

Her heart was being pulled in two different directions: come back to life, and stay numb.

The next hour—or maybe more—went by in a blur as hospital staff worked on warming her up. Finally, they left her, wrapped in a cocoon of a heated blanket.

Beyond exhausted, she slept.

Faith woke up feeling the most beautiful sensation of warmth, but also a feeling of disorientation. That smell…

She opened her eyes, slowly. She saw a light blue privacy curtain and an IV pole, and heard the unmistakable sounds of a hospital—codes being called, shoes on squeaky floors, the hum of machinery. The smell was that mixture of disinfectant and despair that she had come to know too well.

She struggled to sit up. If there was one place she did not want to be…

There was a strong hand across her arm, staying her. She turned her head. Brad Daniels was sitting in a chair beside the hospital bed.

"Hey," he said.

It was really unfair that he had aged so well. He was one of those men who was getting better as he got older. It felt like such a terrible weakness that she was glad he was here, despite the fact she had asked him not to come.

"Hey," she said back, and sank against a cushion he put behind her back. The effort it had taken to sit up drained her, so she closed her eyes again, and just let an exquisite feeling of contentment float through her, replacing that moment of panic when she'd realized where she was.

"Feeling okay?" he asked.

"Yes, so good. Warm. You didn't have to come."

"Of course, I didn't *have* to. But I knew your clothes were wet."

She suddenly remembered him pulling her soaked clothes off her. It felt horribly embarrassing. She kept her eyes closed.

"I wasn't sure where you were staying so I didn't know where to go to retrieve some dry things for you to put on when they discharge you."

He laid a package on her lap, and she opened her eyes again, and looked at it, instead of him. Looking at him made her feel weak.

Swamped by memories.

Of a younger Brad, his lips on hers, awakening something in her that she had never known before.

Or since, if she was going to be completely honest about it.

She told herself, firmly, that what she'd had with Felix was so much better than fickle, youthful passion. It was steadiness, security.

"I've got your jacket and sweater, but I didn't bring them here. I think it's going to take about a year for that jacket to dry."

The package was wrapped in brown paper and tied with hemp twine, the way very exclusive shops would have done it. The paper had *Cobalt Lake Resort Boutique* subtly embossed on it, and a little green sticker that attested to its environmental friendliness.

She had barely cried since Felix had died, six months ago. Today, she was making up for it. Now, as she slid her finger under the twine, it felt as if she was, once again, choking back tears.

Faith drew out the items, one by one. Brad had obviously gone way beyond her basic needs. There was a beautiful new down jacket and a soft woolen toque in the same shade of sage green.

This was followed by a pair of navy blue yoga slacks, a plain T-shirt and a light zip-up hoodie that matched the slacks. Like the packaging, each item had a sticker on it attesting to how it was doing its part to save the world.

"Sorry about the leisure wear," he said. "They're kind of one-size-fits-all, so it felt like a good bet, since I don't know your sizes."

"No," she said, "it's perfect."

For someone who didn't know her sizes, the last items in the bag were underwear—a lacy white bra and matching panties. A quick glance at the label showed them to be sustainably produced, breathtakingly expensive and her size *exactly*.

She dared a glance at Brad and saw he was blushing, ever

so slightly. It was endearing. Was he remembering things best left in the past?

She quickly tucked those items under the brown paper and ran her fingers over that raised, tasteful embossing.

"So is the Cobalt Lake Resort still in your family, Brad?"

"Of course," he said, reminding her he was one of those enviable people who had always known what his future held.

"I don't remember there being a boutique."

"It was one of my wife's ideas."

It was one of the very questions she had wanted answered about him. Of course, he was married. No surprise there. The Daniels family was nothing if not traditional. In fact, it was *good* that he was married, a comfortable barrier for the niggling of attraction she felt for him, still, after all these years.

Or maybe it wasn't attraction at all. She was probably experiencing some kind of psychological phenomenon, some kind of bonding to the man who had, after all, just saved her life.

Faith slid a look at his ring finger to confirm. A band of gold rested there.

"Did your wife help you pick things for me?" That would put the *sexy* things in a different light.

He twisted the band.

"She died," he said. "Two years ago."

So much for the different light. He had chosen those things.

Still, Faith noticed Brad's tone was flat, as if he was deliberately trying to strip the emotion from it. But she saw an anguish, the kind that she was very familiar with, flash through the deep brown of his eyes.

Something in her went very still. What were the chances of this? Of the craziness of their reunion and then this interesting twist? That both of them had lost their life partners?

"I'm so sorry," she said quietly.

So many questions. How had his wife died? Did they have children? What directions had his career taken him in? Were his parents still alive?

Had he been happy with his choices? Or had his family's expectations—his domineering mother, to be precise—dictated them to him?

Suddenly, she felt as if she wanted to know everything about him. What had the last three decades held for him?

She could see the same curiosity in him as those dark eyes rested on her, inquisitive.

Her close call in the lake had made her feel weak. His thoughtfulness had made her feel weaker yet.

Faith was appalled to find she craved connection with Brad Daniels.

But life had taught her the inevitable link between connection and loss—even the companionship of a cat was destined to cause pain—and she could not leave her poor battered heart vulnerable to that.

She had vowed that her children, and her grandchildren, would be enough for her at this stage of her life, even as her daughter, Maggie, looked somewhat panicked at the idea of being her mother's raison d'être.

Mom. You've got to find yourself again.

Maggie wanted her to find herself, but ironically, didn't even want her to travel alone to the place she had spent some of her high-school years.

And maybe that concern was not completely unjustified. Look at the chance she had taken, racing out on that ice for a dog.

Faith felt a sudden jolt of panic. Maggie!

CHAPTER FOUR

"WHAT TIME IS IT?" Faith asked, after twisting her neck to look frantically for a clock in the hospital cubicle.

Brad slid back his cuff to reveal a gorgeous watch. While she and her husband—he'd been a university professor, until his retirement, and she had been a teacher—had always been comfortable, there had never been room for watches like that in their lives.

Brad's watch was probably worth more than the down payment on their beloved downtown Toronto bay-and-gable, pre-World-War-Two-constructed house had been!

"It's just after five."

"Oh! I was supposed to let my daughter know when I got here."

When Faith had arrived in Whistler her hotel room had not been ready so she had decided to delay calling Maggie until she could do so from the comfort of her room. Since she had not been able to check in, she had left her suitcase—with her dad's ashes inside it—in a secure storage room.

"Mom," Maggie had said, "I don't think you can just travel with, er, human remains. Or spread them wherever you want. I think you have to get permits."

Her daughter, the lawyer, would think of such things. But

for once in her life, Faith was not going to do it right, or follow the rules. Her father would have approved. One of Max's favorite expressions had been "it's easier to beg forgiveness than ask permission."

So Faith had left the suitcase and then gone for that fateful walk around Cobalt Lake.

Another thought struck her, and her rising sense of panic increased.

"Where's my phone?" she asked. "My purse?"

Brad's brow furrowed, as he obviously was trying to remember the scene.

"I didn't have my purse when you pulled me out of the water?"

"Definitely not then."

"I hope I left it on the shore."

"I don't recall seeing a purse there. But I wasn't looking for one."

"What if my purse—and my phone—are at the bottom of Cobalt Lake?"

"You likely threw the purse down," he said, and there was something about him that was just so reassuring. "Do you remember where you entered the lake? Off the dock? Your purse might be there."

"I don't know where I went out onto the ice. Or if I threw or dropped the purse as I ran. It's all kind of a blur. All I remember, clearly, is that woman screaming for Felix."

"The dog."

"Yes."

"And something more?" he asked softly.

After a moment, she nodded.

"Who is Felix?" Brad asked, in a voice that felt as if it could call all her secrets from her.

She sighed.

"That was my husband's name. He died."

Brad drew in a sharp breath as he, too, recognized the coincidence in their shared tragedies.

Faith was aware she didn't need to offer anything else. But the close call, the weariness, now the loss of her purse—one blow after another—seemed to be lowering her barriers.

"Recently?" he asked quietly.

"Six months ago."

"I'm so sorry, Faith."

"Felix, my husband, had a horrible condition. A form of dementia most people had never heard of, until that action film star got it. It was a behavioral variant. It affected his personality, his judgment, his empathy."

She was slightly in awe of herself for managing to sound so clinical about something that had been so utterly devastating.

"Oh, Faith." Brad did not appear to be falling for her matter-of-fact tone. His deep voice was gravelly and showed genuine caring. His eyes on hers seemed to invite her to fall into what they offered: the understanding of someone who had also loved and lost.

She ordered herself not to say one more word. She ordered herself to remember the danger of connections, particularly to another human being.

Particularly given her shared history with Brad. But even as she tried to warn herself of the dangers, she kept talking. She glanced at the IV dripping into her arm. Was it possible there was something in that?

"He left me a long time before he actually died. I couldn't save him. No matter what I did, he just drifted further and further away from me."

The clinical dispassion was leaving her voice. There was a little wobble in it. This would be a really good time to stop talking.

"I couldn't save him," she whispered, "but when I heard that woman calling his name, it felt like maybe I could save something."

Why was she saying this? It had to be the IV making her say

things she shouldn't. Feel things she shouldn't. For instance, she shouldn't feel as if she *knew* Brad. As if she could trust him with her grief and vulnerability, as she had trusted no one else, not even her daughter, or her son. You didn't know someone because they had been your *first*.

Well over thirty years ago.

There was probably nothing resembling truth in those first passionate encounters between Faith and Brad.

But even if she had not known him fully back then, she could not deny she the raw genuineness in him, coming out on that ice and rescuing her. Everything he was had been on full display, with no filters. Strong, brave, compassionate, wise, willing to put himself at risk for someone he had thought was a stranger.

It had also felt like raw truth in his eyes when he had told her about the death of his wife.

Still, obviously, she was in some kind of shock, or on drugs, which had made her blurt out personal details of her life like that.

And then, her defenses completely crumpled, and she was crying *again*.

Faith had an awful thought. What if she had come all this way, thinking fulfilling her father's final wish would help her find herself, and the hard truth was that the self she would find was weak and needy and given to sharing confidences with people she didn't know?

Well, that was not exactly true.

She *knew* Brad Daniels.

Or a version of him.

She didn't know him now. Ridiculous to feel as if she did, based on his heroics on the ice.

"Scoot over," he said, and she could no more disobey this command than the ones he had given her out there on Cobalt Lake.

He came up on the narrow bed beside her. Despite all her warnings to herself about the dangers of connecting, she did not tell him no, she did not push him away, she did not try to avoid contact with him.

She *liked* the feeling of his weight sinking down on the bed beside her. She *liked* his scent—subtle, masculine, mountainy—tickling around her nose.

He didn't draw back the thin blanket that covered her, and so his thigh was on one side of it, and hers on the other.

Still, the contact—the connection—was there. Subtle heat from his leg, her leg lying against the hard length of solid muscle.

And she liked that, too.

It had been so long since she had shared a moment like this with another human being. Except her grandchildren—Maggie's two daughters, Chloe and Tanya, four and six—who snuggled into her as she read them bedtime stories.

She had been away from home less than a full day, and suddenly she felt melancholy, homesick.

"I think there's something in the IV drip," she said with a loud sniff.

"There probably is," he agreed.

"I'm glad we got that sorted. That I'm being drugged. That I'm not like this. At all."

"Like what?" he asked huskily.

"You know. Needy. Weak. Talkative."

"I don't see you as any of those things," he assured her softly, then he drew her head to the exquisite broadness of his shoulder and let her cry as he murmured soothing words. It felt as if she had never known anyone in quite the same way she knew Brad Daniels.

"I'm really not—"

"Shh, give yourself a break. You've had a shock. You're probably mainlining muscle-relaxants."

She giggled at the suggestion, and relaxed into the comfort he was offering.

Finally, and with what seemed like just a touch of reluctance, Brad extricated himself from the bed and handed her some tissues.

She was glad it had been quite some time since she had put on makeup, because had it survived the lake it would not have survived this deluge of tears.

While she dabbed at her eyes and tried to stop the heaving of her chest, she watched as Brad took charge of everything. He was a man that had so obviously come fully into himself. He'd always been confident, but now maturity had added weight to that confidence. She could not help but admire how he handled himself as he made calls to the resort and sent staff out to look for her purse and her phone.

His manner was friendly, but also firm. There was an unmistakable power in him. There was an invisible line, even on the phone, that made him one-hundred-per cent the boss.

This is what she needed to remember, since it felt so good to just surrender to being the one taken care of—once she had been staff at his family resort.

And his mother had not had the people skills her son had. Deirdre Daniels—always Mrs. Daniels to the staff—had been rigid and condescending, possibly the worst boss Faith had ever had.

And that was before Mrs. Daniels had made it known, in no uncertain terms, that there was no room for a chalet girl—and probably particularly one with the last name Cameron—to have a place in her son's future.

But all that seemed a long time ago and far away as Faith let this next-generation Daniels take charge of her life.

When he was done making his calls, Brad handed her his phone. "Call your daughter," he said. "Let her know you're okay."

He kindly exited the room to give her some privacy.

His phone was still warm where it had been cupped in his hand. What an utterly ridiculous thing to find appealing.

She glared accusingly at the IV drip before punching in Maggie's number. Of course, her daughter did not pick up, either because of the time difference—bath time for the babies, there was that sensation of homesickness again—or because it was coming up as an unknown number. Either way was a blessing, because Faith did not want to confess to her daughter that she had nearly brought more tragedy on the family, or tell her about the predicament she currently found herself in, or the circumstances that had led up to it.

It would just confirm all those doubts that had flashed through Maggie's eyes when Faith had announced her mission. She could practically hear the exasperated, worried, *Oh, Mom.*

"Hi, honey, safe in Whistler," Faith said with artificial cheer, leaving a voice-mail message. She glanced around the cubicle, glad it wasn't the video chat she would normally have used to connect with Maggie, Chloe and Tanya. The backdrop would have been a dead giveaway, that left to her own devices for the first time in years, Faith had managed to make a mess of it.

"Sorry to be letting you know so late. I seem to have misplaced my phone."

I knew she shouldn't go by herself, Maggie would say to Sean, when she heard that message. *How do you misplace your phone?*

"I bumped into a high-school friend who loaned me theirs," Faith continued. "I'll check in with you tomorrow."

She disconnected, thankful that her son, Michael, was away at university in Scotland and there was no need to keep him updated as to what was going on. She'd sent him a text about her upcoming travels, but she was not sure it had even registered with him.

Faith had the feeling that Michael had been grateful for the physical distance separating them when Felix was ill. The last time he had come home it had been a fiasco. It felt as if his sense of family had been deeply compromised by the trials of the last few years, and he had chosen a chilly withdrawal. When she'd told him she was thinking about selling the house he'd grown up in, he hadn't responded at all, as if that part of life—and happier times—was far behind him.

And then there was Maggie, who cared too much.

How could she begin to repair so much damage to her family? Could she?

She sighed, and looked at Brad's phone, willing to take advantage of the diversion from the troubled state of her own thoughts. She was *not* the kind of person who would give in to the temptation to check out a few photos on the unlocked device.

Of course, she wasn't the kind of person who dashed out on the ice after a dog, either. Or unloaded emotional baggage in front of strangers.

Maybe she didn't know who she was at all anymore. Wasn't that at least part of the purpose of this mission that already seemed to be going so badly awry?

Of course, nobody would be more delighted by things going *awry* than her free-spirited dad.

Faith decided, even if she was choosing a new her, it wouldn't be someone who snooped on someone else's phone. She did like the wallpaper on Brad's lock screen, though. It showed a beautiful young woman with silvery hair, sitting in a mountain meadow and looking toward the camera with undisguised affection.

His daughter, she assumed, studying the similarities in the bone structure. The woman didn't exactly look happy—she had lost her mother, after all—but there was both strength and confidence in the set of her chin, and shoulders, in the directness of her gaze.

He had raised his children well.

She scoffed at herself for reaching that conclusion on the basis of one photo. She didn't even know if he had a daughter, or how many children there were.

It could even be a niece, though that wouldn't explain the resemblance. Brad had been an only child, like Faith, so if it was a niece, it was on his wife's side.

When the door of her hospital room squeaked open, she hastily put the phone on the table tray in front of her as if she was a spy who had been caught looking at a file!

CHAPTER FIVE

IT WAS A doctor and a nurse, not Brad, who came into Faith's room. It was a sign of how much the world had changed since she was young—in good ways—that the doctor was a woman and the nurse was a man.

The nurse, who introduced himself as Adam, began to remove the IV.

"Is there something in that?" Faith asked him, as the doctor laid a very cold stethoscope on her chest.

"Yes, it's a heated intravenous solution of salt water. It helped warm your blood."

"And that's all?" Faith heard faint skepticism in her tone.

"That's it," Adam said with a smile. "If you're feeling not quite yourself—"

Whatever that was, she thought silently.

"—it's probably because your body sustained quite the shock. You're very lucky."

Lucky. Of course, she was. She had made a stupid, irresponsible decision and been saved from the consequences.

And yet, she was deeply suspicious of luck. Luck—chance, fate—had also selected her and Felix for a journey into heartbreak so breathtakingly painful nothing could have ever prepared her for it.

Still, with her rescue from the icy water of Cobalt Lake, her poor family had been saved from yet another blow, and for that she really did need to be grateful.

Even as she hoped they would never find out what she had done. The very thought of Maggie's tone, the look that would be on her face, made her cringe inwardly.

"Thank you for all your hard work," Faith said to the medical team. "I feel lovely now."

Except for the fact she had just discovered she had no excuse for confiding so deeply in Brad, for accepting the comfort of his body next to hers on the bed, his broad shoulder to rest her head on.

Faith was stunned by how much she missed those kinds of everyday intimacies. But those yearnings could make a person weak when they most needed to be strong.

"You'll need to take it easy for the next few days, but I think you're good to go," the doctor said.

But that was a dilemma. Go where? With no purse, no ID, no credit card, no phone? She wouldn't even have clothes if Brad had not supplied them.

The medical team left the room and Faith got out of bed, shocked by her lack of strength. Her legs felt as boneless as pudding.

She ducked into the tiny bathroom that adjoined the room with the clothes that Brad had given her. She pulled off the hospital gown—even that small effort sucked the strength from her—and sorted through the items.

She found herself blushing at his choice of undergarments. So feminine. Maybe even sexy. She had given up on sexy a long time ago, even before Felix got ill. Comfort had seemed way more important.

But even if it had been a long time since she'd worn anything but the most utilitarian underwear, she was too old to blush.

Still, she'd spent thirty years with the same man, so putting on undergarments purchased by her old high-school sweetheart felt oddly intimate, just like Brad beside her in that bed. But how had he gotten the sizes so right?

Her sense of embarrassment deepened as she recalled him yanking those sopping, cold clothes off her on the shore of the lake.

She hoped he was so busy in rescuer mode that he hadn't noticed that she wasn't eighteen anymore. Was rounder than the lithe teenager she had been.

But Brad wasn't the kind of guy who missed a thing.

Which included the scars of life, stretch marks and wrinkles, and things she had really thought she would never be brave enough to show another man in her life.

And yet, in this really lovely underwear, it seemed as if all her flaws were minimized. For the first time in a very long time, Faith felt exquisitely feminine. She realized why a woman might be tempted to spend so much money on lingerie.

She slipped on the yoga slacks and top. Both were products of a well-known designer—made from sustainable bamboo—and, as Brad had promised, one size fitted all, though maybe it was a bit on the snug side, hugging the curves of a body that had not been in a yoga class for at least twenty years.

Would yoga classes be part of her journey to find herself? Faith glanced in the terrible warped mirror above the sink.

The harsh hospital light wasn't helping, but she really did look awful. Her natural curls—dark brown threaded through with the odd strand of gray—were crushed to her head in some places and sticking straight up in others.

She pulled on the toque—the label said it was hand-knit by a local artisan—and that hid the worst of it. Her lips still looked faintly blue and she looked as pale as the death she had come close to experiencing.

She was annoyed at herself that she felt like she would have killed to get her hands on that little makeup kit tucked away in her suitcase.

Faith exited the bathroom. The small effort to get dressed

had increased the sensation of heaviness in her limbs. She sank onto the edge of the bed, and ran her hand over the bamboo fabric of the slacks, trying to think what to do.

First and foremost, she had to break this sense of connection with Brad.

They were now, and always had been, from different worlds.

He was from a world of wealth and good taste. His mother had made it abundantly clear that a chalet girl—Mrs. Daniels's euphemism for a chambermaid—had better not have designs on her son.

Those had been her words, spat out, snooty and cuttingly judgmental. Her tone had been lady-of-the-manor to maid-who-emptied-the-pots.

Have designs.

Those words could not have come at a worst moment in Faith's life. Despite the bliss of loving Brad, real-life problems had been pressing up against her. Only a few days before, her dad had confessed he'd gambled away the money he had scrimped and saved for her college fund for as long as she could remember.

She had never seen Max cry before, but he had cried when he had told her, "I thought it was a sure thing. I thought I could at least double that money. That you could have gone off to UVic and lived like a princess instead of a pauper. It was a pony named Faithful Fate. I thought it was a sign..."

Could Mrs. Daniels have known about Max Cameron's terrible mistake? It seemed she did. Whistler remained very much a small town.

Because Mrs. Daniels had then held out the single carrot that Faith had been unable to resist. She had offered to pay all Faith's expenses—tuition, housing and a small allowance—for her entire four years at a prestigious university in Eastern Canada, a long, long way from where Brad would be going to school at the University of Victoria, on Vancouver Island.

Faith had been accepted at UVic, as well, but even with scholarships, after her dad's confession, she had been contemplating the financial aspects of pursuing a higher education with terror. She would be on her own. Though she had always excelled in academics—she loved to learn and knew early on that she wanted to be a teacher—she knew no matter how she stretched, or how many part-time jobs she managed to land, she wasn't going to be able to do it.

And, of course, by accepting Mrs. Daniels's offer, she hoped to somehow alleviate her father's shame and pain over his awful mistake, too.

To fix it.

Look, Dad, it all worked out.

Faith had insecurities—and plenty of them—before those words, and that offer, from Mrs. Daniels. By the time they'd arrived in Whistler, when she was in grade eleven, they had moved so many times.

Despite his horrible mistake gambling away her college money, Max had had only one addiction. It had been spectacular. It wasn't as if he didn't like booze and gambling, but those paled in comparison to his grand obsession.

Max Cameron had been a powder hound. It always seemed the place he thought he would be happiest was wherever he wasn't.

And so they had followed the promise of snow. Max had worked at Lake Louise, Sunshine Village, Aspen, Deer Valley, Jackson Hole and a multitude of others, loving how the one guaranteed perk of working at a ski resort was either free or discounted skiing.

He'd had great dreams for Faith, but she had never developed his love of the sport, possibly because it had cost her so much in terms of stability.

Instead, she had loved books and school. Max had eventually given up on a ski-racing career for her, referring to her affectionately as his little bookworm.

Books, though, didn't provide a complete barrier from the

knowledge she had grown up with, of how resort towns worked. She was well aware that she and her father were on the bottom rung of a caste system, and that was before his many eccentric escapades were figured in.

Ski villages hosted very rich people who came for extended stays or owned the fanciest homes, and availed themselves to the posh resort lifestyles. They skied and hiked and went to spas, and sipped expensive wine in front of fires. If they had families, their children mostly went to private schools.

Then there were the business owners, like the Danielses in Whistler, who sold accommodations, or fine art, or exquisite furnishings, or designer clothes made out of bamboo. They were heavily community-minded, and that included supporting the local schools.

At the bottom of the resort-town heap were the people, Max said, with a grin and a shrug of his shoulders. Like the Camerons, who actually kept everything running, the maids and the store clerks and the lifties and the mountain guides and the ski instructors.

These people couldn't actually afford to live in most of the famous ski resorts in North America, unless they were lucky enough to get staff housing. Otherwise, it was trailer parks and basements suites, or houses shared with other employees. Faith had grown up experiencing all of those options at various times.

Max had been a seasonal worker, a chair-lift mechanic, and the absolute best at what he did. He had also been a true free spirit who had never conformed to what society expected from him.

He had been a single dad since Faith's mother had died when she was three. He had embraced that role with a startling joie de vivre.

She could remember him bursting in the door of her first-grade Christmas concert—where had that been, Big Sky in Montana?—looking panicked because he was late, his hands still black with grease and dressed in his work coveralls.

But the pride on his face, the love in that lopsided grin, had made her world. Though as she got older, it hadn't always felt like enough. Her dad's work could be as sporadic and unpredictable as he himself was. Especially in high school, when she had become aware money was tight and taken the job at Cobalt Lake to help out.

She'd been the new girl—again—and didn't have the right clothes or shoes, couldn't afford a good haircut and certainly didn't live at the right address. The money she'd earned helped pay the rent, it didn't buy baubles.

And so, when Brad Daniels—wealthy, athletic, popular, a member of the Whistler elite—had first shown interest in her, Faith Cameron, daughter of a lift mechanic and a lowly employee at his family's resort, she truly had felt like Cinderella, with a real live prince and a chance to dance at the ball.

She'd met him at school, not the resort. Having many experiences with moving, Faith had known the way to meet people was to join something, preferably not something that cost extra money. And so she had joined the school paper...and been mortified when her first assignment was to interview the athlete of the month, who had been Brad.

With his good looks and his athletic prowess, she had been expecting arrogance and superiority. Instead, she had found someone who seemed unaware of his social standing, or of hers. He was funny, humble and genuinely interested in people. He was one of the easiest people she had ever talked to. Sometimes it felt as if he was interviewing her, since he was so interested in all the different places she had lived.

Originally intimidated by him, she'd asked him for half an hour of his time. An hour later they had ended up going for sodas together at a local café.

He'd asked her, almost shyly, at the end of that time, if he could see her again.

She'd taken a deep breath, and admitted she worked as a chalet girl at his family resort. She would never forget the slow, sweet smile that had come across his face.

"Oh, that's wonderful," he'd said. "It means I'll see even more of you."

As if her station in life, and his, meant absolutely nothing to him. And it never seemed as if it had.

Faith had allowed herself to get caught up in the fairy tale of first love and to believe good things could happen to a girl like her.

But then, as it turned out, even if Brad genuinely did not care about the differences in their circumstances, *somebody* had, and she cared very much.

Brad's mother.

She had flung those stinging, life-altering words at Faith. And then made her that offer.

That offer. She knew it was a deal with the devil.

Three days had passed without eating or sleeping. Crying until her eyes swelled nearly shut.

And then, Faith had done what she had to do. She accepted the terms—all of them—dictated by Mrs. Daniels.

Dealing with moving was nothing new to her. But dealing with heartbreak was. She missed Brad so much. She was dying to call him, to explain, to just hear his voice.

And Faith missed her dad, as well. He had been the constant in her life, and yet he seemed broken by the choice he had made, and the choices she had made as a result. Nothing she said or did when she called him seemed to make him feel better. Brad was out of her life and her father was drifting away from her.

She threw herself into her studies, blocking out heartache, trying to outrun that not-good-enough feeling. That, and the guilty awareness that she had somehow sold out. She had done what her father would never have approved of. Chosen security over happiness, the safe way over the unmapped route.

It had taken years to feel she belonged in her solidly middle-class life, especially with Max in the background, leaving

Whistler at the same time she had, and going back to Banff. And then to Colorado. For a while, he'd been in Europe.

She'd had to send him airfare to come to her wedding, the first time he had met Felix. He'd taken her aside and suggested she "rethink" Felix, proclaiming him as dull as yesterday's porridge. Though he'd never been much of a drinker, he'd made an exception on that occasion. Max had gotten drunk and made a toast to a "boring and conventional life."

She'd been glad to put Max back on the plane, glad his presence in her boring, conventional life was sporadic. Because she loved *everything* about that life.

She had the life she had always hoped for—her own career as an elementary-school teacher, a husband who was stable and doting and, finally, motherhood.

Faith *loved* every single thing about family life and motherhood.

She loved it that she and Felix had aspired to the most ordinary of dreams. To have children, to buy their own house, to have a warm holiday in the middle of winter and to save their money so that Maggie and Michael could go to university, worry-free.

That life—those, oh, so ordinary goals—had slowly made Faith *finally* feel she was okay, that she was worthy of good things.

But then those good things had been snatched from her, in a dizzying flurry of tragedies. Her father had been diagnosed with liver disease—after ignoring the symptoms for years—and come home to her, only to die within weeks.

At about the same time, Felix's baffling changes in behavior had accelerated alarmingly.

And so, all those old insecurities seemed as if they had not been put to rest at all. They had just waited, patiently, for this past boyfriend to show up in her life and make her feel, at fifty-five, when she had really hoped to be beyond such things, insecure all over again.

It was not exactly, she thought wryly, what she had come back to Whistler for—to find herself in the grip of events that had happened well over three decades ago!

And she needed to remember the goal in her quest for discovery. Despite the insecurities of growing up in class-divided resort enclaves, when she was young, she had been so aware of her strength.

There had been a period when she had felt as if she could overcome any obstacle. During those romantic months of first love with Brad, at the end of their senior year, Faith had had a sense of being on fire with life, immersed in the moment, embracing the possibility that anything could happen.

So the ghosts of her former self had drawn her back here. That insecure girl wanted to find the roots of her self-doubts, exacerbated by Felix's illness; and that confident girl who thought she could do anything wanted to be coaxed back out.

Brad chose that moment to come back into the room. In light of the thoughts she had just had, Faith saw him through a new filter.

He carried himself with an enviable vigor for life. The air around him was practically shimmering with his amazing energy. He had an unshakable sense of himself, an innate self-confidence. It was in everything about him, in the way he dressed, in the way he carried himself, even in the polished cut of his silver hair.

The color of his hair was undeniably sexy on him. He looked like Gregor Watson. Only better, because he carried his looks without a hint of arrogance.

She did not want to be noticing anything *sexy* about Brad Daniels. But, given their recent close encounters—and his choice of underwear for her—how could she not?

"They tell me they're releasing you. Can I give you a lift?"

Of course, he could not give her a lift! She had to stop this right now! But what was she going to do? Walk back to her hotel? When her legs felt as if they were barely functioning? And then what?

"Yes, a lift would be nice. I'm not sure what I'll do about checking in. Without my wallet."

He tilted his head at her.

"I just arrived here in Whistler a few hours ago. The room wasn't quite ready for me so I left my luggage, but I'll have to see what the hotel has to say now that I'm without ID or a credit card."

He considered this.

"Maybe you should come back to Cobalt Lake with me until your things are found."

Such a bad idea.

Terrible.

Given the softness he was making her feel in places that had gone hard. That she had hoped were impenetrable for forever more.

That's exactly what she was afraid of.

That and the growing connection, if she allowed him to rescue her again.

"I keep a cottage at Cobalt exclusively for use of visiting executives. There's no one in it currently. You'd be welcome to it, until we sort out your difficulties."

It was a relief that he wasn't actually asking her to stay with him. That relief was somewhat nullified by his casual use of the word *we*.

It had been such a long time since she'd had a partner to help her with her decisions and difficulties. The kids had done their best, but it wasn't the same as this.

Someone to lean on.

"No," she said, with convincing firmness, "I've put you out quite enough. If you drop me at my hotel, I'll figure it out from there. I'm sure they've had guests lose things before."

CHAPTER SIX

BRAD WAS TRYING very hard not to stare at Faith. The outfit he'd hastily picked up for her from the boutique was made for someone with straighter lines than hers.

Her generous curves seemed beautifully womanly to him. Cynthia had been an athlete, all hard muscle and sinewy strength. She had never had a hair out of place, and her makeup had always been perfect, even when she stepped in, fresh off the slopes.

Faith, understandably, was having a bad-hair moment, that even the toque couldn't hide. Wayward curls were escaping out from under it, some sticking up, some flattened against her temples. Her face was makeup-free and her skin was so pale. It made her eyes look huge.

There was something distinctly waiflike about her. She was definitely vulnerable and he could not forgive himself if he just dropped her off at her hotel to cope when she was in a more fragile state than she seemed to realize.

There was something else about her, that he remembered from their shared past. In high school, that place that celebrated *sameness*, particularly in girls—same hair, same clothes, same fingernail polish—Faith had stood out.

She had not been the same.

The first time he'd ever even noticed her was when she'd interviewed him for the school paper.

Her wayward curls, that tentative smile, those huge earnest eyes, the *questions*. Nothing he'd been expecting.

If you could have a conversation with anyone, living or dead, who would you choose?

If you were stranded on a deserted island, who would you want to be stranded with?

At that point, he'd known Faith Cameron five minutes, and the answer to both questions had been *you*. Not that he had dared to admit that out loud. He had never been so completely captivated before.

And maybe, he realized, not since, either. Was there anything in the world that matched the thrill of first love?

There had been something about her...and still was. Something fresh and wholesome, wonderfully original and surprising. His mind settled on the word *real*.

He remembered, with startling clarity, the first time he had tasted her lips, how sweet and plump they had been, how she had been both innocent and eager. As he himself had been. They had discovered the brand-new world of passion together, with curiosity and boldness and reverence.

And joy.

Maybe especially joy.

He was appalled with himself when he realized he was comparing Faith to Cynthia. His guilt was instantaneous. Still, he needed to reassure Faith in no uncertain terms.

"It's not putting me out, Faith."

Brad contemplated the storm of feelings—oh, those most dangerous of things—that he was feeling. *Put out* was not one of them.

Aside from the guilt of catching himself comparing his wife to another woman, Faith's rescue had breathed to life a dying spark within him. The spark was that need a man had to be the warrior—to protect those around him.

Rationally, he knew he had nothing to do with Cynthia's decisions, the ones that had led to her accident and death, but a part of him felt, acutely, a sense of failure.

A powerlessness no man wanted to feel.

He had carried that sense of failure and powerlessness within him until that very moment he had succeeded in pulling Faith from the water.

Is that why he didn't want to let her go now? He wanted to relish this sense of having wrestled with fate, and won, this time?

He was being too complicated, he admonished himself sternly.

Faith Cameron—no, Saint-John now—had made it abundantly clear she didn't want any more help from him. Or at least, that's what her *words* said. But the *feeling*—there was that pesky thing again—that he was getting from her couldn't be more different than those words she had just spoken.

He wasn't sure what had possessed him to climb into that bed with her, and to take her in his arms, to comfort her, but he had, and it had changed everything.

Coupled with the rescue, he felt protective of her, something he had not felt for a long time, and something he needed to remind himself he had failed at—spectacularly—once before.

Still, it was pretty simple.

She was an old friend. She'd had a shock. She didn't have a wallet or a purse or a phone.

On top of all that, Gopher had been on the front steps of the hospital when Brad arrived.

"I got some great photos of you and that woman out on the lake," the paparazzo had said. "And the dog. The dog angle is the kind of thing that could make it go viral. It could be my break. Maybe even better than some shots of Gregor."

Without saying a word, Brad had pivoted and turned back to the parking lot.

"You could be a hero! I've got a really good writer interested in the story. She's here in Whistler, too, at the moment. But time is of the essence. Nobody will care about it a week from now."

Yay, Brad thought, still walking away.

"If I could just talk to you for a minute, it could make you famous."

Brad could not think of one thing he would like less than being famous. He always felt such pity for Gregor Watson, who could no longer do one normal thing without being hounded. But Gopher, a man who made his living preying on that whole cult of fame, would probably never understand that.

"And her. What's her name?" the annoying man had asked.

Brad had reached his vehicle with Gopher, undeterred, on his heels. He'd snarled at him, "Get lost, before I call the police."

He'd gotten back in his vehicle and made it look as if he was driving away, but in actual fact, he'd pulled into the lane at the side of the hospital.

A staff member on break had recognized him, and used his pass to open the locked side entrance.

"Good job out there on the lake, Mr. Daniels."

Oh, boy, it had never been one of his ambitions to be a hero in a small town.

Still, the notoriety cemented his desire to protect Faith. If ever a person needed a rescue, it was her, and if ever a person had needed to be a rescuer, it was him.

"Um…" he said to Faith now, after she had turned down his offer of accommodation "Do you want the good news or the bad news?"

They had often teased each other with that very phrase in those months they had been together as a couple in high school. He saw recognition dawn in her face, and a smile touched her lips.

It wasn't until she smiled that he realized how haunted she was, not just by the events of the day, but by what life had handed her with her husband's illness.

It wasn't until she smiled that he realized how much he wanted to make her smile again.

"The good news," she decided.

"Damn it," he said.

"What?"

"There isn't actually any good news."

And then she laughed, and it was exactly as he remembered her laughter being, a pure light in a world he hadn't even realized was dark.

"First of all, there's a reporter out on the front steps of the hospital who seems to think your rescue could be story of the year."

"A local reporter?" she asked.

"Unfortunately, no. He's been hanging around trying to catch Gregor Watson."

"The actor, Gregor Watson?"

"Yes, but he's not here anymore, a fact that hasn't caught up with Gopher."

"Gopher?"

"My security staff nicknamed the photographer. Gregor stays at Cobalt when he comes."

"Oh," she said, digesting that, looking at him as if there were facets to him that she had not considered.

"I don't want my children to *ever* find out what happened. Maggie, in particular, would put me on the doddering-old-fool watch list."

He smiled. "My daughter can also be pretty unforgiving of what she perceives as my senior-moment transgressions."

"I think I saw her picture on your lock screen when you loaned me your phone. She's extraordinary, Brad. Is she your only child?"

He felt that rush of pride that Cassandra always made him feel. "Yes, she is. She really is beautiful."

"Yes, I saw that. But there was something about the way

she held herself that made me think she's very confident and strong, a credit to you."

He felt so pleased by those observations.

"She's a great young woman, even if she doesn't allow me to use the word *typing*."

Faith chuckled. "I'm not allowed to correct spelling and punctuation in texts."

"I bet you're encouraged *not* to use them, right?"

"So right! And I was a teacher. It's like swallowing nails not to add a comma here and there. To plunk down a sentence with no capitals. To not scream in frustration at autocorrect."

"You became a teacher," he said, pleased. "That was your dream."

"Yes, it was. grade three and four. When they're still so lovely, and nearly fall over dead if they see you in the grocery store because they can't imagine Mrs. Saint-John actually eats."

It was his turn to laugh, but then he made himself get down to business.

"Aside from Gopher, the other bad news is that I know they can't allow you to check in at the hotel without a photo identification, and a credit card." He said this carefully, speaking from his long experience in the hospitality industry.

She contemplated that for a moment, then drew in a deep breath. "I should probably just go home. I can do what I came here to do another time."

It occurred to him, almost shockingly, that he did not know where *home* was for her.

"Do you think you could check flights to Toronto for me?"

He made no move toward his phone.

"I should just get you to take me back to Vancouver. To the airport." She blushed. "Or arrange for someone to do it. Sorry. It's a long trip. You're obviously a busy guy. Not a chauffeur. It's not like you're staff."

Why had she said it like that, with that funny little inflection in her voice on the word *staff*?

"Actually, if I could just borrow a bit of money from you," she said quickly, "I'll take the sea-to-sky shuttle to the airport. That's how I got here. It's a beautiful drive."

But that drive was two hours long, and it was evident to him that Faith was beyond tired, and practically swaying on her feet. She was in no condition to be making these kinds of decisions.

He decided not to tell her the resort had a helicopter at their disposal—another reason the celebrities loved visiting them—that could get her to Vancouver International in under half an hour.

But getting her to the airport was one thing, getting her on a plane was another thing altogether.

"Um… I hate to be the one to break this to you—" *not really* "—but if you don't have the right documents to check in to a hotel, you don't have the right documents to get on an airplane, either."

Brad watched as Faith figured out exactly how bad a pickle she was in.

"Oh, no," she whispered.

She didn't have to look quite that aghast that she was realizing she was highly dependent on him, at the moment.

"On the other hand, even if you could get on a plane, if you went home early, there would be lots of questions from Maggie, I'm sure."

She gave him a grateful look, for thinking of that angle, or remembering her daughter's name, he wasn't quite sure.

"How long were you planning on staying?"

She had to think about it for a minute.

"I'll be leaving Friday…if I can get things sorted out."

"Then let me look after you," he suggested, gruffly. "Whistler's still a good place, despite how much it has grown. I have every confidence your purse will be found or turned in, but until it is, just come to Cobalt."

Her shoulders heaved. "I guess I have no choice," she said with such genuine reluctance it stung him.

She reminded him, a little bit, of that ungrateful dog, barking at him after its rescue.

He frowned suddenly, remembering their senior year, and how they had discovered each other. He remembered the richness and excitement of first love. *That* feeling—made breathless by someone else's presence—that no matter where you went in life, no matter what other thrills you experienced, that one could never be replicated.

Firsts.

And then he remembered she had hurt him.

And that had been a first, too. His first broken heart. Brad reached back over the years, and the details were surprisingly sharp.

He'd been astonished to find a curt note from her, left at the front desk of the hotel, saying she was leaving Whistler to pursue her life and she wished him well with his.

He'd called her home phone—no cell phones back then—but no one had answered.

He'd driven by that trailer she and her dad, Max, lived in about a thousand times, but it had appeared to have been totally abandoned.

When he'd finally found the nerve to go the door, Max had been shirtless and swigging a beer. His eyes were red-rimmed and he'd looked at Brad with a sadness, as if someone had died.

"She's gone, buddy. Off to school."

"UVic?"

For a moment, had something like pity crossed that man's sorrowful features?

"No, she changed her mind."

Brad didn't want to beg, but he had. A phone number, an address, *anything*.

But her father had shut the door in his face.

Brad looked at Faith now, and saw in her expression exactly what he had always seen in her. Despite her reluctance to accept his help, there was an unguarded softness in her eyes and around the plumpness of the bottom lip she was chewing. She wasn't like that snappy little dog at all. He could see what she was: a person of innate integrity and kindness.

And yet, that note from decades ago had not been either.

The opposite, in fact.

A reminder that he had not *really* known Faith, any more than he suspected now, that he had ever really known his wife.

So, a warning.

To look after Faith, if she accepted his invitation, but to keep his distance, too. To protect himself from his inability to read the heart of the female species.

CHAPTER SEVEN

BRAD, WITH OLD-WORLD manners that did not surprise Faith, held open the door of his vehicle for her. They had exited the hospital through a side door, in case Gopher was still camped out at the front entrance.

She shuddered at the thought.

"What?" Brad asked her.

"Just thinking of my daughter finding out about my escapades because they've become front-page news," she told him.

"It's not 'front-page news' anymore," he informed her solemnly. "It's *going viral*."

And then they were both laughing. It was the second time he had made her laugh. She thought she could probably count the number of times she had laughed in the last five years on one hand.

She noticed his vehicle was one of those very sophisticated, very large all-terrain sports vehicles. She had to step up to get into it.

She slid into the deep leather seat, and Brad shut her door with a click. He came around to the driver's side and started the vehicle with the push of a button. It hummed quietly to life and Faith was enveloped in a sense of luxury.

The scent was heavenly—part Brad, part new vehicle. The

seats were heated, the interior was filled with the notes of a lovely acoustic guitar from a sound system so good the guitarist might have been in the back seat.

Like Brad's watch, the vehicle sharply highlighted the differences in their worlds. Faith drove a subcompact in Toronto. Felix had never been able to part with his old Volvo, which had been secondhand when he'd acquired it.

It was now nearly six o'clock, and the peaks surrounding the village had disappeared behind the shroud of absolute darkness that one only experienced in the mountains.

Brad pulled away from the hospital. "What hotel?"

She told him and then said, "The SUV is a bit of a surprise. If the boutique packaging is any indication, Cobalt Lake seems to have embraced all things eco-friendly."

He glanced over at her and grinned. "It seems like one of those gas-guzzling pigs, doesn't it?"

Had she sounded judgmental? She hadn't meant to. She'd just been trying to make conversation. "I'm sure it's necessary around the resort, and for unpredictable winter conditions."

"A bigger vehicle with four-wheel drive is necessary, but this is actually an experimental vehicle, a prototype that we'd like to produce if we can figure out how to get the costs down. It's an innovation based on hydrogen-fuel technologies."

"You own a vehicle company?" she said with surprise. "I thought you had inherited your family business, the Cobalt Lake Resort?"

"I did, but it never was at the forefront of my interests. I might have even let it go completely after my parents died."

"I'm sorry. I didn't know your parents were gone," Faith said, guiltily happy there would be no chance encounters with an aging Mrs. Daniels at the resort.

"My wife, Cynthia, loved it, and managed to drag Cobalt Lake Resort, kicking and screaming, into the twenty-first century. My daughter, Cassandra, does most of the day-to-day management of it now, so that I can focus on other things."

She heard the pride in his voice at the mention of his daughter's name. She had a sudden horrible memory of Felix brushing past Maggie, pretending she wasn't there, inexplicable hostility stamped in his features.

A reminder of how terribly wrong love could go.

She felt as if she had been punched and left breathless, as was so often the way when these memories surfaced. Thankfully, it was dark in the car, and Brad had that lovely gift for conversation.

"I'm a part owner of the hydrogen-fueled-vehicle company. I'm actually part owner in quite a few ventures. In university, I discovered I had a gift for sniffing out innovation, and figuring out which, of the millions of them, had potential."

This was said without even a hint of conceit, but with the enthusiasm of a man who truly loved his work.

"Right now, the most exciting project I'm involved in is developing an exoskeleton for human beings. It has amazing ramifications for the severely disabled."

Faith glanced over at him. In the light of the dashboard, she could see that he was, despite his losses, all of the things she was not. As in: fully engaged in life.

He pulled up in front of the hotel. "No, you stay there. I'll go get your things."

"I'm sure if they won't let me check in without ID, they're not going to hand over my luggage to a complete stranger."

He raised an amused eyebrow at her. "Stay here."

She watched him go, riveted by the presence he radiated. She saw him lift a hand to people he recognized, exchange quick greetings, once even stopping for a moment. There was a sense of him being where he belonged, and knowing it, in a way she found enviable.

Finally, Brad slipped through the doors of her hotel.

While he was gone, she put down her window and breathed in deeply. The mountain air had a texture to it—sweet, pure—that she had only ever experienced in these mountain villages.

Whistler Village had always been high-end, even in her growing-up years, but the atmosphere had morphed into something out of a fairy tale, an unlikely combination of cozy mountain meets cosmopolitan posh.

There was no snow and it wasn't anywhere near Christmas, and yet there was that holiday feeling with white lights threaded through the branches of every tree, and outlining every window, awning, railing and building.

The sounds of laughter, people chattering, cutlery rattling, glasses clinking, came in her open window and filled the crisp mountain air with happy sounds. Despite the chill of the evening, Whistler celebrated the outdoors in all seasons.

The patio areas of cafés, pubs and wine bars were open, the tables full, heat lamps glowing bright orange. People, colorfully dressed in parkas and toques and scarves, drifted in and out of shops, laden down with parcels. The was an air or excitement, prosperity and vitality.

A few minutes later, Brad emerged, carrying her suitcase by its handle. He was so strong it had not even occurred to him, apparently, to use the wheels to drag it along.

Again, she noticed him exchanging greetings.

He opened the back gate of the vehicle and tossed the suitcase in. He would live in that world of very expensive luggage. But if he had noticed hers was slightly travel-worn and certainly not a brand name, it didn't show in his face.

"I hope they at least put up a fight before they handed that over to you," she said.

"Yes, I did a tug-of-war with the desk clerk."

He laughed. His laughter was so wonderful. It shimmered with a promise of a life that held laughter again.

She wasn't sure if that was a good thing or a bad thing, but she found herself leaning toward a good thing.

"I'm pretty well-known around town," he said. "Not the one they're watching for to make off with luggage that doesn't belong to them. I seem to be especially well-known now. At least three people mentioned what happened at Cobalt Lake this afternoon. It's the talk of the town."

"Oh, no."

"Don't worry," he said, "I'll keep you out of the glare of the spotlight until this all blows over. In a week—or less, if we're lucky—they'll have moved on to something else. Last week the talk of the town was the stray-cat problem. The dog rescue is a little more riveting for now. But next week, who knows? 'Skunk family takes up residence under Banker's Bar? Bear misses memo on hibernation and is chasing tourists through Lost Lake Park…'"

He was making her laugh again. And then they were on the familiar rode to Brad's family resort.

If Faith thought Whistler had changed, nothing could have prepared her for Cobalt Lake.

Like Whistler, it was like something out of a fairy tale, every tree and every walkway lit up with millions of tiny white lights.

The lodge and grounds had been given a complete facelift.

No wonder Gregor Watson stayed here, and Brad appeared to be on a first-name basis with him!

"But where are the chalets?" she whispered, catching glimpses of gorgeous little cottages seeded among the stands of evergreen trees at the base of the ski hill.

"Oh, those old A-frames?"

Yes, the ones, she had cleaned to his mother's exacting standards.

"They hadn't been built properly, and were starting to have issues as they aged. Mold. Frozen pipes. Roof leaks. Decks that couldn't withstand the snow load. Cynthia replaced them with these cottages, one at a time, over the years. All the A-frames are gone now."

He skirted the main lodge, and took a side road that curved through a forest grove, lit with fairy lights. It looked amazing. Faith could just imagine how magical everything would look when it snowed.

Brad stopped in front of a delightful structure, set well away from the other cottages. Faith went to open her door, but he lifted his hand, ever so subtly, and then came around and opened her door for her.

Again, such an old-world courtesy, and she *loved* it.

She stood looking at the cottage, trying not to let her mouth fall open. In what world was *this* a cottage?

It was a house, and a beautiful one at that. A tasteful sign showed it had been named Wolf's Song, and Faith remembered the name of the ski run directly behind it was Timber Wolf.

The Cobalt Lake Resort had always named their cabins, but they'd had cutesy names like All Decked Out, Misty Morning Magic, Mountain Standard Time and the Bear Cub Club. The new name signified a change in direction that was also more than evident in the new face of the resort.

A wide, curved stamped concrete walkway led the way, through manicured shrub beds that held plants chosen to keep color, even in the winter—emerald cedars, miniature mountain pine, dwarf burning bush.

The "cottage" had a craftsman-like style with an imposing stone-and-wood facade. Open trusses, huge and wooden, held up the roof over the covered entryway. Two flickering gas lanterns framed the large front door, which looked majestic and antique.

Brad carried her one shabby suitcase onto the porch and she followed him up the wide staircase. The spacious deck area had four deeply cushioned outdoor chairs on it, black-and-white-plaid blankets draped artfully over them.

Something brushed by her feet, and Faith gave a little squeal and stumbled back toward the staircase.

Brad dropped her suitcase and had her in a second.

"That darn cat," he said, annoyed.

Out of the corner of her eye, she saw a white form dashing away.

He didn't let her go, right away. She felt his nearness, breathed in his scent, and his strength.

"You're destined to rescue me today," she said. She intended it to sound light, but it didn't feel light. She was marveling at the sensation of having someone to lean on, of not having to rely on her own—admittedly quite wobbly—strength.

"My pleasure," he said, stepping away from her. "That cat! Such a nuisance. It's been hanging around here since the summer."

She suspected the cat was being used as a distraction, as if he, too, had felt a shiver of something white-hot with promise pass between them.

Brad punched in a code, and opened the door. He set down the suitcase inside. That poor suitcase had never looked more forlorn, and like it didn't belong.

"It's probably not the kind of luggage you're accustomed to," Faith ventured, as a way to tame down the white-hot-with-promise thoughts.

Brad looked down at the suitcase, genuinely baffled. "What?"

"Like not Louis Vuitton. Or even Samsonite, for that matter."

"Oh," he said, cocking his head and looking at her suitcase, then dismissing it with a shrug. "They all look the same to me. Cynthia picked all that stuff."

It occurred to Faith that maybe she was exaggerating the differences between them—focusing on the watch, the car, the luggage—as a form of self-protection.

But then Brad flicked on a light switch, and stood back to let her pass him. Faith stood in the foyer. No, she definitely was not exaggerating the differences in their worlds. The interior of the cottage was like something on the front cover of a lifestyle magazine.

CHAPTER EIGHT

"This is incredible," Faith breathed.

The decor was mountain-lodge, but in the most upscale way imaginable. It was a completely open plan, with expansive hardwood floors, huge windows, a floor-to-ceiling stacked stone fireplace. Logs crackled invitingly inside the firebox.

"You like it," Brad said, pleased.

And it seemed that was all that mattered to him, that she liked it. There seemed to be no ego—*look what I have*—in his statement at all.

"What's not to like?" she asked. "Did your wife do this, too?"

"She had a designer."

Faith had grown up in rented trailers and basement suites, with secondhand furniture and left-behind art hanging crookedly on walls.

She remembered her and Felix tackling projects in what they had thought would be their first house, with a kind of reckless enthusiasm. It had been modest, large enough, but in much need of repair. Its main selling point had been the location—walking distance to the historic St. George campus of the University of Toronto, where Felix worked, and the elementary school where she worked.

But it had also appealed because it had been on a block lined with mature trees that gave them shade in the summer, and that gave them birds to feed all winter. How Felix had adored coming up with increasingly complex plans to try and keep the squirrels from those feeders!

They had lovingly fixed the leaky basement and painted walls, and prepared nurseries, and bought throw cushions. They went through awful decorating stages, like sponge-painting walls and a Southwest theme and Scandinavian-style furniture.

When the time had come when they could have moved on, Faith, possibly because of her gypsy childhood, had been completely unable to let it go.

Their starter home became their forever home.

It had never—not once—looked like this, or even close to this.

But somehow, they had created a sense of home. And had so much fun doing it. She remembered the time they had painted the nursery in preparation for Michael moving out of the bassinette beside their bed. The color on the paint chip had been fine, but on the walls it looked hideous.

"My," Felix had said, mildly, "he's going to feel as if he's growing up inside an aquarium."

"Lucky boy," she'd said, deadpan.

And then, with paint in their hair and on the tips of their noses, they had started to laugh, and they had laughed until they were rolling on the floor.

Faith suddenly felt sorry for Brad. She bet he'd never had a moment like that in his entire life, poor guy.

She slipped off her shoes.

"You don't have to take off your shoes," he said.

"I can't imagine anything more un-Canadian than leaving your shoes on," she told him. Not to even mention the thought of scratching those beautiful floors could give her nightmares.

She let the great room draw her into it. "Who lit the fire?"

"Oh, I called ahead. One of the staff got it ready."

There it was again. *The staff.* Just in case she had any ideas about trying to forget the divide between their two worlds.

Their house had a fireplace. It had never drafted properly and every time they tried to light it, the whole house filled up with smoke and the fire detectors went off.

And for some reason, that was a good memory, too.

She realized, startled, that *good* memories had not been part of how she remembered Felix, so far.

She and Felix could not have afforded to stay in a place like this in a million years. What would it cost? A thousand dollars a night? Conservatively?

Even if they could have afforded it, she suspected they would have never done it, not even for a special treat. No, they would have opted to spend the money on a new furnace. Or bringing the kids home from university for Christmas, or building up their retirement savings accounts.

Yes, now that she thought about it, it was definitely building the retirement savings account that would have won out instead of a night in a fancy hotel. How important that had been to Felix… She shook off the feeling of sadness that was trying to edge in on her sense of genuine enjoyment of these posh surroundings, her surprise at finding herself here.

"Sit down," Brad invited Faith. "You look dead on your feet."

Not the impression one wanted to give, but she felt the same way she looked, and moved into the great room and sank into one of the deep inviting armchairs that faced the fireplace.

"I'll put this in the bedroom," he said and took her suitcase through a door off the main entrance. "I'm going to head over the lodge. I'll rustle up a cell phone for you, and bring something over to eat."

He was gone before she realized she had not said no.

In fact, she felt powerless to say no.

Faith settled more deeply into the comfort of the chair and enjoyed the flickering beauty of the fire, and the lovely light it cast over the stunning cottage interior.

She let her gaze roam around the room. Despite how undeniably grand it was, with its soaring ceilings, gorgeous light fixtures and priceless art, the room was somehow extremely cozy and welcoming. That's what designers did, she supposed.

She could see those professional touches in the upscale kitchen that was at the far end of the open space. It had a dizzying array of stainless-steel, high-end cabinets, stunning light fixtures. An entire bank of windows looked out toward the ski slopes, though the slopes were just a dark shadow at the moment.

Fresh flowers and a fruit basket were sitting in the center of an expanse of Italian marble that was the kitchen island.

Sadly, it felt like a kitchen not a single person had ever baked cookies in. She thought of Chloe and Tanya, standing on chairs beside her in her kitchen, as covered in cookie dough as she and Felix had once been covered in paint.

Still, as Faith looked back to the fire, she was aware of feeling slightly stunned to find herself ensconced in Wolf's Song.

Since Felix's diagnosis—no, way before that, because things had to become quite alarming before you even sought a diagnosis—she had felt as if she was being thrust deeper and deeper into a carnival funhouse.

Why were they even called that? Those places that kept your world feeling tilted and off balance. Those places of warped mirrors and hideous surprises and false exits. Those places where the panic rose in you as you became more and more lost in the mazes, and became more and more convinced you could never find a way out.

And yet here she was. She had popped out. Been released from the "fun" house nightmare.

She was sitting in this gorgeous cottage, in front of this soothing fire, only because her beloved husband, by now a stranger to her, had died.

How terrible, Faith thought, to feel relieved. To be so *glad* to be sitting here, instead of immersed in the day-to-day tragedies of living with someone who had been afflicted with bvFTD, or behavioral frontotemporal dementia.

She had been flattened by it. Numbed.

Was it the shock of hitting the frigid water that had jolted her out of the trance she had been in? She was aware that, starting this afternoon, for the first time, she had a real sense of leaving it behind her.

This is *exactly* what Maggie had wanted for her. Well, maybe without the dog, the icy lake and the near-death experience.

But this feeling of the flatness leaving her. Being in Brad's cottage felt just like being warmed up in the hospital.

That's what the memory of Felix and his obsession with the retirement savings account had tried—unsuccessfully, it would seem—to edge out.

A sense of the life force creeping back into her.

She felt alive.

And, okay, just a little bit frightened by the feelings Brad was drawing out of her. He had suffered a loss, too. Why did he still seem so vital? So engaged with life? It made her feel as if he had a secret that she needed to know.

She shouldn't really feel compelled to uncover any of Brad Daniels's secrets. In fact, it was dangerous. It felt as if, with the tiniest little shove, things between them might be right back where they had been when they were teenagers. Terrifying, indeed.

But why be afraid?

Hadn't life already done its very worst to her?

"Dad," Cassandra said over his phone, "what on earth is going on?"

Brad's phone was blowing up. It seemed every single person in Whistler wanted to know what had happened on Cobalt Lake this afternoon. He looked at it, alarmed, as the message counter kept ticking up. Fifty-six messages? Fifty-seven. Fifty-eight.

He'd put it on silent mode, but the phone was programmed

to let Cassandra's calls come through. Even if he was screening everyone in the world—which it seemed he was at the moment—he always tried to be available to his daughter.

The signal was really bad—probably because Brad was in the wine cellar. The lodge had its own wine cellar, but this one, below their residence, had been Cynthia's private enclave.

He didn't even know when he'd last been down in this room, but like everything else Cynthia had done, it was beyond exquisite.

"Earth calling Dad," Cassandra said, and he realized he hadn't been listening to her.

"Sorry, Cassie, what? Bad signal."

"I asked you what is going on."

For a startled moment, Brad thought Cassandra must be referring to Faith being tucked away at Wolf's Song.

He realized, given their conversation this morning, he did not want Cassie to know anything about the woman in the cottage. Would his daughter take one look at her, and find Faith perfect for him?

He couldn't imagine anything more alarming that Cassandra deciding to play Cupid. For his own good!

Somehow, it seemed impossible that they had just had that conversation this morning. It felt to Brad as if a lifetime had gone by.

"My phone's going crazy," Cassie told him.

Join the club, he thought.

"So is the front desk. Everybody wants to know about the rescue on the lake."

"Oh?" he said innocently. "What rescue?"

"Dad! They're saying you saved a woman and a dog who had gone through the ice on Cobalt Lake."

"Oh. That. It was nothing, really. You know how people love a great story. Remember when the gondola got stuck on Whistler and that ski-patrol woman went up on the ladder and got all those people off? Heroine for a week?"

"Dad! Don't downplay it. It sounds amazing," Cassie said. "And we still have lots of media people in town and hanging around the resort because of Gregor."

Cassie was usually working with security to protect their guests from the media, not approaching them.

"I could not have set up better publicity for the lodge if I tried," she breathed.

He went very still. "Catastrophe is not a publicity opportunity," he said sternly.

"But it wasn't a catastrophe. It was a disaster averted. From what I'm hearing, you prevented something terrible from happening."

"Leave it, Cassie."

He read her silence on the other end of the line as being slightly stunned.

"Dad?"

"Look, I've got a really bad signal. I've got to go."

With the tiniest niggle of guilt, Brad disconnected from Cassie and looked around the room that had been one of Cynthia's pride and joys.

Like the cottages, and the lodge, and even their private residence, this room had been done by a designer.

A very famous and expensive designer who had her own television show on the home-and-garden channel.

Cynthia had needed perfection.

He had felt indulgent of that need. She had come from a working-class background, and especially in the early days of their marriage, he thought she had felt she needed to prove herself to his parents, his mother in particular.

But had Cynthia lost something in that quest for perfection? Something of herself? Is that why he found Faith so compelling. *Real?*

He'd seen the expression on Faith's face when he'd said a designer did Wolf's Song. If he was not mistaken, it had been faintly sympathetic, as if he had missed something.

This room was beautiful by any standard, and yet now, as never before, he could feel it missing something, too.

Cynthia had loved collecting wine. Drinking it? Not so much. She wanted it "to age." Like everything else about her, the cellar was highly organized, with the rarest wines behind glass on the back wall, soft light sweeping down on the temperature-controlled display racks.

The cellar had been mostly for show. Occasionally, she'd hosted a wine afternoon for "the girls," but mostly, she had just collected.

Is that what he had been, too? For show? Where was her heart in this room? In those impeccably designed rooms? Where had her heart been in the marriage?

He hated these questions.

He wasn't indulging them anymore.

He went and inspected the wall that displayed her most valuable collectibles. Now, he saw there were probably five hundred bottles in this section.

If he drank a bottle every week, it would take him ten years to get through it.

Maybe he should break it out for Cassie's wedding—if his independent, fiery daughter ever found a man who was her equal.

Suddenly it felt ridiculous to "age" the wine, to save it for "special" occasions that never came.

They had *really* never come for his wife.

If there was a lesson to be had from Cynthia's premature death, maybe it was that. The time was now.

Still, he hesitated. Was it a special occasion? It felt like it was. But that was a feeling he needed to fight, not give in to.

But he was going back over there, anyway. Faith had to eat. They both did. Why not bring the wine? It had been a super-tough day. He didn't have to drink it with her—he could just present it to her, as a gift.

Feeling like a rebel—and slightly guilty, as well—Brad randomly selected a bottle from the most exclusive shelf and then made his way up to the restaurant kitchen to collect a dinner for two that Anita, the resort's long-time sous-chef, had put together for him.

He stopped at the front desk. "Hey, Kathy, any word about that purse?"

"No, sorry. Jim had a team out there looking, but they didn't find anything. He left a note here for you."

She passed it to him. Brad glanced at it, then shoved it in his pocket.

"He said your voice-mail box was full."

"Actually, while I'm here, I might as well grab a couple of cell phones."

"Of course." She went to a large cabinet where they kept an inventory of things guests might need, everything from toothbrushes to a selection of specialty pillows.

"There you go, Mr. Daniels. I heard what you did—"

He held up his hand. "That's why I need a new cell phone. Suddenly everybody in the whole village and beyond wants to talk to me."

"That explains the full voice mail. The world does love a hero, Mr. Daniels."

"Huh," he said. He opened one of the cell-phone boxes.

"This is the number," he told Kathy. "If the police call about that missing purse, you can give it to them. And to Jim, if he finds it. No one else. Am I clear?"

"But Cassandra, of course?"

He was shocked that he wanted to say no, but he didn't. He knew Cassie's phone number. If it came up on the caller ID of the new phone, he could decide then if he wanted to talk to her.

And then he stopped at his office and got rid of his own phone. The number of missed calls and texts was becoming ridiculous. Brad felt a startling sense of freedom as he slid it into his desk drawer. People needed to get lives.

As he walked away, he wondered when the last time was that he'd been without his phone.

It wasn't until he was on his way back over to Wolf's Song that he realized taking some back hallways out of the lodge had paid off. For the first time since she'd been born, he was happy *not* to see his daughter.

CHAPTER NINE

FAITH WAS SO glad she had not been able to find the energy to tell Brad no when he'd gone to get dinner for them.

Because the truth was, as the scents wafted off the containers he had brought back to Wolf's Song, she was suddenly famished.

She did wish, though, that she would have found the energy to go rummage around her suitcase, have a quick shower and throw on some attractive clothes, a bit of makeup.

Because it was the first time she'd seen him without a winter jacket on. He was in a plaid flannel shirt, the plaid in subtle shades of gray, almost identical to his hair. The shirt was open at the column of his throat. With it, he was wearing crisp, khaki mountain slacks, belted at his narrow waist.

Though he had obviously changed since the rescue, he didn't look as if he'd put much effort into it. Even when they were young, she never remembered him fussing over his appearance. And still, Brad Daniels looked front-cover-of-a-men's-outdoor-magazine-worthy.

She couldn't help but notice he'd left his shoes on, was a person who had seemingly never once in his life given a thought to a scratched floor, or puddles.

The *staff* looked after things like that. But she waved the thought away, like a pesky fly that was trying to spoil a perfect moment.

He knew his way around the cottage and refused her offer for help, telling her just to sit at the built-in banquette in an alcove nestled in the windows of the kitchen. He opened the wine he had brought with the efficiency of one who had opened fine wines—as in corked, not screw-top—many times.

He poured a splash in two glasses and set them, and the bottle, on the table, then brought over plates and cutlery, and the boxed food, his movements efficient and comfortable.

She noted the tulip-shaped wineglasses had the unmistakable look of hand-blown crystal. The plates and cutlery had a similar aura—yes, he moved in a world where place settings gave off an aura—of being expensive and exclusive.

Finally, he sat down and lifted his glass to hers, and they clinked, the glasses giving off the crisp note that confirmed their high quality.

"What is this?" she asked, after her first sip of wine. It was a white, which was nice. Red always made her self-conscious about her teeth. Faith was certain she had never tasted a wine quite so layered in delightful, exotic flavors.

"Not sure." He studied the label and shrugged, much as he had when looking at her suitcase.

"Taste it," she suggested.

He took a sip. Unfortunately, it made her very aware of his lips. "Hey, that's pretty good," he decided.

That seemed like an understatement. "Have you ever tasted anything like that before?" she asked.

"Um… I don't know. I'm not much of a wine guy."

"Well, you don't have to be a wine person to know this is unbelievable. It's ambrosia."

Again, that easy shrug, dismissing the fineness of the wine in the same way he had barely noticed her suitcase. Brad served the food. It was a Parmesan-crusted chicken on fettucine noodles. The noodles had so obviously been made from scratch, not been dumped out of a box into boiling water.

It occurred to Faith that maybe, just maybe, the reason why the wine and the food seemed so, so good was that it was all part of that intoxicating feeling she had of coming alive.

And part of that was from being with Brad Daniels. Okay, maybe quite a lot of it!

"So what brought you back to Whistler?" Brad asked. "After all these years? You said you had come here to do something."

The chicken was as exquisite as the wine. "My dad wanted his ashes spread here."

"Oh, Faith, I'm so sorry. I didn't know he'd died."

"How could you know? He didn't live here anymore. He hadn't for a long time. He left after I did. But this is the place he remembered with the most fondness. He worked at all of the top-twenty ski destinations in the world, at one point or another, but this is where he said his heart was. When he was sick, he asked me to bring him back here."

"The loss of your dad and your husband... You must be reeling." His voice was soft with compassion, and that same softness was in his eyes when he gazed at her.

It was hard not to fall into softness, like being invited to try a feather bed after years of sleeping on rocks.

"Dad predeceased Felix by about five years. That's why, when I realized I couldn't check into the hotel, I said I could just go home, and try again another time. I'd already put it off for so long, it felt like another few months couldn't possibly matter." She laughed, a little self-consciously. "My dad was a great believer in signs, and things don't exactly seem to be lining up in my favor."

Except, gazing at Brad over the lip of an exquisite wineglass, that didn't seem exactly true.

She had landed on her feet, sitting here with her teenage sweetheart, eating food and drinking wine that was top-notch, in a five-star environment.

"My dad was actually one of the first ones to notice things might be off with Felix. I had so much going on. Maggie, after finishing up her law degree, and in true Maggie fashion, deciding it would be nothing to get married, have a baby and start her career in a three-year period. Things got so chaotic that I kept putting it off."

Brad's gaze offered her what she had not offered herself. Forgiveness for the fact that life had gotten in the way of such a meaningful task.

"I think it's time, Faith. You're here. You'll regret it if you go back without doing what you came to do."

She nodded. "I think you're right. I'll figure it out."

"I can give you a hand."

"Oh," she said, "really, I've imposed enough."

"Did your dad want some place, specifically?"

"He loved the Feeney's Pass area. He mentioned the viewing point. I'll hike up there tomorrow. I won't need a wallet for that!"

"You're not going up there by yourself at this time of year."

She was taken aback by the firmness in his voice. It sounded like those orders he had snapped at her out on the ice. It reminded her a bit of her daughter, an implication she was some kind of incompetent moron who couldn't be trusted to do things by herself.

Not that her first day in Whistler had actually proved Maggie wrong. Or done anything to inspire Brad's confidence in her, either.

Still, she had to discourage him from thinking he could just order her around, despite the fact she had accepted his many kindnesses.

"I grew up hiking mountains all over North America," she said quietly. "I'm not worried about Feeney's Pass."

"Well, you should be." There was an edge to his voice. "There's fresh snow up there."

She felt a surge of annoyance, and realized how truly tired she was. Why else would she be so sorely tempted to tell him to mind his own business, when he'd been so good to her? Her irritability probably had more to do with the events of the day catching up with her than Brad. She checked herself.

Then—while busy biting her tongue nearly in half—she looked at him closely. What she saw on his face was distressing.

"Brad?"

"Cynthia died in an avalanche," he said, his voice husky.

"Brad! I'm so sorry." And so glad she had not reacted to her initial annoyance with him.

"She went skiing by herself. At night. She often did. I don't know why."

She heard so much doubt and pain in that confession. It occurred to her, that despite Brad Daniels appearing to have it all, she did not have a corner on suffering. Or insecurities.

"We've implemented a GPS-tracking-device system here because of it, but even so, I'm not comfortable with you going up there by yourself. I hope you'll allow me to go with you."

Suddenly she saw how important this was for him. She could not refuse him this, even as she saw their lives were tangling a little bit more deeply.

"My daughter thinks it's probably illegal," she said. "She thinks I probably need a permit to spread ashes. I don't intend to get one, just so you know."

"Ah," he said, and lifted his wineglass to her, "so we're to be partners in crime."

"No one would have approved more than my dad."

Brad grinned. She had always loved that grin, lopsided and boyish.

"Max was a legend as a lift mechanic, as you know," he said. "That's why I was a little surprised I hadn't heard of him dying. Ski communities are pretty tight."

It meant the world to Faith that Brad not only remembered her father's name, but had also said such a good thing about him.

"His last job was in Switzerland, until he got sick and came home. Well, not home for him. His home was always on the slopes. He had to come to Toronto, because that's where I was.

"He hated the city and then the hospice. I think he had always just thought when his time came, he would lie down on a mountain, and breathe in the fresh air, and that maybe an eagle would soar overhead. I think that's why he extracted the promise from me to let Whistler be his final resting place."

"I didn't know him well, but I always liked him, Faith—everybody did. He was so funny and outgoing."

"Outrageous," she said with a smile. "A true renegade."

"Here's to the renegades," Brad said, and lifted his glass to her father.

At Max's specific request, there had been no funeral. No words spoken. That casual toast by Brad felt so good, so right, so overdue.

They tapped glasses again, and took sips in memory of her father.

"I'm afraid I'm not much of a salute to his legacy," Faith said with a sigh.

"Don't say that. You are!"

She raised an eyebrow at him.

"Not a renegade, obviously," Brad said, "illegal scattering of ashes aside, but I was always so taken with the way you seemed able to be totally yourself, even given—"

He stopped, clearly uncomfortable. He didn't have to say it. *Even given* that she had been living in a trailer, *even given* that she did not have the good clothes, *even given* that she never had lunch money or even money to go for a Coke with the gang after school.

"I know my dad's legend was certainly not all about his mechanical skills," she said dryly.

Brad said, with unmistakable fondness, "Remember him at World Cup?"

"Oh, yeah," she said. Max had somehow gotten himself at

the start line, and launched himself down the course on his skis. The timer had gone off automatically as he passed it.

She'd been a spectator, and recognized her father's style and crouch immediately. She had never seen anyone, not even all those pro skiers, dance with powder the way he did. But that day, he had not been dancing. It had been a full-frontal attack.

She'd watched, with her heart in her throat, thinking he was going to be badly hurt. But, no, he had finished the course, straightened and waved his poles with a flourish at the roaring crowd.

"His time," Brad remembered fondly, "was the third best recorded that day. Legend."

"Unofficially. He got arrested for his mischief."

"Did he? I'm sorry, I didn't know that part."

"He said it was worth it," she recalled, with reluctant affection. "I was so mad at him at the time, though! And then it wasn't that long after, in the dead of night, that he scaled one of the lift towers."

"The talk of the town!" Brad said. "Forty feet in the air, and he managed to get himself off the tower and onto one of the chairs."

"He wasn't nearly as skillful at getting himself back off, and when they found him in the morning, he was nearly frozen."

"But the guy who found him said Max was quite merry, announced he had just been singing his death song to the dawn."

"In Celtic, apparently."

"Legend."

"It wasn't always easy being the legend's daughter," she said.

"I knew that, even then. And yet, you had some of that in you. The sense of humor, the sense of fun. I really did think you stood out from everyone else."

That had been so intoxicatingly evident at the time. And it was true, despite so many insecurities, that she had been fairly certain of who she was. Somewhere along the way, she had lost that certainty.

"It's because he loved me," she told Brad softly. "My dad had flaws, and many of them, but I always knew how much he loved me. I felt utterly cherished by him, and it did give me a sense of myself."

When had she begun rejecting that sense of herself given to her by her father? Perhaps with Mrs. Daniels's cruel assessment of her as not suitable for her son.

CHAPTER TEN

"BUT THEN, almost in reaction to Max's shenanigans, his free spirit, I became the opposite," Faith revealed, finding herself confiding in Brad. "Desperately seeking normal, liking rules and structure."

When she put it like that, it sounded as if she had become *uptight*, as conventional and boring as her father had once predicted she would be.

"And did you get that?" he asked softly, and there was no judgment in his voice.

"Oh, yes. Felix was one of my professors in university. He was quite a bit older than me. He acted as if he didn't know I existed, of course, which was so appropriate.

"That was one of the things I loved about him actually. He was always so concerned about what was appropriate. It was the opposite of what I had grown up with.

"But a year after I'd graduated and was in my first year of teaching, I ran into him in a coffee shop near my school. I found out later it wasn't an accident. He'd looked for me having let a suitable amount of time go by so that it was *appropriate*—and was kind of checking out the coffee shops in my neighborhood.

"He was most worried about our age difference. He was ten years older than me. But it never bothered me at all. A year later we were married." She sighed. "My father proclaimed him dull as porridge."

She shouldn't have said that! She looked at the wine the very same way she had looked at the IV drip earlier.

She glanced at Brad, a man who would never be called that by anyone! It made the words she had just said feel like a betrayal.

"But he wasn't," she said hastily. "I had the life I dreamed of."

There. That was a good note to end on. But somehow, she was still talking, and she was sure the wonderful wine was to blame.

"And then I didn't. And it's kind of left me wondering where all that adherence to the rules got me. My somewhat unpredictable upbringing made me think about every possibility for chaos and disruption, and head it off before it happened. So much energy spent doing that—and all that time the thing I'd least expected, the thing I could not prepare for, was probably already growing in Felix's brain."

"And that's probably why you dashed out on that lake," Brad said. "Leaving all those fears behind you."

"My dad would have approved of the doggy dash," she said. And it occurred to her that he would have. Not just of her giving in to an impulse, after a lifetime of controlling them, but of everything that had happened after.

Her unexpected reunion with Brad.

The loss of her purse, forcing her to adapt, to accept that the unpredictable was part of life, and that it could be a good part.

Look at where she was!

Something shivered along her spine, almost as if Max was sitting at the table with her, laughing. And then it felt as if she heard his voice.

Don't you love it when a plan comes together?

She really was way too tired. She really could not even have one more sip of that wine. She really could not spend one more moment with Brad. She shivered.

"You're still chilled," Brad said. "Let's move in front of the fire."

She shouldn't. She needed to beg off. To say she was tired, to wish him good-night, to go to bed.

But there was that question again.

All her life of doing everything she *should* do, and where had it gotten her? Since they were going to spend more time together, anyway, why not just surrender?

They moved to the couch in front of the fire, sitting together on it, nearly shoulder-to-shoulder. His scent was so completely and deliciously clean and male. Somehow, the wineglasses were full again, and he finally took off his shoes, hooking the back of them with his toes and letting them drop to the floor.

He put his feet up on the wooden live-edge coffee table that, from the size of it, must have been made from a thousand-year-old tree.

Faith laughed at his socks, which were bright red with little green monkey faces on them.

"What on earth?" she asked. "You're so cover-of-the-outdoor-gentlemen's-magazine, and then those?"

He wiggled his colorfully clad toes at her.

"Cassie got them for me last year for Christmas. It was her answer to 'what do you get the guy who has everything?' It's a membership to a sock club. They send me a couple of wild and crazy pairs of socks every single month. It seems to just tickle Cassie that I actually wear them, so I do."

Faith loved all the things that told her about Brad's relationship with his daughter. She was aware of feeling a drowsy sort of contentment. It was so much like it had been when they were young. It was easy to be together, the conversation flowing as naturally as a river.

She found herself telling him about the nursery painting disaster, and baking cookies with her grandchildren.

"You know," he said, "I've never baked a cookie."

"Come on."

"No, really, never."

For the second time, Faith felt something like pity for Brad

Daniels, the man who seemed to have everything. He'd never painted a nursery the wrong color, never painted at all, in fact. And never baked cookies.

So she told him about some of that, about Maggie and Michael growing up, about the delight of grandchildren, about Maggie becoming a lawyer, and Michael following his heritage back to Scotland to get a doctorate in Scottish history.

"I've worried about how employable that degree will make him."

Brad laughed. "He'll probably end up a professor, like his dad."

She liked it that he seemed to listen so carefully, and that he spoke of Felix with the respect of someone who had not seen, firsthand, the horrible consequences of his illness, and how it had changed the relationships he'd had with everyone who knew him.

She encouraged him to share stories about his daughter, and Faith loved the tenderness and pride in his voice when he talked about her.

They laughed easily together, as they always had.

Somehow, silence descended, and into that silence an aching awareness of him rushed in. Faith glanced at the fullness of his lips.

Memories tickled along her spine.

Brad held her eyes, and then his gaze drifted to her own lips. He reached out with his thumb and scraped her cheek, and then the fullness of her lip. She should have pulled away from that thumb, but she didn't. She leaned into it.

Brad, to his credit, pulled away. He actually looked at his hand as if it was a soldier that had disobeyed a command.

"We're both tired," he said. "It's not the best time to make a decision."

Did that mean he did think the time was coming? To make a decision? About touching each other's lips? And possibly more than that?

He was right.

It was not something to be decided lightly, not something to fall into because they were both beyond exhaustion, in the grip of the dramatic events of the day, and the surprising sweetness of their reunion.

Brad got up off the couch and stretched. It showed off the broadness of his chest, and a rippling of lovely muscles in his arms. His shirt lifted and showed the hard contours of his tummy.

It was breathtaking.

Faith reminded herself, sternly, that her tummy did not have hard contours. Thank goodness, they had backed off on what was developing between them before Brad had made that discovery!

"Oh," he said, "I brought you a phone." He picked it out of his pocket and laid it on the table.

"You just happen to have extra cell phones lying around?"

"It's probably the number-one thing our guests lose or break, particularly during ski season. Supplying loaner phones was one of Cassie's—Cassandra's—ideas, always offering that little extra service to the guests." He chuckled. "In the spring, though, it's a full-time job picking dead cell phones out of melting snow drifts."

"Thank you," she said, not opening the box just yet, and making note of one more example of her indebtedness to him.

She was shocked to see it was nearly midnight. Way too late to call Maggie. It would be 3:00 a.m. in Toronto. Really, was there anything worse than middle-of-the-night phone calls?

She felt a certain guilty relief about that.

"I had to grab a new phone, too," Brad said. "Mine is blowing up. Over the rescue thing."

"Oh, no!"

"I'm doing my best to keep the lid on that."

"Thank you."

"Why don't I come by around ten tomorrow morning, and we'll head up Feeney?"

He was taking charge of everything. She knew she should protest. But she wasn't going to.

"Thank you," she said again. "That sounds perfect."

He hesitated for just a moment. And then he bent, and dropped a quick kiss on her cheek. Completely platonic. Almost European.

"It's so good to see you," he said huskily.

Her silly heart, the one that was supposed to be frozen, had let the fire and his nearness warm it right up.

He slipped his shoes back on and was soon out the front door. She heard him locking it with the keypad. Another small gesture that, like the phone, and the meal, and everything he had done, made her feel intensely taken care of.

It just felt so good not to be the one in charge, to let go.

Faith went into the bedroom. Like the rest of Wolf's Song, the space was opulent, a luxurious symphony of soothing neutral shades and rich textures. The bed was a king. Who needed a bed so large?

She was suddenly so exhausted that it was a huge effort to get her nightgown out of the suitcase and wash her face.

The bathroom had a swimming-pool-size tub in it. There was a chandelier over the tub, hundreds of teardrop-shaped crystals suspended from it, winking with light. In the bathroom!

Finally, back in the bedroom, she pulled back those crisp sheets and climbed into that huge bed. There was a switch beside the bed to turn off the lights.

She was plunged into the kind of complete darkness that city dwellers tended to forget existed.

The expanse of the bed made her feel small.

And very, very lonely.

When she closed her eyes, instead of falling into deep and exhausted sleep, the events on the lake replayed in her mind's eye. She had a terrible night's sleep, and despite that, Faith found herself awake early. She realized her internal clock was refusing to reset from eastern time.

It was nine o'clock in Toronto. She went out into the main area of the cottage and found where she had left the cell phone on the table. She looked out the windows. It wasn't raining, but it was a gray day in Whistler. The mountaintops were swathed in clouds.

She spent a few minutes figuring out the new phone, and then tapped in Maggie's number.

Unlike yesterday, her daughter picked up the unfamiliar number on the first ring.

"Hi, sweetie."

"Mom! I've been so worried."

Faith thought she'd seen that on a bumper sticker once: Live Long Enough That Your Children Worry About You.

"But I called you and told you I'd lost my phone."

"I tried your hotel, and they said you hadn't checked in!"

Faith had not considered that possibility.

"Can you imagine how that made me feel? So then I tried to call that number back, and I reached a message from a man named Daniel. I told him who I was and asked for a call back. I said it was urgent that I speak to you, but he never called me back. What kind of person is that?"

Faith remembered Brad saying he had put his phone away because of all the calls about the rescue.

"He just didn't have his phone with him."

Her daughter, from a generation that practically had their phones growing out of their hands, harrumphed with disbelief.

"And how would you know that?"

"We had dinner together."

"Daniel could have phoned me when you finished. I said it was urgent."

"His name isn't Daniel, it's Brad, and I'm sure he could figure out a three-hour time difference might not make calling back the best idea."

"But how would he know there was a three-hour time difference?"

Faith could feel Maggie shifting into lawyer mode, and prepared herself for the cross.

"Shockingly, where I'm living now came up in our conversation."

"You never said your friend was a *man*."

"I didn't think it was pertinent."

"Mom, where are you? Are you really in Whistler?"

"What?"

"I'm scared," Maggie said. "I know there's something you're not telling me. I could hear it in your voice, in that message you left. You're vulnerable. And you're a woman of some means. Awful people troll the internet looking for people just like you."

Faith looked around at her beautiful surroundings, and almost laughed out loud. If only her daughter knew she was hanging out with a man who was the least likely to be an internet troll looking to prey on a weakened woman.

"You're right," she confessed, aware already she had no intention of confessing all of it. "I didn't tell you everything. I am in Whistler—of course, I am."

She almost said, "I would never lie to you," but realized an omission could be a lie and there was no way she was going to be telling her daughter about going out on the ice after that dog or anything that had happened after.

"I didn't just lose my phone," she continued carefully. "I lost my whole purse. So I didn't have any ID, which is a requirement for checking into a hotel. My friend, whom I've known since high school, and indeed is a man—*as is half the world's population*—put me up for the night."

"At his house?" Maggie breathed, aghast.

"No, sweetie. At the Cobalt Lake Resort. In a private cottage, like a VIP suite."

There was silence. Faith heard her daughter's fingers tapping away, and knew she was busy fact-checking. There was a reason she was such a good lawyer!

Finally, Maggie spoke.

"Mom," she said, "you know what comes up when I put in Cobalt Lake? Gregor Watson. Is he there right now?"

"Rumors abound," Faith said, tickled that her superpragmatic daughter was just a little bit starstruck.

"It's a gorgeous place. I'm on their website now."

"It's very beautiful," Faith agreed.

"Is it decorated for Christmas? Because it's absolutely spectacular at Christmas."

"Um…not yet." Last night that was one of the things Brad had told her his daughter was working on for the first time since her mother had died.

Her voice a whisper of pure discovery, Maggie said, "Brad Daniels is…"

Faith waited for Maggie to share what she'd found out. That Brad Daniels was the owner of that resort. That he owned quite a lot, actually. That he was most likely a billionaire.

But with all that information at her fingertips, that was not what Maggie said.

She said, "Mom. Brad Daniels is gorgeous."

CHAPTER ELEVEN

HER DAUGHTER'S ASSESSMENT of Brad was fresh in Faith's mind when he knocked lightly on the door and let himself into Wolf's Song.

He *was* absolutely and utterly gorgeous. He was obviously ready for an excursion in the great outdoors, in a down jacket and multipocketed canvas expedition pants. He had on light hikers, so she couldn't see what his sock selection for the day was.

Faith was glad she had freshly showered, done her hair, applied a bit of makeup. She'd chosen her outfit with care—a pair of slacks suitable for a hike, a beautiful white cashmere sweater that maybe was not exactly hiking material.

And she had not chosen the outfit just to send off her father, either.

"Hey," Brad said, "how did you sleep?"

She smiled inwardly. Brad was no more aware of the differences in her hair and makeup, the way she was dressed, than he had been of aware of the quality of the suitcase or that wine he had brought over.

And yet, when he took her in, that smile playing across the beautiful curve of his lips, she felt completely *seen*.

"Restless. I'd forgotten how quiet it is in the mountains. And how dark. You'd think those would lead to a better rest, but I think I missed the noise and light of the big city right outside my window. You?"

"Same. Restless. Had trouble letting go of the events of the day."

His arms were full and he went by her and set a bag and a drink tray with two steaming cups on the kitchen island. He opened the bag and pulled out a selection of croissants and bagels, and little pots of jam and cream cheese.

"That smells heavenly."

"Still take it black?" he asked her, passing her one of the cardboard cups.

Who remembered how you took your coffee after thirty some years?

"Yes. You're spoiling me."

He met her gaze. "You know what? You deserve some spoiling."

It should have made her feel as if she had confided too much in him, and had earned his pity, but that's not how she felt, and it was not pity she saw in his eyes.

It was such genuine caring it took her breath away. She went over and took the coffee he offered.

"Do you still take two creams and a sugar?" she asked him. Ridiculous to feel as if that was flirting.

But his grin told her he found it endearing that she remembered, too.

"You want the good news or the bad news?" he asked her.

"Good, of course."

"There isn't any."

She laughed and blew on her coffee.

"The staff searched around the lake extensively. No purse. I checked with the police first thing this morning, and no purse had been turned in there yet, either."

She considered the logistics of that. How was she going to

begin the process of replacing at least enough things to get her home?

"Also, it's not a perfect day for going up Feeney. It's not snowing or raining, but it could start. It's cold and damp out there. You're still okay to go?"

"Yes." Considering she had put off this task for so long, it now felt weirdly imperative that she do it.

"You can add to this morning's list of *not-so-good news* that my daughter is very annoyed with me."

"Hey!" he said. "Mine, too."

And they bumped their coffee cups, in silent congratulation for achieving the goal of having become an irritation to their children.

"It never occurred to me Maggie would call the hotel to try and track me down. I'm afraid the next time you check your messages on your other phone, you'll find a few from her."

"That's too bad that she worried."

"Takes after her mother more than she cares to admit."

Brad smiled at Faith, as if the worry gene was adorable. Then reached into a front shirt pocket and put a card down on the table.

"What is that?"

"It's a preloaded credit card."

"I can't take that!"

"What are you going to do then? Call me every time you want a cup of coffee?"

"That's a good point." His thoughtfulness was so compelling. "I'll pay you back as soon as I have access to funds, though."

He lifted a shoulder, clearly uncaring of whether or not she paid him back.

"I came on a quad," he said, referring to the four-wheeled all-terrain vehicles that were commonly used in the mountains before there was enough snow to bring out the snowmobiles.

"I wasn't sure if you'd prefer that to hiking, since the weather isn't that good?"

"Oh, I'd love that!"

"I'm glad you said that, because I wasn't sure about going as far as the viewing point on foot if it's going to snow."

"I haven't been on a quad since I left here."

"Really?"

"I'm afraid for the last thirty or so years experiencing the great outdoors meant taking a book and a picnic to St. James Park on a sunny afternoon."

Felix had been *not outdoorsy*, and not the least apologetic about that, either. Once, she had talked him into a camping trip with the kids. It had been a fiasco from beginning to end: mosquitos, poor-quality sleeping bags that had left them cold and the hotdogs burned to the point of being inedible over the campfire.

Startled, Faith realized that, little by little, she had surrendered her own interests to Felix.

But isn't that part of why she was here?

Not just to honor her father's last wish, but to discover some lost part of herself? The part of her father that was deeply ingrained inside her? Outdoors. Adventure. Challenges.

"Actually, I can't wait to get back on a quad," she said.

"We can get you your own, or you can ride with me."

"I don't know if after so long I'd be confident riding one solo, especially up the steep parts of that pass."

There was some truth to that, but even more truth to the irresistible nature of sharing the seat of a quad with him.

An hour later, Maggie would have been shocked to see her mother, in her puffy new parka, sitting astride a quad, her arms wrapped tightly around this fabulously good-looking man.

Faith had her nose buried in Brad's rather gorgeous shoulder as they traversed the rocky, steep trail.

A box of ashes, in a velvet drawstring sack, was on her lap, squished tightly between them, and that was all that prevented Faith from being pressed even more intimately into Brad Daniels.

She was glad for the warm coat Brad had provided her with

the day before, and for the fact he had given her gloves, as well. It really was a cold morning.

She was also very glad she had left the driving to him. Despite the thick, cold mist, every now and then she would catch a heart-stopping glance of the steep drop-offs beside the trail.

Soon, the warmth radiating off Brad and the pureness of her surroundings edged out the chill.

It was replaced with a sense of exhilaration, almost homecoming, as they headed into places so high and wild that few people ever got to experience them. The moist morning air was scented heavily with pine and cedar.

The quad was quite quiet, humming along the difficult trail, instead of growling.

As Brad guided the vehicle confidently over the steadily increasing steepness of the rugged trail, the grayness around them began to thin, as did the trees.

Faith realized what had seemed like cold fog was actually a cloud. And then they drove right through it, and came out on top of it, into dazzling sunshine and a bright blue sky.

They were just a few feet from the viewing point, which looked out over the steep valley that separated some of the most majestic peaks of the Fitzsimmons Range of the Coast Mountains.

Brad stopped the quad.

Even though it had not been very noisy, once the sound of the engine was gone, the silence of the mountains and the forest below them was immense. Faith slipped off her perch behind him, resting her precious cargo on the seat while she took off her helmet.

Then she picked it up her father's ashes, hugging that humble velvet bag to her. She walked to what seemed to be the edge of the earth.

She had forgotten how sacred these high places felt, the air beyond pure, the world swathed in clouds below them, the snow-capped, formidable mountain peaks marching off into infinity around them.

Brad came and stood beside her.

"Do you want to be by yourself?"

"No, actually, I think he'd like it that you were here. He liked you."

She took a deep breath. Her fingers, despite the gloves, were cold. They trembled on the drawstrings.

Without asking, Brad—just knowing what needed to be done—helped her with the strings, and then held the sides of the bag, peeling it back as Faith pulled out the plain white cardboard box that was inside.

She wondered if she should tell Brad this humble container was her father's wish, not hers.

But a glance at his face told her he was no more aware of the humbleness of the container than he had been of her suitcase.

In the hospice, Max had handed her an envelope thick with cash.

"This is to pay for it. A cremation. Don't put me in the ground," he'd insisted. "And don't let them talk you into any of their scammy stuff, funeral-home nonsense—fancy urns, and stupid cards with pictures on them. There's enough there to do it simple and to take me back to the high places."

"Dad! You don't have to pay for it yourself."

"Oh, Faith, what would I do with money where I'm going?"

She couldn't argue with that.

"It's the least I can do. You know, I never forgave myself for betting your college money."

"I know, Dad. We don't have to talk about it—"

"You let me say my piece. The worst of it was I played right into that wicked witch's hands."

"What wicked witch?" she'd asked, stunned.

He snorted. "I knew Deirdre Daniels couldn't stand it that her son loved you."

"I had no idea that you knew about Brad and me."

"I might not be great at playing the horses, but I was always good at reading people. I knew what was going on between you and the Daniels kid. I liked him. More evidence, as if I needed it, that rotten parents can have good kids."

His gaze had rested on her a little too long.

"You weren't a rotten parent!" she'd said.

"I gambled away your college money."

"Oh, Dad, everything worked out in the end. It's not as if Brad and I were going to go on and get married and have kids. Neither of us was ready for that. I was seventeen, for Pete's sake, he was eighteen. I've been happy with Felix. I wouldn't have changed a thing."

Again, his eyes had been on her face, so direct. He'd hesitated.

"You know there's something wrong with the old guy, eh?"

She hated it that he always called Felix that. "Wh-wh-what?" she had stammered.

"When was I here last?"

"Two years ago, at Christmas."

"Oh, yeah, that's right. The year I worked at Schweitzer. That's a good hill. You should go there sometime. Take Maggie and Michael. It's in Idaho."

He hadn't said it with recrimination, but she was pretty sure it bothered him that his grandchildren didn't ski, hadn't experienced the high places.

"You're not noticing," Max had said, his voice a tired whisper, "because it's probably happening slowly. But for me, not having seen the old guy for two years, the changes can't be denied. Can't miss them. I'm tired, pet. Maybe you can come back tomorrow."

But there had been no tomorrow.

And then she *had* seen the changes. Once she did start seeing them, she was not sure how she had missed them. Maybe because of a full life: graduations, a marriage and babies, her dad's illness, work.

But after Max had passed, it had been like there were alarm bells clanging in her head, accompanied by red and white flashing lights.

Felix's curious lack of affect about the death of her dad, and then about the birth of Maggie's baby, their first grandchild.

His increasingly insensitive and inappropriate remarks.

How could she have not noticed Felix, of all people, being inappropriate?

He started being mean. Last Christmas, after he complained childishly about the turkey being dry, he shook his head sadly at Maggie, and said, "I never thought I'd have a fat daughter."

Michael, who had traveled all that way to be with them, had set down his cutlery quietly, and said, "I've had about enough of you sniping at Mom and Maggie. You've been doing it since I got here."

In a blink, Felix had been out of his chair, towering over the seated Michael, his fists clenched. "What are you going to do about it then?"

Faith had had the shocking feeling that they were about to become *that* family, the one where the police arrived at their house on Christmas day.

The exact kind of family she had seen in Deirdre Daniels's judgment of her all those years ago, that she had spent her whole life trying to outrun.

"Are you okay?" Brad asked her now.

Was she okay? Her father had noticed the changes in her husband long before she had, but he had probably noticed the toll those changes were taking on Faith, too. Even before Felix's illness, Max had thought she was giving up parts of herself.

Was that why he had sent her on this mission back to Whistler?

To let him go?

But to find herself, too?

CHAPTER TWELVE

"I'M OKAY," Faith reassured Brad with a nod.

And then, she opened the box. She had not opened it before. Inside it was a thick, clear plastic bag, fastened with one of those impossible zip ties.

Without saying a word, Brad slipped a knife from one of those many pockets in his mountaineer pants. As cosmopolitan as he was, he had been born and raised traversing these back-country trials. He would no more be caught in the wild places without a knife than he would be caught without water.

He slit the top of the bag open, and then he stepped back and behind her.

She was aware it was a physical gesture, but it felt symbolic, too. Brad had her back.

She lifted the bag up and away from herself. Slowly, she tilted it upside down. Some of the ash was light, like dust, and hung in the air, floated upward, suspended, almost glittering in the strong sunlight.

Some was picked up by the breeze and carried away.

And some fell into rocky crevasses and onto rugged outcrops. As she shook the last of her father's ashes from the bag, there was an incredible sense of relief, of rightness, of peace.

As if Max was finally home.

"Look," Brad said quietly.

And then from behind her, he put his arms around her waist, and she leaned back into him and tilted her head up to look at the intense blue of the sky.

Together, they watched as the bald eagle, possibly the largest one she had ever seen, danced and soared on the wind currents above them.

"In the end," she said softly, "this is what was left of a man."

"No," Brad said. "You're what's left of the man, Faith. You're his legacy. And you're a good one."

So it was not just her father who had come home.

With Brad's arms around her, and his voice stirring her hair, Faith felt she had come home, too.

She had expected she might cry when she let go of Max this final time. Instead, she felt a sense of closure, and having done right by her father.

He would have *loved* this.

Instead of feeling devastated by fresh grief, Faith felt an unexpected sense of euphoria and release as she silently wished Max well on his journey, and thanked him for all the gifts he had given her.

Among the best of them: to embrace the moment in all its unpredictability, to embrace the unexpected joys life gave you.

Brad contemplated how deliciously right it felt to be here on the mountaintop with Faith. It felt like such a grave honor to be trusted to help her with this most sacred of responsibilities.

"Do you feel the way I feel?" he asked her, finally releasing her. The eagle had vanished, riding a wind current up and up and up, until it was but a speck in the sky and then they couldn't see it at all.

She turned and looked at him. "Like a part of something bigger than us all?"

"Exactly," he breathed.

"Yes, I do. I feel at peace. And oddly happy."

"Exactly as Max would have wanted," Brad said. He felt oddly happy, too. To be with her, to be in the mountains, to feel such intense connection to all things.

He flattened the now-empty box and stowed it in the pannier of the quad. He saw her tuck the velvet bag inside her jacket, next to her heart.

"Do you feel ready for a hot drink? I brought a thermos with hot chocolate."

"You're spoiling me," she said again.

"I know," he said. "I like it."

Her eyes misted up. She was a woman who had not been spoiled nearly enough. At least not for a long time.

"Maybe not just yet."

Her eyes drifted to the trail, not the way they had been, but where it began to twist downward on the other side of the pass.

"Should we keep going then?" Brad asked. "We can see if we can get as far as the Mud Puddle, or if there's snow that will turn us back before we make it there."

The locals had created a tiny but beautiful rock pool around a hot springs that bubbled naturally out of the rocky earth around it. The water flowed in and out of that pool constantly, making it pristinely clean. Where it sloshed over the rock walls, it had created a decadently warmed mud bath, worthy of any spa.

It was probably the best-kept secret in all of Whistler. The locals did not tell. Anyone. Ever. It was code named the Mud Puddle, so that casual reference to it did not give away the fact there was an extraordinary secret up there in Feeney's Pass.

Some longing flashed through her eyes.

What was he doing, exactly? It felt like something more than just trying to draw that carefree part of Faith back to the surface.

"I can't," she said.

Thank goodness, Brad thought, that Faith was intent on being the reasonable one.

Still, he heard the reluctance in her voice.

"Why not?" he asked, pressing her.

She sighed heavily. "I have to start figuring out how I'm going to get on my flight on Friday if my purse isn't found. I'm sure there's an overwhelming amount of phone calls that have to be made and paperwork that has to be done."

There. Get back on the quad, and fight all the things his arms wrapped so tightly around her were causing him to feel, and drop her off to do her tasks.

It would be the safest thing.

Safe. Not the choice that would honor her devil-may-care dad.

And yet, he could not miss the longing in her eyes as her gaze drifted again, not to the trail the way they had come, but the other way. To where it went.

He saw how she had carried the weight of the whole world on her shoulders for so long. "You can leave all the responsibilities behind. Just for today."

He had, after all. He'd sent Cassie a quick text this morning, from the new phone, telling her he would be out of cell range for the whole day.

"Nothing would please Max more than that," Faith said pensively, mirroring the thought Brad had just had.

It wasn't quite a yes. He nudged. "Do you want me to see if we get cell service here? I can call the resort and have someone start doing the legwork about getting on a commercial flight without documents."

"No, don't bother with the cell."

He was relieved by that because he was sure if he opened that new phone there would be a dozen messages from Cassie.

"Come to that, I'm sure Maggie is all over it, already."

"There's another option, too. I can get you home, Faith. I have a plane."

She looked at him, startled. "It's a long way in a small plane, especially at this time of year."

"Uh, it's not a small plane. It's, um, a jet." He needed her to know he was problem-solving, not boasting. "I mean I have access to a jet, I don't own one."

But then that felt dishonest, as if he was trying to downplay himself, and he was aware of wanting one-hundred-percent honesty between them.

"I probably would own one," he confessed, "except that my environmentally sensitive daughter would disown me for the hypocrisy of asking our guests not to have their sheets washed every day, while I'm indulging myself for the sake of convenience. She might say male ego."

To his relief, Faith laughed.

"Our daughters," she said, with a shake of her head. "Why are they so hard to please?"

"Because we raised them to not be afraid to have their own opinions," he said.

"True." And then she added, "And don't worry about the private jet! That hydrogen-fuel technology will probably be applicable to planes someday."

And the best possible thing happened.

They were laughing.

"What's one more day?" Faith said. "I'm sure I'll get home one way or another. Yes, let's see if we can get to the Mud Puddle."

He surreptitiously turned off the tracker that was clipped on to his jacket. Somehow, he did not want his daughter, unable to get him on his phone, looking at a GPS map, watching the little red dot that was him move closer and closer to the Mud Puddle.

It would just lead her to asking too many questions. Questions he was not in any way ready to answer.

He wasn't even sure if he had an answer, beyond following an impulse, and what kind of answer was that?

Faith got back on the quad behind him. The box that had provided some separation on the way up to the viewing point was gone.

Every bump and every rock brought her into closer contact with him. He could feel how snugly he fit between the V of her legs. He could feel her curves, even through the pillowy shape of the jacket she wore.

He could feel her heat.

And her heat seared him.

It filled him with something he had not felt for a very long time.

This was way more than an impulse. It was a *wanting*, raw and powerful, like a man who had crawled across the desert wanted water, or like a man who had not slept for weeks wanted to lay himself down, close his eyes and be taken by the abyss.

The snow, thankfully, blocked the trail before they reached the Mud Puddle, which would bring a lot more challenges to his impulses that he was not quite ready for.

They got off the quad.

The moment he was out of close contact with her, it felt—thankfully—as if the spell had been broken.

"End of the line," he declared.

Faith took off her helmet, ran her fingers through her messy hair. The spell threatened to curl around him again, like wisps of smoke coming up from a fire.

"It's not much farther, is it?"

"No, but it'll be slippery."

"Should we try it on foot?"

He cast an experienced glance at the trail. The snow was not deep enough to worry about avalanches, and yet, he felt that reluctance to give himself to the wild places that had so betrayed him.

"I didn't really come prepared for that. I didn't bring towels...or bathing suits."

His eyes met hers. She cocked her head and looked at him. She did not seem like the vulnerable woman who needed his protection. She seemed to know exactly where this could lead.

And what she wanted.

Of course, she had wanted to rescue that dog, too, which showed her decision-making skills might not be the best...

"Maybe it's not—"

"I can't believe you let me down like this, Brad. You've rescued me, you've fed me, you've given me a place to stay and money. You've offered to help me get home, but now this. You've forgotten the bathing suits."

She was teasing him. If felt wonderful. She smirked when he got it.

"Okay," he said, "turning in my Boy Scout hero badge. A bit of a relief, I must say."

"My dad used to say the Puddle was a healing place. That even the animals knew. That a sick animal would go lie down in the heated mud. I can't imagine being this close and not going there. What do you think?"

What he thought was alarming. He was not sure he could refuse Faith anything.

"Sure," Brad said. "We don't actually have to get in. Maybe just stick our feet in the mud."

"Does that make you a stick-in-the-mud, Brad?"

Was she suggesting she wanted to do more than stick her feet in the mud? His face felt suddenly hot.

"Am I remembering wrong?" Faith asked. "I don't remember anyone wearing bathing suits in the Mud Puddle, because the mud just wrecked them, anyway."

No, she was remembering that with one-hundred-percent accuracy. Was she actually trying to make him blush?

What else was she remembering? Because he was remembering youthful exuberance, laughter, both of them being kind of shy and kind of bold, the slipperiness of the mud, kisses hotter than that sulfur-scented water.

She rummaged around in the pannier and pulled out the thermos. He found a couple of bottles of water. With her free hand, she took his free hand, as if that was the most natural thing in the world. They began to make their way up the slippery trail.

They pushed and pulled and clawed through the snow, and

over the icy patches, until they arrived at their destination, breathless.

Brad was pleasantly surprised by how this, his first venture into this kind of country in a long, long time, did not feel anxiety-provoking.

The opposite.

He felt his soul soothed by the pristine atmosphere of the high alpine, where the Mud Puddle was located, well above the tree line. Its smell—strong and sulfury—like rotten eggs, alerted them to how close they were before they actually saw it.

It was tucked behind a wall of rocks, well off Feeney's Pass, which was probably why the locals had succeeded in keeping it a secret so long. The slightly beaten path to it could have been mistaken for an animal trail, and indeed, there were some animal footprints in the snow, but no sign of human activity.

Brad watched Faith's face as they squeezed through the tiny little opening in the rocks and found themselves in an open area on the other side, a breathtaking view of the mountains around them.

"You know how some things aren't quite as you remembered them?" she breathed.

"Yes."

"This is better than I remembered it." She sat down on an outcropping and removed her light hikers and socks. She rolled up her pant legs and then sank her feet into the mud.

"Oh, my," she said and made a sound in her throat of deep and sensual pleasure. Then she opened her eyes and looked at him. "This isn't going to be good enough," she told him solemnly. "I can't come all the way here, and not get in. I would regret it forever."

CHAPTER THIRTEEN

BRAD QUESTIONED IF he had ever really thought they were going to get up here and just be satisfied to soak their feet and drink hot chocolate.

Twenty-four hours ago he certainly could not have predicted being at the Mud Puddle with Faith Cameron. Saint-John.

In fact, everything about his life with Cynthia had been ordered. Predictable. If you had asked him, he would have said he liked it that way.

But then the way she had died... Who could have predicted that? It was as if it was in total defiance of her own highly structured life.

He thought of that eagle soaring on the updraft, just letting life take it.

Live, something whispered to him. *Live*.

He took off his jacket and cast it aside. Now what?

She was looking at him to show the way. He could see it in her eyes, that she was wrestling with the insecurity of not being young anymore. Neither of them were young anymore. And they had both probably seen plenty of bodies in various circumstances.

"We can pretend we're Icelandic," she said, but her uncertainty was endearing. "That whole country is covered in hot springs. I don't think anyone worries about bathing suits."

"I've been there. On business. They're global leaders in geo-thermal technology. You're right about there being hot springs everywhere. Almost every town, even ones so tiny you wouldn't expect it, has a pool heated geothermally. But everywhere I went, people had on bathing suits."

"Oh," she said. "Did you go to the Blue Lagoon?"

"Yes. It's amazing. There are pockets of white mud in it, called silica, that you smear all over your bathing-suit-clad body."

She laughed. "It's on my bucket list. What's on yours?"

He'd lived an extraordinary life, he realized, where if he wanted to do anything, he had always been able to make it a reality.

He was surprised to hear himself reveal something. "I hope someday I'll be painting a nursery for Cassie."

He realized she was looking to him for leadership. He took a deep breath and stripped to his shorts.

The mountain air bit into his skin. He tried to keep his eyes to himself as beside him Faith peeled off item after item of clothing, until she was in her underwear, too.

"It's no different than being at the beach," she said bravely.

"Exactly."

"Except I haven't worn a two-piece since my first baby. So don't look!"

He tried hard not to look. Despite the fact they were barely dressed, Brad felt oddly comfortable with Faith, as if they had been married for a hundred years, as if being like this together was as natural as those springs bubbling out of the earth.

His hand found Faith's once again, and together they went to the edge of the pool.

It felt closer to the very edge of the earth than they had been at the Feeney's Pass viewing point.

* * *

"The silica in the Blue Lagoon can't have anything on this," Faith said, sliding down into the mud, until she was completely prone, letting its delicious warmth ooze over her body.

She was grateful that this morning, after just a moment's hesitation, she had chosen the underwear he had given her yesterday, unable to resist how pretty it was in comparison to the utilitarian offerings in her own suitcase.

Funny, how what a woman had on, where no one could see it, could make her feel pretty.

Sexy.

Of course, now he could see it, but he was being a perfect gentleman and not looking at her at all.

She scooped up handfuls of mud. It was going to wreck the underwear beyond repair, but she could buy new things. Things more delicate and feminine. Maybe she'd even use that credit card he had given her and check out the Cobalt Lake Boutique before she went home.

She gave herself more completely to the mud, and covered herself thoroughly, partly shy and partly because the warmth of it was so compelling.

She contemplated the fact that with all her imperfections, here she was, nearly naked, in a very sensual setting, with the very gorgeous Brad Daniels.

What would her children think if they knew that after a less-than-twenty-four-hour reunion, she was frolicking in the mud, in her rather sexy undergarments, with her old high-school lover?

Faith decided, firmly, she would not go there. She had long been captive to what other people thought and she would not give away one second of this experience to the imagined recriminations of others.

She had played it safe her entire life.

Where had that gotten her?

She was so tired of being the responsible one. Setting the example, being so damn *good* all the time.

Objectively, she and Brad were just two mature people giving themselves over to enjoying an unexpected experience.

She slid a glance over at Brad. He had stepped out in the mud, sinking in to his ankles. His broad back was to her. He had on boxer briefs, and was choosing not to lie down, but was standing, bending, cupping his hands in the mud and pouring it—it had the consistency of thick gravy—over himself.

It didn't really feel *racy* being in their underwear together. They were both now also clad, from the tips of their toes to the tops of their heads, with brownish-gray mud.

He looked like the clay form that they cast bronze around. And he was beautiful enough to be replicated into a statue.

Brad was a perfectly made man. Age had not diminished that. If anything, he seemed to have come even more into himself. Broader. More solid, with his long legs, wide shoulders, deep chest, taut belly. Even clothed as he was in mud, she could see the dimples above the band of his shorts, at the small of his back. The little indents were just above the lovely cut of lean buttocks that showed quite clearly through his mud-plastered shorts. Faith was surprised by how clearly she remembered that feature.

She had loved those dimples then. It had felt like a wonderful little secret she knew about him. Her sense of delight seemed undiminished by a very long hiatus!

Should she feel guilty? What was there to feel guilty about? It wasn't as if she had to submit a report to her children or to anyone else.

It struck her, in a way that it had not before, that she was free. To do and be whatever she wanted.

And at the moment, she was delighted to discover a sense of the mischievous in herself. When was the last time she had been playful, if her grandchildren had not been involved?

Even then, because of the stress of Felix, sometimes it had felt as if she was just going through the motions, playing the role of cheery granny, but not feeling it. At all. Her mind always elsewhere, her heart always numb.

She raised herself on her elbows, picked up a fistful of mud and tossed, aiming toward one of those dimples above his backside. It landed with a satisfying splat, square on one of his broad shoulders.

He turned and gave her a narrow look. At first, she thought he clearly expected more maturity, but then, she saw him gathering his own great fistful of mud.

"Prepare for a muck smush," he said, and stalked toward her, his expression theatrically menacing.

Laughing, she tried to get up, but the mud held her captive. She tried harder and then, with a great slurp, the mud released her and she moved to dash out of his reach. But it was impossible to build any speed with the mud sucking on her feet.

His hand found the middle of her back, and he gleefully ground mud into it. She bent to swiftly reload with a mud missile. When she turned around, he was already sloshing away, throwing taunts over his shoulder.

And just like that, she and Brad were playing like the children they had once been.

Sliding, shrieking, throwing mud balls. Soon, not an inch of skin was visible on either of them. Their hair was caked with mud. Her belly actually hurt from laughing.

He had just dodged her again, and with the mud dripping off him in twisted ropes, he looked like a mythical, hairy beast.

"You're the Sasquatch people claim to see in this area!"

"It's true," he confessed. "My mud-wrestling name in Sasquatch Sam."

"And here's me without my phone! That's a million-dollar photo right there."

"Absolutely not! I protect you from publicity, you protect me and my true identity."

It was pure silliness, and she welcomed it like parched earth welcomed rain.

She closed in on him again, arm raised to slam him with mud, but then when he pivoted to run, his feet skidded out from underneath him, and he was down, sliding through the mud on his butt.

Chortling, she lunged after him, and hovered over him. She was going to get him right in the face.

"Have mercy," he cried. "Man down."

"There is no mercy from the world-famous mud-wrestler, Greta the Barbarian. Prepare for annihilation."

He drew in a deep breath and closed his eyes, as if he was a warrior surrendering to his fate.

Faith chuckled and cried, "Victory!"

But before it was a complete victory, an unbelievably strong hand snaked around her ankle. When she tried to kick free of it, her balance tilted, then tottered, and then she was falling, their mud-slicked bodies coming together with a dull smack.

She was sprawled on top of the whole length of him. The mud-slicked underwear was a poor barrier, indeed. They might as well have both been naked. Slipping and sliding against each other, Faith thought it might have been the most sensual thing she had ever felt.

Only the whites of their eyes showed as they stared at each other, creatures from the deep, warm mud oozing out from between where their bodies were pressed together.

"Greta, I surrender," he whispered.

She freed an arm from between them, and with her thumb, cleared the mud off his lips. But before she could claim them, he slipped out from underneath her, stood and held his hand out to her.

Hand in hand, they walked to the small, rocked-off pool. He helped her slide in, then went and retrieved the thermos. She ducked under the water, and felt the mud melt off her hair and body.

He came, set down the thermos on the ledge and then slid into the pool beside her. He ducked under the water and came up restored to himself. The pool was tiny, with only one way to sit in it, side by side, and shoulder-to-shoulder.

After their dunk, the water turned the same color as the hot chocolate that he'd poured.

But, because it was constantly fed from the spring, it slowly cleared.

Utterly content, they sat on a ledge within the rock pool, water up to their chins, naked shoulders touching, stinky steam rising around them, sipping their hot chocolate.

"I needed that," he said, smiling at her, his dark eyes dancing with merriment. "To laugh like that. To let go."

"Me, too. I can't tell you how much."

"You don't have to. I get it."

And Faith suspected he was the one person on the planet who did get it, entirely. How sorrow was a cloud you walked under, thinking it would never break. That you would never see the sun again.

And yet, right now, both literally and figuratively, she could feel the sun again. She lifted her chin to it and closed her eyes.

CHAPTER FOURTEEN

"CAN I ASK you something?" Brad said to Faith, after a long comfortable silence.

"Or course."

"I've always wondered," he said, and she could hear the caution in his voice, so at odds with the carefreeness they had just experienced, "what happened all those years ago. One minute, we were like this—" he motioned at the pond and the mountains, a gesture that included them "—and the next you were gone."

What was the point, after all these years, of throwing anyone under the bus? Her father's terrible error in judgment, his mother's ability to pounce on an opportunity to control the unfolding of her son's life?

"The money for school just dried up," she said, her tone as careful as his.

"But why didn't you tell me that? I could have helped."

Over his mother's dead body.

But, of course, Mrs. Daniels was dead. There was no sense sullying her memory now.

"I was embarrassed," she said, "and scared." That was so true.

"But what happened? You just disappeared."

She hesitated. "A benefactor came along and tossed me a life rope. A full scholarship at U of T. It was a once-in-a-lifetime thing, and I had to make some hard decisions really fast."

"I still don't understand why you cut off contact so completely. Not a phone call, or a letter. Not even a Christmas card?"

Because Mrs. Daniels had made the terms abundantly clear.

"Brad, it's a long time ago."

She didn't realize her brow had furrowed until he pressed his thumb gently into it.

"Yes, it is," he agreed. But she could see the pain in his eyes.

"I'm sorry if I hurt you. I really am."

"That's part of what I couldn't understand," he said quietly. "It seemed so unlike you. To hurt anyone."

"I'm sorry," she said again.

He looked at her, deeply, as deeply as anyone had looked at her for a long, long time. It felt as if he could see the *truth* of her, even though most days—though not today—she felt she didn't know that about herself.

"I thought you loved me," he whispered. "As much as I loved you."

I did, she said silently.

Out loud, she said, "Brad, I was seventeen. You were eighteen. So young. I don't think we realize how young that is until we have our own children, and watch them hit those milestones. How would you have felt if it was your daughter, making decisions that could alter the course of her whole life based on that fierce, unflinching first love?"

"That's true," he said with a sigh. "I felt like she was a baby at seventeen. Sometimes, I still do. But you have a good point. Still, I feel as if there's something you're not telling me."

"Let's just leave it," she suggested quietly, though part of her wanted to trust him with all of it.

Brad sighed.

"You're right. Let's leave it. It's all a long time ago."

There was simply no point in saying to him *My dad gambled away my college money, and your mother was waiting like a vulture to pick over the bones of our lives.*

She had said to her father, on his deathbed, that it had all worked out. And yet, she was aware, in this moment, that didn't mean she didn't feel a residue of resentment around it.

But she didn't need to influence Brad's vision of the world, and his family, by sharing that with him.

For a while, the deep silence of the mountains was comfortable between them.

"Did you have other plans for your stay in Whistler?" he asked her.

She smiled. "I was going to go have dinner at the Mountain Hideaway where my dad would have never been welcomed. And tomorrow I was going to hit some of the shops and buy a few things he would have never been able to afford."

Because, she remembered sadly, Max was saving for her college, a noble gesture that he had spoiled with one impulsive decision. The worst of it was not his decision, but his guilt. He'd put walls around himself, imprisoning him in ways he had never allowed himself to be imprisoned before.

"I guess I was going to kind of thumb my nose at Whistler for Max Cameron. But now, I won't."

"If it's because of funds—"

She held up her hand. "It's not. It's not because of the lost purse. I'm pretty sure that credit card you gave me would cover even a breathtakingly expensive dinner at the Hideaway. But sitting here, where the world is so pure, and so wild, and so free, I don't want to do those things anymore.

"It feels almost as if it would dishonor him. If there was one thing my dad was not, it was into the *show*. To him—" Faith swept her arm over the views all around them, much like Brad had done earlier "—this was true wealth. Living fully. Experiencing creation deeply."

"Maybe it's just as well not to have dinner at the most well-known place in town given the interest of the media in locating the damsel in distress, the hero and the dog."

"Just tell them your hero badge had been revoked, remember?"

"If only it were that easy. They're hounds and the fox is their story. I don't think decency or sensitivity is part of their world."

"Thank you for being decent and sensitive in a world that isn't, Brad."

His hand found hers, and squeezed. She felt the length of his leg touch hers through the heat of the water. She felt a jolt of primal hunger go through her that was both alluring and alarming.

She stroked his leg. In response, he turned to her, gazed at her for a moment and then dropped his lips, nuzzling her neck before pulling away.

"I'm sorry. It just feels so much the way it always felt with you. As if you are steel and I am a magnet, helpless against your pull."

"Don't be sorry," she whispered, stunned—but delighted—that he still found her as attractive as he once had.

Brad's lips on her neck had awakened her awareness that there was a need inside her, not just to be seen as attractive, but to be a woman again. To feel a deep awareness of her own body, to feel that rush of desire, that exquisite moment of fulfilment.

To feel the tenderness of a man's lips, the rasp of his voice, the worship of his hands, the power of his need.

To experience physical intimacy.

All those things suggested hope for life.

Faith felt the enchantment of the world she found herself in—more, she felt healing blossoming inside of her.

Some barrier—some adherence to the rules she had followed her entire life—dissolved inside Faith with all the resistance of sugar meeting hot water.

"If it's too fast," he told her, "we can slow it down. We don't have to—"

But she put her hand behind Brad's head and drew his lips down to her own, and silenced him. His lips were so soft and so beautiful.

How was it possible to remember a sensation this accurately? And yet, she did—she remembered exactly what it had been like to be with him. And, at the very same time, as the kiss deepened, it felt brand-new and exquisitely exciting.

Her hands explored the water-slicked silk of his heated chest. His belly. She reveled in his hard lines. In letting her hands *know* him.

"Faith," he whispered huskily, "do you know where this is going?"

"Oh, yes."

"Are you sure?"

She laughed against the delicious column of his throat, nibbled it and then reached up and nipped his ear.

"Of course, I'm sure. It's not as if I can get pregnant."

"I was hoping," he growled against her ear, "it was because you found me completely irresistible."

"Ah, yes, and that."

And then they were laughing together, but the laughter was heated and breathless. He lifted her with astonishing and easy strength, setting her on a rock shelf as he stood before her.

Brad reached behind her, and his hands found the snap on the bra. It fell away, and his eyes drank her in.

Not seeing imperfections at all.

She found the band of those lacy panties, and both of them tugged them off. He stepped out of his shorts.

Faith did not feel self-conscious as his hands took ownership of her, as his eyes worshipped her, as his voice anointed her with blessings.

She wrapped her arms around his neck, and her legs around his hips, and he pulled himself into her.

You are so beautiful.
You are a miracle.
You are so good.
You are so strong.

After, they lay side by side, on a cold, smooth rock, the heated vapor coming off the pool and their own supercharged skin keeping them warm.

"So," she said, utterly content, "this is what it feels like to be a sinner."

She wondered, really, why she had waited so long. All through Felix's long illness, people had told her what a saint she was, until she had hated that label.

"If we're sinners," he said, "why do I feel I'm right at heaven's gate?"

The sinner and the saint, she thought, resided side by side in most people, probably in about equal measure, circumstances drawing out one or the other.

It was life in balance, really.

Like this rock they were lying on, hot and cold residing side by side in the perfect unison of healing.

A phrase ran through her head, and she was vaguely aware it was from the story of Adam and Eve.

They were naked and not ashamed.

Since the beginning of time, this was what a man and a woman had been meant to feel together.

The sacredness of connection.

It seemed as if the creation that was at the heart of that story was thrumming with life around them. The entire universe felt as if it was in harmony right now.

Joy and sorrow danced together, like the motes of her father's ashes caught in sunlight, until they melded together, until she could not tell one from the other, and they became neither joy nor sorrow, but that substance that made up life itself.

Hope.

* * *

There was such a sense of *rightness* to the way Faith's arms felt, wrapped around Brad, as he guided the quad back down the mountain.

Realistically, it was not that different than when they had headed up Feeney's Pass, but she was not trying to be proper anymore. She was giving herself fully to their connection, nestled comfortably into the back of him, her cheek resting on the back of his shoulder.

Brad was freezing. He had given Faith his shirt to towel off with as best she could, but now that wetness next to his skin was a terrible thing. His hair was also wet, under the helmet, which intensified the feeling of being cold. He hoped he was blocking the worst of the icy wind from her.

Protecting her.

It felt good to be protecting Faith.

Had he been so protective of her when he was young?

He thought, suddenly, of her words: *It's not as if I can get pregnant.*

He slammed to a halt so abruptly that her chin jabbed into his shoulder. He cut the engine, twisted to look at her.

Her hair was ice-tipped where it poked out from under the helmet.

"You weren't pregnant, were you?"

"What?"

"When you left?"

She shook her head, bemused. "No, Brad. I was taking precautions."

"Did we talk about it?"

"Brad! You're making me feel as if I'm on the witness stand for a cold case." She changed her voice, and it became deep, stern. "And what exactly was Mr. Daniels wearing on June sixteenth, thirty-some years ago?"

Not a condom, apparently.

"Sorry," he muttered. He turned back abruptly, facing forward, feeling guilty.

She was taking precautions.

Where had he been? Had they talked about it, or had his brain just been completely on hold, in that stupor of first love, or more bluntly, first sex, that pushed every single other thing out of the way?

Of course, the *first* aspect of it wouldn't explain why he'd gone on to repeat the very same pattern with Cynthia. She had told him she was protected and he'd happily left that responsibility to her.

He restarted the engine and piloted them down the hill. It was nearly dusk when they pulled up outside of Wolf's Song.

Faith slid off the quad. He could tell she was cold, despite him blocking the wind.

"You look like you need a hot shower," he said.

She pulled off the helmet and ran her fingers through her crushed hair. The curls sprang back, and she grinned at him in a way that made her seem unchanged from her seventeen-year-old self.

She tilted her head and grinned at him. "Are you joining me?"

CHAPTER FIFTEEN

THE TEMPTATION TO join Faith in the shower was nearly over-powering. But Brad made a decision that he was not going to be the same self-centered, instinct-driven jerk he had been when he was eighteen.

"No," he said, his firmness directed at himself more than at her. "Have your shower. I'll find us something for dinner."

Did she look faintly disappointed as she turned and went into Wolf's Song?

Here was the thing. She hadn't been pregnant, but she could have been. Funny, he had not once considered that possibility.

He recalled himself in those younger days. He'd said he loved Faith. And she had pointed out that, at that age, really, what did they know of love?

He had relished every moment with her, but when she had left, she had not trusted him with the truth that her family was in financial distress. He probably hadn't been worthy of it. Full of himself, enjoying the moment, reveling in the exquisite, all-encompassing sensation of his first really physical relationship.

He remembered going to see Max, all those years ago, asking where she was, pleading for information.

In retrospect, Brad was shocked Faith's father had not punched him in the nose. Because that's what he would have done if some young jock had gone after his baby, which he could now clearly see Cassie had been at seventeen.

But now, Brad thought, as he contemplated how he and Faith had slipped so naturally back into intimacy, he had the rarest of things.

A second chance.

An opportunity to get it so right this time.

Did he love her? Despite the self-centeredness of his eighteen-year-old self, he had been sure he loved her then.

Sure, almost from the first minute he'd seen her, the new girl in town, when she'd arrived at their school at the end of the eleventh grade.

He remembered saying to his mom, getting ready for senior prom, "I'm going to marry Faith Cameron someday."

Since then, though, love had taught him so many hard lessons about loss and powerlessness.

Maybe the new mature him didn't need to think of Faith in terms of love. Instead, he would see that he'd been given an opportunity to have a relationship with his equal, and an adult.

To treat her with respect.

And honor.

To spoil her rotten.

He didn't recall spoiling her rotten having anything to do with their twelfth-grade romance. He recalled almost everything in his young—and, admittedly, exceedingly horny—mind had been being about finding ways to be alone with her.

No wonder she had left without a backward glance.

And yet, he had felt as if he loved her madly, and beyond reason. Still, he was aware, again, he would want to kill anyone who had treated Cassie the way he had treated Faith.

After he had dropped off Faith, he parked the quad at his place. He raced in, and after changing into a dry shirt, and brushing his teeth, and running a comb through helmet-flattened hair, he took out his replacement phone and looked at it for the first time all day.

It occurred to him that it might have been years since he had not looked at his phone for this many hours.

It felt amazing. Freeing.

There were several messages. The first was from the police saying Faith's purse had been turned in.

He contemplated his sense of disappointment. No doubt that meant she would be able to go home Friday, as planned. Today was Tuesday. That would mean only two more full days to-gether.

Somehow, he had hoped to stretch out that *spoiling time*. And maybe he still could. He could just ask her to stay longer, couldn't he?

The other message was from Cassie. Thankfully, she sounded annoyed rather than frightened by his sudden disappearance.

What should he tell her?

Nothing.

The loss of Cynthia had made him and Cassie unusually close, but maybe it was time to back off from that a little.

His daughter did not need to know all the details of his per-sonal life, particularly given the fact she might place herself in charge of a romance project, and she also seemed to think his and Faith's experience out on the ice could be used to benefit the lodge.

He called her.

"What's going on with your phone, Dad?"

He told her about it blowing up over the rescue on the ice so badly he'd had to put it away and temporarily get a new number.

"I've seen pictures of that rescue now. That photographer posted some on social media, with the caption 'do you know these people?' It sure looks like you. The other person looks like a little kid, but I hear it was a woman. The whole town is talking about it."

Yay.

"Another media person posted an interview online with the lady whose dog it was. Its name was Felix. So adorable!"

"That dog was about the furthest thing from adorable that I can think of."

He didn't like it, one little bit, that something that was so highly personal to Faith—her husband's name—was out there in the public. Was it just local, so far? Or was it spreading?

It felt as if the jackals were circling, playing on the fact that everybody would think that was a heartwarming, poignant story. They would only like it *better* if they ever discovered that she had gone after that dog because it shared the same name as her now deceased husband.

But her pain being on display for the world would cause Faith so much suffering. She specifically did not want her daughter to know. He was going to have to look it up himself and see if the story was gaining steam or if it had stalled. He didn't want to ask Cassie because the less he expressed interest in it with her, the better.

"Dad, you should talk to them."

"Them?"

"The media. That photographer was in here again today."

"Did you let him know Gregor's gone?"

"No!"

He wished there was a way to tell Cassie that Faith needed the same kind of protection that his daughter went to such lengths to give their celebrity guests.

But how to make that request without letting on how deeply he was getting involved?

"Because they're going to run with it, anyway, and you probably have the best perspective of the whole thing."

Yes, he did, and knowing the secret of why Faith had gone out on that ice was something he planned to keep to himself.

He didn't like it that they were circling, closer and closer, to Faith's life.

"I'm not talking to them," he said firmly.

"I still think…"

He let her tell him what she thought, but didn't offer any comment. She sighed.

"You're so stubborn sometimes!"

"Now you know where you got it from."

She laughed, forgiving him.

"How was your day?" he asked her, and just as he had hoped, it threw her off the scent of the rescue-on-the-ice story. He listened to her talk about Christmas, how she was going to start on the cottages first—she was thinking of changing out the lights from white to colored around Cobalt Lake, she couldn't find some ornament or other, but she had found the perfect tree...

He was aware, a little ashamed, that he wasn't really listening to her. No, he was ticking off things he needed to get done in his head.

The first thing he did when he hung up was look for the rescue story online. It didn't pop up immediately, which was a good thing. When he found it, the video was pretty lousy. Maybe Gopher needed to improve his skills if he was looking for a break, instead of preying off the talent of others. It had about five thousand views, which in the online world was next to nothing. All it meant was that half the population of Whistler had had a look.

Relieved, he refocused on his mission of making up for the callow young man he had once been.

He snagged another bottle of wine from the very fine collection and then called the Hideaway and placed an order.

Brad hopped in his vehicle and headed into the village. First stop: the cop shop. Though technically the purse probably shouldn't have been surrendered to him, because he was the one who had reported the loss and had standing in the community, and was this week's hero, it was handed over to him without question.

His next stop was the floral shop on Main Street. They were getting ready to close, but again, he was able to use both his community standing and his local-hero status to coax an extraordinary bouquet out of them.

"Something special," he said.

"Any particular color?"

"Maybe just white."

"Budget?"

When was the last time he had purchased flowers? It had been too long, he thought. He wished he would have made small gestures that let his wife know how much he'd appreciated her more common. Marriages would be in a different place if everyone had the awareness he now had, that time was not a guarantee.

"Don't worry about budget," he said, "just the prettiest bouquet you can make."

He exited with a huge paper cone, stunning white blossoms peeking out of it. He wasn't sure what they were, but his whole vehicle filled up with the fragrance.

Then, finally, he stopped at the Hideaway and picked up the dinner he'd ordered for two. By the time he pulled up in front of Wolf's Song, Brad was feeling exceedingly pleased with himself.

Faith opened the door for him, before he even knocked. As if she had been waiting for him.

That did something to his heart.

She had showered and done something with her hair that made all the little curls stand up individually. She'd put on a hint of makeup, which made her eyes look huge and her lips look luscious. She was wearing a white turtleneck sweater, and slacks. It was casual and yet it made her look so feminine and womanly that it would be way too easy to forget his mission, and behave like a besotted teenage boy all over again.

But what he liked most was when he saw the light in her face when she took the bouquet from him and buried her nose in it.

"Did you buy the whole flower shop?" she teased him.

"I tried," he confessed.

"Gardenias!" she said. "They last about three seconds, so such a treat! Hydrangeas and roses. All my favorites!"

He would have liked to have been able to say to his daughter, *See, Cassie? Panic room? Are you kidding? The old man doesn't need any help from you in the romance department.*

"Do you want the good news or the bad news?" he said, stepping back from the door.

"Okay," she said, "I've fallen for this twice, so give me the bad news."

He laughed. "There isn't any."

Well, that wasn't exactly true. There was the video that had popped up online. He reminded himself to look again later and assess what was happening with the number of views. He didn't want her to worry if it was nothing, a local story that stayed that way.

He held up a finger to her, then went back to the truck, and came back up the walkway with the bag of food from the Hideaway. He had tucked the bottle of wine inside.

Faith took the bag, looked at the restaurant label on it and met his eyes with gratitude.

And then, he turned back once more to his vehicle, and came up the walk with her purse. Her mouth fell open. She nearly dropped the bag of food—with that very expensive wine in it!—but she caught herself, and instead, she set it down, took her purse from him and hugged it.

With those huge eyes so intense and soft on his face, she said, with the faint disbelief of someone who no longer believed good things could happen to her, "It really is all wonderful news."

Brad felt as if it had just become his life mission to keep it that way.

Faith could not believe she was holding her purse! It was such a relief and such a gift. She had just finished a conversation with Maggie, on the borrowed phone, before Brad had arrived.

She had been right about one thing. Maggie had spent much

of the day figuring out how to get her home. It involved filing police reports, swearing affidavits, showing up at the airline customer-service hours before the flight. It had felt overwhelming, and like it would take up a great deal of the time she had left here.

And now, she had been granted a reprieve. She could just focus on *this*.

This really being *him*.

She had told Maggie, briefly, about the beautiful releasing of Max's ashes, but nothing else about the day.

Well, what was she going to say?

Oh, by the way, Maggie, you know that guy you thought was so gorgeous? He's actually my first love from high school and we did a very sexy version of mud-wrestling and I can't wait to see what the evening has in store.

Even a sanitized version would have probably given Maggie fits and led to stern advice-giving. It seemed like there was a growing list of things she was keeping from Maggie.

Well, she could let her know one thing that would reduce Maggie's worries. While Brad carried items to the kitchen, she pulled her phone out of the side pocket on her purse. Amazingly, it still had a tiny bit of battery life, and so Faith sent a quick text.

Purse found!

She added a few smiley faces.

"What can I do?" she asked, following Brad into the kitchen.

"You can sit right over there, look beautiful and try this wine."

Faith felt like the princess her father had once wanted her to be, as Brad completely pampered her. He poured wine and set the bottle on the table. It was even more exquisite than it had been the night before.

"Do you need to charge that phone?" He flipped open a panel behind her that completely concealed a charging station.

Was there anything they hadn't thought of at this resort?

She plugged in her nearly dead phone, and then decided to look up the wine. Maggie would be impressed if she served such an impressive vintage at Christmas dinner.

She stared at her phone, disbelieving. They certainly wouldn't be having it with Christmas dinner.

Now, she wasn't sure what to do. She didn't want to appear gauche, but surely he must have opened this bottle by mistake.

"Brad," she squeaked, "do you know what this wine is worth?"

"No," he said, unconcerned.

"It's worth eight thousand dollars a bottle."

He stopped what he was doing, obviously as startled as she had been. And then he started to laugh. "Oh, well, we can't put the cork back in, so we might as well enjoy it."

"But where did it come from?"

"We have a private cellar, separate from the resort. I'm afraid I have no idea what anything in there is worth. I told you, I'm not much of a wine guy."

She got it. Like the suitcases, the wine must have been his wife's thing.

"I don't think I can enjoy it, now," she said. She used her phone to do some quick calculations. "It's approximately fifty-three dollars and thirty-three cents a sip!"

"All the more reason to enjoy it," he said. He took a small taste out of his glass. "Ah. Fifty-three, thirty-three." And then he took another one. "One hundred and six, sixty-six. One fifty-nine, ninety-nine."

She started laughing. "Please stop."

But he didn't. "Am I impressing you with my math skills?"

"Brad," she said with a sigh of surrender, "you're impressing me in every possible way there is to be impressed."

He grinned at her, pleased, and she found herself relaxing, as he set the table, lit candles, plated the food.

There was an awareness of him, physically, that was startling.

The squareness of his wrists, the shape of his fingers, the sensual curve of his lips, his economy of movement as he worked in the kitchen, his innate air of confidence.

He was really so out of her league in every single way! And yet, here she was, Brad Daniels's lover.

CHAPTER SIXTEEN

"BON APPÉTIT," Brad said, setting a plate in front of her with a flourish, and then sliding onto the deeply upholstered bench seat beside her, so close their shoulders were touching.

The scent of him mingled with the scent of food.

The afternoon's escapades—never mind drinking an eight-thousand-dollar bottle of wine—seemed to have left her senses heightened, acutely so. Even though she was wearing a sweater, she could still feel the fabric of his shirt against her shoulder, and beneath that the sinewy strength of him.

She sighed with pleasure, and took a bite of the food.

"This is delicious," Faith said. "I don't even want to know what it cost."

"In comparison to the wine? Peanuts."

"Thank goodness." She took another bite. "I think what we had last night was just as good."

"Take that, Hideaway. I'm going to tell Anita, our chef who prepared last night's meal. She'll be so pleased. Our restaurant is a little competitive."

Faith liked these small things about him so, so much. He was a man with an eight-thousand-dollar bottle of wine in his cellar and an innovation investor with a portfolio that was probably worth billions, and yet, Brad would take time out of what was no doubt a very busy schedule to make sure one of the staff felt valued.

Unlike his mother, she thought, but brushed the feeling away. Tonight, particularly with her purse back, it felt like she needed to just relax. Enjoy what was being given to her.

He insisted on cleaning up after, and she let him, since really, it just involved scraping the plates and loading the dishwasher.

The fire had not been started, and Faith liked watching Brad's easy competence with it. Paper, kindling, small pieces of wood, match, then a slow feeding of larger pieces until a cheery fire crackled invitingly.

Then he settled on the couch beside her, and threw a companionable arm over her shoulder, kicked off his shoes and put up his feet.

She admired his socks: bright yellow tonight, with orange and black.

He squinted at them. "I think they're ducks," he said, wagging his feet at her. She looked more closely. Definitely ducks!

"You know what duck rhymes with?" he whispered evilly in her ear.

"Truck," she ventured, pretending innocence.

"Exactly!"

After a moment, he leaned over and said, his tone husky and suggestive, "Do what you're dying to do."

What she was dying to do was so X-rated it made her blush.

"I mean we're halfway down that road, anyway," he whispered. "With ducks and trucks."

She held her breath, thinking of the word she *never* said, that rhymed with both of those.

"Go ahead," Brad said softly, pulling away from her just enough to let his gaze slide to her lips.

She leaned toward him, her eyes half-closed.

"We both know what you're dying to do. That's a fast charger. Your phone is probably ready to go. So show me the pictures of your grandchildren."

Faith burst out laughing. She loved it that he was teasing her. She loved how easily the laughter came. She gave Brad a solid thump on his shoulder. "That's not what I thought you were going to say."

"Really?" He lifted a sexy eyebrow. "Dirty mind."

"Maybe we should give the phone a little longer to charge," she suggested.

Without another word, he lifted her against his chest, and she curled her arms around his neck, and snuggled into him. He carried her down the hall and into that bedroom as if she was light as a feather.

He put her down on the bed, and they undressed each other, with wonder and deliberation. This wasn't something that was *just happening*, as it had been at the Mud Puddle. This was a choice.

They used every inch of that bed, which just yesterday, she had thought was so ridiculously large.

This second time, there was an exquisitely slow tenderness to their lovemaking. They were two people who had been cast adrift, who had found each other. Who were rescuing each other, who were celebrating being pulled back from the abyss of a dark, roiling, endless, uncertain sea.

Much later, Brad, completely naked, completely confident in his nakedness, padded out of the room to retrieve her phone. Oh, those dimples!

Faith was pretty amazed by how she didn't feel self-conscious, either. Was there an opposite to self-consciousness?

If there was, he had drawn it out of her. With his hands and his lips and the look in his eyes.

It might be, she mused, with him out of the room, a good time to ask herself where all this was going. But the truth was, she didn't care.

She had cared all her life. She had made plans, lived by rules and behaved a certain way, and despite her best efforts, nothing had turned out the way she expected it to, anyway.

Now, for once, she would try to just breathe. To just enjoy, to the fullest, the pure sensual sensation of being in the moment.

He came back in, gave her her phone. Clothed only in sheets, she opened it and showed him some pictures.

"This is Maggie and Michael," she said. It was a picture taken of them in front of the Christmas tree, last year.

"They're extraordinarily beautiful," Brad said. "Maggie looks a lot like your dad. Your son has your hair. Look at that mop of curls. I bet he has to fight the girls off."

When she looked at this picture, though, she didn't see how gorgeous Michael was. She saw the tension around his mouth, the baffled anger. Would she ever be able to overcome the barriers he had erected around himself, as if family was so painful for him, he no longer wanted to be a part of one?

"Everything okay?" Brad asked, pushing a little strand of hair away from her forehead with his thumb.

He was so sensitive to her.

"Felix being so changed was really hard on the kids. I can see it in Michael's face in this picture."

"You are undoubtedly an extraordinary mom. I'm going to say you gave them what they needed to come back from it."

How had he happened on the most perfect thing to say?

"These are my grandchildren, Tanya and Chloe."

"There's those curls again," he said, as if those curls were the most amazing thing in the entire world!

The image was of them in the kitchen, the girls on chairs, in aprons she had made them for Christmas, wooden spoons raised to lips, a big green bowl between them.

"That's the cookie bowl," she said, and then glanced at him. In his glamorous world, did it all seem just a little domestic and dull?

But if the smile tickling across his lips was any indication, no.

"Your face," he said, handing her back the phone, and touching her cheek with a fingertip, "when you look at those girls."

"You'll know someday."

He sighed. "I hope."

"Show me your daughter."

"I'm still on the temp phone."

"Oh, no. Is your phone still blowing up?"

He shrugged. "I haven't looked at it all day. Such a sense of reprieve. I'll grab the temporary one, though, and see if I can pull up her social-media page."

So Faith and Brad sat in that huge bed—it could have been a twin for as much of it as they were using—backs propped up on luscious pillows, swathed in crisp white Egyptian cotton sheets, admiring each other's families.

When she yawned, he turned off the phone. "Sorry. I forgot the time difference. I'll head out."

"Please stay," she whispered.

He sighed. "I was hoping you'd ask."

And he settled back in the bed beside her, gathered her in her arms and took her all the way home.

Just before she slept, she thought of how just last night this bed had seemed too big and too lonely. In her journey through grief, this is what she had least expected.

How swift and bright was the light of hope. With those thoughts swirling around her, Faith thought she would have the best sleep ever.

Instead, she woke to pitch-blackness, trembling from the remnants of a terrible dream.

"Hey," Brad said softly, and Faith found his arms around her. "I think you had a bad dream. You were yelling."

He pulled her close to him, nuzzled her neck, buried his nose in her hair.

"I did have a bad dream," she said, shaken, so comforted by his arms and his warmth in the bed.

"Tell me," he invited huskily, and nudged her to turn over and face him. Her eyes were adjusting to the dark, and she took in the lines of his face, the sweep of his lashes, the curve of his lips.

She felt safe, the opposite of how the dream had made her feel.

"Tell me," he said again.

And so she did.

"I was out walking in a park in Toronto," she said, taking strength from the beautiful calm of his dark eyes. "It was a nice summer day, and there were lots of people in the park. Families picnicking, young couples strolling hand in hand, little kids laughing. And then this loose dog came toward me. He was quite lovely, a big dog with a thick brown fur coat, and soft eyes. It was really friendly, wagging its tail, its tongue hanging out, almost like it was grinning.

"I stood still and the dog came to me, and I was so delighted, like somehow it had picked me out of all the people in the park that day.

"But when I reached down to pet it—more like to welcome it—it turned into a bear. And it stood up on its hind legs and it grabbed me in this hold. It was so strong. It was crushing me. I couldn't get away. That's probably when you heard me yelling because then I woke up."

"That's powerful," he said. "I see a pretty clear meaning in it."

"I agree. I have variations of it, all the time. This is the first time with the dog, though. It's a dream where I think I'm safe and happy, and I'm amazed I'm the one having this experience.

"But then there's some danger lurking, or something familiar becomes extraordinarily terrifying without warning. Once I dreamt I was in my kitchen, making cookies, and a gunman burst in, and started shooting everything, my beautiful kitchen being ripped apart by machine-gun blasts."

His arms tightened around her. His silence encouraged her to continue.

"I guess my subconscious is trying to help me deal with my

life. Everything that I thought was safe, this feeling of being blessed by love, suddenly being wrecked, turning into something dangerous and unpredictable."

"Faith," he whispered. "I'm so sorry. Did your husband...? Was he dangerous and unpredictable?"

"That was the hardest part. That this kind and dignified and gentle man became a complete stranger to me. It happened slowly. At first, he'd say or do something strange, and I'd just brush it off. 'He's tired. He's stressed. He hasn't been eating right.' My dad hadn't seen him for two years when he came back to Toronto, sick. And he noticed right away that Felix had changed a great deal.

"And then I wasn't so quick to dismiss things. It was quite alarming, watching how reckless he had become, agitated, like a hyperactive child. Forward motion with no thought. So there were accidents, like catching a frying pan on fire, and incidents like getting caught shoplifting in a neighborhood store. He became so unbelievably nasty. He had no filters, whatever he was thinking he just said. He had no comprehension that he was hurting people. Last Christmas, he challenged our son-in-law to a fight. So, yes, I guess he did become dangerous and unpredictable.

"It was even worse because I felt as if I couldn't tell anyone what was going on, because I wanted to protect him. I didn't want people looking at him through the lens of something I had said about him."

"How lonely was that for you?"

"You have no idea."

But his hand squeezing hers made her think maybe he did have an idea.

"The only people I wanted to tell were doctors. I had this naive idea the medical system would step in and help you if things went sideways.

"But that's not how it works, at least not with brain disorders. A doctor, who would spend ten minutes with Felix, would think he knew way more about him than I did after thirty years together. My calls for help—increasingly desperate pleas—felt as if they fell into an abyss. It was so unbelievably hard to get a diagnosis. Because I couldn't get a diagnosis, the kids just thought Felix was becoming horrible with age, and that I was making excuses for him.

"But in the end, what difference did that diagnosis that I finally got make? There was not a single thing they could do to change it or stop it."

Faith couldn't believe she'd unloaded all of that. She was not sure she had ever told her story so completely.

"You have lived through the nightmare you just woke up from."

"You know what the worst of it was? All these nasty things he was saying and doing? What if the kids were right? What if that's who he always had really been—what if he'd always nursed these horrible thoughts about people—and the disappearance of his filters just allowed it all to come out?"

After a long time, his voice strong, sure, something a person could really hold on to in the dark of night, Brad said, "I don't believe that."

"Why not?"

"First of all, you would have never married a man like that. But second, you know how people are when they're drunk? You know how they say and do all kinds of things they would never normally say and do?"

She could not help but think of her father at her wedding.

"There's a saying—*in vino veritas*. It's Latin, it means 'in wine there is truth,' but I've never quite seen it that way, either. Cassie had a friend once, in her teen years, the sweetest girl you could ever meet. Kind, helpful, quiet. Cassie brought her home one night after they'd had too much to drink. She was so awful. Loud, rude, vulgar. The next day she didn't even remember. But how could anyone look at her and reach the conclusion that how she behaved, for those few hours out of her whole life, was who she was?

"It's an altered state. It's not who people really are," Brad concluded quietly. "And I'm sure that's what it was for Felix, too."

She felt an amazing wash of peace when he said that. A sense of understanding, not just for Felix, but for her father, too.

"Thank you," she whispered to him. "Those are just about the most comforting words anyone has ever said to me about this."

CHAPTER SEVENTEEN

FAITH FELL ASLEEP AGAIN, but Brad didn't. He marveled at the way he felt with her in his arms.

The truth was, he hadn't ever thought he would feel this way again.

Whole.

Complete.

So, so alive.

It was very much like that eighteen-year-old boy who had declared with such fierce certainty, *I'm going to marry Faith Cameron someday.*

He felt wildly and ridiculously in love, as if his every sense was humming, vibrating electrically within him.

He couldn't just come out and say that. A declaration of love at this early stage would scare Faith into next week. After all, he was even scaring himself.

But he could *show* her. Slowly, he could try and heal what the last few years had given her. He could do that by giving her these last two days and making them as carefree, as fun and as full of adventure as was possible.

Wednesday and Thursday. Friday she was supposed to go home.

But maybe, if the next two days went well, he could convince her to stay.

He could see if what he thought he was feeling could stand up to the kind of reality tests only time could give it.

He couldn't change what had happened to her, or the way his teenage self had behaved, but he could make her laugh.

Feel young again.

Have hope.

Embrace adventure.

Feel confident in her own beauty.

Maybe even have faith, as her name called her to do. That life would be good again. That the dogs would not turn into bears, that she could feel safe and secure even if she was doing things that weren't exactly safe and secure.

"What are we doing here?" she asked, the next morning, getting out of his car. Brad had been up since 5:00 a.m. laying the groundwork for this. "What is this place?"

"It's a zip line."

She digested that for about two seconds. "What a terrible idea."

But underneath the words, he heard the fear of a woman who had friendly dogs turn into killer bears in her dreams. And in her real life.

"It's not such a bad idea," he said softly. "An adventure like this is about facing your fears. It's about discovering your competence in dealing with them. Life throws us all kinds of stuff. We can't control that. The one thing we can control is ourselves."

This is part of what he had learned in search-and-rescue.

"The way I see it, life has thrown some unbelievable stuff at you. Stuff you probably thought would crush you. But it hasn't. Embrace that. This lesson is as much for me as it is for you. Do you know I haven't skied since Cynthia died?"

As he knew it would, as soon as he made it about a benefit to him—about helping him—she was right on board.

She took a deep breath, and regarded the course, and then they walked up to the entrance kiosk. It was such an act of trust.

She laughed when she saw the sign on the window, not even trying to hide her relief. "Look, it's closed for the day. A private event."

He laughed, too. "The private event is us."

"What?"

"It's not their busy time of year. I didn't want to have to worry about either of us being recognized."

She actually put her hands on her hips and glared at him. He thought he'd better not smile, even though she looked as adorable as an angry kitten.

"You booked the whole park?"

"I did."

"Don't you think that's unnecessarily extravagant?" she asked him sternly.

"Hey, it doesn't even hold a candle to that wine last night."

"I think your money would be better used for something else."

He was not entirely certain she wasn't just using this indignation as a shield to avoid zip-lining.

"Such as?" he challenged her.

"How about the food bank?" she ventured.

He gave her a long look, then pulled his phone—still the temporary one—out of his pocket. He couldn't remember the accountant's phone number, but he found the website and dialed it that way.

He got by reception with ease.

"Graham. How are you? Brad Daniels here... Cassandra's fine, she's getting the place ready for Christmas. How about Brenda?" After they got the pleasantries dealt with—Graham's daughter, who had gone to school with Cassie, was expecting grandchild number three—he said, "Speaking of Christmas, I'd like to make a donation to the hamper fund at the food bank... Oh. I already have? How much?... Okay. Double that."

He clicked off his phone and put it in his pocket.

"Now, you're just showing off," she said, but a smile was tickling her lips.

"Just trying to impress my lady. Did it work?"

"Oh, yeah," she said softly. She took a deep breath. Her grip tightened on his. "Okay," she said, "I'll do this."

"It's just the beginning," he said. "I have a few other things planned, too."

She regarded him thoughtfully for a minute. Then she said, "Okay, Brad, you can have the rest of today. But tomorrow, I'm going to make the plans."

He frowned at that. He had it all in place for tomorrow night. He looked at his watch. Maybe, he could move it up to tonight.

"If you'll excuse me just a sec, I have to make another phone call."

A few minutes later, he stood on the precipice, harnessed in and wearing a helmet. He helped Faith buckle hers in place.

"If this is so safe, why are we wearing helmets?" she demanded. "And what possible good will they do as we are falling to our deaths?"

"We won't die of a head injury?" he teased her. "You first, my lady."

"No, no, you first. I insist."

"Okay, but you have to promise you won't chicken out and leave me stranded on the next platform by myself."

"Okay," she said. "I promise."

Her promise felt as if it carried the weight of a cargo full of gold.

Brad was surprised his hands were a bit clammy. He couldn't let Faith see that. He'd never get her to go. He took a deep breath, and pushed off the first platform. The harness caught him, and suddenly he was whooshing through the air at breakneck speed.

He realized the sensation of a total loss of control was not one he particularly liked. He had to clamp his jaws shut to keep from yelling his dismay. He was very happy when his feet found the next platform.

He turned and gave Faith a thumbs-up, hoping she wouldn't be able to see the slight shaking in his hands. She squinted at him, took a deep breath and leaped.

What had he done? She was screaming in terror! But then he realized, it wasn't terror at all! She was screaming with laughter.

Her feet found the platform and she tumbled into his arms, gazing up at him with absolute delight.

"That was the best! The wind! The feeling of freedom! It was like flying." She suddenly stopped, and looked at him more closely.

"You didn't like it," she said, despite his best effort at a brave expression.

"Terrified," he admitted, pressing his forehead to hers. Just like that, she was the strong one. He saw exactly how she had gotten through Felix's illness. Because she had a core of pure steel.

She leaned into him, and whispered, "Brad, it's the closest sensation to sex I've ever had without actually having sex."

"That puts an entirely different spin on it," he said.

"I hoped it would."

And somehow, after that, he surrendered to it. To the speed, and the sense of not being in control, and of the bottom falling out of his belly and his world. He loved how she imparted her joy and her confidence into him.

He realized that discovering something brand-new, even if it was frightening, gave the world a shimmer it had not had before. Or maybe that shimmer was from sharing the brand-new experience with her, just as they had when they were younger.

A few hours later, Faith stood in front of him. He helped her unsnap her harness. The look on her face made the private booking of the zip line a bargain. It would have been a bargain at twice the price.

"I *loved* that," she said, unnecessarily, since her enjoyment was shining out of her eyes.

"Me, too," he agreed, and realized he really, really meant it.

"I think that's the most exhilarating thing I've ever done," she told him.

"Since you've already compared it to sex, my ego feels quite deflated," he said, for her ears only, with mock sullenness.

"Okay, the most exhilarating family-friendly thing I've ever done. I'm going to see if there's any zip lines close to us in Toronto. I mean, the girls are too young, but it would be a great thing for Maggie and Michael and Sean and I to do together. It's exactly as you promised, a chance to embrace the exhilarating side of fear."

He liked it *so* much that her first thought was how to share an experience like this with the people who meant the most to her.

"I have something even better planned for tonight," he told her.

"Better than that?" she said skeptically.

"I think so. It's formal, though."

"I didn't bring anything formal to wear."

"Go get something. You never had a chance to use that preloaded credit card I gave you." He sighed at the look on her face. "I'll make another donation to the food bank."

At this rate, the recipients of his generosity would be having steak and lobster for Christmas dinner rather than turkey.

"How formal?" she asked him a little later as he dropped her off in front of Wolf's Song.

"As formal as you can make it." He looked at his watch. "I'll pick you up at six."

Faith entered a Whistler boutique that she would have never ever been able to afford when she lived here. She remembered how stressed she had been going to prom.

She had taken the sea-to-sky shuttle into Vancouver and used her chambermaid earnings to buy an exquisite dress at a secondhand store. She had traveled that distance so that none of her classmates would see her dress and recognize it as one they had discarded.

She had owned many gorgeous gowns since then, for faculty events, weddings, graduations, alumni reunions. And she had never owned another secondhand one. But she had never owned one like this shop was selling, either.

In fact, this was the kind of shop she avoided. The tasteful displays, soft lighting, good furniture, mirrors with gilt around the edges might as well have been neon signs blinking *expensive*. She had always harbored a secret sense that the sales staff in a place like this would know an impostor when they saw one!

But it must have been a new staff member today, because she didn't have the good sense to kick Faith out as not belonging.

In fact, she smiled at her, waved a hand and called, "Let me know if I can help you find something."

Which was probably the same as saying "I won't bother, because I can tell you can't afford it."

She went to a rack of evening dresses, and flipped over a price tag on a midnight-blue one. She tried not to gasp. On the other hand, the man had probably spent the equivalent of a new car on her today.

She could suck it up for once in her life.

The saleslady materialized at her side, as if she knew, somehow, a decision had been made. But she wasn't in the least snooty. In fact, she reminded Faith of one of Maggie's friends who went to the young-mothers group.

"I'm Bridgette," she introduced herself.

"A special-occasion dress?" she clarified once Faith had told her what she was looking for. "My favorite. I've got just the one. I thought of it the minute I saw you looking at this rack. Come with me."

And just like that, Faith found herself in a very posh changing room, looking at herself in the most gorgeous gown she had ever laid eyes on.

A little later, handing over her own credit card, not the one Brad had given her, she was not sure that how wonderful she felt buying that dress could be considered sucking it up.

That parcel tucked under her arm, Faith's next stop was the grocery store. She felt, acutely, the juxtaposition of the dress with her purchases there.

Perhaps she could change her plan for tomorrow. But really, there wasn't time. And in a way, it was a bit of a test.

Hours later, despite wearing a dress about equal to a month's salary when she'd been teaching, Faith felt as nervous waiting for Brad to come as she had felt all those years ago in her secondhand dress for prom.

She looked at herself in the mirror.

The dress was dazzling and elegant. Like Brad's hair, all the shades of gray in the silky fabric reminded her of storm clouds with the light behind them. The dress was beautifully cut, with a deep V at both the front and back, belted at the waist and then flaring out to midcalf. This was obviously why people paid so much for these dresses: the design of it *loved* how women were made. It hugged all the best parts of her and skimmed over others.

She looked beautiful.

And yet, when she looked at herself, she was aware the beauty did not come from the dress, or from her painstakingly tamed hair and her carefully applied makeup.

The beauty was from surviving the lake.

The beauty was from riding behind Brad on the quad.

The beauty was from honoring her father's last wish.

The beauty was from allowing herself to experience every single pleasure the Mud Puddle had offered her.

And the beauty was from having loved—and lost—and somehow finding within herself the courage to try it all again.

The doorbell rang, and, feeling really nervous for some reason, Faith opened the door.

Brad stood there looking very James Bondish, in a black

jacket, a crisp pleated shirt, a bow tie, knife-pressed black slacks and mirror-polished black dress shoes. Gregor Watson did not have a single thing on him.

She was glad for every cent she had spent on that dress, but she wasn't sure even that was enough to bolster her confidence in light of how suavely perfect he was.

"Show me the socks," she whispered.

He lifted a pant leg, and he had on blue socks with purple polka dots. Just like that, he was *her* Brad again, fun-loving, devoted to his daughter, not taking himself too seriously. She didn't need to be the least self-conscious of him.

Tonight, he had a different vehicle, parked in front of Wolf's Song, sporty and low-slung, and nearly as hard to get into as his bigger SUV had been.

Of course, the shoes were unreasonable. But she'd had to have them. And her new best friend Bridgette had insisted.

They weren't in the car very long. In fact, he drove around the corner, to the bottom of the Timber Wolf run and the chair-lift station.

She gave him a quizzical look, but he stopped the car, came around and opened her door. He guided her through the dark to the front of the station.

A voice greeted them. "Evening, Mr. Daniels. Ma'am."

Brad took her hand and settled her on the waiting chair. The lift attendant handed him a thick blanket and Brad put it over her shoulders and his, cocooning them together.

"Thanks, Mel," he said. "Remember—"

"Top secret," the young man said.

Faith shivered with delight. It really was all very secret agent. She loved it. The chairlift hummed to life, clanked once or twice, and then they were riding higher and higher, as the cables lifted them above the ground.

CHAPTER EIGHTEEN

FAITH SNUGGLED INTO Brad and took in the views. Soon, they could see all the way to Whistler. Cobalt Lake and Whistler both looked like miniature Christmas villages, their lights winking in the darkness.

By the time they reached the top station, they were in snow. The moon had risen and the world felt silver and white, as if it had all been designed to match her dress.

It was utterly magical. Adding to the magic, it somehow felt as if taking her to the top of a mountain on a chairlift was a subtle, but beautiful nod, to her father.

The chair halted, and Brad took the blanket from his shoulders and completely wrapped it around her. Even so, it was very cold up here. A path had been shoveled to a small café that Faith recalled served hot chocolate and coffee during the ski season.

Tonight, Brad held open the door for her, and a wall of welcoming warmth embraced her. There was a single, candlelit, white-linen-covered table, set for two, the chairs next to each other, rather than opposite each other, so that they could both face the view.

A formally attired waiter glided out, and filled their wineglasses.

"Don't even ask," Brad warned her.

So she didn't. She didn't ask what the wine had cost, or allow herself to wonder what this exquisite dinner experience had cost him.

The waiter came out again, this time with a tray covered in a silver dome. He set it carefully in the center of the table, and with a flourish removed the cover.

Tears sparked in Faith's eyes. "Oh, Brad," she whispered, as she looked at the two Zippy burgers wrapped in their distinctive red-and-white paper.

"The funny thing is Zippy's is still there, and the place we were supposed to go that night has long since shut down."

It flooded back to her. Prom night. She had felt like Cinderella in the beautiful gown she had managed to pick up secondhand. But she felt like Cinderella in more ways than that. Because Brad had insisted he was picking her up at her place, the run-down trailer on the edge of town.

When she had come out of her room in the gown, Max had stared at her, flummoxed. And then he had bowed before her, and kissed her hand, and asked her for a dance.

Dancing with her dad, she had looked up at him to see the tears in his eyes.

"My little girl," he'd whispered, "all grown up and I'm not ready for it."

And it felt as if it was only then that she, too, had realized exactly what that night represented. A transition. The end of one chapter and the opening of another. High school would be over in a few days.

And then, Brad had arrived, standing nervously at the door with a corsage in his hand, and a limo idling behind him.

Max had put him at ease, chatting and teasing, and then he'd noticed the limo. "Wow," he said to Faith, "you're beating your old man to a first ride in a limousine."

And then Brad, with that amazing generosity of spirit that had made her love him, had said, "We're going for dinner first, Mr. Cameron, why don't you come with us?"

Faith supposed there were some girls who wouldn't have liked that. But somehow, to her, it felt perfect, saying goodbye to this part of her life with the two men she loved most.

And so the three of them had climbed into the limo, her and Max equally as wide-eyed and how luxurious it was. And then Max had said, "My treat tonight, kids." And he'd tapped on the glass and said, "Zippy's and step on it."

And so instead of the dinner at the fancy restaurant where Brad had reservations, the limo had pulled up in front of Zippy's and let them out. It shone in her memory. Maybe because it was so soon after that everything fell apart.

"Funny," she said, "how sometimes when things don't go according to plan, they turn out so perfectly."

"One of the best nights ever," Brad told her quietly, and raised his wineglass to her. "To remembering old memories and making new ones."

After the dinner things had been cleared away, the transformed café was filled with music and Brad held out his hand to her.

They danced together.

Again, she was drawn back to senior prom, to how it had felt to sway against him, how aware she had been of every detail of him: his scent, the thickness of his lashes, the full bottom lip, the way his hand had felt resting on her waist.

She gazed up at him now and felt that familiar intensity.

"You know what I love best about an older Faith?" he asked softly.

"What?"

"Everything," he responded with such sincerity her heart stopped.

"Oh, Brad," she said, "wrinkles and extra pounds—"

He put a finger to her lips. "Life," he said. "When I look at you, I see your life in your eyes. I see the layers of it. I see you holding sick kids in the middle of the night, and choosing a prom dress with your own daughter. I see you and Felix making sacrifices so that she can become a lawyer and Michael can go to Scotland. I see the depth facing sorrow has given you. And I see the courage in your undiminished capacity for joy."

Out the expanse of windows, the stars twinkled above them, and the lights of the village twinkled below.

Faith was so deliciously aware that somehow she had left her real life behind her and stepped directly into a fairy tale.

Only Brad was saying this was the *real* her.

Just as it was the real him. He had grown into his great promise of generosity, of humor, of sensitivity.

She melted further into him, felt the cradle of his arms close around her, and wished for this to never, ever end.

It was the wee hours of the morning before they were back at Wolf's Song. They fell into each other's arms.

Despite the exhaustion, a need was there, that had been building and building as they had danced together on the top of that mountain. It was as quiet as the hum of a bee, as immutable as the waves of the ocean, as powerful as a sudden summer storm.

They undressed each other with reverence, they worshipped at the altar of life. Faith had a sense of each of them bringing everything they had ever been, everything they now were and everything they would ever be.

They began as separate people, kissing, tasting, touching, giving and receiving pleasure, exploring sensuality from a lovely place of maturity. But as the intensity built between them, the sense of separateness was lost.

Not just between them. As they exploded, the barriers of the universe came down, and they collapsed. Into everything.

She lay in the circle of Brad's arms after, feeling the steady rise and fall of his naked chest beneath her cheek.

Beyond content.

Happy.

She was the one thing she had wondered if she could ever be again. She marveled at it. She was happy.

The smallest niggling of doubt pierced that happiness. She'd volunteered to make the plan for tomorrow.

What could she give the man who had everything?

Especially since his daughter had already beaten her to the sock idea?

She could give him the one thing he had missed.

But suddenly, in the light of everything he had given her, her humble, homey idea felt *not good enough.*

Tomorrow felt as if it was going to be a test. She fit into his world. Would he fit into hers? Somehow, she didn't feel ready for that test, or for the possible answer.

But it was too late to make a different plan.

In the morning, she was familiarizing herself with the kitchen when he came in. He was so darned cute first thing with his tousled hair, and sleepy, sexy eyes.

"I'm going to go to my place and grab a shower and a change of clothes. Any wardrobe suggestions for your plan?"

Insecurity clawed at her. No fancy dress required. No quad helmets. No adventure-sturdy mountain wear.

She was going to introduce Brad to ordinary life. After the magical worlds he had invited her into, it was sure to fall flat.

Faith debated canceling.

She debated telling him he could come up with the plan for the day, after all.

But no, it was time to see if their worlds had any overlap at all.

"No," she said, "just come dressed for comfort."

He came and kissed her, full on the lips, and it almost made her insecurities vanish. Almost.

"So what's the plan?" he said, when he arrived back.

Comfy for him was a pair of dark denim jeans, a crisp shirt paired with them. He looked way too sexy for what she had in mind.

She took a deep breath. "We're going to bake cookies this morning."

She watched him closely for signs: that it was too domestic for him, a little dull, boring.

Instead, he grinned at her with such real enthusiasm that she felt her heart melt. In fact, it felt as if any little piece of herself she had been holding back from him, suddenly and completely surrendered.

"Look what I found," she said, leading him over to the counter.

He looked at her find. "I don't have a clue what that is. A device dropped from the ship of an extraterrestrial?"

He was going to make the differences in their worlds seem fun, like exploring a new place.

"It's a stand mixer!"

He inspected it. "As opposed to a sitting mixer?"

"It's a chef-worthy piece of equipment. What kind of vacation cottage is equipped like this?"

"This cottage actually has a commercial kitchen, because it's the largest of the cottages. Sometimes people rent all of the cottages, particularly in the offseason, for weddings or conferences or family reunions. This one becomes the central meeting place, and it's set up for caterers."

Soon, they were measuring ingredients together. He had put on his playlist. The kitchen was filled with sunshine, laughter and music.

She handed him one of the beaters after they had creamed all the cookie ingredients together. She took the other one for herself. She licked the cookie dough off it.

"Oh, my," he said, watching her with narrowed eyes. "So that's how you learned to do all those remarkable things with your tongue."

He closed his eyes, and began to do very wickedly exaggerated things to the beater with his tongue and lips. Soon, he was adding sounds, until he had her howling with laughter.

In fact, she had never laughed so much while baking cookies in her entire life.

Now, the first batch of cookies was cooling on the counter, and the second was in the oven. He was sitting, casually, on the island. She had taken the beaters out of the beautiful stand mixer that was built into the cabinet system.

It occurred to Faith she had wanted to show Brad what ordinary looked and felt like. Instead, he had shown her the extraordinary hidden among the ordinary.

Suddenly, without anyone knocking or the bell ringing, the front door swung open. Brad slid off the counter and turned to it, quizzically.

Faith recognized his daughter. Cassie came in and pecked him on the cheek, took in the cookies, acknowledged Faith with a lifted hand.

Faith noticed Brad had set the beater down, almost as if he was hiding it. In fact, he had a bit of a deer-caught-in-the-headlights look.

"I thought I'd start Christmas decorations over here later this afternoon. I don't like to do the public areas until after Remembrance Day, but I thought I could get a head start on this."

"Sure," Brad said. Faith tilted her head at him. It was their last full day together, and her plan for the afternoon hadn't involved working around his daughter setting up Christmas decorations.

"Dad, you must be in charge of cookies for the next search-and-rescue meeting. I think hiring a caterer is cheating."

Faith waited for Brad to correct his daughter, and make an introduction.

Instead, Brad said nothing.

His daughter came over and offered her hand. "Hi, I'm Cassandra, Mr. Daniels's daughter."

"Hi, Cassie," Faith said warmly. "I'm Faith." She glanced at Brad. Nothing.

"It's Cassandra," she said. The correction was ever so casual, but it put up the faintest of barriers. The *staff* did not call her Cassie. She helped herself to a cookie, as if she owned the place, which come to think of it, she did.

"These are delicious," she said. "Can you make sure Anita gets the recipe?"

"Of course," she said, and heard a bit of tightness in her own voice.

"What time do you think you'll be wrapping up? I won't come in until after you're gone."

Again, here was an opportunity for Brad to indicate Faith was not the caterer, that they were friends. And that the cottage was in use until tomorrow.

When he didn't say anything, Faith said, a little sharply, "Not to worry. I'm done."

Cassandra left with that same surge of busy energy she had come in with.

Faith took off her apron, folded it carefully and set it on the island. "I'm not sure I understand what just happened there, Brad. I thought I was staying here until tomorrow."

She'd also had some pretty hot plans for him this afternoon, that involved that huge, jetted tub in the en suite bathroom, and a container full of rose petals.

"We have lots of rooms," he said with a shrug.

"Why didn't you tell her I wasn't a caterer?" Faith asked softly.

"It just seemed less complicated not to mention it."

Suddenly, it occurred to Faith that the lift attendant last night had been sworn to secrecy, not because of the media chasing a story, but because Brad hadn't wanted his daughter to know about her.

"Really? It never occurred to you that your daughter mistaking me for staff might be hurtful to me, particularly since you didn't seem eager to correct her perception?"

He looked puzzled, the same as when she had mentioned her suitcase not being up-to-snuff.

"I was staff here, once. Do you remember that?"

"You were a chalet girl," he said, eying her uncomfortably, apparently sensing her rising temper and bracing for it.

"A chalet girl. Your mom's euphemism for a chambermaid. You know what I did, Brad? I stripped dirty sheets off beds, and cleaned toilets. I bet you've never done either, have you?"

"I'm not sure where this is going," he said uncomfortably.

"Your mom told me all those years ago that I wasn't good enough for you and I can see nothing has changed. You didn't even introduce me to your daughter!"

"My mom said that to you?" He looked genuinely shocked.

But she had started now, and she couldn't have stopped, even if she wanted to. It felt as if she had been keeping the secret to protect him. But now, she saw she'd been protecting herself, as well, as if the grown-up her might be able to slip into his world, her lack of social standing no longer applicable.

She was telling him *everything*.

"Brad, my dad lost all the money he'd saved for college gambling on a horse. A sure thing, he said. I'm not sure your mother set that up, though I wouldn't put it past her. But she sure didn't let an opportunity get by her to get rid of the *chalet* girl who had *designs* on her son."

"What are you talking about?" He looked angry now.

"You know who my mysterious benefactor was? You know who paid for my college, in the east, far away from her precious son? You know who made a stipulation that I wasn't to contact you *at all*? *Ever?*"

Brad looked utterly stunned.

She marched by him. He reached out to stop her, but she ducked easily out of his grasp and kept going.

She went down the hallway, and into the bedroom. She closed the door and locked it behind her. She ignored his soft knock on the door.

She pulled her shabby suitcase out of the cupboard, threw things in it, including that stupid bag full of rose petals she'd saved from the bouquet he'd bought her. She zipped it shut.

She ignored his rattle of the handle.

"Faith, we need to talk about this."

She pulled out her phone and called the hotel she'd originally had a reservation with. Thankfully, they had a room available for tonight.

The dress she had worn last night was still hanging in the closet. She realized she didn't want it. It was part of a world she could never belong to. One in which she had been an impostor.

She fished through her purse and put the unused credit card he had given her on the dresser.

Taking one last look around, feeling like Cinderella after the clock had struck twelve, Faith opened the double doors that went out to a deck off the bedroom.

She softly closed them and, tugging her suitcase behind her, took the boardwalk around Cobalt Lake toward Whistler.

When she got home, she'd send him a check for the jacket, and the toque and the clothes.

And then she'd burn them.

As she walked around the lake, she could almost see herself, out there, nearly drowning, thinking, laughably, that her father or Felix had somehow taken pity on all her suffering over the past years.

That her fate had been altered.

But she should be way more familiar with fate than that by now.

CHAPTER NINETEEN

IT WAS QUITE a while before Brad realized Faith had left.

He'd gone and sat in the living room, waiting for her to cool off. She would understand when he explained to her that he didn't want Cassie figuring out who she was because of the media thing.

And he certainly didn't want his daughter thinking Faith was a romantic interest.

She'd probably laugh when he told her Cassie would have them locked together in a panic room in no time.

Though if he was going to be locked in a panic room…

A horrible shrill noise startled him and he leaped off the couch. Smoke was roiling out the oven door and the fire alarm was shrieking its outrage.

He went and opened the oven door, and was nearly overcome with smoke inhalation. Brad slammed the door shut, held his breath and then opened it again. He pulled the second batch of now scorched cookies out with a tea towel. In his haste, he burned his hand.

Standing there, sucking on the burn, he waited for the bedroom door to fly open, for Faith to dash out, worried about him. She was the kind who would worry and fuss over any injury.

She'd probably want to look at his hand, run it under cold water, insist on a first-aid kit—it might be just the thing to soften that unfamiliar anger he had seen flare up in her eyes.

But the door didn't open.

And then he knew.

She was gone.

The cookies suddenly felt like an illustration of his life: scorched.

He wandered back into the great room, nursing his hand, and sank back down on the couch. Eventually the smoke alarm stopped shrieking. Brad thought about what Faith had accused his mother of.

He wanted, desperately, for it not to be true. But in his heart, he knew it was. The pieces of the puzzle of Faith's sudden departure from his life just fit together a little too snugly.

His world felt strangely perilous, as he challenged what he had believed to be true his entire life. His mother had been part of that life—one of the biggest parts—for forty years. Of course, he'd known she had flaws. His mother had never been going to win a popularity contest. But he would have never imagined she was capable of something so controlling and so conniving.

How could he possibly have spent that kind of time around her and not know who she really was?

And couldn't the same be said of Cynthia? Twenty-eight years of marriage, and he was not sure he'd known her at all.

And Faith? He'd been wooing her for days. Protecting her. Contemplating a life with her, because he wanted to capture the feeling he had around her.

Of being engaged.

Connected.

Of being alive.

He'd felt he'd been as open and transparent with Faith as he had ever been with anyone. And she thought he was judging her? Not finding her good enough?

It was an insulting misread of him.

But it was certainly more evidence that when it came to the women in his life, he didn't know them at all.

It was good that she was gone, he told himself, because he'd been about to get himself into big trouble with her.

As head over heels—as blindly—in love as he had been when he was eighteen.

He got up from the couch and let himself out of Wolf's Song before his daughter came back.

Faith was exhausted as she walked out of the frosted doors that separated the airline passengers from those picking them up at Toronto Pearson International Airport. She paused for a moment, watching the reunions, people so excited to see one another. Passionate kisses, hugs, greetings.

She realized she was holding up traffic, people streaming around her.

She had to focus on something other than the feeling of her heart breaking. Again. She told herself she had done the right thing.

It wasn't just that she and Brad came from two different stratospheres, that he came from a world that she could barely imagine, and she came from the world that served them.

It was *this*.

This crushing feeling of loss. It was bound to happen sooner or later. Even when someone got a puppy, the sad ending was already looming, waiting...

"Mom!"

Startled, she saw Maggie coming toward her. Her beautiful daughter, her face wreathed in happiness to see her. And just like that, she was part of all of the happy reunions happening around them.

Maggie's arms closed around her. "It's so good to see you."

As if she'd been gone a year, instead of five short days.

"I had no idea you were coming," Faith said. She had fully

intended to call a cab. "It's your busy time of day. Suppertime, and baths, and bedtime stories…"

"I just needed to be here," Maggie said quietly. "I've been so worried about you." She smiled. "Not being able to reach you that first day, and finding out you hadn't checked into your hotel, sent me into worry mode."

Before Felix, Maggie hadn't had a worry mode. Now, they all did, like survivors of a terrible natural disaster, an earthquake or a tsunami.

They walked to the carousel and Maggie spotted Faith's suitcase right away, and took it, then ushered them through the busy airport to her waiting car.

See? Faith told herself. She had family. She didn't need a man to look after her, to give her this sense of belonging and home. Maggie was her home. Maggie was quite capable of spoiling her on occasion.

She watched how Maggie handled the traffic with such aplomb, chattering about the girls and how excited they were as the day care and the school were already gearing up for Christmas plays.

"Chloe's been chosen to be the donkey in the manger scene. She's over the moon. Of course, I have to listen to her practicing her braying every waking moment." She demonstrated the bray and Faith laughed.

It was a reminder that laughter waited, even after the heartbreak, like sunshine waited behind the rain.

Not that her heart was broken!

She barely knew the man.

Liar, her inner voice reprimanded her.

"I was hoping you could help with the costume," Maggie said. "I don't even know where to begin."

Faith felt a warmth growing in her. Because she knew where to begin. She could already imagine the costume taking shape, the comfort of feeding the nubby gray fabric through her sewing machine.

This was her life. Being with her children and her grandchildren, making cookies and sewing costumes, and being in the front row for the Christmas concerts.

Her life was not erotic experiences at secret hot springs, private zip lines, exquisite meals on mountaintops.

In his heart, Brad knew that. That she could not fit into his world. That was why he had gone to such lengths not to introduce her to his daughter.

They pulled up in front of Faith's house, and Maggie parked in a spot Faith wouldn't have even dared to try. Again, she marveled at her daughter's competence, at the lovely feeling, that despite it all, she and Felix had done so much right.

Maggie brought the suitcase to the front door, and Faith found her key. How would she have gotten in without her purse? She wouldn't have thought about it until just this minute, she'd be standing out here in the cold calling a locksmith.

It had been a miracle, really, that her purse had been turned in.

But where had the miracle been when she had most needed it? No, best not to believe in such things.

Or one could think their first love rescuing them from certain death was also a miracle.

She missed Brad. Crazy to miss him so acutely after just a few days of being with him. On the other hand, when she had seen him after all these years, she had recognized a part of her, a secret part of her, had missed him that whole time.

Maggie was looking at her oddly. "Mom, are you okay?"

Secrets felt as if they took too much energy.

"Have you got time to come in for a minute?" Faith asked her. "I have something I need to tell you."

"Of course, I have time for you, Mom!"

Such a simple statement, and yet it brought tears to her eyes.

"What's going on?" Maggie asked a little later as they sipped hot tea—not fine wine. "I knew I should have gone with you. You shouldn't have tried to look after Grandpa's ashes by yourself. And then losing your purse…"

They sat on the slightly worn love seats in the living room, facing each other. Faith felt her spirit flitting around her house. She could see the marks on the doorjamb of the upstairs bathroom where they had measured the kids every year. Over there was the spot where Maggie had drawn on the wall with a permanent marker when she was five, and no matter how often they painted over it, it eventually bled through again.

There was the place, on the carpet, where Felix had spilled his coffee, and the dent in the wall where he had fallen.

"I think it's time for me to move," she told Maggie, surprised to realize she had made that decision sometime in the last few days. "The house is at an age where it needs things I can't give it. I've leaned on Sean quite enough over the past few years. He has his own house to look after."

"Don't make that your reason, Mom. We don't mind."

Her memories of the children were imprinted on her heart, not on a growth chart on the bathroom doorjamb.

"It's not the reason," she said. "I'm just ready for a different life."

She and Maggie's phones pinged at identical times. That meant it was either Michael or Sean sending them both a message.

"That's great news," Maggie said, smiling down at her phone. It was Michael.

I'm going to come home for Christmas. I'd like to see it one last time, in case it ends up being sold.

The timing of the text seemed serendipitous. Almost as if, even though the seas separated them, he had sensed the decision, sensed Faith looking around that space, getting ready to say goodbye…their energy joined in ways she would never fully understand, but was grateful for.

She was aware, as she looked at her phone, it was quite possible she misinterpreted what had seemed like Michael's indifference. While she had been thinking her son was insensitive, was it possible he was the most sensitive of them all?

"Mom? Is that what you wanted to talk about? The house? I'm not sad. I was actually hoping you'd arrive at that decision."

Faith took a deep breath. "No, that wasn't what I wanted to talk about. I want you to know what happened the day I arrived in Whistler."

She wanted, suddenly, for her daughter to know all of it—and maybe all of her—good and bad. Because wasn't that really what home was, not four walls, but being accepted for who you were?

So she told her about her ill-advised attempt to rescue that dog.

As she told it, she was aware she felt it had been an exceedingly stupid thing to do. On the other hand, if she had not done it, she would not have met Brad.

And for all the heartache she was going to feel over the next while, would she trade those days of laughter and adventure and discovery for anything?

The hope they had given her that someday life was going to be okay again.

Maggie was staring at her, open-mouthed. "You broke through the ice and ended up in the lake rescuing a dog?"

Faith nodded. "Please don't say how dumb it was. I already know."

"Is that why you didn't tell me?" Maggie asked softly. "Because you thought I'd think you were dumb?"

Faith nodded. "Getting old. Incompetent. You needing to look after me, instead of the other way around. A repeat of what we went through with your dad."

"Oh, Mom," Maggie said softly.

Faith drew in a deep breath. "There's one more part. The dog's name was Felix."

Maggie was silent for a long time. When she finally spoke, her voice was fierce, and Faith was shocked to see she had started crying when she told her the dog's name.

"Mom, I need you to listen to me. I don't know what's made you feel I think of you like that. Maybe I'm tired sometimes, because of all the things that come from juggling two little kids and a career. Maybe it makes me seem impatient and judgmental.

"But you going out on the ice after that dog? That had Dad's name? That's the bravest thing I've ever heard. You are the bravest person I know. When everybody else, including me and Michael, had given up on him, you hung in there. You got up every single day and did what needed to be done. You went on living, when you must have wanted to just lie down and give up a thousand times.

"You have a warrior spirit. Even when the battles were so hard, even though you knew you could not win, there you were, strapping on your armor and taking up your sword.

"You know what you taught me, Mom? Love can take on anything. Love will get you through things so horrible you cannot even imagine them, let alone prepare for them."

Faith took a sip of tea, stunned by how badly she had misinterpreted how her daughter saw her.

"Speaking of love," she said softly. "There's more. The man who rescued me was Brad Daniels."

"Mr. Hottie," Maggie said, and then it fully registered what her mother had said. "Love?" she squeaked.

"He was my first love, in high school."

And then she told her daughter things she had never told her. About growing up with Max, and working as a maid at the Cobalt Lake Resort, and finally about Mrs. Daniels, letting her know she was not good enough.

And then she told her about Brad spoiling her.

And his daughter finding them in the cottage together, and how she had felt he was ashamed of her.

"Oh, Mom," Maggie said softly. "He wasn't spoiling you. He was romancing you."

CHAPTER TWENTY

FAITH COULD ALMOST allow herself to be persuaded. She had to remember, Maggie was a lawyer. She convinced people of things for a living.

"Until his daughter came along," she said firmly. "And then he couldn't put enough distance between us. I realized he knew I couldn't fit in his world. Ever."

"Out of the hundreds of possibilities," Maggie said gently, "that's what you came up with? Could there be another reason for the way he acted?"

There was that lawyer again!

"I doubt there's another reason for Brad not introducing me to his daughter," Faith said stiffly, almost flinching as she remembered being corrected, and asked to call her Cassandra.

But then she thought, if she was capable of misinterpreting her own son, and her own daughter, had she misinterpreted Brad as well?

"I'm going to tell you what I think," Maggie said, in that tone that let Faith know her daughter was going to tell her, whether she wanted to hear it or not.

"You are that warrior. You are the bravest person I know. But that battle with Dad has left you bloodied and exhausted.

And you feel you can't ever do it again. Did you worry if you did hook up with Brad, that you might end up going through it all again someday?"

First of all, she wasn't going to be one-hundred-percent honest after all, because she wasn't going to confide in her daughter she had *hooked up* with Brad, if Maggie was using the term in the way young people seemed to use it.

But, second of all, she was a little surprised that, no, she had never thought of Brad, not even once, of needing her care someday.

Maybe that had been part of his appeal. That he was so healthy, and so vital, the least likely person to ever become dependent.

"You worry about Michael and I, don't you? Carrying the genetic makeup for it?"

As much as she had not thought of Brad in those terms, Maggie hit a nerve with that one.

"I do," Faith admitted, sorry she had not done a better job of hiding that particular concern.

"I did at first, too," Maggie said. "But then I realized all the worrying in the world wouldn't change what was going to happen in the future. All it would do was steal the joy away from today."

"How did you get so wise?"

"Look who I have for parents."

Parents.

"After you've spent your formative years trying to figure out how to keep squirrels out of the bird feeders, believe me, you got some smarts going on."

Faith was so grateful that Maggie had pulled that memory from all of them. She could remember the three of them—Maggie, Michael and Felix—in the backyard, building bird feeders with an impossible-to-penetrate squirrel obstacle course around them. She could remember the laughter, and the intensity with which their latest creation would be observed. In the later years, there had even been cameras set up.

"In my heart, I was always kind of rooting for the squirrel," Faith admitted.

"Me, too. I think we all were."

We.

The family they had been.

It was worthy of gratitude that the last years of struggle had not permanently stolen from Maggie all the incredible gifts her father had given her, when he was still able.

And Michael was going to come, too. He'd called it *home.* She hoped it was those kinds of memories drawing him here.

"See, Mom?" Maggie said quietly. "We'll start to remember the good things again. And that will make us less afraid."

"I suppose," Faith said, hoping for her son and daughter and grandchildren, but dubious for herself.

"You're afraid of loving Brad," Maggie continued, her voice the same soft voice Faith had always marveled at hearing when she explained something to her children. "You're afraid you can't have a happy ending. You're afraid you don't have the strength to battle the uncertainties that love can lay at your doorstep ever again. I think, as brave as you are, you were looking for an excuse to run away from what the universe has given you."

Faith went very still. Regardless of the fact she had never once looked at Brad in terms of health concerns, loving someone took unbelievable courage. She looked at her beautiful daughter, and saw that she was not only wise, but also intuitive beyond her years.

This, too, was what tragedy did—there were roses hidden among the thorns.

"I think you're right," Faith said. "I have no bravery left."

Maggie smiled softly at her. "Sometimes you have to let other people be strong, Mom. I bet Brad has enough bravery for both of you, to carry you until you're strong again."

"I think you're reading way too much into how he feels about me."

"I hope I'm not. That man was absolutely dreamy."

"Well," Cassie told Brad as she came into his office, set a coffee on his desk for him and settled in a chair across from him with her own, "that was an opportunity missed."

He stared at her, startled. Did she mean Faith? How did she know?

"Gregor has been spotted on the French Rivera, with a new girlfriend. They're all gone. Every media person who was here who was interested in that story about your rescue on the lake has disappeared."

He laughed at that. He was pretty sure it was the first time he had laughed in—

"I guess it was time-sensitive, anyway. No one cares about it ten days after it happened."

Ten days. Ten days since he had laughed, since Faith had left, each day longer than the one before it and not just in terms of the winter darkness that was descending on them.

"Ah, well, Cassie, you did a great job keeping them off Gregor's trail for all this time. They still thought he was here, and they had the possibility of that side story to keep them occupied while they waited for a glimpse of him."

"I know," she said with an impish grin, and lifted her coffee cup to him.

He saluted her back. "You're doing a great job getting everything ready for Christmas."

"It isn't a season," she said, "it's a feeling."

He looked out the window. Snow now blanketed his views. He could see skaters on the lake. The trees twinkled with bright lights and decorations.

One season shifted to another. Grief had already taught him that. Everything kept moving, regardless of how you felt about it. He didn't have the *feeling*. But he wasn't going to tell his daughter that, when she was working so hard.

"It's picture-perfect," he said, trying for enthusiasm and missing.

"Dad, is something wrong?"

"No," he said, and then, just barely refrained from adding, *Don't give too much energy to perfection, Cassie.*

"Christmas," she said, cocking her head at him. "It's such a hard time of year. I miss her, too."

"I know, sweetheart."

She looked at her watch, gasped and catapulted from her chair. "So much to do. Oh, by the way, did you get me that cookie recipe?"

"Uh…sorry, no."

She gave him a look of faux annoyance. "Another opportunity missed. Possibly the best cookies I've ever tasted."

And then she was gone. Brad waited until the door had closed behind her, and then, ever so slowly, opened his drawer and took out the letter. He suddenly had to find out if his wife was one more woman he had never really known.

Beloved

Brad was aware of a faint tremble in his hands as he opened the flap of the envelope, the glue long since dried.

A single sheet of folded paper, as yellow with age as the envelope slid into his hands. He closed his eyes, and unfolded the paper.

And then he took a deep breath and opened his eyes.

Beloved, my beautiful girl, you are now hours old and so utterly perfect.

Relief swelled in him, as well as a trace of self-loathing for his own doubts about his wife. The letter was to their newborn daughter.

I am terrified of the huge responsibility you represent. Is there any hope at all of keeping all this perfection intact as you grow toward womanhood? I feel your father and I did not have good role models for this adventure called family that we have entered.

My mom and dad, already gone, were so hardworking and down to earth. But hugs? "I love you"? As foreign to them as a trip to a far-off land. I grew up with "make yourself useful," not "I stand in wonder of your perfection"!

And your grandmother Daniels! I often wonder how did someone so harshly judgmental and so impossible to please, ever raise a man like your father? He is the finest man I've ever known.

My hope for you, darling girl, is this:

From your father, I hope you get qualities of decency, generosity, calm…and the world's best eyelashes.

From me, I hope you get qualities of order and adaptability, an ability to see what could be, instead of what is.

But my greatest hopes aren't about what you inherit from each of us, but what you discover within yourself. I hope you find courage, and independence, and creativity, and joy. I hope as parents, we give you the gift of being you in the world.

And most of all, beloved Cassandra, I hope when love knocks on your door, you say yes to it.

And now, you are stirring, and our new life as a family begins. I am putting this note away for you. I will take it out when you are thirty, and we will look at it together, and see how much of what I have wished for you has come true.

With all my love,

Mom (the happiest word I have ever written)

Brad held the letter for a long time, humbled by his wife's words about him, her words to their daughter.

He looked at the photo of her on his desk. In it, Cynthia was smiling, but he could see the faint tension around her mouth, the faint wall up in her eyes.

It seemed every question he'd had about his wife and their marriage had been answered by what Faith had said, and what this letter confirmed.

His mother had always been a difficult woman. She'd moved from Austria when she was a teenager, but never lost her accent. He suspected she had been made fun of. Once, in a rare moment of softness, Deirdre had told him something that had happened to her own mother during the war.

After that, he'd seen his mother—whom the staff called an old battle-ax behind her back, and the kids at school the dragon lady behind his—in a different light.

She was in some way a tormented soul, and so perhaps he had forgiven her things he shouldn't have. He'd told her once that he would not tolerate her being bad-tempered and judgmental with his wife.

He had never seen her behave that way toward Cynthia again, but after Faith's story, he wondered if he hadn't just forced his mother's aggression underground.

Looking back, he could see the daggers hidden in comments that had been seemingly innocent, that he had not given a thought to at the time. It occurred to him his mother might have subtly—and even not so subtly—tormented Cynthia when he was not in earshot.

And then Cynthia had felt a need to earn her way into the family. She probably had never once stood up for herself, thinking if she was good enough and perfect enough she could win her place in the Daniels family.

He thought of her relentless quest for perfection, the way she had put on airs, and pronounced things *marvelous* when they achieved her impossible standard.

Impossible, because no matter how hard she tried, she had probably never been able to get out from under the harsh judgment of his mother. She had set herself an impossible task if she'd been looking for Deirdre's approval.

It was even possible his mom had been even more ruthless when, after succeeding in getting rid of Faith, she had come up against the exact same challenge a few years later.

Had his mother made Cynthia pay the price for that accidental pregnancy again and again and again?

And he'd been blind to it all, engrossed in his work, thinking Cynthia was just as engrossed in her life, happily turning the resort into a world-class destination, collecting those incredible bottles of wine.

After Cynthia's death, he'd begun to question the strength of their marriage, but now he saw the flaw so clearly.

His mother had bullied his wife, and he had not seen it, beyond that first time. He should have been more vigilant. Instead, he had not protected Cynthia, not assured her she was absolutely enough exactly as she was.

No wonder, since the early days of their marriage, Cynthia had begun taking those bold midnight skiing excursions.

He'd thought they were out of character for her. She was so controlled, so *not* spontaneous.

But in actual fact, maybe that was the place—the only place—where she had felt free of the oppression of perfection, free to be herself, free to let her hair down, free to scream at the moon if she wanted.

Free to go out of bounds.

Free to shake her fist at all the rules and order that had been imposed on her, first by his mother, and then by herself.

He suspected by the time his mother had died, the patterns had been set. Cynthia had been so far behind the wall of her defenses—making her appearance and the resort and her wine collection so perfect—that she didn't even know that she was behind a wall anymore.

"I'm so sorry," he whispered to the picture. He slid the letter into the top drawer of his desk, added a reminder to his phone for way, way in the future.

He would give it to Cassie, as Cynthia had wanted, on her thirtieth birthday.

He'd known all along that Faith was about second chances to get things right. He just hadn't known how many levels it was on.

He picked up his phone and sent a quick text.

Cassie, are you still nearby? Do you want to walk around the lake with me? I'll tell you what happened that day.

He realized what he was really going to do was ask his daughter's blessing.

She answered back right away.

I'd love that.

Even with her busy schedule, she still loved being with Dad. For all the mistakes he was sure he and Cynthia had made, he could be assured in this.

His daughter was evidence of the triumph of love.

He picked up his jacket and headed out the door. For the first time since Faith had left, he felt optimistic, a stirring of hope chiseling away at the heaviness in his chest.

At the same time, he wondered if what he was about to confide in Cassie meant there was going to be a panic room in his future.

CHAPTER TWENTY-ONE

A PART OF Faith had really hoped that Maggie was right, that Brad had enough bravery for both of them.

But as she clicked off the days of November, it seemed if he was going to be the brave one, there was no sign of it. In fact, that time with him had a dreamlike quality to it, as if it had happened to someone else, unfolded on a movie screen or between the pages of a book.

Real life was enjoying the frenzied excitement of Chloe and Tanya after the first snow. Real life was beginning Christmas shopping, and watching decorations go up, bringing light and color to a dreary time of year.

Real life was helping Michael find a reasonably priced flight to come home.

Real life was starting that donkey costume for the Christmas play, and making paper snowflakes with her granddaughters that were now displayed in every window of her house.

Real life was realizing this would be her first year without Felix, though in truth, she knew she had lost him a long time ago.

Real life was taking action on her decisions about the house.

The house had actually been too big for her and Felix, once the kids were gone. But she had held on to it knowing that those kind of decisions were beyond his capabilities, and also that the familiar brought him some comfort.

Faith thought, with longing, of the woman she had been for a few short days in Whistler: carefree, bold, sure of herself.

She knew letting go of the house that had brought her such a sense of safety was part of embracing that woman.

That sense of safety had been an illusion. Just like in her dreams, the dangers had lurked, benign, in plain sight.

Yes, on that terrible last day with Brad, she had lost that certainty about herself—given in to old, old insecurities—but she knew now, her confidence was right there, waiting for her to invite it back into the forefront of her life.

A week later, she said goodbye to the real-estate agent, closing the door behind him against the snow that tried to swirl in.

So they would have one last Christmas here. One more time, with the kids and the grandkids gathered around the tree, the house smelling of turkey.

She thought she should feel sad, but she didn't.

As she looked around, she felt oddly free. Selling the house would leave her financially secure for life. That short time with Brad had filled her with longings.

All kinds of longings, she acknowledged with a blush, and yet the one that remained was to embrace adventure.

To travel. To explore. To discover.

The doorbell rang. She thought the real-estate agent must have forgotten something, and went back and opened it. But no, Brad Daniels stood on her doorstep.

He was stunning, just the way she would expect a man to look who had just stepped off his private jet.

But underneath that sophistication, she saw he looked exhausted. Gray stubble—that she had such a desperate need to touch, she had to stuff her hand behind her back—dotted his face. He looked faintly haggard. Thinner.

And then she remembered Maggie saying he would be brave enough for both of them.

His number, from that call Faith had made from the hospital would have been on Maggie's phone.

"Did Maggie call you?" she asked, mortified.

What would her daughter have said? *I think my mom's in love with you.*

And Brad, with his need to rescue...

He looked surprised. "Did Maggie call me? No, I called her. Her number was on my phone from when you called her from the hospital."

"She knew you were coming?"

"I wouldn't go that far. But she surrendered your address without much of a fight." He smiled that wonderful, delicious, crooked-grin smile at her.

She stepped back and let him in, aware of how humble her house was compared to the opulence of nearly every space at the Cobalt Lake Resort.

But he did not appear in any way aware of the humbleness of her house, just as he had not been aware of the differences in their worlds because of his watch, his car, her luggage, his ability to rent an entire park, or open up a ski hill for a private dining experience.

He had never been aware of those things, so Faith could suddenly see Maggie had been right.

It had been her who had seen the differences in their worlds, it had been her who had jumped to the conclusion that he had not introduced her to his daughter because she was not good enough.

With that realization, Faith felt the door of her heart squeak open one alarming inch.

Just enough that she said, "Come in, Brad. Sit down. Should I make us tea?"

So different than the expensive wines he had offered her. And yet, he tilted his head, and smiled. "Tea sounds wonderful."

And so, a while later, they sat across from each other, sipping tea from her bone-china thrift-store finds.

Then he set down his teacup, and drew in a deep breath.

"I want to clear the air with you."

"It's not necessary."

"I think it is. I had two reasons to keep you hidden from my daughter, neither of which had anything to do with your perception of not being good enough. First of all, she seemed to think the publicity from my rescuing you would be good for the resort. I knew you did not want Maggie to find out what had happened, so it seemed wise to keep you and my daughter in separate worlds for the time being."

He had been protecting her, Faith thought.

"Secondly, Cassie is very type A. Whatever she does, she does with incredible focus, smarts and zeal. And the very morning of the day I pulled you out of Cobalt Lake, she had indicated that if I was ready to move on, she would be there to *help* me. You cannot even imagine my terror at the prospect."

Faith found herself giggling.

"When I told her I wasn't interested in the awkwardness of dating, she suggested a panic room. A panic room!"

Now, she was laughing.

Oh, how he had a way of doing this to her.

"I was really, really angry when you told me you thought I hadn't introduced you because I felt you weren't good enough. And when you told me about my mother, my sense of shock and betrayal were off the charts. I had been struggling with a feeling of not really knowing Cynthia, and when you said that, I felt like I didn't know you, either. That I was the worst man ever at reading the truth about women.

"What was the truth about you? Twice, you had let me fall in love with you."

Faith felt her heart stop.

"And twice you had abandoned me. But as a week went by, I realized the truth. There's usually something else underlying anger. And for me, it was fear. Not the let's-jump-off-the-edge-of-the-world kind of fear of zip-lining. A deeper fear. A soul fear of the uncertainties of life. Of how you can think every-thing is going just fine, and then have your whole world col-lapse from under you.

"And then I had the thought, if I'm feeling this way, how much worse is it for you? I lost my partner to an accident. But you lost yours in the most cruel way I can imagine. What I real-ized, Faith, was that it's not about being perceived as not good enough for you. It's the terror of saying yes, once again, to the very thing that tore your world away from you."

Somehow, she was getting up and crossing to him. She found herself, not beside him, but on his lap, her arms around his neck, her tears wetting the crisp white linen of his shirt.

To be *seen* so completely.

"I'm scared, too, Faith. Both of us have learned things do not always go according to our little human plans. But we should have also both learned that life is short. Each breath is precious. We are offered gifts beyond what we can possibly believe we deserve. I want to see where this is taking us.

"I want to explore the physical world with you, but also the world of the heart. I feel we can show each other, and our chil-dren, the resilience of the human spirit. We can give them the gift of hope. Yes, bad things happen. Unimaginable things.

"But we pick ourselves up and go on. Not necessarily stron-ger, but deeper somehow. More compassionate. More in touch. More connected. Not less, not pulling back from the world, but going forward into it, saying a loud, impossible-to-miss *yes*.

"To all of it. The good and the bad."

There, in the circle of Brad's arms, Faith came home. To herself, to her heart, to a world that required the bravery, her daughter had seen, and she had doubted.

Until this very moment.

When he whispered, "Let's embrace our second chance. Let's jump into the abyss, hand in hand. I want you to marry me," she said the only word that was left in her.

"Yes."

EPILOGUE

CASSANDRA STOPPED IN the lobby and took a look around. So much to do, and so little time to do it in. Normally, she probably would have taken out her phone and made a few quick notes.

But the truth was, she was a little disoriented.

She had just met her father's girlfriend.

Soon to be more than his girlfriend, if the looks Brad and Faith had been exchanging had been any indication.

Dad had sent his company jet to get Faith specifically for them to meet. The meeting had been so touchingly important to him.

Cassandra had thought it might be awkward to meet Faith. The truth? She was just a tiny bit miffed that her dad had managed his own romance without a single bit of input from her.

From the anecdotes around the table tonight, it sounded as if her dad had not only done it without her, but had also absolutely dazzled his new love.

Well, not really his new love. His old love. His high-school sweetheart.

It had been apparent to Cassandra almost as soon as her dad had taken her for that walk around the lake and told her about Faith, that some sort of destiny was at play here. It was powerful that fate had brought them together on the lake, coupled with the odd fact that the dog she had rescued had born the same name as Faith's late husband.

But now, seeing them together, it was so much more than that. Her father and Faith *fit* in some remarkable way.

Even if Faith had not passed her the cookie recipe, she would have recognized her as the woman baking cookies in Wolf's Song. She didn't even want to think of what they had been doing together in there, besides baking cookies!

Still, she could not have conjured someone better for her dad.

Faith radiated a kind of wholesome goodness. She was the type who made cookies, and she had mentioned she was making a donkey costume for one of her granddaughter's Christmas plays. How adorable was that?

There was a sense of family and sturdy values around Faith, and Cassandra found herself loving the fact that Faith made it so apparent she was going to be welcomed into that thing, as an only child, she had always missed. A brother, a sister, nieces!

A sense of home.

But along with that wholesomeness, that sense of family, there was a kind of quiet strength about Faith. It was the strength of someone who had known suffering and loss as surely as Cassandra and her father had, and decided it was worth it to love again, even if it hurt.

This was the part Cassandra didn't really like: the looks that had flashed between Faith and her dad, the way their hands had intertwined, and their shoulders touched, had filled her with the strangest sensation.

Added to that was how alive her dad had looked. Cassandra wouldn't have even guessed something was missing from his life, until she saw how different he was now that it was there.

It. Love, of course, so evident, shimmering in the air between Faith and Brad like fresh snowflakes twinkling silver in moonlight.

And that strange sensation it had made her feel?

She didn't even want to admit what it was.

Not with Rayce Ryan, her own high-school crush, about to arrive here as their newest ski instructor.

It wasn't quite the same. She hadn't been his sweetheart. Ha. She hadn't even been on his radar. And yet, being near him, catching a glimpse of him in a hallway, had always made her heart race and her color deepen embarrassingly.

And then that one night, their final dance ever, as high-school students, it felt as if he had awakened to her.

Seen her.

And for one astonishing moment in time, she had felt as alive as her dad had looked tonight.

And then Rayce Ryan had wanted to kiss her.

And she had run away!

And, of course, in the years that followed, like everyone else in Whistler, she had followed his racing career with avid interest.

But had anyone else experienced that frightening sense of longing that she had nursed ever since she had run away from his kiss?

Had anyone else wanted to coax the tenderness from that devil-may-care man who had challenged the rules of the universe—and gravity—until he had lost?

Impatiently, Cassandra shook off the residue of yearning that seemed to be clinging to her in the face of her father and Faith providing evidence of happily-ever-afters.

Of course, other people had entertained those thoughts about Rayce! He was gorgeous, he was a celebrity, he was a world-class athlete. He'd probably had women, prone to romantic fantasy, throwing themselves at him for close to a decade. Certainly, he had been the heartthrob of at least half the girls in high school, and maybe more!

Cassandra might have secretly indulged the childish notion of endless love when she was young and naive. But she was not that anymore.

She had a million things to do.

A million.

So why was she going back to her place, to look again at all those clippings of Rayce Ryan's career?

Just one more time.

She was just doing her due diligence on the new employee, she told herself, nothing more. Before she put them away.

And before Rayce arrived. A man like that—with all that energy, who had no patience with rules or the laws of order, who was endlessly and effortlessly charming—could turn a world upside down in one blink.

If you let him.

And Cassandra Daniels was not going to let him, not any more than she had let him kiss her all those years ago!

* * * * *

Their Midnight Mistletoe Kiss

Michele Renae

Michele Renae is the pseudonym for award-winning author Michele Hauf. She has published over ninety novels in historical, paranormal and contemporary romance and fantasy, as well as written action/adventure as Alex Archer. Instead of "writing what she knows," she prefers to write "what she would love to know and do" (and yes, that includes being a jewel thief and/or a brain surgeon).

You can email Michele at toastfaery@gmail.com.
Instagram: @MicheleHauf
Pinterest: @toastfaery

Books by Michele Renae

If the Fairy Tale Fits...

Cinderella's Billion-Dollar Invitation

Cinderella's Second Chance in Paris
The CEO and the Single Dad
Parisian Escape with the Billionaire
Consequence of Their Parisian Night
Two Week Temptation in Paradise

Visit the Author Profile page
at millsandboon.com.au.

Dear Reader,

This was a fun story to write! And what made it even more enjoyable was working with Cara Colter to create the Daniels family and the Cobalt Lake Resort. Cara, who hails from British Columbia, gets all the credit for her knowledge on Whistler and skiing; I've never skied, but having lived in Minnesota all my life, I figure I got the winter stuff right.

This is the first Christmas story I've written for Harlequin, and I simply had to incorporate some of my holiday favorites. I always put a part of myself into my stories, but I'll never reveal those personal touches!

This A White Christmas in Whistler duet starts with Cara's story, which features a billionaire dad, a widower who gets a second chance to romance his high school sweetheart. To continue with the high school theme, I've matched a wounded Olympic athlete with his unrequited high school crush.

Here's to a happy holiday filled with warm and wondrous family love!

Michele

To everyone who has tasted snowflakes and
engaged in snowball fights filled with laughter.
And if you haven't—what are you waiting for?

CHAPTER ONE

CASSANDRA DANIELS SNAPPED photographs of the massive floral display in the Cobalt Lake Resort lobby. It had been delivered an hour earlier and it had taken two delivery men to carry in the heavy vase overflowing with white and red poinsettia, deep red roses, sprays of glittered baby's breath, and sprigs of wispy greens. A plush red velvet ribbon wove in and around the bouquet.

"Marvelous." She studied the few shots and then color-adjusted her favorite to post on the resort's social media feed. "Mom would be pleased."

In fact, her mother, Cynthia Daniels, would only employ her approving "marvelous" when something was worthy of praise. Be it decorations around the resort, a chef's special dinner or even the sound of boots crunching fresh-fallen snow on a peaceful Christmas morning.

With a heavy sigh, Cassandra's shoulders dropped. It had been two years since her mother's death. An avalanche while she was out skiing had taken her from this world much too early. Grief still teased at Cassandra and seemed to attack at the most unexpected moments. Tears in front of the guests? Never. She could hold them back until she retreated to her apartment. Yet the invisible emotional tears in her heart seemed never-ending.

Christmas had been her mom's favorite season. As the re-sort manager, Cynthia Daniels had taken seriously the task of decorating for Christmas. Each year she employed a crew of temporary workers for a week to make it all come together. From the guest rooms to the lobby, the spa, the exterior and all through the outer areas, including the cozy wooden walkway that curled around the lake. Not a patch of property remained untouched by the festive spirit.

Last year Cassandra hadn't been able to summon the spirit necessary to put up more than some interior garlands and rib-bons. Her heart had felt the lack of her mother's presence in those missing decorations. This year she was determined to pull herself up from the grief, rediscover her own joy and create a Christmas that would make her mother declare, "Marvelous."

The outdoor decorating had been completed by a local crew. The trees were kept strung with lights throughout the year, as well as the lake walk. Inside the resort everything sparkled, glimmered and danced with sugarplums, tidy presents, tiny snowmen and snow-sprinkled figurines, poinsettias, holly and the requisite mistletoe. The spicy aroma of cinnamon and nut-meg greeted guests in the lobby. Each guest room was subtly touched with Christmas. And the last of the ornaments were currently being placed on the twenty-eight-foot blue spruce that greeted guests as they entered the lobby.

Cassandra heard someone call her name. One of the night maids had begged to help with decorations because *Christmas was her jam*, and she'd stayed on this morning to help.

"It's finished," Kay announced with a gleeful clap and a Vanna White–like splay of her hand toward the massive tree.

"It looks amazing," Cassandra enthused.

She strolled toward the tree, her eyes moving up, down and around to take it in. She'd given exact instructions on how the decorations should be hung. The ribbons strung evenly, yet art-fully. Tinsel used sparely. No two similar ornaments close to-gether. The red glass ornaments hung equal distances apart...

Yes, she was aware of her need for perfection. But Cassandra never asked for more than was possible. And if she did notice something out of place she'd never call out an employee for what wasn't a mistake but rather a misplacement. Her dad had once let her in on the backroom talk that the employees thought she could be demanding but they didn't mind because she countered it with kindness and respect.

Kindness was never difficult. It should be a person's normal mode; that's what her mom had taught her. And if you put out a warm welcoming vibe, it would return to you in greater amounts.

With a touch to a handblown glass sleigh that she remembered her dad giving her a few Christmases earlier, she then trailed her fingers over the shimmery silver tinsel. Astringent pine filled her nostrils. The ever-present scent of burning cedar emanated from the fireplace opposite the tree. Nearby a trio of peppermint candles sweetened the air. Cap that with the cinnamon sticks hung here and there within the pine boughs. The delicious perfume epitomized Christmas.

Cassandra stood back, hands on her hips. The tree looked Instagram-worthy. More photos were necessary! Could this mean she was almost finished with decorating? Save a few smaller tasks she had on her list—

"Wait." Her eyes darted over the tree hung with ornaments the Daniels family had collected over the twenty-eight years her parents had been married. She didn't see it. The one ornament she'd requested Kay take special care in hanging front and center. "Kay?"

"Yes, Miss Daniels?"

She loved Kay like an aunt who tended to smile at her and then sneak up close to tuck in a stray tag or remove a bit of lint from her sweater. Just as fussy about some things as Cassandra could be.

"Where is the ornament I told you about? It was my mom's favorite ornament. I made it for her when I was eight."

"I didn't see the ornament you described. A wood star?"

"Yes, a star made from twigs I collected in the forest. I glued them together. In the center was a photo of me and my mom. It gets front and center placement every year. It had to have been with the other ornaments. Did you check?"

"The bins are over there." Kay pointed to a rolling cart stacked neatly with clear plastic storage bins. All of them empty. "The boys brought in all the bins labeled for Christmas yesterday evening. Should I send them back to the storage room to check for more?"

"Of course. Or no, I'll do it." They'd done their part. Besides, she was the best person to recognize the missing item.

"This is not right. It's… It can't be Christmas," she said, her voice wavering. The courage she'd summoned to step away from the grief over the loss of her mother began to falter. Her stomach clenched. "Not without that ornament."

She noticed someone near the wall behind the tree bend down. "No!"

The employee who held the light switch box connected to the tree froze, half bent over. He flicked Cassandra a wondering look.

"No light! Not until it's perfect," she said, a bit too loudly. She sucked in her lower lip.

"But shouldn't we check to see that they work?" the startled man asked of her.

Cassandra shook her head adamantly. "Not until the ornament is in place. I'll look for it. You can clean up and return the bins to the storage room. But no one turns on the lights until you get the go-ahead from me. Understand?"

The half dozen employees standing around muttered their agreement.

Cassandra gave her sweater hem a commanding tug and nodded. Christmas simply would not happen until that ornament held the place of honor on the tree.

* * *

Someone seemed very agitated about a missing ornament.

Rayce Ryan observed the commotion in the resort lobby. No one had seen him enter, though that was by choice, given he purposely stood near a frothy display of pine, ribbons and sparkly snowflakes; Christmas camouflage. The entire three-story open lobby was decorated to the nines with red, green, sparkles, snowflakes, wreathes—it even smelled like Christmas.

It had been a long time since he'd celebrated Christmas with family. Memories of cozy flannel pajamas, hot chocolates by the fire and opening presents leaped to his mind and gave him a rare genuine smile. He'd had a great childhood. But when he hit his teen years, life had changed in so many ways. Most of it good. The worst of it? He'd lost the only family he'd ever known.

Might he dream to someday have family again? And along with that, a real home?

Some dreams were impossible. Besides, he'd once had the sweet life. A guy had no right to complain. Even as broken as he was. Rayce had begun to make a new life for himself. To perhaps capture a bit of that sweet life again. And it started here at Cobalt Lake Resort.

Rayce veered his attention back to the lobby. Something wasn't right. And it seemed to circle around the petite blonde wearing a white sweater and slacks. Her hair was silver-white as well. Visions of sugar pixies danced in his head. Er, no, it was plums or snow princesses—he always got his song lyrics confused.

With a swelling of his heart, he suddenly recognized the pale beauty. It had been years since he'd last seen her, but he'd thought of her often in the interim. That she seemed upset by a missing ornament didn't surprise him. She'd always been— what did they call it—type A? Or more appropriately *driven*, as he'd once labeled her.

"Driven and unobtainable," he muttered.

Another grin stretched his travel-weary jaw. His flight

from Florida had been delayed, turbulent, noisy—two crying babies—and alcohol-free. It was mid-afternoon and he was ready for a nap. Or a beer. Probably both. As an Alpine ski racer, he'd once thrived on six hours of sleep and eighteen hours of training, skiing and partying. Now? Life had decided to shove him on his face. Hard. And he was still recovering.

After the snow princess commanded to those standing around the Christmas tree that there was to be no light, she then grabbed a clipboard and turned to look right at him. The recognition on her face was a mix of surprise, curiosity and… disappointment?

A look with which Rayce had become all too familiar. Had *everyone* watched his colossal crash when he'd lost an edge at top speed on the giant slalom at last year's winter Olympics? Well, if they hadn't, they'd likely seen memes of it on social media. His most immense failure endlessly repeated and looped, and even set to farcical music. All because he'd been betrayed by a woman he loved.

Stupid heart.

No, he couldn't be reading the snow princess's expression right. She was involved in taking care of business. Ever busy. Always on the go. Always out of reach.

He waved. She had to know he was due to arrive today. He'd dealt with her dad, Brad Daniels, throughout the hiring process. The man had picked him up from the airport. They had chatted about their hopes for good ski conditions and that Rayce would have to establish his own teaching schedule. Brad had dropped him off with apologies because he'd had to return to town to pick up some parts for one of their snow machines.

Left to himself to figure things out? Not an issue. Rayce was a self-starter and could pick up anything on the fly. This should be an easy gig. Thanks to far too many years of training, he was disciplined as hell. But while his body was in the program no matter the challenges presented, it was his heart that usually ended up bringing him down.

Thus, his reason for standing here in the Cobalt Lake Resort. He'd been hired for the season as their guest ski instructor. Like it or not.

He hadn't decided if he did like it or not. The experience would reacclimate him to the slopes. And, with hope, allow him to start over. To figure out his next step. To…be a normal person for once in his life. Not some guy who had devoted over fifteen years of his life to training, competing, media appearances and giving 200 percent, including blood and sweat. And most of those years without family to keep him grounded and remind him that he was loved.

Rayce missed his grandparents. Was there anyone out there who could show him the immense love and kindness Roger and Elaine Ryan had? If there was, he desperately wanted to swerve in their direction.

With a nod toward Cassandra, he grabbed his suitcase and rolled it toward her, even as she started walking away from him while gesturing that he follow. He remembered her well. They'd attended the same high school in Whistler. He'd been a jock; she'd been all brains and academic achievement. She had been The One He Could Never Have.

He knew because he'd tried. And failed.

But did that mean he had to give up on the dream? No, Rayce Ryan never gave up—until the task injured him so badly he had no choice but to bow out.

Cassandra looked as beautiful as ever. Probably even prettier because she'd done something with her hair; it was snow-white instead of the sunny blonde she'd once been. Her mouth was soft pink. And the sway of her hair with each of her strides, the way it dusted her elbows…

Rayce knew his heartbeats weren't skipping from exertion right now.

"Rayce Ryan!" She paused and turned to shake his hand. "Dad must have just dropped you off?"

"He did, with instructions to take the place in and get comfortable. I know the slopes. I did spend every winter here my entire childhood."

"Right. How many times did my dad have to send out security to rein you in after midnight?"

"Too many to count." He chuckled. "You can't keep a ski bum off the powder."

"No, you can't. But I think you should claim professional over bum."

"Eh. I'll always be a bum, living for the fresh pow and carving my line through the corduroy."

She smiled but caught her mirth quickly and adjusted her mouth to a tight line. "We've set up security cameras now. Just a warning if you have any midnight black runs planned. It's for the safety of our guests. Is that your only baggage?"

"I left my skis and equipment in the side entry where your dad let me off."

"Perfect. You can claim an employee locker later; that should fit most of your gear. If you'll walk with me." She strolled past the reception desk and down a long hallway. What a sensual sway to those slender hips. The woman was obviously a skier. She knew how to move. "I'm a bit busy right now," she called over her shoulder.

Her wavy hair bounced, enticing him to catch up and consider touching it. Admiration from a distance had been about all he'd managed with Cassandra Daniels. Yet seeing her again after nearly ten years did inspire him to wonder if he could broach that distance. Walk alongside those swaying hips that reminded him of a skier's schuss down the slopes.

"I'll get you to your cabin and leave you to take the place in on your own," she continued. "You're familiar with the layout of the resort. Not much has changed since our teen days, though we did add another lift and the outdoor amenities have doubled. Do you have a schedule prepared for next week?"

"Not yet. Your dad said I could take a few days to familiarize myself with the slopes and figure out my schedule for private lessons."

The look she cast over her shoulder judged him nine ways up and down. Rayce was used to that look. From everyone. Often it was accompanied by expectation. Everyone demanded so much from an Olympic athlete.

And he had let everyone down.

With an assessing nod, she finally said, "In a few days I'll touch base with you and get your schedule entered into the database."

Cassandra pushed open an outer door and barely broke stride as she took off down a heated sidewalk that curved around the backside of a high snow-frosted hedgerow. It was only ten degrees today, but she didn't flinch from the chill. Rayce, on the other hand, had grown accustomed to the Florida weather over the past year he'd spent in recovery. Jet Skiing and scuba diving warmed a man's soul in ways a frigid Canadian winter never could.

"This is the employee route," she said over a shoulder. "You're welcome to walk through the guest area, but it's quicker and more efficient this way."

"I suspect efficiency is your superpower."

Another judging glance. Or was it curiosity this time?

The woman had changed little since high school. Still pretty, still put together when it came to clothing and makeup. Still holding her head a level above all others. Because she was smart, or because she felt entitled? Had to be the smarts. The Daniels family had owned this resort since he could remember and held a trusted place in the Whistler community.

As Rayce followed her sure stride, he couldn't resist wondering if he might wiggle under her skin, nudge the snow princess off her throne to see if there was a warm, caring individual underneath the stoicism.

What the heck, man? His heart was interfering far too early. *Keep your eyes off her hips.*

"I mean," he corrected his comment about her superpower, "from what I remember about our high school days. You were driven."

"And you were a star." She marched up half a dozen wood steps to a small cabin capped with an A-frame roof and a frosting of pristine snow. She tapped a digital code into the box by the door. "Here's your new home away from home. The code is 5489. That's your code for all entries around the resort. It's written down in the welcome materials inside."

A home away from home? Rayce hadn't labeled a domicile *home* in—it had been since he'd left his grandparents' house to travel the racing circuit. Since then, hotels, airports and the occasional couch had served as shelter. This cabin was merely another place to sleep and eat while life tried its hand at him.

Cassandra pulled open the door and he walked up. Before crossing the threshold, he stopped and when he tried to meet her gaze, she suddenly seemed nervous, avoiding eye contact and pushing her hair over one ear.

"Are you…okay with me working here?" he asked.

Her pale blue eyes darted between his, speculating, perhaps even making decisions that only the female species made; things he could never comprehend. Her soft pink lips parted in wonder. "Whyever wouldn't I be?"

He shrugged. Because he recalled her walking away from him once. It had been ten years ago. They had been teenagers. Surrounded by friends and anyone who mattered in their lives. Oddly, that moment still hurt his heart. Rejection proved a more brutal wound than failure could ever inflict.

"The Cobalt Lake Resort is excited to feature Rayce Ryan as our exclusive ski professional this season," she said, or rather recited like some kind of marketing promotion.

"But what about you?" he tried. "Are you…excited?"

"I… I'm pleased you're here?"

"Are you asking me or telling yourself?"

"I don't understand the question." She checked her watch.

"I really hate to leave you, but I need to get back to the task at hand."

"Something about an ornament?" That didn't sound so pressing, but what did he know?

"Exactly."

She offered her hand to shake, which he did. Despite the frigid temperature, her skin was warm, and it allowed him a few more seconds to stand in her atmosphere. Take in her beauty. And wonder about the thoughts that were bouncing around inside her head. What did she think of him? Dumb jock? Handsome not-so-strange stranger? Just another employee? Failed Olympian?

Her phone rang and she checked the screen.

"That's my dad. I'll catch up with you later, Mr. Ryan. You have free run of the resort. But do alert security to get an employee badge before you head off to a slope. The GPS in the badge constantly pings the security office, so if there's ever an accident…"

"Will do."

And then she was off, as quickly and efficiently as was possible, the phone pressed to her ear as she chatted with her dad. The moment was so—

Déjà vu struck Rayce with stunning precision. She'd run away from him during the high school dance. After he'd bent to kiss her. In that one precious moment when the world had stopped and his heart had leaped for the stars.

And he had fallen.

Running his fingers through his hair, he watched until Cassandra disappeared beyond the hedges.

"She's going to disturb your heart again, dude."

Or maybe, she'd never stopped.

CHAPTER TWO

"I KNOW, but that ornament means so much to me," Cassandra said to her dad, who had called from the parts supplier in town to see if she needed him to pick up anything. She'd mentioned that the tree was almost ready to be lit. Almost.

"Cassie, the tree is the big welcome to the resort. We have to turn on the lights."

"Just let me find the ornament first. Please? It won't take long. Give me a few days to comb through the resort?"

His sigh reminded her that they'd been through a lot these past few years. He'd been there with an arm around her shoulder and a kiss to the top of her head whenever she'd felt her lower lip wobbling and the memory of her mother emerge. He had gone through the same grief but remarkably had recently been able to welcome his high school girlfriend, Faith, back into his life after thirty years apart. They'd just announced their engagement.

"I'll give you a week," he said. "But that's far too long to allow the tree to sit there dark."

"I promise I'll find it sooner." And now to change the subject… "Can you pick up some of those monster cinnamon rolls from the bakery for me? I know you're going to make a stop there."

"I do love those cinnamon rolls." Despite the Daniels family's love for health and fitness, they were a favorite treat. Who could resist that gooey, sweet cream cheese frosting? "Oh, did you run into Rayce Ryan?"

"Yes, I gave him a quick lay of the land and showed him to his cabin."

"Take care of him, Cassie. He's going to attract new business as our resident ski professional. And the guy's a looker, eh?"

"Oh, Dad, I think I hear a cinnamon roll calling for you. Talk to you later. Bye."

She clicked off and rolled her eyes. A looker? Why on earth would her dad imply she might find Rayce attractive? On the other hand, her dad did have a tendency to tease whenever she'd dated. He thought his jokes were much funnier than they really were.

Well. Rayce Ryan *was* all kinds of sexy.

She opened the back door used by employees and, starting toward the main areas, picked up her rounds that had been interrupted by the missing ornament debacle: ensuring all decorations were perfect.

It had been ten years since Cassandra had seen Rayce in person. Sure, she'd seen him on the news. The bar in the resort always had at least one of the TVs streaming the sports networks and especially focused on winter sports. Over the past decade, Rayce's face had been everywhere. The golden boy. The skiing wunderkind. The Olympic gold hopeful.

The man who fell.

On Rayce's first trip down the giant slalom at the Olympics last year, something had distracted him and he'd crashed. Hard. The viewing public had watched as he'd been carted off on a stretcher, only to surface a few days later to announce that his injuries had been devastating. He may ski again, but never professionally.

Cassandra recalled how her heart had dropped as she'd watched that interview. Tears had even rolled down her cheeks.

To have trained and worked so hard for something and then to have it torn away in literal seconds. It had to have destroyed Rayce in ways she couldn't even imagine.

When her dad had suggested they hire Rayce as their seasonal ski professional, she'd thought it an interesting idea, but hadn't believed it would come to fruition. Was he even ski-ready? Did he want to continue in the sport? Even if only as an instructor? And really, would taking a teaching job fulfill him in the manner that Alpine ski racing had? It could only be a step down for the man who'd once reigned as a local sports hero, and she didn't have to wonder how occupying that lower step might affect his ego. *Cocky*, *charming* and *confident* were the keywords the media often used to label him.

As well, she hadn't said anything to her dad about Rayce having been The Boy She Could Never Have. All through high school she'd been entranced by him. Every girl with eyes and a gushy swooning heart had been captivated by his charming manner. He'd been a jock, a confident cute guy who knew all the girls wanted him and who had used that to his advantage. Rayce must have dated half her senior class at Whistler Secondary.

But he'd never given Cassandra a glance.

Until the Last Dance the night before graduation. When Rayce had walked across the gymnasium floor and asked her to dance, her friend Beth had literally shoved Cassandra forward. She'd been too stunned, utterly at a loss for words. The Boy She Could Never Have wanted to dance with *her*? Following the momentum of that shove, she had moved across the dance floor under the dazzling disco ball as if under a spell. Dancing with the dreamy guy! Hand in hand! Face-to-face!

Yet when he'd bowed his head to kiss her, warning bells had clanged. And she had made a run for it.

Cassandra regretted not accepting that kiss. Because she had always wondered: *what if?*

And she still did. Could they have been a thing? Might the kiss have led to dating and something more? At the time, she hadn't been aware of his plans to move. Rayce had left Whistler right after graduation to devote his life to skiing and travel the Alpine ski racing circuit, so it could have never become serious. But if she were honest with herself, over the years she'd never chased away the fantasies of *what could have been*.

Are you excited I'm here?

Yes, she was. But she'd had the presence of mind not to feed his ego.

Shaking her head and smirking, she shook away her silly thoughts and redirected her attention to the decoration hung on the wall just outside the lobby. There were twelve identical arrangements of blue spruce wreath and red velvet ribbon nestled with green paper presents throughout the resort. This one needed a little nudge to the left...

"Hey!"

Cassandra startled at the deep male voice that, after her initial surprise, settled into her skin as if a welcome burst of sunshine warming the crest of an icy summit.

"Sorry, didn't mean to startle you." Rayce looked over the arrangement, his summer sky eyes bright with enthusiasm. He twisted one of the tiny presents to the left, then nodded. "Perfect."

Cassandra adjusted the present back to the correct position it had been in. "Did you find the cabin to your liking?"

"Yes. I appreciate that I can live on-site for this gig. It's cozy. And the tiny fridge will store my protein drinks and veggies." He tapped the present, tilting it off-center.

Cassandra moved the present again, and this time held her hand over it. "You have access to our chef and the cafeteria. All included in your salary. Feel free to use it anytime it's open." She swatted at his hand as he moved toward the present again. "Don't touch!"

He mocked affront and then chuckled. A laugh capable of making her lose her train of thought. "Did you find the ornament?"

Ornament? Uh… Don't think about his laugh!

"Not yet." And now she had a deadline thanks to her dad. "I'm headed to the supply room now to go over it with a fine-tooth comb."

He hooked his thumbs in his jeans' front pockets. "I'll go along with you."

"What?"

"I'm offering my services, fair lady. The wind has picked up so I'm putting off my survey of the slopes until tomorrow. And lame excuses aside, I'm whipped from today's travel. Two airports with long layovers and screaming babies. I'm good at finding stuff. I once found a snowboarder buried under four feet of snow in the middle of a blizzard."

Cassandra swallowed. The image of a body buried under snow arrested all thoughts about making things perfect, replacing it with a hard press against her heart.

The Whistler ski resorts had their occasional accidents. With the Pacific Ocean so close the weather was unpredictable. Blizzards and avalanches were a part of the deal. She'd grown up with a healthy understanding of safe skiing conditions and when to give Mother Nature a wide berth.

"Cassandra?" He bent to search her gaze.

She didn't want to explain how his casual mention of finding the buried snowboarder affected her. And she had promised herself she'd move beyond the grief this holiday season. Which couldn't begin without that ornament.

"Sure." She nodded. An inhale drew in courage. "I'll accept your offer to help. Come along with me."

"Any day, all the time," he sang as she sailed down the hallway and turned to take a stairway to the lower level where the storage room was located. "So how's life been treating you since high school, Cassandra?"

Descending a few metal stairs, they landed in the basement, and she flicked on the lights. The main room was neatly ordered with storage labels placed high on the walls to designate different sections. Her mother's doing. Everything was neat as a pin.

"Life is fine, as always," she responded. Fine. But not marvelous. Yet.

With a regretful wince, she veered toward the interior decorations. All the plastic bins that had held the Christmas decorations were placed back on the shelves. Some had a few items sitting inside—probably broken ornaments—so she pulled one down and opened the cover. "You?"

"Well, you know, took a little spill recently. Turned my life upside down. Now I'm trying to get back into fighting form."

Nothing but a cracked red glass ornament inside this one. She replaced the plastic bin and pulled down another next to one Rayce tugged out. "Fighting form? Do you intend to train again? For more competition?"

He'd only signed on as the resort's guest instructor for the season. And her dad had thought that perfect. See how he worked out. Then they could decide whether to extend Rayce's contract. Cassandra had thought his injuries had been so serious he wasn't able to ski competitively again. The media had reported he'd gone through numerous surgeries to repair broken bones, torn muscles, followed with intense rehabilitation. Though she noticed no outward signs of damage, no limp or painful movement.

"I'm always training," he said. "Docs tell me I'll never be able to achieve the level I was at, but when someone tells me no…"

She caught his wink. It lifted a gasp at the back of her throat. And something warm did a little spin in her core. The man wielded a useful charm with that wink. And he was very aware of it, she felt sure.

"This job is my introduction back to the slopes. A way for me to test my body, see if it's willing and able to fight back to competition form. I have to give it a go. Prove to myself that it's possible."

"It's good to know you have recovered."

"Recovery is a state of mind. Or so my physical therapist tells me." He rapped the cover of the container. "What am I looking for?"

Reining in the rise of desire his wink had summoned, Cassandra focused on the task. "Star-shaped ornament made from tree branches. It has a photo of me and my mom in it."

With a nod, he checked the bin, then placed it back on the shelf. There were dozens of the containers, which they methodically worked through.

"So you're the manager of the resort," he said as he worked. "I always knew you'd accomplish something great."

"You did?" Which meant…he'd thought about her achieving that greatness? Interesting. "You never gave me a glance in school. I find it hard to believe you had taken a moment to consider my future."

He turned his back to lean against the plastic containers and crossed his ankles. A soft gray sweater stretched across his noticeably hard pecs and abs. Once she'd stared at his blue eyes in a magazine spread and decided to call his iris color *caught* because any woman who peered into his summery blues long enough would surely be so.

Rein it in, Cassandra!

"I thought about you a lot, Cassandra. Watched you, too."

"Seriously? Sounds a little creepy to me."

But really? He'd watched her? No. Impossible. It had been her who had slid the sly glances his way as they'd passed in the hallways, or who had always taken the route from math class to science by the gymnasium so she could peer through the glass doors and catch a glimpse of him spiking a volleyball or netting a basketball. He'd played all sports when not training for the slopes.

"Not like stalker watching you," he said. "But every time you passed me in the hall? I gave myself whiplash."

She laughed, then caught herself. How to handle such a revelation? Of course, it meant nothing now. If only she had known ten years ago that they'd been secretly exchanging glances. Might her fantasies have come to fruition?

"You don't believe me?" He reached for the highest bin, which was filled with ornaments, and set it down for her. He bent beside it and watched as she sorted through the damaged and faded pieces.

With his proximity, she inhaled. He smelled subtly of cedar, but more so of pine and an icy winter day. Which was about the best scent ever.

"You're hard to not notice, Cassandra. You were smart. Pretty. Still are. But your hair has changed, and I like it. Very snow princess."

She paused in her sorting. After high school she'd decided to brighten her natural blonde hair, and now she regularly went to the salon to touch up the few places where some strands of gold fought to be seen. She liked the platinum look. It suited her. Snow princess? She'd never thought of it like that, but she did have some repressed need to *let it go*.

Or at the very least, get on with life and stop allowing memories of her mom to bring her down. This Christmas would be filled with joy and happiness. If it killed her.

"What'd I say?" He tilted his head wonderingly.

The man's blue irises were edged with black. Stunningly sexy. Add to that his stubble and messily cropped hair that looked as if Christmas elves had run wild through it, and he was everything and more. There was a reason why all the sports magazines had featured him on their covers. Why major sports products had paid him millions in sponsorships. And one of the largest cologne manufacturers had tagged him to hock their product. Women melted when Rayce Ryan looked at them.

Cassandra was not immune to such melting. Every part of her felt warm and loose. *Caught*. If he were to lean closer…

"I think I've lost you." He thunked her forehead with a finger. "You in there, Snow Princess?"

The rude touch prompted her to lean away. "Don't do that. I was just thinking."

"Yeah? I know, you're thinking about that night we danced, aren't you?" His voice lowered to a husky baritone, which teased at her inhibitions. "I still think about that dance once in a while, too."

So did she. And yet. She was an independent, capable woman, and certainly not prone to romantic delusions. "Why? That was ten years ago. We were in high school. We've grown up now, Rayce. We've moved on. We've..."

So why was she making a big issue about him asking now? Did she still have a thing for Rayce Ryan?

Of course you do, and don't deny it!

And they were not delusions. Romance was...something she hadn't taken time for in years. And she felt the ache of that lacking connection and emotion as strongly as she grieved for her mother. Though certainly she didn't have the time or heart space for a romantic liaison right now.

"I wish I'd had the courage to ask you out," he said. "But you occupied an echelon I could never manage to reach no matter how high I jumped." He shrugged. "Guess it served me right that you wouldn't kiss me."

A delicate glass ornament clinked against another and Cassandra shoved the container aside, standing. She'd analyzed that unclaimed kiss in the days following the dance.

"I couldn't kiss you," she explained. "Did you expect I'd put on a show for the whole class? We were standing in the middle of the dance floor. Everyone was watching. I..." She stepped away from the bin and wandered toward the door.

And really? He'd left town but days later. She would have been left with a kiss and dashed hopes for something more. She'd made the right decision. At the time. She did not live in the past and would not respond to the regret that rose with memory.

Before leaving, she said, "I wanted my first kiss to be special. I didn't think it meant anything to you at the time." She made a show of checking her watch. "I need to be somewhere. Meeting. I'll catch you later."

She fled. Just as she had fled the dance floor ten years ago. And it felt as silly and heart-wrenching now as it had then. She didn't want to run away from Rayce. She wanted to lean in closer. Inhale his subtle cologne. Savor his body heat. Feel his muscles meld against her body.

Kiss him.

Like she'd dreamed of doing for years.

Her reason for running away from his kiss had been because she'd wanted it to be special? To not be a performance before their entire class?

Standing atop a sunlit slope on his second day at the resort, Rayce's smile beamed brighter than the sun. If he'd understood Cassandra correctly, she *would* have kissed him if the conditions had been right. Which meant she hadn't fled his kiss because she hadn't liked him or because he'd somehow offended her. She had simply required the right moment.

Who would have thought? Since that night of the dance, Rayce had carried her rejection in the back of his heart, and it had often peeked out when at a party and he'd wanted to approach a woman. Would she like him? Would she want to kiss him? Or would she run away, leaving him standing there, the laughingstock of all those around?

Despite those anxieties, he had dated a handful of women over the years. But none of those entanglements had ever been so serious that his heart had relaxed enough to allow in contentment. Those women had been friends, lovers. A few weeks of excitement and fun between training camp and traveling from country to country. But dating seriously while he'd been on the racing circuit? Not easy. Except for that one time that had resulted in the ultimate betrayal.

Never date a team member, his coach had often advised. But had Rayce listened to that stern warning?

"Stupid heart," he muttered.

Now he was encouraged to learn that the rejection hadn't been because Cassandra hadn't liked him. Could he possibly find that moment with her once again? The perfect moment that would allow her to kiss him without an audience or the feeling of putting on a show.

He liked to make goals and exceed them. But this felt like more than a goal. It was…a quest! For a snow princess?

"Yes!" With a deciding nod, he pushed off down the slope.

His skis glided through the fresh powder. His plan this morning was to take things in, assess the runs he hadn't skied for years. There were hundreds spread across two mountains and various ski resorts. He'd take it slow and steady and focus on those closest to the Cobalt Lake Resort. He wasn't going to admit it to a soul, but a healthy fear made him cautious. One wrong move and the scarred muscles in his back would scream with pain. Not to mention his wonky leg.

The finest doctors had put him back together after his crash, but medical miracles weren't always possible. And while the surgery on his hip had been successful, the pain associated with the surgical scarring could quickly go from barely there to excruciating, shooting up and down his spine. It made him too cautious, fearful even, and that was never a good thing when racing down the slopes.

Rayce Ryan was broken. Yet admitting that to himself felt defeatist. Like giving up. Had the doctors been right? Would he never again achieve competition form? Was he really out of the game for good?

He knew those answers. But his heart was playing stubborn and didn't want to accept that his future may look exactly as it did right now. Playing the role of ski instructor at a swanky resort.

He'd not trained for more than half his life to teach others how to navigate the bunny hill, or even to give cocky young ski-racing wannabes tips on how to hold their balance and find the fall line. But here he was. Life had dropped the Cobalt Lake Resort in his lap.

Might he possibly put back together his broken pieces here? Teaching required he listen and give others suggestions and approval. Yet how to get that personal coaching for himself? Was there anyone left in this world to pat him on the back and offer him the reassurance and love he craved?

That he'd included love in his mad-making thoughts surprised him. Yet it was the truth. He'd been alone for the last year. Perhaps for much longer than that, when he considered that racing, while surrounded by millions of spectators, was an insular sport.

Rayce craved the emotional support he'd once received from his grandparents. And no, he'd never felt close enough to any of the women he'd dated to call it love. Rayce wanted a mixture of the approval and adulation racing had served him but with an even bigger portion of quiet acceptance. Maybe even respect.

And most certainly love.

Might he find that with Cassandra? She seemed to keep herself at a distance from him. There had even been a few moments when he thought she'd gotten lost in her thoughts—ah, shoot. He recalled his conversation with Brad on the way here. He had lost his wife, Cassandra's mom, two years ago in an avalanche. He'd mentioned Cassandra was still finding it hard to move forward, that grief was playing a real number on her.

And stupid Rayce had gone and said something about finding a person stuck in the snow after an avalanche.

"Idiot," he admonished himself.

Jabbing a ski pole into the snow, he shook his head. He might have already spoiled things with Cassandra, but that would never dissuade him from trying again and again.

CHAPTER THREE

THE NEXT DAY, while Cassandra waited for Kathy, the receptionist, to print up a copy of an invoice from a recent delivery, she adjusted the display of tiny resin snowmen featured at the check-in point. Five snowmen were seated around a fake fire warming their mittened stick hands. She couldn't remember if her mom had picked it up or it had been a gift from one of the guests. They were always receiving tokens and gifts from people who returned to Whistler year after year to spend their holidays here at the little boutique resort tucked between two larger establishments.

The Cobalt Lake Resort was a ski-in, ski-out that catered to an elite and moneyed clientele. They hosted many celebrity guests. Their security detail was top-notch, and Cassandra prided herself on the fact that not a single paparazzo had managed to invade their walls for a sneaky shot. They didn't close their doors to such individuals, but they did make it difficult to snag a room when certain high-profile celebrities were booked.

Rayce was considered a celebrity and she and her dad had discussed whether the hire would be wise. Certainly his presence would attract more guests, but for what reason? Merely to snap a shot with the famous skier? No, they'd decided Rayce would add another layer of polish to the resort's excellent reputation with his skills and easy charm. Fingers crossed, they would not be disappointed.

"What's up, Snow Princess?"

Cassandra jumped and one of the snowmen toppled. Was it the man's life purpose to sneak up on her?

"Must you do that?" she asked.

"I think I must. I like to shake things up. And you need to be shaken," he said with a huge helping of sly charm.

Shaken or caught in that beautiful blue gaze, she wondered. Feeling her jaw fall slack, Cassandra quickly noticed her swooning reaction and straightened.

Kathy, who stood over the printer, glanced over her shoulder at them. Cassandra did not miss the receptionist's bemused smile.

Rayce turned a snowman to face away from the fire. Cassandra turned it back to sit in line with his fellow snowmen.

"There's always one in the crowd that goes against the grain." He turned the snowman again. "Gotta have those sorts. They make life fun."

She curtly turned the snowman back. "Life requires a certain amount of order and..."

She almost said *control*. The need for order and perfection was naturally embedded in her DNA. Her mother had passed that gene on to her. And she would never *not* want to be like her mother.

"Talk to you later, Kathy," she said and resumed her morning route.

"I took a tour of the slopes." Rayce followed her through the lobby. The next stop was the spa to ensure they'd received the laundered towels and check that all the decorations were in perfect order. "Place looks great. You guys updated Lift Number Three. It's smooth. And a hot chocolate bar at the bottom of the Surf's Up run? Genius."

"We have three hot chocolate bars and a s'mores bar near the fireplace out on the patio. They are always busy."

"Your man, Eduardo, mixed me up a spicy cinnamon hot chocolate." He kissed his fingertips and followed with an, "Ahh…"

"You'll never get back to racing form if you indulge in those decadent treats."

"Eh. I'll work it off."

Out the corner of her eye she noticed him ease a palm down his thigh. The injured leg? She wanted to ask, but she also wanted to respect his privacy.

"I'm going to do a run-through of a private training session tomorrow," he said. "Work out my game plan before you unleash me on your guests."

"That sounds like a good idea."

"It does, right? But I need a guinea pig. Someone to role-play the guest. Can you spare anyone to fill the role of newbie for me?"

"I'm not sure. Tomorrow we're training some new serving staff. Most other positions will be running extended shifts as the holiday rushes in on us."

Rayce spun around in front of her and landed his palm against the spa door. His eyes slowly took her in from head to toe in a manner that touched every nerve ending she possessed. Tiny fires ignited at each point. For once Cassandra regretted that she always wore white. The warmth suffusing her skin— was she blushing?

"What about you?" he said with a waggle of his brow. A suggestive move. And not at all businesslike.

Must she draw a line about lusting after employees? The resort didn't have any fraternization rules. It seemed an unnecessary intrusion into a person's private life. But how to stop sexy thoughts of Rayce when his wink was engineered at a DNA level to make a woman blush?

"Me? Uh…" Surely there was an employee she could spare for a few hours?

"I know you're busy. You are always on the go," he added. "I was thinking of asking your dad. I probably should—"

"I'll do it." Her heart answered before her logical brain could stomp a foot down in protest. Because really? There was nothing whatsoever wrong with working with the man to ensure he had his game down right. The bonus would be that she'd have reassurance their instructor had been a worthy expense. "I can mark some free time into the afternoon."

"Awesome. Find me on the bunny hill tomorrow. You can play my newbie skier."

"I'll see you then."

"Not if I see you first." She caught his wink as he opened the spa door for her and gestured grandly that she enter. "On the slopes, Snow Princess. I can't wait."

The door closed behind her, and Cassandra stood there a moment in the steamy, humid atmosphere to register what had just happened. The man had seduced her into working with him. She wouldn't call it anything but. Trying to resist that sexy wink and his charming manner had been futile.

And yet. The practice session may be more than an employer assessing an employee. Especially if that wink were doing its job correctly. And yet…skiing. She hadn't been on skis since her mother's passing. And she wasn't sure she was ready for it yet. Would it seem rude if she canceled? No, she didn't want to cancel. And it wasn't as though it were a date. Just a friend helping a friend.

Oh, how she wanted to allow a man into her life. Thing was, she wasn't sure her heart was in the right place to handle romance when grief still managed to overwhelm her at the oddest of times.

Honestly? Cassandra Daniels was incapable of change.

On the other hand, spending more time with the exuberant and charming Rayce might inject a little joy into her life. And that was a necessity.

* * *

Cassandra lived in the family wing of the resort, whereas her dad lived in the family home in town. Occasionally she considered moving back into town, finding a nice cozy condo, but the job kept her busy and staying close to work was key.

Or that was the story she told herself. She was no busier than most resort managers really, and she could have managed time off and even a vacation if she'd wanted it. But without children of her own, or even a boyfriend, it had been easy enough to lose herself in the job. Owning a home equaled a settled heart to her. Only a dream.

Her top-floor apartment looked out over the tiny Cobalt Lake and consisted of a bedroom, a small kitchen, a living area with a balcony that she spent a lot of time on even in the winter months, thanks to the heater, and an office corner, where she now sat going over the day's to-do list. It was the morning of her practice lesson with Rayce. Concentrating on the list was difficult due to the nervous flutters in her stomach. Why had she agreed to a ski lesson? Of all things?

A quiet knock on the door was expected. And a welcome distraction from *other* distractions.

"Come in, Anita!"

The sous chef stopped in every morning at seven o'clock with a pot of thick creamy hot chocolate. Cassandra had never asked her to do so; it was simply a continuation of what Anita had done for her mother. After Cynthia's death, Anita had taken a few days off, then quietly returned to work. Cassandra still hadn't spoken to her about her mother's death. They knew they shared a mutual grief and that was enough.

"With a touch of peppermint today," Anita said as she set the tray beside Cassandra's elbow on her desk. They never chatted overmuch. In the mornings Anita was busy prepping the day's meals for hundreds of guests. She turned to leave, but at the door paused to say, "The surprise is not my fault."

With that, she quickly closed the door.

"Surprise?"

Cassandra twisted her mouth as she studied the tray. A white porcelain pot of hot chocolate and an upside-down cup. A serving of Chantilly cream always accompanied the drink, and a mint cake sat beside it on a small plate. That woman would fatten her up sooner rather than later with all her sugary offerings.

Turning the cup over Cassandra gave a start and almost dropped it but managed to catch the cool porcelain before it clinked against the plate. Sitting under the cup was a tiny resin snowman. The very snowman Rayce had wanted to turn against his fellow snowmen sitting around the fake fire.

"Seriously?"

Shaking her head, she plucked up the figurine. What did this mean? It had certainly come from Rayce. And the fact that he'd learned where, exactly, to place it, and who he needed to know to do so, must have taken some sleuthing.

Interesting. Did that mean he was pursuing her? Or just making fun?

Probably the latter. And yet he'd told her he'd noticed her in school. A lot.

Cassandra pressed the snowman against her heart. "I should have never run away from that kiss."

On the other hand she was a private person. Even as a teenager she'd had the sense to be cautious. Had she kissed Rayce Ryan on the dance floor in front of their classmates, surely the gossip would have blazed. And in those situations it never ended well for the girl. And then with him leaving a few days later?

She'd made the right choice. At the time. But might the opportunity for a kiss again present itself?

"I wouldn't run away if it did."

With a nod, she set the snowman on the tray. Pouring the hot chocolate, she then topped it with a plop of Chantilly cream. It was a recipe from a famous Parisian restaurant that the resort paid to use exclusively. It was literally the reason some guests stayed; for the rich soul-hugging hot chocolate.

With a sip of the thick sweet concoction, she closed her eyes and remembered the first time her mom had told her about the Paris she dreamed about visiting, and how someday they would visit together. They'd climb the stairs to the top of the Eiffel Tower, stroll through the city's many formal gardens and share a pot of hot chocolate, even if it was summer.

They'd never gotten a chance to go to Paris. Tickets had been purchased for a spring trip. The spring following that deadly winter two seasons ago.

With a sigh, Cassandra caught her chin in hand. She'd gifted those tickets to a friend and her new husband as a honeymoon trip because she hadn't been able to bear going alone or with anyone else. She was trying to honor her mother with the beautiful decorations this season, but every time she thought about Cynthia Daniels's bright smile and tendency to use the occasional French word because she thought it was chic her heart dropped.

"I miss you, Mom."

And no amount of decorations—no matter how perfect—would ever bring her back.

Her dad had fallen in love with Faith, his new fiancée, just a month ago. Brad Daniels was moving forward in life. And Faith had two children Cassandra's age. She was going to be a stepsister! And that felt exciting. Yet every so often, if she were honest with herself, she felt as though her dad were cheating on her mom.

Silly, really. Her mom and dad had been not so much a perfect couple as a perfect team. Yet Cassandra, being an astute twelve-year-old who learned a lot about relationships from social media—and who could add and figured out she had been conceived months *before* her parents' marriage—had asked her parents if they'd *had* to get married because of her. The explanation had been simple: on the same day as their engagement party they'd also found out they were pregnant. Best day ever! Since then Cassandra's life had been filled with love and happiness. Brad and Cynthia Daniels had shared twenty-eight years together. Happily.

Yet even knowing her mother for twenty-eight years, it had still been too short a time. How to move forward as her dad had? When Cassandra felt memories tugging at her, she tended to grow straighter, become more controlling. While her dad had tended to head out for a run to be by himself with his memories.

The stress of the past few years, of holding back her sadness, had begun to weigh on her. She'd exploded over a missing ornament. She should have never done that in front of the employees. And this silly little snowman didn't have to be facing a specific direction to look inviting and cute to the guests.

Always one that goes against the grain.

Like Rayce Ryan?

Yes, the man—an adrenaline junkie to the core—went against everything her heart agreed was safe. But why did she require safety? Why not enjoy a little fun with a guy who made her smile? It didn't have to become a relationship. She hadn't the room in her heart for that right now.

Cassandra sighed. "Not yet. But…"

Maybe sooner than she expected?

Rayce had joined Brad Daniels for an impromptu lunch. Meeting him as they'd turned to walk the same hallway, Daniels had invited him to try the new hot Cuban sandwich the chef had created. They currently stood in an alcove attached to the kitchen, which was stacked with cases of wine and a trolly loaded with fresh produce. The sandwich, spicy yet loaded with cool sweet slaw, had hit the spot.

"Ready to hit the slopes?" Brad asked.

"You bet. You've got some smooth runs. And the powder you're making on the Blackout run is nice and dry. Perfect conditions."

"How's it feel to get back out there?"

Rayce's back twinged but it wasn't from pain, rather expectation. He knew what Brad was implying. Are you capable? Am I paying for a wounded instructor who won't be able to give it 110 percent?

"I'm at ninety percent, Mr. Daniels. Honestly? I can't take the runs at top speed, and my balance sometimes goes out because..." The pain made him leery. No one was going to know that. And honestly? That 90 percent was closer to 80. "I've developed a workout routine. I'll be getting good use out of the weight room. I hope to live up to your expectations."

"Don't push too hard, Rayce. I don't have any expectations. Just give it what you've got and represent the resort with kindness and respect. The guests aren't expecting you to medal in their presence. Sharing your knowledge and demonstrating good skills is what they are looking for."

He fist-bumped Rayce, then nodded to the chef who had been lingering nearby for a few seconds.

"I have to give the chef my report on the sandwich. You good to go?"

"Thanks, I am. I've arranged a practice session later to work on my teaching skills."

"Sounds smart. I knew I hired the right man. Tell Cassandra I approve of the new menu item when you see her." He winked.

"I, uh, sure." How did he know Rayce was going to see her soon?

Before he could ask, Brad wandered into the kitchen and started chatting with the chef.

Rayce shrugged and made his way out the back of the kitchen and down a hallway that led him to an outer door. He stepped out into the crisp winter air. The sun was bright and after that conversation he felt weirdly bright himself.

The man didn't have expectations? Everyone had expectations of Rayce Ryan. He'd lived his entire life to achieve goals, meet expectations, then crush them all and soar beyond.

It felt unusual to hear someone say to just do what he could. Almost as if whatever effort he put in would be acceptable. And yet how to function without the approval of a job well done? A goal achieved? A time smashed by a tenth of a second?

This not-meeting-expectations was a new experience for Rayce. And navigating it was going to prove a challenge.

CHAPTER FOUR

IF A PICTURE were featured in the dictionary depicting *snow bunny*, then the vision walking toward Rayce would hold place on the page. Dressed in white snow pants and jacket, with a fuzzy pink hat topped by a big pink pom-pom, and spills of her snow-white hair falling out across her shoulders and back, Cassandra's pink lips drew his attention like a target. Each time he saw her, he felt like the high school jock who had zero chance with the smart girl all over again.

Of course Cassandra was hiding grief under that bright smile and carefree demeanor. During the interview, Brad had mentioned she hadn't hit the slopes since her mother had passed. That was crazy. But Rayce knew grief. It could level a person. He'd be cognizant of her feelings. But as well, he couldn't bear knowing she might never step into a pair of skis again. This could be good for both of them.

"I wasn't able to find an available employee," she said as she neared him, "so you're stuck with me."

She'd been trying to find a fill-in so she wouldn't have to work with him? Yikes.

"*Stuck* is the last word that comes to mind." He winced. Had he sounded too eager, too excited that he would get to spend time with her? Could she sense his growing warmth and the need to unzip his jacket—but he wouldn't do that, because what would he tell her? She was so beautiful. And she kept dashing her gaze from his like a gazelle dodging the hunter. Cute.

And yet she'd tried to find a replacement.

Chill, man. The woman isn't interested in you. Pay attention to your job.

"Feels like we're getting some snowfall soon," she commented. "Maybe it'll hold off until nightfall. I want the snow groomer to make a run over the slopes before then."

Rayce nodded in approval. "I do love a night storm. Especially when there's a full moon."

"Oh." Cassandra dropped her gaze and studied the snow. In fact he sensed from her body language she didn't want to be here right now. "Well, I don't think it'll be an all-out storm. Just some flakes."

Had he said something to upset her?

Keep it professional, idiot.

He did want to try out his instructing skills on a stand-in before the real thing happened, so he'd do his best to keep her smiling. "Should get enough to make guests happy campers come sunrise, eh?"

"Huh? Oh. Yes." She shook her head as if jogging something from her thoughts. "So. Here I am."

Oh, yes, she was. The one woman who seemed capable of throwing him off-balance with a mere look. Or a pause in her thoughts.

He had to focus.

"Okay, class!" He clapped his hands together, which lifted her chin, and earned him a small smile. Whew! "I understand you've never skied before, is that right?"

"Right," Cassandra answered astutely.

"Well then, we're going to spend a little time learning the basic maneuvers, ways to move and how to coordinate hands with feet before we even put on skis. It's all in the hips!"

He gave his hips a sway and that got a laugh from her, which made the pain that shot up his spine bearable. Just get through this, he coached inwardly. Don't let her see you fall.

"I knew you had a smile in there somewhere, Snow Princess. Show me your hip action. Let's go side to side and then in circles."

For the next twenty minutes he worked through basic motions that would allow someone new to the sport to get connected with their body and understand how certain movements would affect their placement on the snow. He kept it simple; if he sensed a skier was experienced, he would adjust his instructions accordingly.

Standing behind and near Cassandra was the best position to teach. And the occasional touch to her elbow to correct her arm position, or even to her shoulder to lower her line of balance thrilled him more than it probably should. It wasn't like he was touching her skin. But their intimacy teased at him. Her shiny hair beckoned for a nuzzle. And she smelled like flowers blooming under a crisp winter snow.

Keep it cool, he reminded. *Save the flirting for later, yeah? The quest for a kiss must be achieved.*

"Do you think that's helpful or a waste of time?" he asked when she laughed at another of his exaggerated hip swings.

"Very helpful. I see so many people stiffen up and try to prevent falls. If they were only taught the basics of body proprioception, they might not struggle so much. And we'd have less sprained wrist and ankle reports. Good call on the basics."

"That means a lot, coming from you."

"Oh, please, you're the Olympic athlete." She gave him a gentle punch to the bicep and he responded with mock outrage. "You know what you're doing."

"Sure, but I've never taught before. And was I kind? I distinctly recall your dad using that word. Be kind to the guests."

"You are a mix of kind and sensual—er, I mean…" She twisted her mouth. "You're a natural, Rayce."

Sensual, eh? That had slipped out before she'd caught herself.

Interesting. So maybe he was getting through to her in the manner he'd hoped for? Was it possible that her repeatedly asking him to readjust her stance with his hands to her hips had been not so much because she had no clue what to do, but rather because she'd wanted him to touch her?

"Good," he said around an inner grin of triumph. Wouldn't pay to get cocky while in practice mode.

Remain professional.

Was that even possible? "I hope my limp doesn't show too much. Wouldn't look good coming from someone who's supposed to be a master at the sport."

"I hadn't even noticed it!"

"Really?" Even if she had said that to be nice, it relieved a niggling self-conscious worry. "It only bugs me now and then."

"Will you tell me about the injuries you suffered? The press made it sound like you'd never walk again. Yet here you are, looking like you could do the giant slalom and the super G on the same day."

"On a good day? I might take that bet. On a not so good day, my entire left leg seizes up. I've got some pins and titanium rods here." He tapped his upper thigh. "And a plate that's still holding my femur together."

"Yikes. Can you feel all that hardware?"

"No, but I do get good Wi-Fi reception."

Her jaw dropped. Then she quirked a wondering brow.

"I'm teasing," he insisted. "But I had you fooled for a second there."

"Fair enough."

Man, she was gorgeous. And not like the ski bunnies he was used to hanging around and on him. There was something about Cassandra Daniels that set her apart from any woman he'd ever had eyes for. It went beyond her beauty. She was perceptive, listened and seemed genuinely interested in what he had to say. Yet she wouldn't agree with him for agreement's sake. The woman had a mind of her own and wasn't afraid to use it.

"Have you had physical therapy to help with the pain?" she asked. "What about medication?"

"Too much physical therapy. Spent a lot of time in a recovery unit. And then a rehabilitation house. I'm on my own now. Incorporating all that I've learned from physical therapy. I have some chronic pain from the hip surgery, which compromised my skeletal alignment. It's crazy. As for drugs, no way. I didn't want to take painkillers too long. So don't worry, I'll pass the resort's drug tests."

"We don't do that. And we wouldn't dream to do so. It's good to hear you're managing the injury. Just don't push it too hard. You've already shown the world what you are capable of."

"But did I?" Rayce stabbed the ski pole, which he'd been using to demonstrate balance, into the snow. "I crashed on my first jump out of the start house, Cassandra. That's hardly showing the world my stuff. It's a hell of a lot of failure if you ask me."

"Oh, come on, Rayce. Is that all you use to measure your success? How many World Cup Championships do you have?"

Two. And the World Cups were the sport's standard of excellence. Rayce had garnered the best and highest paying sponsorships from his World Cup wins. And by investing wisely, he had saved more than enough to live comfortably.

"The Olympics isn't the be-all and end-all," Cassandra said.

"Actually, it kind of is. If you can't medal in the big O, then you're nothing according to the media. Especially after your sponsors have invested so much in you. Millions, Cassandra. They certainly didn't get their money's worth from me."

"I guess I know that the energy drink dropped you."

"And the sportswear line. And the ski-gear line. And the protein drink that was going to be modeled after my own recipe."

"Yikes. I didn't know about those others. That's gotta be…"

"A mean slap in the face."

She sighed and nodded. "But you're not a failure, Rayce.

Failing is not getting back up and moving forward. Failing is lying there and accepting it."

Her words sounded good. In theory. But. "Failure is not winning."

"Winning is everything?"

He blew out a breath. "Yes."

Winning used to be everything. But was it still? Of course it was.

And yet he knew that ultimate win was now out of his grasp. Much as he wanted to fool himself with training and therapy, the pain reminded him every morning that he could never go back to what he once had. No more World Cups. No more Olympics. He. Was. Broken.

"Whatever." He gestured dismissively. "I'll never come to terms with it. And I'll always pursue the next approving pat on the back. There's nothing anyone can say to change that. So!" He clapped his gloved hands together. "How about we strap on the skis and try the bunny hill?"

"Sure, but... Rayce, this probably doesn't mean much..." She lifted her eyes to meet his and he swallowed awkwardly. A certain truth glinted in her blue irises. It felt real, and familiar. *Comfortable*. "Whether or not you believe it, you have accomplished so much more than the average person. You don't need to prove anything to me, or my dad. We hired you—"

"Because everyone wants to train with Rayce Ryan. Don't deny it. And I get it. I am taking the paycheck."

"It's not all like that."

"But some of it is, right?"

She shrugged. His mood had soured since the conversation had switched to a focus on his weaknesses. And he didn't like to show that side to anyone, especially not a woman he was interested in.

And yet her father had said much the same. That Rayce didn't need to prove himself to him. He still didn't know how to process that declaration. But he'd have to learn if he wanted to glide toward the future instead of laying sprawled on the snow in the past.

"Skis," he said and handed her a pair.

He clicked into his own skis and waited as Cassandra set hers on the ground and took position with her boots placed on either side of them, ski poles in hand. She stared down at the skis for such a long time he wondered what she was thinking about. And then he knew. This was a test for her. Brad Daniels had said his daughter hadn't put on skis since her mother's death.

Due to an avalanche.

Was it too soon? Had his invitation been thoughtless?

"I can't do this." With a sudden jerk of the poles, she stabbed them into the ground and stepped away from the skis. "I'm sorry. I…just can't."

She turned and walked off, her pace quickening to a jog.

Every bone in Rayce's body wanted to rush after her, but he'd felt something in her tone. A deep sadness. Tinged with fear. He knew that tone and that feeling. Man, did he know fear. He'd lost a part of himself during that Olympics' crash. He knew she had suffered a huge loss as well. It wasn't simply the lost ornament that was keeping her pinned to her grief; it was the memories of her mother, too.

He should go after her, make sure everything was okay. But the sadness in her voice reminded him so much of his own pain. A pain that had been with him far longer than since the accident. There were days he could barely deal with it himself. How could he help anyone else when he couldn't help himself?

Turning and stabbing his poles into the snow, he debated taking a run on the bunny hill. His leg didn't bother him today. Navigating the beginner hill would be like talking in his sleep: a no-brainer.

But.

Something compelled him to swing a look in the direction Cassandra had fled. Gathering the skis and poles, he put them away in the equipment shed, then went in search of Cassandra.

CHAPTER FIVE

THIRTY MINUTES AFTER she had fled the practice session with Rayce, Cassandra heard a quiet knock on her apartment door.

She swore softly and tugged the thick chenille blanket tighter about her shoulders. As soon as she'd gotten to her apartment, she'd kicked off her boots, shed her winter wear and plunged onto the couch. The tears that had been but a trickle had exploded and she'd engaged in a good sob session.

Now she sniffed softly and lifted her head to stare out at the sun falling behind the mountain. Her entire life had revolved around those mountains and the ski-bunny lifestyle. It had given her the greatest joy.

And it had devastated her family.

"Cassandra, I'm coming in," Rayce announced as he opened the unlocked door. He spied her sitting before the balcony doors. "No, don't get up. Is it all right that I'm here?"

Was it? She hadn't expected him to let himself in but asking him to leave felt rude. "Sure."

She nuzzled her chin into the blanket. No time to worry if she had red eyes or looked a mess. The man of her dreams carefully approached in the dimly lit room. Less than an hour and it would be completely dark outside. Still, the pale light seemed to outline his rugged jaw and even glint in one eye, softening him.

"I was worried about you," he said. He glanced around the room.

Everything was neat and in order. As it should be. All was well. Except her heart. Her grieving heart.

"Is it okay if I sit with you?"

Yes. No! She wasn't sure what she wanted right now. She'd never been one to share her emotions with others. And the only times she had, had been with her mom when they'd chatted over a hot chocolate. The Daniels family was not emotionally demonstrative.

But with Rayce's expression bordering on worried, she couldn't allow him to suffer.

She patted the couch beside her. "I'm sorry, I had a weird moment out there. Had to get away. I didn't want you to see me break down. And yet…" She shrugged and splayed her palms up in defeat. "Here you go. Cassandra Daniels. Undone."

"I'm sorry. I, uh… Your dad mentioned your mom's death during the interview. He also said you hadn't been on skis since then. So when I asked you to help me, well, I thought maybe if I could get you back on skis…" He sighed. "It was too soon. I shouldn't have pushed you."

She flashed a look at him. That he was so perceptive of her emotions startled her. It wasn't merely the light that had softened him; perhaps he did understand her. And it wasn't too soon, it was simply difficult. That he'd nudged her in an attempt to help meant a lot.

"I'm sorry, Cassandra. Losing a parent can be rough. Enough of a reason to need to get away when life zaps you with memory. Is that what it was out on the bunny hill?"

She sighed heavily and tugged up the blanket around her neck like a protective piece of armor. "Mom and I were close. We shared clothes, spent weekends shopping and enjoying spa treatments. We were best friends. We were extremely type A and—

fine, I admit it—controlling. But together we were a dream team. That's what dad always used to call us."

Rayce sat on the couch beside her, facing the balcony doors. Snow had begun to fall in thick goose down flakes. That she had allowed him in and shared something so personal with him startled her. She hoped he wouldn't overstep and delve too deeply into her pain. She didn't know how to open up completely.

Yet at the same time she was thankful he knew about her loss. His presence comforted her. She was glad he'd thought to check in on her.

"Your mom must have been beautiful," he said. "I mean, look at her daughter."

"She was gorgeous. Always dressed in gray and black. Very elegant, and looking like, well…if I'm the snow princess, she was the snow queen."

"I sit in the presence of royalty."

She chuffed. The man had lightened her mood by being himself. Letting down the blanket, she turned to face him, leaning her shoulder against the back of the couch.

"It was the skis," she confessed. "Standing there, looking down at them. The last time I skied was on a sunny afternoon with my mom."

He smoothed a hand over her knee. Patted it gently. But that he didn't try to offer condolences or empty sympathy meant so much. After the funeral many had come up to her and said *let me know if you need anything* or *call me if you need anything*. Really? Why couldn't they simply *do something* for her, without her having to put herself out there in her most vulnerable time and ask?

Rayce's silence shimmered as if gold. Like the best gift anyone could have offered regarding her loss. And she relaxed, settling into the couch.

"I'm not sure I'll ever be able to bring myself to put on skis again," she said quietly. "I… I see bad things when I even think about it."

"Bad things?" Now his gaze didn't so much catch her as offer her a soft place to fall.

She gave a deep exhaled breath laden with sadness. "My mom loved to ski at midnight. Under the full moon."

"Aw, Cassandra, I'm sorry. And I made that thoughtless comment about—I shouldn't have said anything."

He had said something about nighttime snowstorms. Which had been a catalyst to her mood swiftly changing. Yet she'd tried to remain light, not show him her angst, and paying attention to his teaching had helped some. There had even been a few moments of subtle flirtation she hadn't ignored.

"One night Mom went out alone." She spoke the words before her brain could hold her back from the confession. "She triggered an avalanche. It was hours before Dad realized she was missing. This was before we started using the GPS badges. Rescue crews worked through the night. We couldn't find her until the following morning." She buried her face in the blanket.

Her heart seized and her throat felt too narrow to breathe as her sobs renewed. She had cried often in those weeks following her mom's death. And every week after. Though the tears had lessened, the loss still felt the same in her heart. There was a hole now. In the shape of Cynthia Daniels. And nothing could fill that empty shape. Not even a silly ornament. That was still missing. The clock was ticking toward the turning on of the tree lights. She'd searched all the storage bins again, and the linen storage room. Would she ever find it?

Rayce gently squeezed her shoulder. Dare she ask him to wrap his arms around her? To hold her? It's all she had ever desired during those long winter nights following the funeral—to be held. Of course she and her dad had hugged, but he had been mired in his own grief. And initially neither of them had known how to interact with the other.

"Thank you for telling me that," he said quietly.

She wiped the tears from her cheek and braced her palm against the side of her head. "I hadn't expected such a visceral reaction to standing over the skis and looking down at them. Guess I know now that skiing is not in my future."

"It makes me sad to hear you say that," he said. "Skiing is such a joy, a passion, a way of life."

"I know." The sport affected a person not only physically, but also mentally. It provided health. Activity. Utter joy. To completely abandon it seemed unthinkable. Even Rayce, who had been damaged irreparably by the sport, had not given it up. "But I don't know how to be comfortable with it again."

"You don't have to put on the skis," he said. "Not yet."

She tilted her head, one eye revealed above the blanket. He brushed the hair from her lashes. That touch went a long way in broaching the soul-encompassing hug she desired. They were friends, but not yet close enough to ask so much from him. Just having him sit beside her calmed her worries.

"Someday you'll have to put them on," he said. "You can't run from it forever. Trust me. I know grief, Cassandra. It's a deep pain. But it softens over time. And I promise, when you're ready, I'll be there to hold your hand when you glide down the slope. I'm sure your mom would wish the same for you."

She'd never thought of it that way. Cynthia Daniels would never want to see her daughter in such emotional distress. So why had she done something so stupid as to go out on her own at midnight when she'd known the dangers and risks? Her selfishness had changed Cassandra's life forever.

"Is there anything I can get for you now?" he asked. "Some tea? A box of tissues?"

She smiled at his genuine concern. "I'm going to be okay."

"Good, because it hurts my heart to see you sad."

"I wouldn't want to be the cause of a man's wounded heart."

"I heal fast." He rubbed his thigh. "Some parts of me do, anyway. Hey, I was thinking about taking a walk around the lake once it's dark. Check out the lights. Do you want to join me?"

"I'm…"

"Not sure. I get it. I shouldn't intrude any longer. I know grief can be so personal." He stood and then picked up the blanket that had fallen to the floor with his movement. He tucked it on her lap. "I wanted to make sure you were okay."

Cassandra inhaled his delicious winter scent. It distracted her from her sadness. The man was handsome, talented *and* compassionate? There had to be something wrong with him—but what?

"I'll, uh…be at the path to the lake in an hour. If you want to join me, I'll see you then."

When he stood at the door she called, "The snowman under my teacup was evil!"

Rayce smiled a wicked yet sexy grin. "Yes, yes, it was. I did tell you I was here to shake things up."

"Mission accomplished."

"Don't give me any high scores yet. I'm just getting started. See you later, Snow Princess."

She was thankful for his quick exit. And while she should have asked for that hug, she felt the little she'd given him had been an opening into her soul. And that opening beamed out some light.

Spending time with Rayce made her less sad. And all he had done was listen to her. But he had said he knew about grief. Perhaps they were kindred spirits who could help one another?

She dared to think that could be possible.

CHAPTER SIX

AN HOUR LATER Cassandra bundled up for a walk in the chilly weather and headed outside. A sudden *meow* distracted her, and she caught a glimpse of that darn cat. The stray that had been scampering around the Cobalt Lake Resort grounds since summer. Snow-white, it was difficult to see against the snowy landscape and tended to surprise her. It was becoming a nuisance, stalking the birds who conglomerated at the various feeders and leaving tracks across the guests' snow angels. And she was pretty sure she'd found cat hairs on the cushions around the outdoor fireplace. But she had a resort to run so there was no time to consider pet patrol.

Wandering across the patio where the fireplace blazed and a few guests sipped hot chocolates before the amber flames, she felt drawn toward the interesting safety Rayce offered. When she arrived at the head of the wood-paved pathway that circled the small lake and sighted the handsome athlete, she could only smirk. He was doing it again!

"Seriously?" she announced as she approached Rayce.

The man adjusted the big red weatherproof bow attached to the wood railing. Dozens of the bows were posted along the pathway. Christmas lights were strung between them. The glow from the lights reflected off the glass ice pond in fairytale glimmers. Cassandra would never tire of the photos guests posted on social media along with comments that the lake walk was *magical* and *enchanting*. One couple had even gotten engaged on the covered dock at the halfway point around the lake.

"Now it's right," he said with a pat to the now-crooked bow.

Cassandra tilted the bow to the right. Perfect. Then, feeling the best way to win the argument was by distracting him, she started walking. "You like to disturb the norm!" she called back.

He joined her, their winter jackets brushing softly as their arms touched. "I like to push boundaries."

"I'm aware of that."

"Why is it you are so satisfied with normal?"

An interesting question. She did like to be challenged. Yet there was a certain safety in familiarity. "What's wrong with normal? You make it sound dirty. Taboo."

"Nope, you've got that wrong. All the taboo things I can think of are far from normal. And some involve whipped cream."

Cassandra's jaw dropped open as she met his grinning face. With a waggle of his eyebrows, she realized he'd done it again. He was tossing out zingers to see if he could get a rise out of her. Disturbing her norm. Inciting a tremor of desire.

"I love whipped cream," she volleyed, taking a bit of pride in the quick reply.

"Then you and I are going to get along just fine."

They reduced their walking pace to a stroll as the path curved and overhead the tree branches danced with colorful lights. Pinks, blues, greens and reds reflected in the snow, dusting the branches and shimmering across the glassy lake surface.

"This is incredible," he said. "It feels like a fancy light show yet cozy at the same time. And Christmas music?" A melody softly echoed through the speakers placed along the trail. "Love it!"

She pointed toward the center of the lake. "As soon as we get safe ice thickness, we'll open it for ice skating and pond hockey."

"Nice. I love an aggressive game of pond hockey."

"Yeah? We'll see how talented you are with the stick when we meet on the ice."

Rayce nodded in surprised approval. "I think you just challenged me, Miss Not So Normal."

"I suppose I did."

"So I take it you're not a puck bunny?"

"Please." Puck bunnies were over-styled fashion victims who fawned over professional hockey players and flirted their way into their beds and sometimes earned an expensive and sparkly gift. "I'd never be caught swooning over the players from the sidelines. I like to get into the action."

"I never would have guessed that of Miss Astute and Perfect."

"Don't call me that. And I'm not Miss Not So Normal, either."

"Sorry. But can I use Snow Princess? Pretty please?"

She made a show of thinking it over, then nodded. "If you must."

"Yes!" Rayce glanced over his shoulder. "But that ribbon…"

"Fine!" She skipped ahead and turned to face him as they walked. "I admit that I have perfectionist tendencies."

His swagger drew attention to his hips. Relaxed, easy. So sure of himself. "You like to control the world."

She performed an evil laugh and then pressed her pinkie finger to her lips. "Or perhaps just a small portion of British Columbia."

He laughed and jogged up to her, clasping her hand. "I love an evil plan. Now here's mine. Race you to the dock?"

"Doesn't sound very evil, but…" Dropping his hand, Cassandra took off. "I'm in!"

After a burst of energetic running, she arrived at the covered dock that had been built to showcase its Nordic design; it was made of clean pine, with traditional rosemaling along the rafters. Another couple leaving hand in hand nodded to her and she called to them to have a good night. That left the dock to Cassandra and Rayce.

Stepping up onto the cozy retreat beneath the glowing lights always lifted her mood. Spending time with Rayce seemed to do the same. Was it his teasing at her boundaries that felt so exhilarating? How odd. And yet she did enjoy inching closer to his idea of shaking things up. And she hadn't given a moment's thought to—no, she'd cried enough earlier. Time to take a vacation from work and her grief, if only for the evening.

With a leap over the two steps, Rayce landed on the dock floor with arms splayed triumphantly. "He makes it in a single bound!"

"I'm very impressed. I noticed your limp earlier and I thought you were in pain. Everything all right now?"

"Eh, there's some muscle twinges, but I'm still standing. And performing that stupid leap may seem silly but considering I couldn't even walk a year ago? I'm taking it as a win."

"You can have it."

"Thanks. That'll go a long way when I know I'll be suffering in the morning."

"Oh, Rayce, then why do you do such things?"

"How can I not? I'm stuck with an injured leg and tweaky back while all I want to do is push my body to the limits. If I keep pushing maybe my leg will take the hint and get over this stupid pain."

"Either that, or you'll cause more damage. Sorry. I shouldn't be a naysayer. What do your doctors say?"

"That I need to take it easy."

"Even the sports doctors? The ones who work with the Olympic team?"

He shrugged. "I lost access to them a month after being in the hospital."

"Really? That hardly seems fair."

"I don't want to talk about the politics of it all. I've survived and that's what matters."

"Fair enough." She tapped one of the hanging icicle lights. "So what do you think?"

"This place is cool." He looked out over the pond. Red and

green lights dazzled the circumference, and a fancy laser light painted a show of Santa's sleigh being pulled by reindeer across the iced surface. "Promise you'll include *The Little Drummer Boy* on the playlist for me?"

"Oh?" She assessed him. His eyes sparkled in the glow of the white icicle lights. And that hair…always tousled and so tempting. She'd like to run her fingers through it. Tug him closer and— "Is that your favorite Christmas song?"

"It is. I like the story of the little boy playing his simple drum for the newborn Christ. It…" He shrugged. "Gets me right here every time." He thumped his chest. "But don't tell anyone Rayce Ryan has a soft spot."

She crossed a finger over her heart. "Promise."

"I suspect you are an excellent secret keeper."

"The best. But if that's the only secret you've got…?"

"Eh, I have plenty. The press exposed most, though. Crazy how the paparazzi became so interested in a regular guy from a small town, isn't it? And yet I make one monumental mistake, and they've ghosted me."

Cassandra hadn't realized it but, yes, about a month after the Olympics snafu, all news of Rayce Ryan had fallen off the radar. What fickle allies the press could be. And the public, for that matter.

"Does that bother you? Not getting the attention anymore?"

He leaned against the railing, cocking his head to the side. Their breaths condensed before them in tiny puffs. "I am a guy who likes to put himself out there, be seen, make connections, talk to anyone willing to talk to me. The media fed that need. It's the part where my coach ghosted me that really cuts."

"Your coach? Seriously? You mean you haven't talked to him since…?"

"Not since about a week after the accident. He stopped into the hospital. Tossed a wilted bunch of flowers at the end of my bed and proceeded to tell me how disappointed in me he was."

"Oh, Rayce, I'm so sorry."

"Eh." He shrugged. "I deserved it. The man invested a lot of time and money in my training. And look what he got."

"He got a double World Cup champion is what he got. Not to mention you were rated number seven overall in Alpine racers. That's an accomplishment."

He sighed and scruffed his fingers through the hair she wanted to feel against her skin. "I know, but that didn't seem to matter much in that moment when he stood in the doorway to my hospital room. Coach had been there for me since I was a teen. He wasn't exactly a replacement for my grandfather, but he was protective and stood up for me and had my back. Until I crashed. He blamed me for making a stupid mistake. And he was right on the mark."

"Rayce! How could he have possibly blamed you for that? It was an accident."

His heavy sigh spoke volumes. "My mind wasn't in the game. I forgot that my goal was to please others. And now? Who will approve? Cheer me on?"

"You need the cheers but without the flashes," she stated.

"Maybe? But I'm not here to talk about my screwups," he said. "I thought we were talking about our social skills?" He slapped his chest. "Super extroverted. Complete opposite of you."

Cassandra conceded to his sudden need to change the subject. Though she wanted to know more, to delve deep into his soul and—really? She wanted to go soul-deep with the man? What had happened to just friends?

That charming smile and easy demeanor is what happened. Rayce defined irresistible. And that made her want to learn as much about him as she could. And might that abandoned kiss be claimed?

"I'm not an utter introvert," she said. "I can turn on the smile for our guests and clients."

"But I suspect you're happier when you get some downtime. You go all day, make the world perfect, and then...?"

That he pinned her so easily made her wonder if it was as obvious to everyone else. Of course she'd observed as much about her mom. When Cynthia Daniels turned in for the evening, she shut down. Soak in a hot tub, sip some tea and forward all work emails to the *save* file. That had also been her time to spend with family. And while her mother had worked sixty-hour weeks, she had still found time for Cassandra, and made that time special.

But Cassandra had no one to give her attention to so pushing her workweek to seventy hours had been a natural progression. A social life? What even was that?

"After the world has been perfected," she said to Rayce's question, "I shelter in my room and have a cup of tea or hot cocoa and relax."

"Ah, so you are capable of relaxing."

"Oh, come on! I'm relaxed right now." She waggled her shoulders, letting her hands flop. The tension that usually strafed the back of her neck was, surprisingly, absent. "See?"

"Well, and there are no people watching right now." He made a show of casting his glance around them in a one-eighty.

Cassandra glanced around the pathway that circled the pond. The night glistened like a fairyland. The atmosphere around them encouraged her to be present, completely. To accept what life wanted to give her. "No, there aren't. But what—?"

"I did bring this." From his jacket pocket Rayce tugged out a plastic piece of greenery with white berries—mistletoe.

"Where did you get that?" She made a grab for it, but he easily dodged her. "You broke it off from some display—"

She swallowed back her protest as he held it high. Above and between the two of them. The unspoken question was so loud: *do you dare?*

"Don't run away this time." His voice was laced with a quiet request to meet his heart halfway. A heart that had been battered, beaten and put through the ringer.

In his eyes shimmered a softness. Gone was the cocky, confident skier who had once held the world's attention and who had thrilled the crowds with his swift and agile performances. The part of him that called out to her now felt almost innocent. Lost.

Similar to how she felt when grief overwhelmed her.

Stepping up to him, she eyed the piece of green plastic that dangled a few white berries. Suddenly they stood in the center of the high school gymnasium, disco lights flashing across their faces. Hands sweating. Heartbeats thundering.

But this time, they stood alone. No audience to dissuade her hopeful fantasy.

Cassandra tilted onto her tiptoes and—a snarling *meow* parted them both. Rayce spat out something about "a critter" and dodged to the left.

Cassandra now saw the white cat had gotten tangled in the Christmas lights strung along the pathway. It struggled manically. Crouching, Rayce approached the creature carefully.

From down the path some kids shouted to, "Catch the snow monster!"

With a quick move, Rayce succeeded in untangling the cat and it leaped from his hands, landing on the glassy lake surface. The cat struggled to find its footing on the slippery ice.

Two teenagers jumped onto the dock and raced to the railing to watch as the cat scrambled away.

"You guys weren't chasing that cat, were you?" Rayce asked in a surprisingly parental tone that impressed Cassandra with the added innuendo of admonishment. "Leave it alone."

"We won't hurt it, mister," one of the kids responded. "We just want to see if it makes it across the lake. It slipped! Did you see that?" He poked his friend in the arm.

The look Rayce gave her said exactly what Cassandra was thinking: once again their kiss had been foiled. And it was obvious their window to try for another kiss would not return out here.

He held out his hand and she took it. They started toward the resort at a slow stroll. Little was spoken. The tension was palpable. The desire heating her neck had not lessened. She had been so close to finally kissing the one man who could knock her out of her self-imposed boundaries.

That darn cat!

When they neared the patio with the blazing fire, Rayce tugged her to a stop and she turned to look up at him. His skin and eyes glowed from the reflected Christmas lights.

"I'm not sure I'll be able to walk within your vicinity without wanting to kiss you," he said.

Same. And yet logical Cassandra leaped out to take control over mushy romantic Cassandra. "That wouldn't be wise in front of the employees."

His smile dropped. "You worried about some kind of fraternization thing? Because if you are, I'll quit the job right now."

"You haven't even begun!"

"I know, but that's the choice I'd make. Just so you know."

"It's not that. We're not so fussy about telling our employees who they can date. I'm a private person. I like to keep things like…" *their almost kiss!* "…that…sacred."

He stroked her cheek. "I get it. You're not into cameras flashing while I sweep you off your feet and into a kiss?"

The thought horrified her. To see her mug splashed on some front page, or worse, go viral online? No, no and most definitely, no. She shook her head.

"Well, the paparazzi are no longer interested, so no worries there." He twirled the plastic mistletoe. "But I may attempt the sweeping part again when you least expect it."

She snatched the mistletoe from him. "I would expect nothing less from the man sent to shake up my life. Now, from where did you steal this?"

He grabbed it back and stuck it in the back pocket of his jeans. "Not telling."

"But if there's a hole in a display somewhere…"

"That'll keep you on your toes!" He took off walking on the path.

"Rayce!"

"Merry Christmas, ya filthy animal!" he called back, then sped up, his chuckles echoing in the chill night air.

Cassandra shook her head. But then she smiled. Quoting one of her favorite childhood Christmas movies? The man was certainly all kinds of crazy mixed with charm and a dose of dashing.

And he had almost kissed her.

Let the shaking up of her life begin.

CHAPTER SEVEN

ANITA SET THE serving tray on Cassandra's desk and left with a few kind words to have a great day. Finishing off a letter to the local scout troop who had requested a field day at the resort, Cassandra then turned over the cup and gave a little chirp to see a little drummer boy figurine smiling up at her.

She chuckled. "Oh, he's good."

She tapped the drummer boy's head. "You are almost as cute as he is. But he is handsome. And sexy. And..."

She sighed. Oh, that almost kiss. Closing her eyes returned her to the dock, standing so close to Rayce. His outdoorsy scent had filled her senses. The soft melody of Christmas music played in the background. One more inch and their breaths would have mingled, their lips would have touched.

Her heartbeats thudded now. She sighed and caught her cheek against a palm, eyes still closed.

What was happening between them? Were they flirting toward something greater? The thought did not put her off. And it encouraged another smile. What a perfect way to spend the holiday season. With a man who intrigued, excited and surprised her. Cozy snuggles while sharing a blanket before the fire? Yes, please!

Of course she wouldn't expect anything more than a fun time.

He had, after all, only signed on for the season. And certainly she wasn't prepared to begin a relationship, what with—well. She hadn't the time for that.

And yet, why *not* indulge while he was here? She'd seen the happiness return to her dad's eyes after he'd fallen in love again. It was a special spark that only lighted when a person's heart sang. And there was no reason she shouldn't seek a relationship. Her workload wasn't so immense she couldn't devote time to another person.

What was stopping her?

She glanced to her daily list. The top item was *find ornament*. How many days had she left on her dad's ultimatum to find it? Half a week had already passed.

Was searching for the ornament a means to fill the hole in her heart? Could she fill that hole and make room for another living, breathing person? Why couldn't she be satisfied with memories of her mom, and just forget about the wood star? There were many more ornaments on the tree that her family had gathered over the years. Each with a different memory. Why not stroll out to the lobby right now and flick on the Christmas tree lights? Begin the holiday proper?

Something held Cassandra back. Pushed her toward the quest. And it was a different place in her heart that needed filling than that which was currently being entertained by Rayce Ryan.

It was the feeling.

Christmas isn't a season; it's a feeling.

Cynthia Daniels would often quote her favorite movie as Cassandra would follow her about the resort, helping to tidy.

That ornament had brought joy to Cynthia Daniels's heart. And by placing it on the tree this year, Cassandra would honor her mother's memory and move forward.

Only then could she exhale and allow another person into her heart space. *And feel.* For now she would steer clear of anything serious with Rayce Ryan.

* * *

They were eighty years old, the pair of them, and had been married for sixty years. Neither had skied a day in their lives. But it was on their bucket list, along with sky diving. That adventure was going to happen next week after they hopped on a flight south to Arizona.

Rayce got a kick out of watching Mr. and Mrs. Thorson glide down the bunny hill. Hands clasped to support one another, their elated hoots echoed in the crisp morning air as their extremely slow journey seemed to stir up more joy than any person should contain.

He shouted an encouraging, "Whoo!" and kept a careful eye on the twosome. They'd be fine. They wore enough winter clothing that should either topple, they'd probably roll in the thick snow like giant marshmallows.

With their general lack of ability and hearing, Rayce had taken his time with them, making sure they understood the movements and correct balance before allowing them to step onto their skis. He'd felt a flush of pride when they'd taken their first sweep down the hill. And not fake or false pride like an approving word that must be earned through hard work, pain and repetitive motions.

Now that he thought about it, Rayce wasn't sure he'd ever taken pride in his accomplishments. All his life he had known nothing but skiing. He'd read about it, talked about it, eaten on the slopes and dreamed about the powder through the night. His grandparents had pushed him down a hill when he was four and since that auspicious first descent, he hadn't stopped seeking the next thrill. What else existed beyond skiing? It wasn't as though he were qualified for a desk job or retail work. He didn't know how to exist away from the slopes.

The thought was crazy. And he knew it. But that didn't loosen the fear in his bones. Who was Rayce Ryan without the skis?

"Heck if I know," he muttered.

He winced as a step to the side tweaked the muscles in his

back. That was the real fear that had become embedded in his bones. The pain made him tentative on the snow, even disconnected from his body at times. It challenged his balance. And ski racing was all about balance.

Was he a has-been? A loser? He didn't want to wear those labels. But the only way beyond them was by rising and taking back the win. Through immense and uncompromising pain. A win that he wouldn't know how to appreciate. So would it even be worth it?

A triumphant shout from the bottom of the hill redirected his thoughts.

Pushing off and taking the hill in a quarter of the time it had taken the Thorsons, Rayce arrived beside them as they both settled on a bench to rest after their strenuous but successful journey.

"You two rock," he announced. Mr. Thorson met him with a fist bump. Rayce hoped to remain as young at heart when he reached their age. "See you tomorrow same time?"

"For sure!"

"Glad you had a good time. Go have some hot chocolate!"

Helping them out of their skis, he then sent them off in the direction of the hot chocolate and s'mores bar. He collected their skis and poles and skied over to the rack to leave them for the groundskeeper who made a sweep every so often to return equipment to the warming room.

Thinking about hot chocolate reminded him of the clever message he'd sent Cassandra this morning. Hey, it was the little things, right? Deviously, he knew she'd spend time trying to figure out exactly where that figurine had come from.

At the sight of Rayce's cocky smile, Cassandra straightened from inspecting the massive wreath hung on a wall in the lobby. It was filled with tiny festive figurines. Yet nothing seemed to be out of place.

"Not from that one," he said as he joined her side. He beamed.

So proud of his intrigue. "But I've got some mistletoe in my pocket if you want to learn where that came from."

"You think you're so clever?"

He shrugged. "I do have certain talents."

Cassandra exhaled. Yes, he did. And the idea of utilizing said mistletoe flourished in her brain to a full-on make-out fantasy. No stray cats struggling in a tangle of lights to stop it, either. But with a glance to the reception desk, she quickly swept away that titillating thought.

Kathy set down her headset and with a wave got Cassandra's attention.

"What is it, Kathy?"

"I got a call from Lift Four. The Torgerson twins are at it again. I tried to contact your dad but he's in a meeting right now."

"The Torgerson twins?" Rayce tilted a questioning glance toward her.

"They are young, rich, spoiled and tend to hit the slopes drunk. Anyone hurt?" she asked Kathy.

"No, but the attendant at the bottom of the lift said they've planted themselves on a snowbank and are loudly booing the skiers' landings."

"They need to be redirected," Cassandra said. "I'll round up one of the grounds men to help me coax the twins toward the nightclub. It's a bit early for dancing, but I'm sure they'll appreciate the atmosphere in there."

"I'll help you."

She gaped at Rayce, but then realized he may be just the person to help her out. The twins were celebrity chasers, and she was quite sure they lived only to see and be seen with everyone who was anyone.

"You may be the bait we need to lure them away from the lift," she said. "Come on."

Half an hour later Cassandra and Rayce said goodbye to the twins and headed outside to walk the path toward the lake. A guest had reported seeing animal tracks on the path. Possibly a bear? Cassandra doubted that, but she'd give it a look.

As soon as the twins had seen Rayce, they'd asked for autographs. Rayce had signed the sleeve of the one's ski jacket. After some polite conversation, and Rayce hinting that all the ski bunnies were in the bar warming up by the fireplace, they'd convinced them to take their hijinks inside.

Cassandra exhaled for a job well done. With a lot of help from their resident celebrity. But watching Rayce chat about his World Cup wins and his secret maneuvers hadn't felt like witnessing an ego show. In fact, the ego that had always puffed up his chest and set back his shoulders during after-race interviews hadn't been evident. And she wasn't sure if that saddened her or if it was just Rayce taking a new turn. Had the accident crushed his ego?

Before thinking, she blurted out, "What did it do to you?"

Rayce slashed a gloved hand across a pine tree, releasing a storm of snow across his face. He turned and tilted his head. "What are you asking? About the twins? They're all right guys. Just needed some attention."

"I mean the crash." She shrugged. "You were so kind to the twins. I would have expected grandstanding and boasting from Rayce Ryan, especially with two devoted fans of the sport."

"Boasting? You think I'm cocky?"

"Rayce. The whole world knows that."

He bowed his head but couldn't hide his smile. "Fair enough."

"Yes, but since you've been here at the resort I've noticed, well…you seem calmer. Maybe not so quick to grab the spotlight?"

He clapped his hands together and studied the wood pathway. No animal tracks yet. She'd made him uncomfortable. But it was too late to take the question back. And she genuinely felt he was a different person than the one who'd skied competitively a year ago.

"I told you about my mom," she said. "It changed me and the way I interacted with others."

"Really? Because you seem like the same go-getter I once used to notice in high school. Still on the fast track, everything perfect, woe to all those who don't meet your standards."

That was a shocking statement. But before Cassandra could reply that he was being hurtful, he put up a hand. "Sorry. That was, well, it was the truth. But that doesn't mean I haven't noticed your kindness toward the employees and your general goodness. You are a snow princess, like it or not."

"Does it come with a crown?"

He caught her teasing tone and winked. "Made of snowflakes. But you're right about me not grabbing the spotlight. Well. There are no spotlights to be found here at the resort."

"We keep a tight rein on the media."

"Appreciated. By all your guests." He scruffed his fingers through his hair, an action that always made Cassandra's fingers itch to do the same to him. Then he said, "You're right. This past year has changed me. Is it for the better? Not sure. What do you think?"

"I think you're…" sexy, alluring, and oh, did she want to kiss him "…doing well with the guests. And the staff. You've won them all over. Especially Anita. You and Anita have a weird thing going on."

"We do have a secret alliance. Does it bother you?"

She thought about the surprises that appeared under her morning cup. "I'm not going to tell you who you can befriend and who you can form secret alliances with. Anita was good friends with my mom."

"I picked up on that from the chats I've had with her. She's very proud of you. Following in your mom's footsteps. You know, that's the only thing I've ever wanted to feel about myself."

"What? Pride? You don't feel pride in your accomplishments? Rayce!"

"If I don't have a coach yelling at me to do better, change an angle, do it again and again and again, I just…" He shrugged and his shoulders dropped. "Maybe I won't ever get back to racing form again. And maybe I don't want to."

That was a stunning confession. What else was there for an Alpine ski racer like Rayce Ryan? Guest ski professional at a local resort didn't seem to land even close to what he was accustomed to.

"Really? What do you want?"

"I can't tell you. It's…"

At that moment, a rustle came from beneath the pine tree, which spat out a snarling white cat. It leaped out and dashed between them on the path and scampered off.

"That darn cat. Again!" Cassandra declared as she studied the ground. "Those are the smallest bear tracks I've ever seen." And what terrible timing the critter had. Would she ever find a moment alone with Rayce to fulfill her fantasy of kissing him?

"You should catch it."

"Oh, no. The last thing I need is a pet cat. It's feral, I'm sure."

"Yeah, but what if it wanders onto one of the slopes? When there are skiers out there? I'm sure you have accident insurance, but I'm also sure you want to avoid any lawsuits."

"I hadn't thought about that. But what would I do with the cat if I did catch it?"

He shrugged. "Take it to the pound. They can rehome it. It could be someone's pet. Maybe they are looking for it."

He had a point. "I'll get one of the employees on the task. Uh…" He had been about to tell her why he didn't think he wanted to race again. She wanted to hear that. But she was starting to feel the chill. If a body didn't move in the winter air, it felt the cold much faster. "Are you hungry?"

"Always."

"Would you like to join me for dinner as thanks for the suggestion about the cat?"

"I'd like to join you because you want to spend time with me."

"Oh. I do want to spend time with you," she said breathily. "Meet me at my room in half an hour. I'll have a meal brought up."

"It's a date." He wandered off toward the employee cabins.

Cassandra muttered what he'd said. "It's a date. Is it? Maybe. I suppose. Yes." She settled into the idea of it with a swoony smile. "Yes, it is."

CHAPTER EIGHT

THE YARD LIGHT positioned above the big outdoor fireplace high-lighted the thick fluffy flakes in their magical freefall. They'd eaten a fantastic meal and shared a large slice of Triple Threat chocolate cake, dense and layered with cream cheese frosting and crumbles of chocolate bits and cherries. Cassandra only ate a few bites. When she'd pushed the plate across the table, Rayce had eagerly finished it off.

Now what better way to enjoy the snowfall than with a bottle of wine, while wrapped in a cozy blanket. The chilled fruity red hit her just right and she smiled as she relaxed deeper into the pillows propped behind her back and shoulders. This couch was deep and comfy, and placed before the windows for the perfect view of the mountains.

Rayce had commandeered a red-plaid blanket and sat close enough that she could breathe in his crisp winter scent and won-der how long it might be before they kissed. They were safe from any feline interruptions here.

"Favorite Christmas movie?" Rayce asked.

They'd been sharing their favorites while watching the snow flutter in the golden beam of light. Favorite sports, adventure spot, music, food, color, all the standards. It was a nice way to get to know him better. And that he had a favorite dance—the tango—had surprised her.

"'Christmas isn't a season, it's a feeling'", she quoted from her and her mom's favorite movie. "Of course *It's a Wonderful Life*," she added. "It's such a feel-good movie. What about you?"

"*Home Alone*. 'Keep the change, ya filthy animal!'" Rayce laughed at himself. "So I'm juvenile. Sue me. I can relate to the little boy being left home alone."

"You can?" She turned to face him. Relaxed and wrapped in the red-plaid blanket, he seemed like an old friend. It was so easy to sit and talk with him. But his relating to the movie bothered her. An abandoned little boy? And the little drummer boy from his favorite song had been all on his own, too. "Have you been left alone, Rayce?"

"Not like in the movie. My grandparents were always there for me." Behind the couch was a long high table and with a finger he teased the little drummer boy figurine she'd set there. "Gramps and Grams died when I was in tenth grade. I was... nearly sixteen? I was left alone for weeks after that while the family tried to sort out who would assume guardianship of me. There was only the one aunt in Hawaii and a distant cousin in Europe. Neither were interested in taking in a teenage boy. It was a rough time."

"I can't believe I never knew that in high school. It must have been terribly difficult for your studies."

He shrugged. "I was a jock. Got by on my sports skills and good looks."

"And your devastating charisma, surely. I can't imagine any teacher flunking you after the Rayce Ryan–charm treatment. So who in your family finally decided to take you in?"

"None of them." He chuckled nervously. "When they started talking about child protective services, my coach stepped in. He gave me a room in his basement. I found an apartment after I graduated. By then I was already racing the Master's circuit and had nabbed a few local sponsorships, so I actually had an income to cover basic living expenses. But once I was out of school I moved into full-time competition and the World Cup series. Didn't need much of a place to stay. Just a bed to collapse on after a hard day of training. It's not so bad as it sounds. Don't give me those puppy dog eyes, Cassandra."

"I know training and competition is a full-time job. And you were incredibly lucky to have a coach to take you in. But I suspect living with the coach was more of a business arrangement than getting a replacement family?"

"Yeah, I would have never called Coach Chuck family. At least not when it came to an emotional connection. I don't think it was necessary for the life I was born to live, what with competing and all that."

"Sure, but Rayce, did you have *anyone* to love you?"

He tilted his head. The light that shone through the balcony doors glanced across his eyes, flooding them with a clear sadness. "That's a weird question. What do you mean?"

"Family is there to put their arms around you when you need it. To give you hugs, as you said. To love you."

"My grandparents loved me." He shifted on the couch and propped an elbow to rest his head against his hand. "They were the only parents I've ever known. They raised me because my parents weren't interested in the job after about four months of trying."

"What? Rayce..." Her heart thundering, Cassandra couldn't imagine something so awful. And he explained it with an utter lack of emotion. She immediately thought of what it would be like to never know her parents. Her mom...

"Don't worry, Snow Princess, I had a great childhood. I assumed you knew the story. News media likes to blast all that tragic stuff. It makes for a good lede. But from what my grandparents told me, my parents were hippies who wanted to travel the world in a van and live off the land. They weren't into kids. Something like that. And Grandma always said they showed me the most love by allowing them to raise me."

"So you never knew your parents? Do you see them?"

"Haven't heard from them. Ever. Nor did my grandparents, though I suspect Grandma tried to find them a few times. And after I started hitting the newsstands and had my ugly mug plastered on product displays, I wondered if they'd try to contact me. But no." He shrugged. "Grams and Gramps were the best. When they died, my world was shattered."

"I can't imagine losing them both. At the same time?"

He nodded. "The carbon monoxide detector needed a new battery. They didn't suffer. Passed away in their sleep. I had been away in Denver for a weekend training course."

"Oh, Rayce." She gave his arm a squeeze. "Your heart must have crumbled."

"That's exactly how I felt. And I'm not sure it's ever been put back together in the right way." He took her hand and kissed the back of it. "When I told you I know grief, I meant it."

"So how did you manage such tremendous grief and at such a young age? If you'll share that with me."

"You thinking about your mom?"

She nodded. Tears felt imminent but she fought them back. Now she felt the need to be strong for him, and to listen, to witness the emotional pain he suffered and may have never had opportunity to share with anyone else.

He stroked her hair and the soft touch threatened to make those tears spill. Was he aware of his easy kindness, his genuine concern? If so, that should have filled him with pride.

"I think of them every day," he said. "It used to crush me. But my constant and relentless training schedule forced me to find a place in my heart for them that wouldn't completely send me over the edge. So I put them here." He patted his chest. "I think about them when I need support and guidance. And when I do, I can only smile."

A tear spilled down Cassandra's cheek. "That's lovely. And very strong, especially for a kid who was forced to take care of himself at such a young age. I like that. Finding a place for them in your heart."

She pressed a palm over her own heart. Her mom had always been there. Yet now she felt the hole where she had once been. Could she do the same as Rayce had done? Keep her mom in a compartment that would allow her to move through life without always needing to cry or yell at others because silly things were not right, not "marvelous"?

He touched her cheek to wipe away a tear. "You'll find that ornament," he said. "But if you don't? She's always with you. I promise."

The promise felt real, and it settled into her heart like a warm hug. If Rayce could manage his life and get beyond his grief at such a young age, then surely she was capable of moving forward, too. With or without a silly ornament.

"We got into some deep stuff." He picked up the figurine and gestured with it as he asked, "You okay?"

She nodded. Whew! Even when she had been trying to be strong for him, her heart had stolen that moment to break down.

"Time to change things up. You want to watch a movie?" he asked. "You know I am calling this a date, so a movie generally follows dinner."

His wink seemed to disguise the inner struggle that he'd just revealed to her. Cassandra could feel his yearning desire to change the atmosphere in the room that had gotten heavier with his confession.

Wiping away another tear, she said, "I'm actually exhausted. It's been a long day of business and wrangling of drunk twins. Is it okay if I take a rain check on the movie?"

"Not a problem. I should probably head out. Keep my eyes open for that darn cat while I'm at it, eh?"

"Please do."

"It's been a long time since I've spent such an exceptional evening with a woman."

"Really? I agree it was nice, but it was also…emotional."

"Yeah, sorry about that." He tucked her hair behind her ear. Watching him study her hair and take her in filled her with a heady rush of desire. But acting on that feeling didn't feel right. "Are you going to be okay?"

Always in his presence. "Of course. What about you?"

"Eh… I tend to land on my feet. Usually." He winked. "We're survivors. Even if it doesn't feel that way to you now, you'll rise when the time is right."

The man was charming and outgoing and…always brought out the best in people. But to the detriment of his wounded heart? Was that his means of hiding his pain? His loss? By charming everyone into liking him? Perhaps cockiness was his armor? No, every move he made was genuine.

Standing, she grabbed his hand and walked him to the door. When he pressed his back against it, she felt compelled to make a connection with him. But a kiss didn't feel right. It was too sensual for the mood that lingered over them and with the ghost of her mother haunting her thoughts. And surely he needed some emotional space as well. But the moment demanded touch so… she hugged him. She made it quick, not allowing her body to respond to his warmth, the utter hardness of his muscles, the—

Cassandra stepped out of the hug. "Thanks for a lovely evening."

He marveled at her. "That was nice. We should do it again soon. I mean the date. But also the hug."

"I'm…" always busy and yet, not so busy as she liked to believe she was. Busyness had been her armor. Rayce had loosened it "…free most evenings."

"So am I. And we do live close to one another. Would be a shame if either of us sat alone in our places eating or doing whatever when it could be done with someone we enjoy spending time with."

"A very astute observation. Dinner tomorrow?"

"I'll bring the mistletoe."

CHAPTER NINE

THE SNOWSTORM DISSIPATED in the early morning hours. Snow-plows were dispatched and snowcats from all the area's resorts set out on the slopes to groom the runs. Walking paths had to be cleared by hand. Thankfully Cobalt Lake Resort employed a crew of talented interns, whom Cassandra quickly dispatched, shovels in hand.

Fresh snowfall always worked like a beacon as skiers headed out early to enjoy the slopes.

From her balcony overlooking the back patio, Cassandra spied Rayce with his clients. He was an easy spot thanks to his neon-green gear. He'd started wearing the color after contracting with the energy drink. Their logo had been a riot of green splashes. They had also been the first to drop him after his accident. It must have been rough for him. And his coach dropping him while he'd still been in the hospital? That was nothing less than vicious.

Yet there he stood, out on the slopes, trying again. In a different format, but he was doing what he could in the profession he loved. He was not a quitter. His grandparents had raised him right.

That he'd opened up to her last night meant a lot. The information about his teen years, and the loss of the only family he'd known, helped her to understand him better. Despite the obstacles he remained determined.

She glanced to the table behind the couch. The drummer boy figurine was gone. He must have slipped it into a pocket on the way out. It was his totem, she decided, even if he didn't realize it. A boy alone in the world, determined to make his way and give what he had to others.

That day she had fled from him in fear of putting on skis returned to her. Later, when he'd come to her room, he had said something so wise. She would have to step into a pair of skis sooner or later.

Rationally she knew he was right. It wasn't because as the manager of a ski resort she needed to be seen participating in the sport. Rather it was because it had been a part of her life until her mother's death. Skiing felt like breathing. And she did miss it.

But later felt much safer, and more doable, than sooner. Because, when looking down at those skis as Rayce had waited, fear had jittered in her throat like the lump that had settled there that morning she'd learned her mom had been crushed by the avalanche. They'd closed the resort for a week, then finally her dad had made the tough decision that they couldn't risk further lost income, or disappointing guests, and had reopened. The show of support from the Whistler community had been incredible, as well as that from people all over the world. They'd been booked solid through spring, and most guests had sent notes with memories about Cynthia Daniels. It had been heartwarming, but also too much.

Following her mom's death Cassandra had wanted to take some time off. Like a month. But she'd also been aware of her father's pain. He'd lost someone he had loved for twenty-eight years. It would have been selfish of her not to stand by his side and keep the resort running. And her mom would have insisted they do as much. Admittedly last Christmas had been dull and lackluster to the guests. No fabulous Christmas Eve party, or even half the usual decorations.

By clinging to her grief, Cassandra was depriving others of something special. Of their own Christmas memories. Which was the very reason they came to the resort in the first place!

Could she fill the mom-shaped hole in her heart and make it like that place where Rayce kept memories of his grandparents? Always there, but not a heavy weight that overwhelmed her and insisted on keeping her down.

"I can do that," she whispered. "I have to do that."

But how? She already held her mom in her heart. It was the need to cling desperately to her memory that had put her in this funk. She needed to open her fingers, relax her grasp and know that the memories would never flutter away.

And it must start with the daily operations around the resort. She wouldn't allow her grief to interfere with the guests' enjoyment of their vacations. Cassandra decided that with every decoration she hung she would be saying "I love you" to her mom. Even making such a decision seemed to lift the heavy weight from her heart. But a small weight remained.

The missing ornament. How many days had she remaining to find it? A day or two, according to her dad's ultimatum. The email she'd sent to all employees last night to keep an eye out for the ornament had not resulted in a discovery. And every nook and cranny she'd checked only produced another letdown. She needed to resign herself to the idea that it wasn't going to be found. And while it was important to her, what really mattered in the long run was that she remembered making that ornament for her mom and the expression of joy on her face every time she had hung it on the tree.

With a nod and an inhale, she decided today would be a good day. A new day. One that would hold her mom's memory in a special place while also making room for everything else. She would not be a doom-and-gloomer, like Mr. Potter from her favorite Christmas movie.

A knock on the door prompted her to invite Anita inside.

"I brought you a new brew that we're thinking about adding to the menu. It's a creamy chai with lush vanilla bean and a kiss of orange. Really lovely."

"Ooh, sounds intriguing. I love chai." Cassandra inhaled the spices and immediately detected the vanilla.

The sous chef set the tray on Cassandra's desk. On it sat an upside-down cup and a porcelain pot. As usual.

Anita wandered back to the door but paused with her hand holding the door open. "The email said you were looking for an ornament?" she asked. "Did anyone find it?"

"Not yet."

"I will check the kitchen storage," Anita said. "You never know. Odd things end up in there on occasion."

"Thanks, Anita."

After the chef left, Cassandra inhaled the spicy aroma. It made her think of foreign places and exotic fabrics and designs. Someday she'd love to travel to Morocco to see the sights and marvel over the culture. She could manage a week's vacation, especially in the summertime when her dad, ever busy with his many business ventures, enjoyed a break from that busyness and liked to take more control of the daily management of the resort.

Catching sight of a spray of glittery snow from the corner of her eye, she wandered to the patio doors, which were edged with snow. It looked like a frame around a Christmas postcard. Must have been a hunk of snow dropping from the roof.

A flash of neon green caught her attention. Rayce skied slowly beside the Thorson couple. He met with them daily, and each time Cassandra happened to walk near the elderly couple, they regaled her with the ski instructor's kindness and fun manner.

Her dad's idea to hire Rayce had been spot-on. But for as much as she felt her heart loosening to allow him into her life, she had to remind herself that he'd only been hired for the season. Come spring he'd be gone. And she did not want to step

THEIR MIDNIGHT MISTLETOE KISS

into any sort of attachment that would eventually be broken. She'd lost too much lately.

Turning to the desk, she followed the spicy scent of chai. Turning over the cup, she gasped, and then laughed. Sitting on the plate was a figurine of a blond kid wearing a Christmas sweater. Upon closer inspection, she realized it was the boy from Rayce's favorite movie.

"Where did he get that? First the little drummer boy and now this guy? I know we don't have this decoration in the resort." Unless it was something one of the employees had brought in? Very possible.

Wherever he'd found it, it made her smile, and laugh when the movie mom's declaration of "Kevin!" struck her thoughts. She tucked the figurine into a pocket then poured the creamy chai. The first sip was amazing. This was definitely going on the menu!

A *ping* on her laptop alerted her. Twelve messages had been forwarded from reception. Good thing she had a pot of chai to get her through the afternoon.

Rayce could see her watching him. From this distance he couldn't quite make out her expression, but a figure dressed in white stood before the patio doors looking in his direction. Heh. She liked him.

More than a few times, as he'd traveled the world by planes, trains and buses, he'd allowed his thoughts to drift back to the good old days of high school, and that beautiful girl he'd always admired. Heck, he'd crushed on her hard. And then she'd run from him.

She wasn't running anymore. Now to get that kiss.

Where *was* he headed with Cassandra? Because it felt like a dating kind of situation. Last night had involved some intense conversation, and stories that he'd never shared with anyone. That stuff had been personal. But he'd felt comfortable opening up to Cassandra. She hadn't made him feel as though he were less than, or wrong for having grown up with a different family structure. And when he'd told her about his grief, it had been real and from the heart.

Yet the last time he'd tossed his heart into the ring, disaster had struck. In the worst way possible. It had robbed him of an Olympic medal. Because the woman he'd thought he loved had kissed another man.

"Stupid heart," he muttered as he glided over the fresh powder toward the Thorsons.

That couple had been married for sixty years! They were respectful and caring toward one another. Man, he'd love to have something like they had. Maybe he should ask for some pointers?

Having clicked out of her skis, Mrs. Thorson lifted a boot for him to loosen the bindings. Rayce knelt before her and made some adjustments.

"You're a good fellow," she said. "You always take your time with us, when you could be out there teaching the youngsters and zipping down the slopes."

"There's no place I'd rather be right now." He set down her boot and stood, only to have Mr. Thorson shake his hand.

"Good stuff, for sure," the old man said.

Rayce lifted his chin. The praise swelled in his chest. It felt like nothing he'd ever experienced on the racing circuit. These two were genuine and honest. They didn't care that he could take the giant slalom in a mere two minutes.

"Tell me your secret," he said to Mr. Thorson. "How have the two of you stayed in love and for so long?" He cast Mrs. Thorson a wink.

Mr. Thorson sat on the bench beside his wife and tilted his bright purple-capped head onto her shoulder. "She's always right. And if you have to go to bed angry, just be sure you're both happy by the morning."

Mrs. Thorson laughed at that seemingly personal comment, while her loving husband hugged her.

Rayce put up his hands in mock dismay. "All right, you two. Let's keep it safe for the kids. I hear they've got a new hot chocolate flavor with honey and caramel in it over at the nearby stand."

"Ooh." Mrs. Thorson immediately made a beeline for the stand that Rayce had pointed at.

Mr. Thorson slapped him on the shoulder and said, "Just be honest and kind. That's all they want from us." With another wink he went off after his wife.

Honest and kind. Rayce liked that. Simple rules for an amazing marriage.

When he was with Cassandra, their connection felt promising. Her smile. Her laughter. That lush snow-white hair that swept softly across his face when he sat close to her. And the genuine care he recognized in her eyes and her voice. It did things to his stupid heart.

A guy should be more careful. Heck, he was only here for a season. Getting involved would not prove wise. But Rayce Ryan never got anywhere by playing it safe.

Was it love he wanted? Cassandra had seemed worried that he hadn't gotten love in his life. He had. From his grandparents. Familial love. But what might it feel like to fall in love with a woman and to completely abandon his heart to that romantic feeling? Could he do that again? Without fear of injury, rejection or losing the ability to compete?

"Honest and kind," he muttered with a glance toward Cassandra's balcony. She no longer stood there. Was being with Cassandra worth losing his focus?

What *was* worthwhile to him now? If this broken body of his couldn't bring home a gold medal, he'd have to find something to replace his need for adrenaline and competition. The cheers and adoration. The acceptance.

Her absence made his heartbeat stutter.

"Damn it," he whispered. "You're going to go for it, aren't you, stupid heart?"

CHAPTER TEN

A FIRE BLAZED in the outdoor fireplace and the s'mores stand was open for guests. The hot chocolate bar currently offered a dozen different flavors. Cassandra loved the white chocolate cherry version. And who could say no to the dark chocolate and orange spice?

During her rounds she frequently stopped to chat with the guests. But her focus would never be dissuaded. Was the hot chocolate bar clean and inviting? Was the outdoor music set at the right volume? Was all the soot cleared away with not a hint of it on the stone patio? All seemed in order, and the right amount of snow had been heaped behind the cozy chairs. A blanket closet was also heated to provide guests with a comforting wrap of cozy warmth.

"Marvelous," she whispered, hearing the word in her mother's voice.

Yes, Mom, it is marvelous. And...with or without an ornament, I can keep you close. I can do this. I can move beyond the grief. I am capable of changing...

"What's that?"

Spinning around and landing in Rayce's arms, Cassandra felt a brief effusion of joy that was quickly replaced by decorum. "Rayce, I didn't see you behind me."

"Keeping you on your toes. That's my job. So, what's marvelous?"

"Oh, nothing really. And everything. Well, not everything. It's what I strive for," she explained as she began to walk the path and he accompanied her.

A trip completely around the lake wasn't necessary but she did like to walk up to the first observation point to do a scan and make sure all the lights were working.

"You strive for marvelous," he recited. "Sounds unattainable."

"It's something my mom used to say. She was very fussy. Everything has a place and position. She would spend hours daily going through the resort, making it look perfect. The guests expected it."

"So that's where you got your need for perfection."

"There's nothing wrong with wanting the best and creating a memorable experience for others."

"Fair enough. So marvelous is the ultimate goal?"

"Absolutely. And… I think I've come close this year with the decorations. I just want to make my mom proud." She clasped her hands before her mouth briefly. "But that ornament."

"I can help you look some more?"

Once at the observation point, he stopped alongside her and leaned his elbows onto the banister where guests could walk out and gaze over the lake in the summer. The bench seating had been recently swept and weatherproof seat cushions were neatly placed in a cubicle for guests to use. While there wasn't an attendant posted, there was an abundance of treats in a small cabinet to satisfy any snack attacks.

"After our chat last night, I had a talk with myself about letting it go," she confessed.

"How's that going?"

A heavy sigh felt like a mutiny of her determination. "Letting it go is… It's become this *thing* that I need to clutch or accomplish or even defeat. I don't know how else to put it."

"You mean, letting go of the thing that connects you to your mom? And you'll never reach that particular marvelous if you don't find the ornament?"

She hadn't thought of it quite that way, but he was spot-on. She nodded and bowed her head. That he understood her always surprised her. He wasn't the unattainable golden boy she'd once put on a pedestal. Rayce seemed so normal, not like the celebrity persona he'd embraced with open arms. Had the accident brought him down or was it that he was new here and hadn't found his footing yet? Maybe the real Rayce Ryan would rise soon enough.

"So, what are we doing out here?" he asked. "Beyond listening to Elvis croon about Christmas?"

"Making the evening rounds before I turn in. One final check for—"

"Marvelous?"

"You got it. Let's walk back but take the path around the fireplace so I can check on the shoveling situation to the employee cabins."

"I can tell you right now it's all good, but I suspect you need to see it to believe it. I don't mind." He stretched out an arm, his hand open in invitation. "You can walk me home."

He winked at her and clasped her hand. She was wearing thin gloves and he wasn't. Never had she wanted to rip them off more than now to feel his warmth, the sureness of his skin against hers. When had she last walked with a man and held his hand? Such a silly thought, yet it was something that went beyond mere friendship. So…why not?

Tugging from his grasp, she bit the finger of her glove and pulled it off, tucking them both in her pocket. When she clasped his hand again, she said, "Much better."

He gave her hand a squeeze. "You always have been the smart one."

Smart, or rather hungry for his warmth and the feel of his skin against hers?

"How's the coaching going?" she asked.

"Better than expected. I really want to take Mr. and Mrs. Thorson home with me when this gig is over."

"They are a sweet couple. Oh. Do they remind you of your grandparents?"

"Maybe? They're just good, fun people. Honest and kind."

"Those are the best sorts of people."

"They make me think. A lot."

"About what?"

He jumped ahead onto the first wide log step that led upward to the employee cabins. It was well-swept and edged with bright strip lighting to prevent accidents in the dark.

"I don't know," he said. "Just life and love and things like that." He dashed up a few more of the massive log steps and she followed. When he pulled her to him, her heart leaped. "You're easy to be around, and that is a new experience for me. I like you, Cassandra."

It felt as though he were declaring his love for her, but she wasn't so foolish as to believe that. It was a delicious feeling, though, to hear that from him.

"You make me feel less broken. Come inside," he said with a gesture toward his cabin. "For a few minutes?"

Unable and unwilling to conjure a quick excuse, Cassandra nodded and followed him down a shoveled pathway to the small single-room cabin.

That word he'd spoken swiftly and softly—*broken*—disturbed her. Is that what he thought of himself? She supposed it was inevitable after what he'd been through. But it put an ache in her very soul to hear his confession.

Before following him inside, she heard a *meow* and turned to spy the white cat scampering across the path they'd taken.

"Is it that darned cat?" Rayce asked.

"Yes, but he darted away. I told the grounds crew to keep an eye out and catch it," she said, closing the door behind her. "Surely, someone would like to adopt the thing. It's so fluffy."

Rayce shrugged off his jacket and tossed it to the couch, but it missed and landed on the floor. "I haven't gotten groceries yet, but I do have snacks and beer. Want a bottle?"

Cassandra picked up his coat and carefully laid it over the back of the couch. "Sure."

He handed her an icy bottle of craft beer from a local brewery. "Have a seat."

She sat on the couch, finding it surprisingly comfy. When she was little, she'd followed her mom from cabin to cabin, helping her to straighten things out, take inventory and order new pillows and linens when necessary. All she could recall was bouncing on this couch, never actually sitting in it like a normal person.

"I know, right?" he said as he settled onto the couch beside her and put his feet up on the coffee table fashioned by a local artist who used fallen lumber rescued from the forest. "It conforms nicely and embraces you like a hug without being understuffed and uncomfortable."

"Wow. I just learned who the resident couch connoisseur is."

"When you spend your late teen years couch surfing, you develop a talent." He tilted his bottle against hers. "To big comfy couches and good conversation."

"What did you want to talk about?"

"Anything and everything, as long as it's with you. We've done the favorite things." Head tilted against the back of the couch, he turned his gaze to her. His summer sky eyes caught her instantly. Could a woman ever tire of staring into them? "Tell me something I don't know that no one would guess about you."

Cassandra considered that one as she sipped. "I'm not so fussy as I appear."

"Doubt it," he countered. "You couldn't let my coat stay on the floor."

"That's aesthetics. I'm a terrible mess in the bathroom. I leave towels on the floor, beauty supplies sitting everywhere."

"You're an absolute heathen." He chuckled. "Come on, give me something good."

"Like what? We've both shared our grief. Hmm, what about a true confession that doesn't involve a family member? Just about you. Personally."

"Fair enough."

He shifted to face her and she danced her gaze over his face. He had mastered the sexy stubble and finger-combed hair. No wonder he'd been on every magazine cover; the man gave good face.

"I'm not good at recognizing emotion," he finally said. "I mean, stuff like love and anger and indifference."

"Really? I would think anger an easy one."

"You'd think, but I've walked into more fights than you can imagine. People tell me I'm too easygoing. I like to joke and prod at people. It's a means of pushing them out of their comfort zones. I think I picked it up from Coach. He was always pushing me to see what I was capable of. Guess it makes me kind of one way or the other."

"I don't understand."

He shrugged. "Things are always either too far to the left or right. Too good or too bad. It's rare that I'm balancing in the middle. It's what I know. I'd like to be in the middle more often. To be more balanced."

"But I thought you enjoyed competing? The challenge. That must weigh heavily to the good."

"Actually it weighs on both sides. Competition is rough stuff."

"That's probably what trained your brain for those two extremes. I wouldn't think the middle ground would satisfy you."

"Right? But, well…" He let out a heavy sigh. "It's something I need to explore. After spending half my life in the extremes, I wonder what I've missed. Can I be a normal guy?"

"I don't think you'll ever qualify as normal, and I wouldn't want you to be so. You're too interesting, Rayce."

He leaned in closer and fluttered his lashes at her. "I think you like me, Snow Princess."

"Of course I like you."

"Do you like me enough to kiss me?"

Her mouth dropped open. Cassandra quickly closed it. And the first words out of her mouth were, "Where's that mistletoe?"

He dug in his back pocket and produced the plastic frond, which was growing crumbled and bent.

"Do you carry that everywhere?"

"If there's one thing I've learned over the years, it's to always be prepared."

"Scouts?"

"No, it's the 'not being willing to get the seat next to the bathroom if I'm late for the bus, train, or plane' kind of preparedness training."

Her laughter escaped in a burst and when she came down from it, Rayce met her with a kiss. Their skin still slightly chilled from the outside air, their initial connection caused a deliciously cool spark. It ignited and shivered through her system, quickly racing through her body to awaken all nerve endings. The crowd cheering in her head was really the thrill of her soul dancing to this moment.

Finally, it shouted. *That kiss you regret walking away from is finally yours.*

As they deepened the kiss, Rayce slid a hand along her cheek and cupped the back of her head. It wasn't tentative or shy. They had connected. And the intensity of the moment surprised her. He knew how to move and met her with an initial softness that then became a little firmer, even daring. Yes, he dared to go deeper, to draw her in closer, to defy her to push him away. Of course she should expect nothing less from the man who was determined to shake up her world.

There wasn't an excuse in existence that would tempt her to push him away.

Reaching up, she glided her fingers through his hair. It was just as soft as she'd imagined it would be. The move pressed them even closer and she laughed a little as they tilted their heads to reconnect differently. The sudden rush of heated passion brewed the moment into a delicious and electric embrace.

As quickly as she had fallen into the joyous surrender, he pulled back and smiled at her.

"No audience," he whispered, with a dart of his eyes to illustrate their quiet surroundings. "It was a long wait, but I'm glad it finally happened."

"I am, too." Giddy swirls spun through her system. Her shallow breaths came as fast as her heartbeats. "I think…one more."

Gripping him by the sweater, she pulled him to her. This kiss was the one she'd craved for years. The one she'd regretted never accepting. The one she'd always wondered about when kissing anyone else. The one she would never refuse. This kiss melded them in a clasp of desire that she wasn't about to destroy by running from it.

But as well, this kiss answered her deep need for connection. For that hug she'd been missing. For an intimacy that fed her soul in a surprising manner, that went beyond mere attraction.

Rayce bowed his forehead to hers. "Something has started here."

Really? Because she was wont to believe that it had started a long time ago. At least in her heart.

"Another?" he asked.

She nodded.

They'd learned one another's mouths and moved quickly to kisses that were deep and long and, oh, so satisfying. And when the hand he had pressed against her back moved around to caress her breast, Cassandra arched forward against his body, wanting…

So much. And yet how dare she take such pleasure when she should be focusing on other things like honoring her mother by making the tree marvelous through the addition of the ornament? She had intended to get that settled before losing herself in a relationship.

Relationship? Why was she even *thinking* that word?

Breaking the kiss, she stood and tugged down her sweater. "I gotta go. Sorry. I'm… This…can't go any further tonight."

"Okay. Yeah. Sorry. That was moving a little fast."

"Just a little." She grabbed her coat on the way to the door.

When she gripped the doorknob, she bowed her head. She was attracted to Rayce. Her entire body screamed for more, more and more! And she wasn't so precious that she wouldn't allow herself to get involved with the man simply because he was an employee. It was her life; she could do as she pleased. And she did crave intimate contact with his naked body, the ultimate deepening of their connection.

"It's not what you want," he called from behind her. "I'm sorry. I was going to be smarter about romance. I think my stupid heart has overstepped."

Smarter about romance? His stupid heart? No, it wasn't stupid. It was being cautious. He'd been through so much in his lifetime. And they understood one another on the grief front. But this side of their relationship was—not so much a challenge as a step in a new direction for her. She wasn't sure what she wanted from Rayce. Or rather she did want something from him—body contact, his hand on her thigh, his mouth on hers—and she didn't know how to take it. Would it be fair to only take that from him without committing to something more?

Oh, she didn't want to talk now. She needed to be alone to sort out her feelings about him.

"It's not you, Rayce. See you tomorrow," she called, then closed the door.

At the bottom of the log staircase, she paused and turned back to the cabin. Soft downy snowflakes fluttered before her. She'd fled from him once again. And this time, she felt even more confused by her conflicting emotions. What did grief over her mother have to do with allowing Rayce into her heart? Surely

she had room for both of them there? And since he'd arrived at
Cobalt Lake Resort, she'd relaxed her staunch work habits and
begun to enjoy herself.

So why the escape from what could have turned into a heavy-
duty make-out session? The man could kiss! And she had waited
ten years for him. Not that she'd stood around waiting. No, she
thought she'd never see Rayce again after high school. But the
fact that he was back in her life, in a surprisingly intimate way,
made her flush warmer than a sip of hot chocolate.

Rayce had been right about one thing. She did reach uncomfortable quickly. She shouldn't have fled.

Was it too late to turn and go back inside?

"It is," she whispered.

Returning to Rayce's embrace would stir up a new conversation that would involve going deeper into her heart than she
could manage right now.

CHAPTER ELEVEN

BRAD DANIELS CHATTED with the electrician who had stopped in to go over the resort's electricals with him. The twosome shook hands and he directed the man to take off on his own—he knew the building—then turned to face Cassandra.

"Dad, how's the wiring and all that important electrical jazz?"

"Just jazzy," he replied with a killer smile that always seemed to turn the heads of the female guests. But the addition of jazz hands went a bit too far.

Cassandra clasped her hands over his to make it stop. "Fair enough."

"So now we can flick on the Christmas tree lights."

"Uh…" She had been coaching herself to move beyond her grief and accept she may never find the ornament, but her heart still hadn't quite gotten the memo. Last night's desperate escape from the arms of a sexy man who had only wanted to get closer to her was proof of that.

Her dad's gaze switched from the massive, beautifully decorated tree, back to her. "The electrician said there's nothing wrong with the remote or any of the connections. It's the big welcome to the resort."

"Yes, but I still haven't found Mom's ornament. And I do have a day or two left on your ultimatum."

"Right. I forgot about that." He shrugged. "Maybe it's already on the tree. Got stuffed deep inside on a pine bow somewhere?"

Did he have no idea which one it was? Or how much it meant to her?

"No, I looked."

He rubbed his salt-and-pepper stubbled jaw. "It's just an ornament, Cassie. Don't you want the guests to *ooh* and *aah* over the fabulous lights? Your mother would appreciate that more than some silly little ornament."

"It's not silly!"

Startled at her outburst, her dad initially cringed, then he pulled her to him for a hug. As much as she didn't want anyone to witness such a moment, Cassandra's body leaned into the much-needed hug and she tilted her head onto his shoulder. The sudden rise of endorphins coursing through her body switched from manic anger to a soothing stream of comfort. Her dad was her rock, the man who had held her hand at the funeral and promised her she would survive, that they both would.

"I know you miss her, Cassie," he said with a kiss to the top of her head. "I think of her every day."

That was the same thing Rayce had said, that he'd thought of his grandparents every day. Was it easier for men to move on? No, that sounded ridiculous. Obviously her dad finding new love had helped immensely on the *moving on* front.

"But you've started a new life with Faith."

"I thought you were happy about Faith?"

The two had gotten engaged after a whirlwind romance. They had known one another from high school and reconnected after years apart. And Cassandra did approve of Faith. She was kind, smart and independent enough to not take any of her dad's nonsense. Not that he had an ounce of it in his bones, but he did have his trying moments.

A bit like Rayce and his needing to push her. Hmm… Was

she attracted to a man who reminded her of her dad? Nothing wrong with that, especially since Brad Daniels was one of the best.

"I am happy that you're happy, Dad. I just… I'm moving slower than expected on this whole 'letting Mom go' thing, I guess."

"You don't ever have to let her go, sweetie. She's still right here." He patted his heart. "Got a nice little nest where she resides."

Cassandra spread her fingers over his chest, feeling his heartbeat, and imagining her mom so close. She felt much the same when things were just right—*marvelous,* as her mother would grandly announce. And Rayce had placed his grandparents in the same manner, right there, in his heart. It was beautiful. She could do the same…

"Give me another day to find the ornament," she asked more than told him. "It's…" She sighed. A weird, ineffable thing she honestly couldn't put into words.

"I get it. But think of our guests. And, you know your mother would not be happy to see the tree lights dark."

He was right: Cynthia Daniels *would* be upset about the dark tree. "One more day." Cassandra held up a fist and he met her in agreement with a fist bump.

"All right, I have to find Faith. She's convinced we need to start wedding planning sooner rather than later. Fancy invitations to order. Silly colors to pick out."

"Have fun with it, Dad."

"Speaking of fun, how's Rayce working out?"

"With the job?"

"Uh, yes? Is there anything else I'd be wondering about? Like maybe the fact that I saw you two walking the path last night? Hand in hand."

Oh, bother, and here she'd thought they'd been all alone and unwatched. But they hadn't kissed outside. Nothing to give her dad reason to suspect they were anything but friends. Except the hand-holding.

"I like him, Dad. Both as a professional ski instructor who has been getting rave reviews from our guests and…"

He put an arm around her shoulder. "Anything that makes your face light up and your eyes sparkle is okay in my book. Maybe we'll have a double wedding, eh?"

"Oh, please, Dad, we're just…"

What *were* they? What did she want them to be? During their make-out session last night, she'd abruptly fled Rayce's cabin. By the time she'd returned to her apartment, she decided it had been nerves.

But she couldn't get what Rayce had said out from her thoughts: *I was going to be smarter about romance.* And he was always calling his heart stupid. What did that mean? It couldn't reflect well on her if his heart had chosen her in a moment of stupidity.

"I have to run, actually." She tapped her watch that blinked with a reminder. "I've got an appointment for…something or other. Talk later, Dad!"

She left swiftly, with her dad's chuckles trailing in her wake. He knew exactly what she hadn't been able to put into words. That she and Rayce were more than simply friends.

And when she considered it, she did want more from Rayce. But she wouldn't label them boyfriend and girlfriend. And certainly not lovers. Taking things slowly was all right by her. But it was not knowing how Rayce felt about the two of them that would drive her mad with wonder.

She owed him an explanation for her quick retreat last night. And with hope, he'd let her a little further into his psyche so she could understand what sort of challenge Rayce Ryan's stupid heart presented to her wanting soul.

Standing at the top of one of the medium challenge runs, Rayce's thoughts were on the snow princess whom he'd kissed last night. Three kisses actually. He had been counting. But then he'd gotten cocky and made a move that was too fast for her. He'd scared her off.

"Not cool." He needed to be more respectful of her needs and...desires.

Never before had he been so cognizant of his actions, of how one wrong move might destroy something he wanted with increasing desire. He must follow Cassandra's lead. It felt like the right way to proceed with her. She required patience, honesty and kindness. Just like he needed the proverbial pat on the back.

He'd grown up knowing that unless he performed a skill perfectly, the pat would not be forthcoming. And...he didn't get them anymore. Not in the form of a coach nodding their approval, the cheer of an audience as they watched him speed by or even the flash of paparazzi cameras as he smiled for the fans.

Life had been so focused, and yes, rushed. If he hadn't been training, skiing or traveling with his coach, he was listening to performance audio tapes and practicing various martial arts to maintain a level of flexibility and skill that was unparalleled by his opponents. Always his eyes had been on the prize. Take a photo with the ribbon, medal or fake gold cup. On to the next event. Not a moment to savor his accomplishments. Not when he had to best himself the next race by a tenth of a second.

Now any chance of earning such pride had been stripped away, leaving him but a man who had lost a dream and who wasn't certain how to move forward.

Life had changed the moment he'd crashed out of the Olympics. And in what had seemed like a split second, all the fans turned to look at the other guy, the newest Alpine racing sensation. The cameras had ceased their blinding flashes in his direction. And even the media, after the routine interviews in the hospital about the pitiful damaged skier, had tucked away their interest and moved on. Along with Coach Chuck. Rayce had never considered Coach a replacement grandparent, or any kind of family member, but he had been his mentor and guide and influenced his every move for so long.

While the cameras and attention had seemed to fill him up at the time, now he realized he did not miss the frenzy, the surface adoration and the false worship that had come along with it. None of it had been real. It was all a show. And he'd been the star of that show for a short time.

But if he didn't feel the innate pull to put on another show, what came next? Race, crash, recover, repeat had been his mantra throughout his competition years. He didn't feel compelled to *repeat* now. And that wasn't as alien a feeling as it should be.

Because lately, when he was with Cassandra, he experienced a different but similar feeling to the racing euphoria. Acceptance. Importance. Not being judged, but rather feeling he could fill the space and simply exist alongside her and she would make him feel like he had done something right.

Cassandra made him feel like he was a little less broken.

It was a feeling he wanted to chase, to inhale and absorb like oxygen into his muscles. But he didn't want to make a mistake and risk crashing out of what they had started. This could be something, and he had to recognize that and honor it without being thrown for a loop by the woman. And sacrificing his stupid heart.

"It is stupid," he muttered. "It's not smart enough to know what's real and what is just a game."

Cassandra didn't play games. Yet her abrupt departure last night after those amazing kisses had tugged at his softening heart, pulling it to a stretch until it snapped back with a sting. She hadn't wanted to remain in his cabin one moment longer. Had he done something wrong? He'd thought she'd wanted that kiss as much as he had.

Stabbing a ski pole into the snow, he flipped down his goggles. Here behind a line of trees, no one at Cobalt Lake Resort who happened to be standing out on their balcony could see him. Rayce didn't need Cassandra to see him; this was about proving to himself that he could do this.

With an inhale, he stretched his back. The twinge of pain didn't bite too sharply. And his leg wasn't bothering him at all. Excellent. He wasn't going to slow this one down. He needed to push himself, to test his limits.

Pushing off, Rayce tucked his poles back and his body bent and lowered to minimize resistance. The slap of the brisk winter air on his cheeks was the best thing in the world. Icy and biting yet burning a heat flash in its wake. A shift of his weight took the gentle curve and then he headed into a swift schuss toward the bottom.

Yes! This felt like his old normal. Free and always racing downward and striving for a goal. The goal right now? Make it to the bottom in one piece.

Laughing at his thoughts, he neared the base of the slope and…his thigh muscle twinged. Fear gripped his senses and his body tilted. His ski angled at the same time as a volt of pain strafed up his spine. A fall was imminent.

Knowing how to take a fall, Rayce readied himself. He landed against the snowbank at the edge of the run in a graceless collapse and roll that spat up sprays of snow. His body settled lying on his back, face up, skis splayed and feet turned outward.

No one around to see that beautiful disaster, thankfully.

"Idiot," he muttered and pounded the snow with both fists. His hip burned. Pain scattered up and down his spine with sharp prickles that made him grit his teeth. "You think you can compete again?"

Who was he kidding? He'd never again be as effortlessly fearless on skis as he once was. He gritted his teeth and eased his fingers over the cramping thigh muscles. A reminder of what he had done to himself. Through emotional stupidity. One moment of self-absorption had cost him so much.

Rayce swore and slapped the packed snow. In truth? It wasn't that he *couldn't* do this; he simply *didn't want* to do this. He'd had a good run. Time to move on.

Because his life had changed.

Staring up at the icy blue sky, his breaths condensing before him, he recalled what Cassandra had said about her mother. Cynthia Daniels had triggered an avalanche. These mountains were dangerous. And with the ocean so near, the weather could change faster than a snap of fingers. Even the most experienced skiers risked death by a sudden avalanche. It would be an awful way to go. Buried alive. If it ever happened to him, he prayed his lungs would be crushed by the incredible weight of the snow, instantly taking his life.

Cassandra must have been inconsolable in the days following her mother's death, just as he had been when he'd learned about his grandparents' demise. Grandpa had been meaning to buy a carbon monoxide detector for over a year. Following that dreadful news, he'd wanted to skip training. Coach Chuck had given him a week, then convinced him training was the best thing for his mental health. And his grandparents would be proud to know he hadn't given up.

Coach had known all the right things to say. And yet... Would Rayce have been better off if he'd taken a little longer to mourn and grieve the loss of the two most important people in his life? There were days he wished he would have, but honestly he could never know if it would have changed his future in any way. Coach had been insistent he return to training. But when things had come down to the wire, Coach had revealed his true colors in the hospital after Rayce's crash.

"You screwed up," Coach Chuck had said. The man's severe, unemotional tone was as clear as a bell in Rayce's memory. It was the foul language—something Coach had never used—that had shocked Rayce. "All that work. And for what?"

Coach hadn't stopped by again after that admonishment. And when Rayce finally called him, the man said he needed to step back. Give Rayce some room.

Rayce hadn't realized it at the time, but it had been Coach Chuck's way of dodging a bad situation. And of accepting a younger skier under his tutelage that he'd been talking to for a year and hadn't mentioned to Rayce. He'd learned about that from the media.

And now who was left in this world to care for Rayce Ryan?

He sat up and stabbed a pole into the snow. He hadn't twisted his ankle. He'd fallen correctly. He'd just feel a little sore for a while. Feeling sorry for himself was more stupid than throwing a race because he'd seen his girlfriend kissing another man.

Cassandra would never use his heart in such a cruel manner. She was true and kind, if a little perfectionist. But he liked that about her. And she gave him the emotional connection he'd lost following the accident. Or possibly it was a connection he hadn't felt since his grandparents were alive.

Who do you have to love you?

That was the real question, wasn't it? He'd succeeded in kissing The Girl He Could Never Have. Now, to trust his heart and follow it to the end? Or would he let her down as he seemed to let down everyone who had ever walked into his life?

CHAPTER TWELVE

NIGHT HAD FALLEN and the view from Cassandra's balcony boasted a fairyland of sparkles and colored lighting. The fireplace below had coaxed out dozens of guests despite the falling snow. It was that big fluffy, soft stuff that looked like goose down and she would swear to anyone that it tasted like candy.

It had been a while since she'd caught a snowflake on her tongue. Wrapping the chenille blanket tighter around her shoulders, she remained on the balcony watching the guests. And when a snowflake fluttered closer, within reach—a knock at her door startled her from catching it.

With a frown she padded inside to answer the door. Her thick knitted calf-high slippers with rubber grips on the soles made squidgy noises on the gleaming hardwood floor. She never expected anyone after ten in the evening so it could only be...

"Rayce."

He tossed and caught the plastic mistletoe a few times. The man was a master of the easy yet cocky smile. But that smile dropped when he noticed her expression. "Really? Is that disappointment? Way to make a man feel welcome, Snow Princess."

"No, it's not. Come in!"

"Are you sure? Because your face—" he gestured before her face with the mistletoe "—is saying something different."

She tugged him across the threshold, then led him through the living room to the open balcony door. "I was standing outside, trying to catch snowflakes on my tongue when you interrupted me."

"Oh." Seeming reassured he hadn't been the problem, he stood on the threshold. "And here I thought you were over me after last night."

"No, I—" They'd have the conversation about her fleeing him, but first things first. "Grab a blanket from the couch and join me!"

A moment later he stood shoulder to shoulder with her, blankets cozily wrapped about them. He leaned over the railing, tongue thrust out.

"It's not as easy as it looks," he said.

Cassandra tilted back her head and opened her mouth. Snowflakes *plished* on her forehead. A cool one melted on her nose. And… "Yes!" It melted on her tongue with a sweet kiss of winter. "I love that flavor."

"What flavor is that?" Rayce pulled her close and she hugged against him.

"The flavor of childhood," she decided. "I haven't tasted a snowflake in that long. It's a good memory."

"I'll remember that next time I do a face-plant in the powder."

She laughed. "I suppose you eat snow all the time, like it or not."

"I've consumed more than a man should, and never voluntarily. Maybe even recently—"

"Did you fall?"

"Eh… Took a stumble. Sometimes the ole leg…" He sighed. "We're not feeling sorry for ourselves tonight. So, can I see if the flavor of a snowflake still lingers on your tongue?"

Their gazes dropped to mouths and with a nod, she leaned in to meet his lips with hers. The winter kiss started with the sweet nip of chill, which quickly warmed. The change in temperature at their mouths was framed by the cool air, the hush of snowflakes dusting their faces and hair. *Magical* was an easy word to describe the moment. Maybe even… No, it couldn't possibly be… *Marvelous?*

"Kissing you is better than tasting snowflakes," he said against her mouth.

"I agree." She pulled him in for another kiss that could melt snowflakes in an instant. Was it possible to achieve the ultimate approval in a kiss?

Rayce's kiss lured her closer and she snuggled against his chest. He opened his blanket and she spread her hands around his back, as he did at her waist. His touch burned in the best way, warming her faster than the fire below. There was a certain perfection to their embrace that defied logic. He was the opposite of her, wild and cocky and a seeker of attention; she preferred the background and order and yet wasn't afraid to share herself when the moment was right. Like now. Rayce brought out things in her she had always known were there, but hadn't seen much of recently. Like passion and curiosity.

With a nuzzle of his nose along her cheek, he slid away the hair from her neck and glided a kiss to her earlobe. Erotic shivers tickled from her neck, over her scalp and down to her toes. Yet they stood outside on the balcony. Anyone below who looked up…

Rayce's hair was capped with white. She brushed off the snowflakes. "It's starting to pick up. Let's go inside."

Both shook out their blankets before going inside. "I want to check out that massive fireplace one of these days," Rayce said. "There's always a lot of people huddled around it."

"Making s'mores and singing Christmas carols. So did you just stop by to kiss me?" Cassandra asked as she wandered to the kitchen to see what she had for wine or beer. A half bottle of red? It would serve. She grabbed two goblets and joined him on the couch. "Sorry. Leftovers."

"That's fine. Maybe I did come over just for a kiss," he said. "Or two. Or three?"

She clinked her goblet against his. "I'm in for three. I saw you this morning standing out on the Harmony run."

"Yeah? You can't keep your eyes off me, can you?"

"It was the glare from your ski visor that caught my attention. But... I admit you're not so terrible to look at."

"You say that as if a forced confession. Who's holding a knife to your throat, Snow Princess?"

"Sorry." Over a sip of wine she met his gaze. Using her best sultry tone she said, "You're very handsome. How's that?"

"And?"

"And? A great kisser. And very..."

He lifted a brow, awaiting her summation.

"Annoying, actually." She moved aside and poked him in the thigh. "What is that sharp thing? Seriously? You carry that mistletoe with you everywhere."

"It's my good luck mistletoe. Hey, my mistletoe maneuver got me another kiss."

"Have you ever used it on anyone else?"

"Never." He made a show of crossing his heart with a finger. "Promise. There's not a woman in this world who could lure this mistletoe above her head, except you."

He tugged the pitiful thing from his pocket and adjusted the wired branches but there was no saving the crumbled tangle of green plastic leaves and fake white berries. "I bet the real stuff would get me—"

Cassandra choked on a sip of wine. "Would get you what?"

They stared at one another as the silence caressed them with an intimate tension. She suspected he would have said *in bed*. And guilt did shade his expression. Though she suspected there wasn't a lewd comment in this world that would make Rayce Ryan blush.

Nothing wrong with expecting they move to the next level of intimacy. That kiss on the balcony had certainly stoked something inside her. Sleeping together was not off the table. Especially on a night like this. Cold outside but cozy inside. Goose down flakes falling softly from the sky. And moonlight enhancing it all.

"I didn't mean…" he started.

"I know what you meant. And you don't need real mistletoe to get that, either."

His brow quirked. On the other hand he wasn't going to be here forever. And she'd flinched the other night when his hand strayed, seeking a more intimate connection. And yet on the other, borrowed, hand she was a big girl. She could do what she wanted.

"Rayce, why are you tiptoeing around me? We can have sex like two adults if we want to."

"I… Right. Of course we can. I just…" He spread his arms across the back of the couch and put up his feet on the coffee table. "Well, you kind of ran away from me last night."

"Because you implied you were doing the dating thing wrong."

"I didn't—oh. Right. Don't take it personally, Cassandra. It's my stupid heart."

"I don't understand why you keep calling your heart stupid. It doesn't reflect well if it was stupid enough to kiss me."

"Kissing you is not stupid, Cassandra. That's the best thing in the world. I'm sorry." He shrugged. "I say that because my heart tends to get me in trouble. Big trouble. And I want to be careful with it. Not follow it too closely into danger."

"All this interaction between us, the dinners and romance, and the utilization of mistletoe, involves some risk. Danger, as you put it."

"I know." He took her hand and kissed the back of it. Summer sky eyes met hers over the top of her hand. How could he possibly believe danger was involved in their interactions? "This is different, Cassandra. I want to do everything right."

"Does my need for perfection prompt that?"

"Nope. I find that part of you adorable. It's… I really like you. And I don't want to send you running."

"Have you had many women run from you?"

"My stupid heart will never tell. Listen, Cassandra, some truths here? I'm not a big dater."

"Seriously? Because every time I've opened a magazine or scrolled online these past few years, I usually saw you with your arm around a woman."

"The rags! Half the time those dates were set up. Makes for good press."

"But what about the Grammys? I distinctly recall seeing you with Aliana Garnet."

"Ah, the infamous 'leaning in' pic that surfaced online and the whole world thought I was kissing her. In reality, we'd been set up for the evening. We didn't click. At all. She smelled like fancy perfume and the scent made me dizzy. And I was too short for her, even though I was inches taller. Those crazy high heels she was wearing! Anyway, that photo was taken when I was whispering something to her about needing to find a bathroom."

Cassandra laughed. "Really?"

"Hey, when a guy's gotta go… Aliana was not at all impressed with me. I didn't even score a kiss. Not that I wanted one. That *date*—" he crimped his fingers in air quotes "—was all for show. She should have thanked me, though. Her TikTok numbers soared. And I'm pretty sure I scored the *Rolling Stone* interview because of it."

"So it was a…business date?"

"Exactly. Super boring. Both of us were working the angles, making sure it served our own bottom lines. Admittedly I have had a few real girlfriends that I thought cared about me, and in turn I cared about them. But nothing that ever lasted. You may have noticed I have a big ego. If I'm not the star, then no one else can be. At least that's what one of them shouted while she was throwing shoes at me and telling me to leave her place. I caught one and took it with me. She texted me to return it, but… I can be a jerk sometimes."

Sounds like the woman may have deserved the theft if she

had been throwing things at him. On the other hand there was always two sides to every story.

"Then why the job here at the resort?" she asked. "Seems insignificant for a man of your ego. The media are not allowed, and you're never going to get your photo on social media for being seen coaching an octogenarian couple on the bunny hill."

"Isn't that the truth! Honestly? This job was all that was offered to me. After the accident I lost my endorsements and the whole world forgot I existed. My manager tried to find me some action but other than a few movie roles—"

"Movie roles? Why didn't you take those?"

"I am not an actor. And I don't need the money. I've saved a good portion from my endorsement deals. And one thing I can do is invest wisely. I'm set for life."

"That's good to know. I'd hate to think you were destitute. What about the fame and attention? I know you miss that."

Letting out a hefty exhale, Rayce toyed with the blanket that he'd tossed across his lap. "I do like the attention. Crave it. But…"

"But?"

"I don't know." He scruffed his fingers through his hair. "I've only been at the resort a little while and have worked with some interesting guests. I was thinking about it as I lay at the bottom of Harmony."

"You were *lying* on the slope?"

"Had a minor misstep. My leg is intent on reminding me I'll never get back to racing form."

"Rayce, you have to be careful."

"Don't worry about me. Besides, I wear that GPS tracker badge when I'm out there. Resort rules, don't you know."

"Those trackers give me and my dad peace of mind. We've had to utilize them more than a few times."

"They are smart. But as for me and Cobalt Lake Resort, I like the smallness of it. The slower pace and personal attention and taking my time to show someone how to do something right.

Don't get me wrong. If I sensed a camera within smiling distance, I'd slap on a grin and pose. That's nutty, isn't it? What's wrong with me, Cassandra? I don't want to be that guy who needs validation from others to exist."

"Seems like you're taking a step in a direction that may not require such validation. If you're enjoying the coaching?"

"Watching Mr. and Mrs. Thorson take their first run down the hill was a hoot. They even clasped hands. It was cute. And, I don't know, it made me…feel."

"Feel like what?"

"Just feel."

"Oh."

It was half sad and half good to hear him say that. Had the man never experienced the joy of helping others? Of being validated simply for existing and not because he'd accomplished a task or won an event?

"You think I'm a nutjob. I can see it in your eyes."

She touched his jaw. The thick stubble enhanced the sensory appeal. Rugged on the outside yet a bit softer on the inside. Rayce Ryan did not cease to surprise her. And that he shared those complicated parts of himself with her meant so much. And yet…

"I'm a little sad that you haven't had moments of validation outside of your sport," she said.

"I have. My grandparents were loving and kind and always there to cheer me on. Even if it was walking in the Sunday school parade dressed like an Easter lamb. Life changed a lot after they passed. I don't know if I can ever get back to that place of comfort and love." He exhaled. "Will I ever have a family? Someone to care about me? Can I ever have a real home?"

"Rayce, you are worthy of all that and more. And you'll find your family, people who care about you. You've had a rough time of it this past…well, probably all during your competition years."

"I wouldn't call challenging myself rough. The physical part of it was awesome. It's that emotional stuff that baffles me. Like right now with you."

She tilted her head against his arm, which rested on the back of the couch. "It's safe to talk to me. I'm glad you've been so open with me."

He inhaled and closed his eyes, nodding. "That's a validation I can embrace. Thanks, Cassandra. For listening."

"Anytime." She snuggled up closer to him and spread her arm across his chest, hugging him. "This is nice. I could do this every night."

"Same. But. I need to know something. Maybe a few things."

"Like what?"

"Do you have a boyfriend?"

She squeezed him. "Do you think I'd be hugging you like this if I did?"

"Right. Also, *would* you like a boyfriend? I mean, a guy you could hang around with, date, spend time with—"

She kissed him to stop him in his struggle to find the right words. And because she wasn't sure how to answer that question. *Did* she want to be his girlfriend? Well, yes, part of her jumped for joy over the label. But another part tugged her back and waggled its finger.

You don't have time for this! Where is that ornament? Why aren't you thinking about your mom right now? And really, he's only here for the season!

Outside the patio doors a flash of brilliant sparks caught their attention and they broke the kiss.

"Sparklers," Cassandra said with growing excitement. "Dad must have brought out the party fireworks. And is that…" They both listened and the sound of a guitar and people singing rose.

"It's our guest musician! Let's go listen." She tossed him the blanket and he grabbed it.

"We could do that or…we could make out some more." He glanced toward her bedroom.

Cassandra bit her lower lip. Yes, that did feel like the next step. The most handsome boy in the school had asked her to be his girlfriend. And there hadn't been a crowd to whisper and gossip and make it wrong. She should take that win. But something wouldn't allow her to rush into What Came Next. While her body craved Rayce, her mind pulled on the brakes.

Rayce nodded. "Music and fireworks, it is." He tossed the blanket over his shoulder and offered his hand. "My stupid heart is thankful for your common sense."

"Who's to say my heart isn't as stupid? I may regret not snuggling with you in a big cozy bed tonight."

"You won't." He opened the door and gestured she lead the way out.

"How do you know?"

"I don't. But I do know that the offer will come again. You can't get rid of me that easily, Snow Princess."

"I wouldn't want to."

They clasped hands, and this time sharing a blanket, they watched the impromptu concert dazzled with sparklers.

CHAPTER THIRTEEN

THE NEXT AFTERNOON the white cat mewled, dodged Rayce's grasp and scampered across the snow-frosted patio stones. He raced after it but turned right into Brad Daniels. The man held an armload of cut wood. Despite his salt-and-pepper hair, and the fact he was at least twenty years older than Rayce, he looked fit and strong. And Rayce had learned he jogged most mornings and was on the Whistler Search and Rescue team.

"Mr. Daniels, you need some help with that?"

"I got it. Looks like you're on critter patrol."

"I want to catch that cat before it does some damage on one of the slopes."

"Good call. Did Cassandra ask you to do that?"

Rayce shrugged. "No, but I like to help out. Do things that make her happy."

Even weighed down by the wood, Brad's smile beamed. "I can see that you do. Let's talk about Cassandra."

Uh-oh, what had he stepped into? Would the man be upset he'd kissed his daughter? Well, he didn't have to confess to that. Unless Cassandra had told him. Why would she do that?

Why was he panicking?

"Cassandra," Rayce said slowly. "Yes. Your daughter. The resort manager. My, uh…boss."

"Chill, Rayce, I know you two like each other."

"You do?" Rayce winced. "Sorry?"

"What for? I haven't seen Cassie smile so much in years."

Whew! He'd won the father's approval? One major hurdle in the quest accomplished. Come to think of it, he'd achieved the quest of kissing Cassandra and altered the goal to something only his heart could describe.

"But I'm worried about her."

"Why is that, Mr. Daniels?"

Brad shifted the weight of the wood in his arms. "The lobby tree lights are still dark. She's holding on to the grief."

"Yes, we've talked about her feelings about her mom. I think Cassandra is coming around. Well, I mean, everyone grieves differently. I'd never ask her to stop..."

"Sure, and I didn't mean it like that. I just..." Brad sighed heavily. "I wonder if I moved too quickly with Faith? Does my upcoming wedding bother Cassie more than I'd expected it would? It's not like I'm replacing her mother."

"I don't think she views your engagement like that, Mr. Daniels. She did say she was happy for you two. It's just that ornament holds a special meaning to Cassandra."

"You'll help her find it, yes? I did give her a deadline, which I believe is today. That tree needs to be lit. It's the focus. If you can help her find it, and in the process, if the two of you fall in love..." He let that sentence hang. Rayce wasn't sure he was supposed to reply so he didn't. And then Brad gave him a stern look that appeared more forced than anything. "Don't break her heart."

"Oh, I won't. Promise."

"Uh-huh." The man's assessing gaze did not preach trust.

As any father had the right, Rayce decided. And even if he were just playing with him, the implied warning had been received.

"I should get back out on the slopes. Got an appointment soon. Don't tell Cassandra about our conversation, please?"

Brad shrugged. "She's a big girl. She knows when a guy is genuine."

With that, the man strode off, arms easily supporting the heavy load, leaving Rayce behind in the cool shadows of the shed.

Did Cassandra know that he was genuine? *Was* he? What did that even mean? *Honest and kind*. The keys to a happy relationship.

His confession to her last night about having difficulty adjusting to a life lacking in fame and attention had been from the heart. Honest. She had seemed to support him. But she hadn't wanted to sleep with him. As well, she'd dodged the question about if she'd like to be his girlfriend. That had stung.

What was wrong with him? Sure, she could be taking things slow with him. Nothing wrong with that. In fact it was smart. He should follow her lead and do the same. Ignore the prodding thoughts that insisted he would never earn the nod of approval from her. Could he ever get beyond that need for validation and start to trust his own heart?

Because he'd never win the girl if he didn't get right with himself first.

The Grammy-winning musician staying at the resort had returned to the fireplace for another impromptu concert. He'd been doing so every day at random times. Two dozen guests, including Mr. and Mrs. Thorson, had gathered, hot chocolates and mixed drinks in hand, roasting marshmallows, tossing snowballs in the background.

Lured by the singer's raspy baritone, Cassandra had donned a cap and mittens and a plush comfy sweater that hung to mid-thigh to head out and enjoy the music. Thanks to their elite guest list, pleasant surprises like this happened on occasion.

The crowd was respectful, and surprisingly she only saw a few phones recording. She nodded to the security guard posted by the door and he got the hint. The resort respected everyone's wishes for privacy; they should do the same for others. When all phones were tucked away, her shoulders relaxed. Joining in on the chorus of a famous song that everyone knew, the make-shift audience raised their arms and swayed amidst the magical glow of snow-covered pine trees.

The next song, a romantic tune, lured some to dance with their partners before the massive stone fireplace.

"Would you like to dance?"

Cassandra spun to find Rayce standing behind her. His smile grasped her by the heart and squeezed. And his beautiful blue eyes made her sigh. *Caught*. And so happy for it. She nodded and as she hugged against his reassuring warmth they began to sway.

"I love this song," she said.

"Yeah, it's sappy, but the girls like it."

"Yes—" she tilted her head onto his shoulder "—we do."

With a slow twirl, they caught the Thorsons' attention. Mr. Thorson put out his fist and Rayce met him with a fist bump. The elderly couple smiled warmly and focused back on their dancing.

"Love that couple," Rayce muttered as he slid both palms across Cassandra's back and his body heat melted through her sweater. She swayed in the arms of a sure warrior. Every part of him was hard and strong, yet lean and agile. His sinuous strength made her feel protected, yet small inside his secure embrace. Like a bird protected from the wind. Closing her eyes, she succumbed to the moment.

In Rayce's arms nothing else mattered. Not the everyday troubles and astute commitment to detail required of her job. Not even that evasive ornament. And thinking that made her cling to him tightly. She didn't want this to end. He was kind, funny, and whatever was happening between them…mustn't stop. *Did* she want to be his girlfriend? At any other time she would have answered with an eager *yes*.

Why was it so difficult to step beyond her self-imposed

boundaries? Were they even legitimate boundaries, or were they just silly fences erected to keep the grief inside?

Whoa. Now that was an interesting way to think about it. Was she keeping the grief in for a reason? What was it she didn't want to face?

"Song's over," he whispered as they continued to sway.

Beside them Mr. and Mrs. Thorson also still swayed to a slower tune.

The crowd sang along to a catchier tune now. Cassandra slid her hand into Rayce's. "Want to slip around the hedge?"

"Sure. Lights check?"

"No." *Move beyond that fence and kick down a few slats, Cassandra.* "Just a romantic nook."

"I am in."

Around the end of the snow-frosted hedgerow, they found a cove with a bench but they didn't sit on the padded cushion. Instead, they stood, hand in hand, in another slow dancing sway. The singer's melody echoed up and over the hedge. Christmas lights from the distant lake walk blinked in a colorful background. If Cassandra saw fairy dust fluttering in the air right now, it would feel perfectly normal.

Rayce spun her under his arm and danced her a few steps. "I like dancing with you," he said. "I don't think I've danced since high school." He got a funny look on his face, realizing something. "With you. That was my last dance."

"Really? And I ran away from you like a—"

"Like a princess who needed to beat the clock. I get it now that you've explained. But we're all alone again. And I kind of get the feeling you like my kisses?"

"Where's your mistletoe?"

He patted his coat pocket and then the back pockets of his jeans. "Darn it."

"Don't worry." She slid a hand up along his stubbled cheek. "I'll issue you a rain check on the mistletoe."

A kiss in the middle of fairyland. A dance in the arms of a

man she was beginning to realize held a certain soul bond to her own. They shared so much emotionally.

"Cassandra, getting to know you has been amazing. And I think about you all the time. It feels weird to say, because it sounds so juvenile, but I like you. A lot."

"Like a lot?" She laughed. "Same."

"Really?" He bobbled the yarn pompom on the top of her white cap. "Well, what do you know. The snow princess likes me."

With a pump of his fists and a shout to the sky, he gave a hoot like the one he always shouted at the end of a winning race.

Cassandra glanced nervously toward the hedge. A crowd of guests stood just on the other side.

"Don't do that." He turned her head to face him.

"Do what?"

"Worry what others think. You're allowed to kiss a man around other people. It's not salacious. It's kind of sweet. We're not high schoolers anymore. The mean girls aren't going to whisper about you and the jock isn't going to tell all his friends he made out with you."

"I…wasn't worried about that in high school, but now I wonder if I should have been. Seriously? You would have kissed and told?"

"No, Cassandra, I mean, we're grown-ups now. We can do what we want when we want. Or is it that you don't want anyone to know you like me? Oh, that's it."

"No, it's not."

"It's an employee thing, then, right?"

"No, Rayce, I already explained—" She decided kissing him was the easiest way to end what had no strength as a viable argument. "It's just uptight me. I need to loosen up."

"I've noticed that," he said calmly, not accusingly. His eyes danced with hers. So easy to fall under his spell. Save for the one thing tugging her off course.

"Yes, well, everything surrounding me this time of year makes it hard to relax and…accept."

He took her hand, tugged off the mitten and kissed her rapidly cooling skin. "You want things perfect for your mom. I get that. But can you manage a few moments here and there for the guy who thinks you're the greatest thing since the giant slalom?"

That race had been his masterpiece. He'd never gotten the opportunity to show that to the world in the Olympics.

"I want to."

"But…?"

"But nothing." She released her breath with a nod. "Right. I'm a big girl. I've got this. And I need to stay in the moment. Right now I am standing before the sexiest, kindest, goofiest man I know, and I don't want him to think I'm not interested."

Another kiss ended what might have become an endless pep talk.

Rayce whispered aside her ear, "Let me walk you back to your room."

She hooked her arm with his. "Gladly."

Once inside Cassandra's dark apartment, they swayed before the balcony doors. The outdoor lights beamed a romantic glow across the living room.

Rayce nuzzled his nose into her hair that smelled like snowflakes, tasted sweet, with a tinge of memories. Everything about her was soft. Even her heart. Because he knew if they detoured toward the topic of that ornament, the mood would flip and he'd be spending the night in his cabin.

That wasn't going to happen. It couldn't. The moment felt right. And when she looked up into his eyes and smiled, then began unbuttoning his shirt, he leaned in to kiss her behind the ear and down her neck. Her soft sigh turned into a wanting moan.

"Stay," she whispered. "Please?"

Rayce nodded. "Wasn't planning on leaving."

CHAPTER FOURTEEN

STARTLED AWAKE, Rayce tapped the off button on his watch alarm, and turned on the bed. Cassandra slept still, tucked between the cozy white flannel sheets. Beautiful, peaceful, gorgeous, sexy Cassandra.

Wow. That had been some sex. He really should snuggle up and—nope. He had a 7:00 a.m. appointment with a guest out on the slopes. Which was twenty minutes from now.

Swearing under his breath, he carefully slid from the bed and gathered his clothes, dressing as he made his way across the room. The curtains were pulled but subdued morning light permeated a crack between them and glowed across the bed. It dashed a line across Cassandra's pale hair.

Did he really have to leave her looking like a sleeping beauty? He'd love to wake her with a kiss and glide right back into making love. He'd be a fool to do anything but.

And yet she was so peaceful. For as hard as she worked, and all the stress she'd been dealing with regarding her mom, she probably needed the sleep. As well, if he wanted to keep this job, he'd best make his way directly to the slope. He'd detour through the dining room on the way out. Anita would have waffles or pancakes and some form of protein to fuel his day.

Pulling on his shirt and buttoning his jeans, he stepped into his shoes at the door and wondered if he should leave her a note. Sneaking out felt a little...sneaky.

Then...he had a better idea.

Waking in the bed by herself was normal for Cassandra. But it shouldn't have been so this morning. Rayce had snuck out without even saying goodbye. Before allowing anxiety to even stir, she had the common sense to glance outside and spotted his neon green winter gear on a slope. He must have had a guest appointment this morning.

After a long hot shower she wrapped a robe about her body and wandered to the desk to check her schedule for the day. Usual rounds and then some thank-you notes, along with gifts to their best guests. This time of year her mom had always sent out gift baskets to a list of dozens. Champagne, chocolates and pastries made by local artisans, and a set of Cobalt Lake Resort branded cozy slippers and a winter scarf along with a handwritten note.

Assembling everything and writing the notes would keep her busy all day.

A knock at the door was followed by Anita slipping in. "Good morning!"

"Thanks, Anita. How's your day so far?"

"Busy. No time to chat."

"Do you have the chocolates boxed for the thank-you gifts?"

"I do. I'll have Zac bring them up right away."

"Thanks!"

The door closed and Cassandra put her feet up on a padded stool and leaned back in her chair. A relaxed coziness had encompassed her since she'd slid out of bed. Like she hadn't a care in the world. There was no rush to get things done. No one required her approval or answers to resort-related questions. She could simply exist.

Then she realized this feeling was that of having been well-pleasured last night. Had it been that long since she'd had an utterly soul-shuddering orgasm? The lingering dopamine was truly the best kind of anxiety medication. Seriously, she needed to take care of her physical needs more often. With Rayce.

She wondered if he felt the same? Had it been difficult for him to leave her this morning? Or had he snuck out, relieved to have escaped the awkward "morning after" chat?

She hoped it was the former. But there was something about Rayce that he kept closed off. Not that she expected him to reveal all and be super open—everyone had their secrets—but… she was putting too much measure on their having slept together. Maybe?

Most definitely. Let it be fun and exciting, she told herself. Just like the Christmas season should be.

With a sigh she tugged up the thick robe and closed her eyes to imagine Rayce's hands gliding over her body. His kisses tasting her. Their heat melding in a hot and heavy lovemaking session. She wanted more than lighthearted fun and excitement.

But what did that mean? Did she desire a relationship with the man she hadn't known very long but whom she had dreamed about on occasion over the last decade? A man who was only here until spring?

She had no grand designs on her future regarding relationships, but it was a "back of the mind" goal to someday have a husband, some kids and a house at the base of a mountain. Never far from the resort. This place was truly her life.

But was it her home?

That odd question startled Cassandra. Of course, the resort was her home. Well. It was her workplace. The apartment was—no, it wasn't a home, exactly. It was where she landed after work, and continued to work, and…

"I don't really have a home," she whispered. Much like Rayce. The realization sunk heavily in her chest. "I want one." But that would involve…

Moving forward. Leaving behind the things she'd become accustomed to calling a home. Opening her heart to more than work. Letting go of some of the control. Sharing herself with another person in every way.

The thought that her mother would never be able to watch her walk down the aisle saddened her. And that switch to memory reminded she did still have a mission.

"Guest thank-you boxes to assemble," she said, "then one last ornament search before Dad realizes I've stretched the deadline by a day."

Turning over the cup on the tray, this time she sighed and caught her chin in hand at the sight of the little drummer boy. A second appearance? He could show up in her life all he wanted.

Rayce noticed Cassandra walking from the direction of the storage room. That ornament haunted her like—a precious lost mom. He'd allow her that need to hold a piece of memory in her hand. He hadn't anything but photos on his cell phone to remember his grandparents by, and he cherished them.

He wasn't sure if he dared talk to her now when she had clearly been looking for the ornament. She might be in a fragile state of mind. And him walking up to her and asking if she'd enjoyed last night would not exactly go over in the resort lobby and—who was she talking to now?

Cassandra greeted a man at the reception desk. Then he leaned in to *kiss her on the cheek*.

"What the heck?" Rayce murmured. That had been more than a friendly European greeting. And they were not in Europe.

Anita strolled toward Rayce with a tray of what looked like stacked egg cartons. She nodded acknowledgment. When she drew parallel, he asked, "Who's Cassandra talking to?"

The sous chef paused and glanced over a shoulder, her eyes taking in the pair at reception. Then she chuckled. "Oh, him! He comes every December to see her."

"What? Why? Who is he? He looks about our age. And he's…" He didn't want to admit it, but the guy was handsome.

In "a crisp white shirt and slicked back hair" kind of business-man way.

"She used to date him. For a season? I don't recall how long."

Used to was good. But. Rayce's neck muscles tightened. A flash of seeing Rochelle kissing the American skier made him wince. The catalyst to his crash.

"Do they...still have a thing?"

"A thing?"

He shrugged. "You know."

How to explain, or simply ask the woman if Cassandra was getting it on with the tall handsome man she had just hugged?

"Not sure," Anita said. "Like you mean sex?" She winked.

He managed to nudge up his shoulders in an "I could care less" manner. "Not that it matters."

"Oh, it matters to you." She smiled as she walked away and called back cattily, "It matters!"

Yeah, it mattered. Because he didn't sleep with women just because he could. Despite the way the press had portrayed him as a rogue of the slopes, Rayce was a gentleman and he never slept with a woman unless he thought there was something between them. Like he had with him and Rochelle. And he'd thought that something existed between him and Cassandra. Really, they had established a connection that felt genuine.

He watched from behind a frosted white wreath smelling of spiced oranges as she led the man toward the back patio door. Really? She was going somewhere with him? Should he walk out there? Introduce himself? Or play it cool and observe them from afar?

Since when did spying fall on the *cool* side of the scale? Rayce shook his head. They looked cozy. And if they'd once dated...

Shoving his hands in his pockets, he turned the opposite way. Just when he'd thought he'd gotten on a good run, found some-one special, he'd crashed. That had been a fast fall.

With a sigh and a lift of his shoulders, he shook his head. "No," he muttered. "I will not fall this time."

It was late by the time Rayce completed his guest appointments and gathered the necessary accoutrements to visit Cassandra's room. The fresh flower arrangement in the café was now minus a long-stemmed red rose, but he'd been sneaky and squished two flowers together to hide the spot. He'd combed his hair instead of sliding his fingers through it a few times. And he'd shaved carefully so there were no nicks. He smelled like a cedar cabin—subtle, one spray of cologne—and he wore an ironed shirt.

Now he knocked on Cassandra's door, holding the flower behind him as he waited.

After seeing her talking to that man in the lobby, he'd initially grown angry. And defeated. The horrible memory of watching Rochelle kiss another skier had made it difficult to breathe. But then something inside him had sat up. That stupid heart of his? Yeah, it had grown smarter over the past days. And it suggested to Rayce the man he'd seen talking to Cassandra had probably been a friend, or a guest she'd known for some time. Nothing for him to lose his cool over. Not worth his anger.

But something niggled at him still. The twosome had walked outside together. And Cassandra had not tried to find him this evening. She knew his schedule. Which made him wonder if she was avoiding him. For what reason?

The door opened and Cassandra, standing in a fluffy white robe, smiled at him. "Rayce. I was hoping I'd see you again."

"Again? I do live here at the resort. Why would you think you wouldn't see me again?"

Her smile dropped. "What's up with you?"

Don't let your heart grow stupid again and ruin this. Be honest. Be kind.

"Sorry. Nothing's wrong. Well. Can I come in?" He whipped around the rose and offered it to her.

"Oh, that's beautiful." She stepped aside to allow him entry as she sniffed the flower. "Wait a minute. Where did you—"

He turned and winced just as she realized the answer to her inquiry.

Putting up a palm, she shook her head. "Doesn't matter. It's the thought that counts, right?"

"It is." Whew! He'd narrowly avoided that little tiff. "So it looks like I caught you getting ready for bed." He looked around. Low lighting in the living room. The humid scent of a recent shower lingered. "You have a busy day?"

"It was a long one. A bunch of reservation switcheroos and we've a high-profile celebrity staying in a week. I've already received a call from the local newspaper wanting the scoop. One of the most difficult parts of my job is detouring the media. How was your day?"

She wandered into the kitchen and found a vase for the rose. Rayce rubbed his jaw. How to ask about the man? Was it really necessary? He should ignore it—but his heart couldn't. He just needed to do it, get it out of his brain, and then he'd know it was nothing and that he could trust her.

"My day was great," he offered. "The Thorsons have grad-uated from the bunny hill to Harmony. They're going to be world-class skiers in no time. I love that couple. They've taught me a lot."

"Really? Like what?" She sat on the arm of the sofa, pull-ing a blanket over her legs. Undone and fresh from a shower, she looked so simple and perfect. He wanted to pull the robe from her shoulders and kiss her skin. Inhale her "flowers under snow" scent.

Concentrate, man!

"Uh…right. The Thorsons have shown me that I can be proud of some things. I taught them how to ski. That is an accom-plishment."

"Of course it is. You have many things to be proud of, Rayce."

"I like that you're on Team Ryan, but…" He exhaled. He probably didn't have to bring it up.

Just move on. It was nothing.

"But?"

He scrubbed the back of his head, then blurted out, "I saw you talking to a guy at reception earlier. He…gave you a kiss."

"A guy? Kissed me? Oh! You mean Clint?"

Clint? Ugh.

"It wasn't a *kiss*-kiss," she said lightly, unaware of his inner emotional torment. "Clint is just a friend. Oh, wait. Did you and your stupid heart think otherwise?"

He winced.

"Oh, Rayce."

"Hey, you can do whatever you want."

"Really?"

He shrugged. "Not like we're dating."

"We're not?"

What was she getting at? He *wanted* them to be dating. They'd made love, for heaven's sake! But… Clint?

"Rayce, I don't sleep with any man who crosses my threshold."

"Well, I just—"

"Is that what you think of me?"

Her outrage stung, and he checked his cocky attitude. "Of course not. Cassandra, I thought…"

But his heart held a rein on his tongue, not allowing him to state what he really wanted. Because this felt like a race he'd forever fail.

She stepped up to him. Her soft blue eyes melted him like a snowman puddled before a bonfire. Rayce recalled the slip of her silken hair over his skin last night. Too luxurious. A treat he hadn't deserved. And yet the woman made him feel less broken.

"You thought?" Testingly she repeated his last words. "You thought what? That we *are* dating?"

He nodded subtly.

"So did I!" she declared with a gesture of her hands. "I never sleep with a guy unless there's something there. Something I want and like and well—no. I'm not going to beg for your forgiveness, Rayce. Especially since there's nothing to forgive. Clint and I did date. Years ago. But Clint stays at Cobalt Lake Resort every December. I ran into him at reception and he told me about his engagement. From there I walked with him for a while as we caught up on the past year. So if you need to do the he-man affronted act after learning that, then I guess you're not the man I thought you—"

Hearing that information snapped his self-imposed reins. Rayce slid his hands through her lush hair and pulled her in for a kiss. An urgent kiss that he'd been holding back since he'd opened the door to see her standing there like a lost snow princess desperately in need of a warming hug. She shivered in his embrace. That wasn't from the cold. Because the same shiver shuddered through his system and warmed him from the inside out. Kissing Cassandra never felt wrong. Had he been angry with her? Thought she'd gone behind his back with another man?

"I'm sorry," he said and bowed his forehead against hers. "It's my stupid heart."

"Stop calling it stupid, Rayce. I can understand how you might have taken seeing Clint give me a kiss on the cheek. But you're the only man I'm interested in. We shared an amazing night last night. I wanted to find you all day but was so busy and I know you worked late."

He kissed her again. "My he-man gene reared its ugly head. I'm a guy, Cassandra. I don't like seeing my girl with another man."

"Your girl?"

He shrugged. "I'd like that, but…"

"But?"

"It's this." He took her hand and placed it over his heart. "My luck with women tends toward the life-destroying."

"Rayce, what are you talking about?"

Could he be completely honest with her? It would allow her to know exactly where she stood with him. And why he'd reacted so strongly to seeing her with Clint. If he didn't confess now, he may lose her. And this wasn't a race he was willing to forfeit.

"Sit with me."

She snuggled up beside him on the couch. The moment was too intimate to destroy with his truth, but it was now or never. He'd come here to make sure he did not stew in anger over something he'd been mistaken about. He owed her his truth.

"The reason I keep calling my heart stupid?"

He peered into her beautiful gaze and his anxiety lessened. *Safe here with her.*

Never had he felt so sure of that.

"It's because it doesn't know how to judge a good thing from the bad. The last girl I dated resulted in my crashing at the Olympics."

She twisted in his embrace to stare up at him and did not assault him with numerous questions, and that made a difference. He needed to exhale and summon downright bravery for the next part. Would the truth change the way she thought of him? Would it send him crashing again, only this time metaphorically, but in an even more painful manner? The idea of another rejection after he'd experienced so much letdown following the accident tensed his muscles.

When her fingers threaded with his, Rayce closed his eyes and focused on the warmth of her skin. Cassandra helped him to think forward instead of wallowing in the past. She would never do anything to hurt a person or manipulate them in any manner.

"I was secretly dating a girl on the Canadian team," he started. "Rochelle. Thing is, Coach had a rule about us dating while on tour. He said dating a team member was bad news. He even encouraged us not to date at all because we're always training and competing. Intimacy before a big race? It doesn't work for some people. It's never affected me. Until I let my stupid heart into the act."

The squeeze of her fingers silently reassured him in a way he couldn't believe he deserved. When had a woman ever sat quietly with him and listened to him spill open his heart? Never.

Because he'd not trusted someone until now.

"It had only been a few weeks of us sneaking around behind everyone's backs, meeting in dark freezing start houses, slipping into a bathroom at restaurants. I really liked her, thought it was more than sneaky stolen moments behind Coach's back. My heart thought she loved me. And I thought I loved her. Maybe I did."

Tilting his head against the couch, he then shook it, utterly amazed that he'd allowed himself to soften like that. Race, crash, recover, repeat could be construed as date, crash, recover, repeat. He'd been given a hard lesson, that was sure.

"On the night before the giant slalom at the Olympics, she broke it off with me."

"Seriously? How awful!"

"Yeah, well. In hindsight we were both in it for the sex."

"But what about your stupid heart?"

"My stupid heart thought something was real when it wasn't."

"Love is love, Rayce. It comes in all forms. You probably were in love with her."

"Maybe." Yes, at the time he had thought he was in love. Yet dismissing that feeling was the only way to set it aside and turn his back on it. "But that wasn't the most devastating part. The next day, as I made my way to the start house for the big race, I saw her standing on the sidelines. I winked at her, because even though it was over..." He sighed. "Stupid heart."

Cassandra slid her hand across his chest and hugged him closer. She was so sensitive to his need for a listening ear!

"Anyway," he continued, "when she saw me, she turned and kissed the guy standing next to her. He was on the American team and my biggest rival. And it wasn't a short peck. It was—"

He swore quietly. "It ripped at me. It shouldn't have, but it did. I didn't want to believe she did it on purpose to mess with my race. I mean, we were on the same team. My loss was her loss! But it happened."

"So when you went down the slope…?"

"I thought my head was in the game, but seeing that kiss messed with my focus. I couldn't maintain my balance when my right ski hit an ice ridge on the seventh gate. I can't even re-call how I went from upright on two skis, to lying on my back, sprawled, staring up at the sky. And as I lay there in a man-gled mess, in pain, all I could think was, you did it to yourself, buddy. You shouldn't have been fooling around. Coach Chuck warned you. Your stupid heart."

"Oh, Rayce, I'm so sorry. I can't believe… Have you talked to her since?"

"She stopped into the hospital—" he swiped a hand over his face "—with the American skier. She acted like that side-line kiss never happened and we had always been just friends. It was another sound blow to my heart. I know I should have been stronger, but I'd never had anyone toy with my heart like that before."

"I can't imagine how that must have felt."

"Worse than the pain of the accident."

"Sorry, Rayce." She rested her head against his shoulder. "Thank you for telling me that."

They clasped hands over his heart. That she wasn't admon-ishing him for his stupidity and loss of focus over something so ridiculous as seeing a woman kiss a man meant the world. No judgment. Just a quiet acceptance.

"Yeah, well, it wounded me. Beyond the scars and surger-ies and all the physical therapy. It hit me here." He tapped his heart. "The pain from the scarring puts an unwanted fear in my bones every time I hit the slopes, but I think that betrayal twisted its way into my soul. I don't want to crash again because some woman touched my heart and then crushed it. So when I saw you talking with Clint…"

"I understand. But I hope you realize it's not the same thing. Clint is engaged. The two of us are old news. I would never do anything to make you crash, Rayce. Promise."

"That sounds…like something my heart needs to hear."

"But you don't believe me?"

Yes, he did. Most of him did, anyway. One thumping section of his heart still held back. "Maybe I need to put on the brakes and take it a little slower. Make sure my heart…"

"Your heart isn't stupid. It's real and wanting, and—I can imagine how you must crave love and attention after all you've been through in your life."

She rested her chin on his shoulder and placed a palm over his chest. Right over his thundering heart. He'd never told anyone about seeing Rochelle kiss the American skier. Never wanted anyone to know it had been his stupid romantic heart that had caused him to crash and literally alter his life forever.

Did she really understand that he had to be careful with his heart now? It had been him who had pursued her. Another quest, like a race, he'd had to complete. Chasing after something that might have given him the love he desired? Was that it? *Did* he crave love and attention? That sounded so needy. And yet he felt good when with Cassandra. Less broken. He didn't know if she loved him. But he did know it felt great to be with her. To receive her attention.

How could that be a bad thing?

"I care about you, Rayce," she said quietly. "And I never would have slept with you last night if you didn't matter to me. So you know, I consider us a pair."

"Yeah?"

"And if you don't, then we're going to have a different discussion."

"I like being a pair with you. But…" There was another elephant in the room that he couldn't be sure wouldn't trample them both. "Is *your* heart really in this?"

"What do you mean?"

"I know what it's like to lose someone, Cassandra. Two someones. Can your heart be in this pair with the distraction of grief?"

"You don't think I can care about you while also grieving my mother?"

"I'm sure you can. It's just, I don't want to step into a situation where you're trying to work something out, and then make it more difficult by introducing romance and love and all that jazz."

"All that jazz sounds kind of nice. But you're right. I am having a hard time of it." Twisting to settle her side against his, the back of her head nestled against his shoulder. "I know it's not about the ornament. But my heart is convinced it is. I've thought about making a special and private place in my heart for my mom, but it feels like shoving her away and reducing that heart space for her. It doesn't feel right. What am I doing wrong?"

"You're not doing a single wrong thing." He kissed the top of her head. "Everyone grieves differently, Cassandra. I can't tell you how to do it. But I can say that for myself, it was a process. I mourned. I screamed. I kicked things. I had the distraction of training to not let me get mired in falling apart after losing the two most important people in my life. But I also believe they would have been upset to watch me fall apart. The way Gramps and Grams died was an accident. But me holding a candle for them without seeing the world around me wasn't right.

"I thought about it one night. What if my mourning for them was somehow keeping them tied to the earthly realm? What if every thought I had about them anchored them to me and kept them from moving onward, going to Heaven or a new life? The best thing I could do was release them. Not from my heart. But from the part of me that needed to hold tight."

"That sounds—" she swallowed "—difficult."

"It's an adjustment. I still thought about them before every race. Gave them a nod. Gramps, who was an armchair astronomer, believed we are all stardust. I like to think the two of them are out there…stars in the sky."

"So you think I need to release my mom's memory to move onward?"

"No, you should always hold on to the memories. Don't be afraid to live your life. Don't you think that's what your mom would want for you?"

"Yes. She'd be angry to see me moping about some silly ornament."

"It isn't silly. It's something very personal to you. But you remember it, don't you?"

She curled up against his side. "I remember getting the glue all over my fingers and being so worried it wouldn't be perfect. But it was. Mom hugged me for the longest time after I gave it to her."

"That's an awesome memory. One you'll always have, even without the ornament. Just give it a think, Cassandra. I'll be here for you. But I don't want to get in the way of you finding what works for you and the memory of your mom."

"That's the kindest thing anyone has ever said to me," she said with a sniffle. "At the funeral everyone was like, *let me know what you need.* Well. I'm not going to reach out to anyone and say help me or hold me. That feels too scary, and needy. I wanted them to just do it for me without being asked. It's so weird when someone dies."

"Same happened to me. I wanted someone to hug me and make me dinner and clean my house."

"What?"

He shrugged. "My place was a mess after the funeral. I'd been out of town for months beforehand. And I wasn't in the headspace to do any cleaning. It's the little things that matter."

"That's so right. I laid in bed for days following the funeral. Then Anita knocked on the door and set a tray with hot chocolate on it by the bed, kissed my forehead and said she'd see me tomorrow morning to start the rounds my mom usually did. And you know? I did see her the next morning."

"Anita's a good one."

"She and Mom were close. I—gosh, I should talk to her about Mom someday. She's never said much. And I haven't known how to talk to anyone about it other than my dad."

"It might be a meaningful conversation for both of you. Anita knows things. She's a keeper."

"You have a weird relationship with her."

Rayce chuckled. "I think I've charmed her."

"That's one of your talents." She hugged him. "Will you stay with me tonight? No making love, just…us?"

"Definitely."

CHAPTER FIFTEEN

SLIPPING OUT OF BED, Cassandra tiptoed into the kitchen and pulled out a pitcher of orange juice. They'd slept in their clothes, snuggling until they'd fallen asleep. That quiet embrace had seemed even more intimate than sex now that she thought about it. Trust had grown between them.

With no breakfast food in the fridge, she decided that making an order with the chef would be best. Peeking into the bedroom, she saw Rayce was awake. "You hungry?"

"Always." He rolled onto his back, stretched out his legs and wiggled his feet covered with thick wooly socks. "What are you making?"

"Oh, dear one, you need to know I've become very reliant on the chef since I made the resort my permanent home. I can call Anita and put in an order for us."

"Sounds like a plan…" He glanced at his watch and winced. "Shoot. It's quarter to nine."

Had they really slept that late? She'd been so utterly comfortable lying beside him, like being with him was the only place she belonged. "Lesson?"

"In fifteen minutes. I'm sorry, I don't have time for food." Swearing, he tumbled out of bed. A few swipes of his fingers through his hair worked his coiffure into place.

Were they destined to forever see him fleeing the scene following any night of shared intimacy? It was funny to consider.

"I can't have the boss knowing I was late because I was sleeping with his daughter. Even if it was just sleeping."

"You most certainly cannot. I'll…"

"What's so funny? You've got a laugh just waiting to escape."

She took in his unruly hair and noticed the crinkled skin on his cheek from sleeping on that side. So cute. Utterly cuddly. And about the sweetest guy she'd ever known. "You're adorable. I'll have breakfast sent out to the slopes. Something you can eat on the go."

"Thanks." Rayce grabbed his jacket and threaded in an arm. He stalked over to her with one boot on and bent to kiss her. "I gotta go! The Thorsons need me!"

As he rushed to the door, Cassandra called out, "Your grandparents would be proud of you, Rayce!"

He paused with the door open, still shoving one foot into his boot. "That's the nicest thing anyone has ever said to me."

"I wasn't trying to be nice. I just know they would be. You've got something, Rayce. People are comfortable around you. They trust you. And you're a world-class skier. Put them all together and you make a great teacher."

"Never would have thought I'd want to do what I'm doing now. But I do enjoy it. I only signed on for the season, though. Your dad just wanted to try me out."

"Would you stay longer if he asked?" And if her heart insisted?

"There is a lot here at Cobalt Lake Resort to want to stay for." If he used that wink one more time, she may have to drag him between the sheets and strip him bare. "Meet me later for some real food?"

"Sure. When do you have a break?"

"Not until four."

"Meet me back here then."

"It's a date!"

* * *

The delivery truck had picked up the thank-you gifts, all boxed up and addressed to guests. Cassandra had made up extra boxes, one for each of the resort employees. She'd handed Kathy at reception a box and the woman had eagerly dug into it, swooning over the chocolate truffles and thanking her with a high five.

After a long day, Cassandra recalled her conversation with Rayce as he'd scrambled out the door this morning. They had a dinner date this evening. She called in an order to the kitchen and was on her way to pick it up when she overheard a conversation in the lobby between what looked like an eight-year-old girl and her mother.

"Mommy, can I turn on the lights and make the tree pretty?"

"No, dear, they probably only turn them on at night."

"But it's already dark outside!"

"I know." The mother cast a glance around the lobby. It was obvious she wanted to make her daughter happy and that child's frown was something Cynthia Daniels would have never allowed to slip past her quality control.

A heavy lump rose in Cassandra's throat. She was denying a little girl a simple Christmas joy because of her adamant refusal to do one thing. That ornament may never be found. It could have gotten crushed or broken. Perhaps last year, when the decorations were packed away by staff, someone had decided it was too damaged and tossed it.

Or it was simply missing. And she needed to come to terms with that. She'd already pushed her father's deadline beyond the past due date.

You can do this, she coached herself inwardly.

Rayce kept a place in his heart for his grandparents. Time to arrange that place in her heart specifically for her mom. A place that would allow her room for others—like a sexy ski instructor—and to move forward.

With a heavy inhale, Cassandra drew up all her bravery

and walked over to the pair. "Did I hear you wonder about the lights?"

"Why don't you turn them on?"

"Uh…"

Never lie to a child.

Slipping over to the present at the back of the tree where the controls were kept safely out of the hands of curious guests, Cassandra plucked out the remote. Her mom had always let her do the honors after the tree was decorated. And she'd pronounce "Marvelous!" as Cassandra would step back and display the glowing tree with a sweep of her hands.

"I was just going to turn it on."

I love you, Mom. This is for you.

She handed the girl the remote. "You can do the honors if you'd like to. Maybe your mom will take a picture of you doing it?"

The girl nodded eagerly and cast a glimmering gaze toward her mom, who was already lining up the shot with her phone. Cassandra slipped to the side and crossed her fingers behind her back. An immense welling of emotion flooded her system. The picture that she'd pasted into the ornament had been of her laughing in her mom's arms. A precious moment forever preserved. They'd shared so many of those moments. And she remembered them all.

Out of the corner of her eye, she noticed her dad standing near the reception desk. His nod and thumbs-up to her spoke volumes. It sent her courage and approval at the same time.

With that reassurance…she relaxed. This little girl would have many memories of her mother as well. Together they may even preserve one of them in a special way, as Cassandra had.

As the Christmas lights blinked on to the cheers of the girl, Cassandra's heart opened a little wider and she embraced the moment with an accepting nod. That special place in her heart beamed.

"Thank you," she whispered, though the girl couldn't hear her through her elated cheers.

Feeling as though she'd received an approving hug from her mom, Cassandra accepted the remote back and clutched it to her chest, watching as the mother and girl took a few more shots before the beautifully lit tree. Behind, at the reception desk, her dad gave a hoot and the few guests loitering in the lobby paused to take it in.

It wasn't perfect. The ornament was still missing. But it was close enough. And maybe this time, Cassandra decided, close enough would do. Because the memory of her mom flushed her system and made her stand tall and smile. All was well.

Mostly. Maybe?

No, she had to accept this. She *could* accept this.

Meeting her dad halfway across the lobby, they collided in a long and generous hug. He kissed the top of her head and then brushed the hair from her face. "I'm proud of you, Cassie."

She nodded, the burgeoning tears making it difficult to speak. "She lives in our hearts."

Yes, she did.

At that moment, Rayce strolled into the lobby, spied the lit tree and his eyes met hers. She shrugged. He smiled and tilted his head in a gesture that suggested she join him.

Giving her dad's hand a squeeze, she thanked him in a whisper as she kissed his cheek. "Thanks for always being there for me." They bumped fists and he wandered over to talk to the mother and her daughter while Cassandra met Rayce beside the hot chocolate dispenser.

"You just turned those on?" he asked as she joined him. "Did you find the ornament?"

"No."

He kissed the back of her hand, then held it against his cheek for a moment. "It's a good thing, Snow Princess. The tree is beautiful. Are you going to be all right?"

He understood the struggle of emotion she currently battled and knowing that settled her rising anxiety.

"Yes, I think I am. I made a place here." She tapped her chest over her heart. "For her. And I couldn't deprive the guests of such an iconic Christmas sight any longer. But that doesn't mean I'll give up my search."

"Is that where you're headed right now? On the search?"

"Actually, we had a date, didn't we? I was going to pick up our dinner and head to your cabin."

"Sounds perfect. How about after we've eaten, we drive into town and catch a movie? Like a real date?"

The hopeful tone in his voice made her smile. They hadn't gone on an official date outside of the resort.

"Sounds like the perfect way to spend an evening," she said.

His smile beamed so brightly that it extinguished any remaining anxiety she'd had about lighting the Christmas tree. With a wave to her dad, she left the lobby holding Rayce's hand.

After the movie the twosome strolled a sidewalk in Whistler Village. Christmas decorations adorned the streetlights, storefronts and even the trash receptacles, and enhanced the festive atmosphere. Rayce had spied a cozy café on the way in and wanted to stop for something sweet following the buttery theater popcorn. He'd let Cassandra pick the movie and it had been, as she'd called it, a rom-com.

"That was a cute movie," she said, clasping his hand.

"It was…too easy," he decided. "I don't think life is like that. It's more messy. Hearts and emotions can change on a dime."

"Are you talking about the movie right now? Because it sounds to me like you've switched to real life and you're not entirely convinced that what we're doing here is going to work."

"Sorry, I guess I zoned out after the hero offered to make cookies to help her win the competition." He sighed and lifted her hand to kiss it, even though she wore a glove. "Yeah, real life, eh? I want it to be like in the movies. Believe me, I've thought ahead. Like years ahead."

"And what do those future thoughts involve?"

"I think about how I'd like to have a family and what that might look like. Having a home, for sure. I'm not going to tell you much more. Don't want to jinx it."

"A home…" Her tone went wistful for a moment, but she snapped out of it in astute Cassandra fashion. "I never think much further ahead than the day or the week's schedule."

"You're kidding me? You must have princess dreams of wearing a white dress and walking down the aisle like the chick in the movie?"

She wobbled her head. "Eh."

"But white's your color!" he said more as a prod than in disbelief.

"Okay, fine, but I've always thought a simple summer ceremony would suit me. Wearing a floral dress. Barefoot. Flowers in my hair."

Now she was just being romantic. Rayce swallowed as the image of Cassandra Daniels adorned in flowers and twirling down a grassy aisle toward him gave him some kind of hopeful quiver right…there. He caught a hand over his heart.

"What's wrong?" she asked while simultaneously pointing across the street toward the café. "All that buttered popcorn acting up?"

"Yep." And he was sticking with that story. Wouldn't feel right to confess he'd had a romantic thought about his future. A future that included his snow princess.

"Let's pick up some fancy treats to take back with us." He tugged her ahead to a chocolate shop that displayed bonbons in the window.

"You do know the way to my heart."

Honestly? He *was* navigating some sort of passageway toward her heart. And it felt like a fresh run down a new slope:

adventurous, a little risky and filled with the unknown around every slight curve. But that was exactly the kind of risk Rayce Ryan liked to take.

CHAPTER SIXTEEN

THE FOLLOWING MORNING, Rayce had lingered in Cassandra's bed. They'd kissed. Made slow and intense love. Dozed off in one another's arms. Then repeated. The man did like to practice a thing until he got it right.

He most certainly did get her right.

Bright sunlight finally coaxed them to rise and get dressed. Rayce had offered to pick up something in the café and bring it up to her, but she declined. She had morning rounds to make and he did have a client. It wasn't a rush out the door to make the appointment, though. They'd kissed all the way to the door, and when he'd gotten ten feet down the hallway, he'd spun and rushed back to give her one more long lush kiss.

Getting it right.

Now she stood before the vanity mirror after having blown out her hair and put on some makeup. She'd never felt so utterly relaxed and at the same time *desirable* in her life. It was a heady feeling. Better than Christmas morning.

The best present she had received so far this holiday season was rediscovering Rayce. Being able to share things with him. Talking about both the good and bad times. He seemed to understand her, and she understood him. They had bonded through grief. But she wanted it to go beyond that. And it did.

They shared amazing chemistry between the sheets. And even when dressed and walking hand in hand or eating or enjoying life, they seemed to fit in one another's atmosphere with ease.

Finding love couldn't be so easy, could it? Because, when she thought about it, she cared about Rayce and adored every little thing about him. From his cocky grin to feeling he needed to wield the plastic mistletoe to get a kiss from her. And her heart was all in. Which meant...

Was she falling in love? So quickly?

Her dad had done as much with Faith. But he and Faith had known each other since high school.

She and Rayce had gone to school together, too, but hadn't really known one another. That hadn't stopped her from crushing on him. And, apparently, he'd had a thing for her, too. Was it only now that life had decided they should become a couple?

Why fight it? Or better, why not take it day by day and enjoy the moments? Yet the deadline for his departure lingered. If she ransomed her heart to him this winter, would she have to take it back when he left in the spring?

"Don't think like that," she admonished herself.

When he'd mentioned his plans last night, the word *home* had seemed to cling to her. More and more she really did wish for a home away from work. An escape from the place where it felt necessary to exercise control. Yet since she'd begun to loosen the reins on that control, the longing for a place to genuinely relax was real.

Dare she dream of a future with Rayce in a home they'd created together?

"Nothing wrong with dreaming," she whispered.

But the thought wasn't as convincing as it should have been. They were in a new relationship. Anything could happen. It was far too early to start picking out patterned China and silverware.

"But I can allow the fantasy," she whispered with an approving nod to her change toward a more relaxed and open future.

Dressing quickly, she combed her hair and pinned it up in a neat chignon, then headed out for her usual morning rounds.

Afterward, bundled up against the cold, she wandered over the boot-tracked trail that curled around behind the main patio and fireplace. When a *thunk* of cold snow splatted her back, she at first thought it was snow falling from the pine trees. But a distant whoop of triumph revealed to her she had been attacked. And she recognized that cocky whoop.

"Really?" Cassandra surveyed the snowy ground, spying the best patch for ammunition. When another snowball hit the back of her boot, she swung into action. Bending, she scooped up a handful of moist yet moldable snow and began to pack it. "Are you aware that I am the snowball-throwing champion of the Girl Guides of Canada?"

Rayce splayed his arms out in mock challenge. Then he tapped his chest and lifted his chin defiantly. "Take your best shot!"

He was close enough for the direct hit that she lobbed toward him. Snow dispersing at his shoulder, he took it like a man. But he quickly bent to reload. As did Cassandra.

She threw another, and another, each time landing a hit on her opponent. He missed her a few times because, now that she could see them coming, she dodged like the professional she was. They moved closer and closer, and her snowball craftsmanship grew messier until finally she held two handfuls of loose snow as Rayce ran toward her. She flung them at him, getting him in the face. His chuckles matched hers as he grabbed her about the waist and took her down in the fluffy snow.

Their kiss was cold and silly as they rolled in the snow and took turns flinging loose snow at one another. Kiss. Attack. Kiss. Pleads for mercy as snow began to sink under her scarf and icy water seeped through her sweater.

"Mercy?" Rayce defied as he hovered above her, a snowball in hand.

"Please!" she shouted.

"Then I guess we know who the new snowball champion is, eh?"

"I'll alert the Girl Guides immediately." She flapped her arms out across the snow as she lay on her back, looking upward.

Rayce flopped down next to her, and he started reshaping the snowball he had in hand.

The sky glistened with a beautiful pink tinge that floated at the tops of the snow-dusted pine trees. It had been a long time since Cassandra had lain in the snow and took things in. Lived in the moment. As well, she'd missed the utter abandon of a good snowball fight.

"Turning on the tree lights wasn't as heart-wrenching as I thought it would be," she confessed.

"I'm glad." He worked diligently at his snowball. "I bet it made your mom happy."

At the thought of her mom, smiling and laughing with happiness, a tear came to Cassandra's eye. But she wasn't going to freak about her sadness. Instead she opened that place she'd reserved in her heart and sat with it a while.

"Here." Rayce handed her the snowball.

"What's this for?"

"You."

She took the snowball; it was no longer rounded. He'd formed it into a heart.

"It's my heart," he said lightly. "I trust you'll treat it well."

She carefully held the snow heart with both gloved hands. "I'll treat it as kindly and respectfully as you've treated mine."

He rolled over to kiss her until they were laughing and wrapped in one another's arms, legs and scarves. He smelled like winter cedar and sensual heat. And he tasted like snowflakes and adventure. Amidst their make-out session, she managed to set the heart down.

Rayce looked aside to spy the snow heart. "Let's leave it there so it doesn't melt."

"Deal. Race you back to the resort?"

"If I claim an injured leg, will you give me a head start?"

"Ha!" She pulled herself up and then before dashing off, she bent over the snow heart and drew a bigger heart around it with her finger. "There. Now it's official."

"What's official?"

"Our hearts belong to one another."

"That's freakin' romantic."

"Yeah? Well, this isn't." She blasted him with a kick of snow, then took off toward the resort.

He followed, his laughter the best balm to the few slivers of grief that the thoughts of her mom had produced. But with Rayce she realized she could hold all those emotions, and still rise to embrace the good times.

He didn't want to wake the sleeping beauty, so Rayce finished a note for Cassandra and set it on her desk. Yes, he'd developed a habit of slipping out of her bed while she slept, but not every time. Invigorated by a night of making love and a newfound intimacy that included trust and honesty, he wanted to challenge himself this morning. And his back wasn't bothering him, so it was now or never.

The sun wouldn't rise for another hour, but he was eager to catch the fresh powder. He grabbed his ski jacket and headed out.

An hour later he landed at the bottom of the run. Exhilarating! The powder was deep and dry. Perfect conditions for a speedy descent. And despite a few painful twinges along his spine, his leg hadn't given him trouble.

But now that the sun had risen, the slope was crowded with skiers. Had he really left a warm, gorgeous Cassandra alone in bed just to catch some powder?

"Fool," he muttered.

However he'd had to prove something to himself. And now that he thought about it, the invigorating feeling that encompassed him may be pride.

"Nice." He could push his body. But as well, he'd learned that he'd hit the limit in those runs. Any faster and he would have been in agony. There were no gold medals in Rayce Ryan's future. No more cheering fans. No more endorsements or sponsorship deals. Retirement was a real thing.

Strangely he was okay with that. Because he'd found something more fulfilling.

With an accepting nod he skied over to the hot chocolate vendor. When he went to flash his employee badge for a free drink, he patted his jacket. Where was the tag?

"Sir?" the elder gentleman manning the bar prompted as Rayce patted down his clothes in search of the badge.

It must have fallen off somewhere. Probably when he'd been flying downhill. Ah, well, he had some cash in his pocket. He handed over a bill and received a steaming cup. It was far from the thick fancy stuff the resort served their guests, but the sugar worked the same, rushing through his system with a scream.

When he tossed the cup in a garbage bin and turned around, his path was blocked by three women wearing various shades of pink and purple. Snow bunnies, each with diamonds glinting at their ears and around their necks. Their sort never zipped up their jackets against the chill. How else would anyone notice their bling? They were not here for the skiing; they were here to be seen and to party.

One of them called him by name and asked him for an autograph. She offered the pink sleeve of her jacket and a black Sharpie. The others joined with their sleeves as he whisked his John Hancock down each arm. Despite the crazy good feeling of pride he was still riding, his ego would never tire of the attention. This retired Alpine racer had to take advantage of it when he could.

"We saw you fly down that slope. You're so talented, Rayce. You make it look so effortless."

The last sleeve was signed and she tipped the capped marker under his chin. Her bright pink lips curled into a seductive twist. "You want to join us in our room for something stronger than cocoa?"

"We have so many questions. If you answer them, we'll make it worth your while," she sing-songed coyly.

Rayce's eyebrows rose. The pheromones coming off them in waves were dusted with perfume and lust. He could feel it permeate his skin.

"Sorry, ladies, I don't think my girlfriend wants me answering questions."

"Girlfriend? The media reports say you haven't dated since the accident. That you were incapable of ever…" She shrugged. "You know."

Now that one stung. And it was a cruel cut at his manhood. The media had never reported any such thing!

As the trio laughed wickedly, Rayce pushed away and slid toward the track leading to the resort. They'd started out amiable enough, but when he'd refused their advances, they'd grown just plain mean.

His mood dove from the high of the early morning fresh powder run to the dredges of a bruised ego.

Cassandra found the note after Rayce had slipped from her bed without so much as a kiss goodbye. It sat next to the little drummer boy figurine and read:

Heading out to catch the fresh powder. See you later.

Seriously? He must have snuck out extremely early because the sun was only just now rising. Which meant he'd hit the slopes before they were open to the public. There was a reason the runs weren't open until the sun came up. They were dangerous; what kind of idiot went out on his own to ski in the dark?

She bit her lip and shook her head. Her mom had gone out at midnight all the time, much to her dad's protests. Such reckless abandon had cost her her life. And while Cassandra knew

Rayce was a professional—it didn't matter. Mother Nature cared little about a skier's skill.

Stepping on something with her bare foot, she winced, then bent to pick it up. It was Rayce's employee badge. She turned it over. A fragment of neon green fabric stuck in the rivet clip. It had torn from his jacket.

She glanced out the patio doors. The slopes were busy; it was always a rush to get to the fresh powder in the mornings. She couldn't see the green jacket out there. Had he gone down a slope before the sun had risen and…had trouble?

A terrible darkness clenched Cassandra's throat. She didn't want to think the worst. But as she clasped the badge and the plastic edge dug into her palm, she could only think of avalanches and skiers missing their mark and careening off the slope to crash into rocks or tree trunks.

Or worse.

She swore. Just when she had been so close to accepting the loss of her mother and moving forward, now this had to happen. *If* anything had happened.

No. He was fine. Right? If an avalanche had occurred, the entire mountain would be cleared and emergency protocol would be instituted. Her dad, a member of the search and rescue team, would have alerted her. Rayce was perfectly fine. He knew what he was doing—but why would he torment her like this? He knew about her fears.

With a swallow she closed her eyes and pressed a hand against her thumping heart. Praying nothing had happened. Her heart may never recover!

Wrapping a scarf around her neck, she stepped into her boots and opened her door to find Rayce standing there with his fist up in preparation to knock.

"Rayce!" She grabbed him by the front of his jacket. "Get in here!"

"Glad to see you, too." He wandered inside and turned to

give her a wink. "Is this urgent welcome because you missed me and need to strip me bare right now?"

"What?" Oh. He was talking about the fabulous sex they'd had last night. But she could not get beyond her fear and anger to soften to that pleasure. "No! You are so reckless!"

His jaw dropped open. "Reckless? Me?"

"Yes, you. Going out before the slopes opened? Were there even any patrols out there? It had to have still been dark. Did anyone see you?"

"Cassandra, are you seriously upset because I—a professional skier—wanted to take a few runs on my own? You know I know what I'm doing, right?"

"The slopes don't care if you're a professional or a newbie. You could have been hurt and no one would have known where you were."

"I left you a note. And I—" He patted his jacket and winced.

"And you left without this!" She held up the badge. "Didn't you notice it missing?"

"Not until after I'd finished my run, and then I got distracted because I was shut down by a bunch of snow bunnies with flashy bling and bad attitudes."

"Snow bunnies?" Her shoulders dropped as she exhaled. So that was what he'd been doing? "You were out there flirting while I was in here worrying about you?"

His smile grew. "You were worried about me? Does that mean you care about me?"

"Of course I care about you. But I don't like that you believe you're so expendable. I would think that the accident curbed your reckless need to endanger your life."

"I am not a reckless skier. And that accident was not due to anything but a broken heart. I told you that!" He swore. "Please don't tell anyone about that. It's humiliating. And now you're chastising me as if I'm a child!"

"Only because I would be devastated if you were injured

or...or worse! I can't believe you don't understand that. After my mom—I thought we had something."

"We do. Cassandra, I wasn't thinking about your mother. I realize now that finding that badge must have freaked you out. You thought I was out there with no means to be found if... if anything had happened to me. I'm sorry. I should have—"

"Yeah? Well, my mom is never coming back because she was reckless. I'll never get to hug her again."

Something inside Cassandra closed. All the emotional work she'd put in since Rayce had arrived sluiced away. Her heart went still as the armor fitted back around it.

She lifted her chin and shook her head. The adrenaline junkie standing before gave her a bewildered look. "I can't do this. You're not the man for me, Rayce. I can't handle any more grief right now."

"Cassandra, I'm fine."

When he made a move to embrace her, she put up her hands in protest. "I need someone stable, Rayce. Someone who is willing to stick around Cobalt Lake for me. Someone who will be there for me and who won't take risks."

He sighed heavily. "Skiing is all about the risk," he muttered. "You know that."

She bowed her head and nodded. "Would you please leave?"

"Really? We have to talk about this, Cassandra. I don't want this thing we've started to end. And I'm not a loser like those ladies on the slopes implied. I can't be. But if I lose you..."

She winced. So much was unspoken in that pause. He'd lost a lot. She should be more sensitive to that. But right now, with her fractured heart, she couldn't handle another heartbreak.

She opened the door, holding it for him. "I'm sorry. I can't do this."

With a heavy sigh Rayce walked to the door but paused alongside her. She couldn't look at him. Or she'd fall into his summer sky eyes and melt.

Without a word he took a mangled piece of plastic from his

jacket pocket and handed it to her. Then he left, closing the door behind him.

Cassandra clasped the mistletoe to her chest. Tears spilled down her cheeks. She didn't want him to go. But she didn't know how to ask him to return.

What was she so reluctant about? It couldn't be because of his reckless behavior. She was bigger than that. The man knew what he was doing. And no matter how safe she attempted to keep her world and those in it, she could never monitor everyone all the time. Accidents were just that—accidents.

She had been so close to allowing love into her life.

Leaning against the door, she crushed the mistletoe against her chest and closed her eyes. "I wish you were here, Mom. I need you."

CHAPTER SEVENTEEN

AFTER AN AFTERNOON class with four kids all under ten years old, Rayce helped an intern return the skis and poles to the storage shed. It had been gently snowing for an hour. Thick flakes quieted the atmosphere in a way those who weren't familiar with a snowy season could never understand. Though the slopes were still packed with skiers, it was as though sounds and conversations were muted. Nature insisted on being noticed.

With an eye to a lift on Blackcomb peak, he shook his head. His back, which had been tight and painful all day, warned him to stay grounded. A deep tissue massage and maybe even a soak in the hot tub felt necessary.

Take care of yourself, buddy. It's the right thing to do. Besides, you're retired, remember?

As well, after the argument with Cassandra this morning, he didn't need a streak of pain in his spine to warn him against taking a risky run. If he'd been feeling low after his encounter with the snow bunnies, Cassandra had shoved him even lower with her announcement that she didn't want him in her life.

As he walked slowly toward the employee cabins, he veered off behind a line of pine trees where the snow blanketed a short length of open field. He'd heard some kids out here the other night making snow angels. And despite the falling snow, he could still see impressions of an angel or two as he walked by.

The pale sky fluttered with flakes. He sighed. His two angels were up there. Somewhere.

"Are you out there?" he asked the sky. "In the stars? Do you miss me as much as I miss you?"

Talking to his grandparents helped him to forget the rough parts of life that tended to sneak up on him. Like an injured leg keeping him grounded. Or an upset woman who had told him she didn't want someone as reckless as him in her life.

The fact that Cassandra had talked about needing someone to stick around long term had been buoying. But at the time his heart sunk. Because in the same breath she'd erased *him* from that possibility.

Cassandra had made a choice. And it hadn't been him. She insisted on swimming in her grief and not allowing anyone to dive in to float alongside her. He could have done that. He thought he *had* been doing that. Talking with her. Sharing his grief with her. Being there for her.

If that badge hadn't fallen from his jacket, he'd be in Cassandra's room right now, holding her in his arms, nuzzling his nose into her hair. Being the man she wanted him to be because that was the kind of man *he* wanted to be.

Eyeing an undisturbed patch of thick snow, he turned and fell backward, arms out. He landed with an *oof* and a chuckle because he'd made an old man noise. At the very least, his leg hadn't done anything weird like twitched him headfirst into a snowbank.

Spreading out his legs and arms, he fashioned a snow angel and closed his eyes to the falling flakes. The taste of them melting on his lips reminded him of his snow princess.

Well, she wasn't his anymore, was she? She'd declared he wasn't the guy for her. That he hadn't cared enough about her to not go skiing on his own. At the time he couldn't have known the angst he was causing Cassandra. It hurt his heart to think that something he had done had upset her.

"She's very special," he said to the sky. "I thought we had something. I…don't want to be alone. I'd give it all up if I could have someone in my life. Someone to love."

He'd already lost it all, so he had nothing left to sacrifice. Was that it? He had nothing to offer someone like Cassandra Daniels. No comfy home. Not even a strong proud warrior of a man who could protect her. An injured leg did not make for a hero.

"I could fall in love with her," he confessed to the sky. "I know what love feels like. You guys made me feel safe, happy and loved. Did I ever tell you how much I appreciated what you did for me? Allowing me to go on those ski trips and funding my training. Buying all my gear. I know you weren't rich. But, Gramps, you never said no. And, Grams, you always had a hot meal and a hug for me whenever I returned home from camp or a ski event. I miss you guys!"

The wind shushed through the pines and redirected a glittering sweep of snow across his face. If that hadn't been a message from Gramps, he didn't know what was. The old man had always been funning with him, trying to get him to laugh.

He sat up and brushed the snow from his ski pants. His cap had fallen off and he twisted to pick it up. He traced a finger over the embroidered Cobalt Lake Resort logo. Could this place ever be a home to him?

"I could settle here and be happy," he said to anyone who would listen.

They were listening. They always were.

"The skiing is first class. And… Cassandra."

His snow princess.

He most certainly was not the best guy she could have in her life, he thought to himself. Not smart enough, that was for sure. And too cocky, certainly. Complete opposite of her careful and neat ways. And…reckless.

But she made him believe his heart was not so stupid. Heck, the darn thing had to be smart. It had led him to Cassandra.

Should he beg her to give him another chance? That's how it worked in the movies. Grand gestures seemed to be a thing in a successful romance. Rayce shoved a hand in his pocket. He'd handed Cassandra the mistletoe in a moment of surrender, of forlorn sadness at having been given the boot. There was no easy passage back into her heart now.

But if a passage still existed, he hoped the gate wasn't locked. "Do I dare fall in love?"

The pale sky was serene and quiet. A few snowflakes brushed his face. Kisses from his grandparents. He knew what their answer was.

Now did he have the courage to live up to their expectations? To show them that he could accept love and give love in return?

The next morning Anita dropped off a tray of hot chocolate as Cassandra was stepping out of the shower. "Have a great day!" she called.

"Wait, Anita!"

"Yes?"

Cassandra pulled on a fluffy robe and hustled out to the living room. She knew the sous chef's time was valuable, but now more than ever she was determined to honor the connection with her mom in any way possible.

"I appreciate you bringing me hot chocolate in the morning. I know you always did the same for my mom."

"Your mother and I..." Anita pressed a palm over her chest.

"You two were close," Cassandra confirmed. "She mentioned you often."

Anita nodded, not looking up. Cassandra could sense her nervousness and heard the catch in her breathing. "I cared about your mother. She was very good to me. To all of us. We chatted in the mornings. Sometimes I would take tea with her if I wasn't too busy."

"That's so nice to hear." Cassandra hadn't known that. Perhaps they'd been more than respectful coworkers, friends even. "I have wanted to speak to you about her since, well, since she passed. I want you to know that you were special to her."

"Thank you, Cassandra. She was special to me. I miss her." Now she tilted her head back and sniffed at a tear. "I know it's hard for you now. And seeing your dad with his new fiancée…"

"It took a while for me to accept Faith, but she's good for my dad. And I look forward to meeting my new step siblings. Are you okay, Anita? I mean…have you ever talked to anyone about…?" About Cynthia.

Anita shrugged and shook her head, and that action compelled Cassandra to hug her. Initially Anita resisted, but then she pulled her into a hug that drew tears from Cassandra's eyes as well.

"She is missed," Anita whispered. "But always remembered."

Cassandra stepped back from the hug and swiped a tear from her cheek. "Yes, remembered. Every day."

"But you mustn't let sadness stick to your bones," Anita said with a deep inhale as she settled her shoulders. "That's not good for anyone."

She'd never heard it put in such a manner, but yes, the grief had stuck to her very bones. And it wasn't good for her.

Anita clasped her hand and squeezed. "Thank you. I needed that hug."

"So did I."

"You are so much like Cynthia," she said. "I know she is proud of you. And you know? I think she would like that handsome Rayce Ryan a lot."

Cassandra chuckled. "I think she would, too. And if she didn't, he'd charm his way under her skin one way or another."

"He is a charmer. So, uh…"

"What is it, Anita?"

"I just think he's falling in love with you."

"You do?" Cassandra wasn't at all surprised at such a declaration. Her heart felt much the same about Rayce. But to hear it declared so simply forced her to own that feeling. "I... Well. Rayce is kind. Funny. We have fun together."

So why had she let him leave? Kicked him out, even? She'd told him she couldn't do this. That hadn't been her talking. Not rationally, anyway.

In that moment Cassandra had allowed fear to rise and overwhelm her. She hadn't been acting in accordance with her true feelings. Rayce calmed her and embraced her every quirk, mystery and even her perfectionist tendencies. Her mom would certainly approve.

Was she looking at Rayce as an option for her future? The other options being...no boyfriend, constant work, no social life, all her free time consumed with work-related tasks?

"Anita, do you think I've lost myself in this job?"

"Honestly? You do spend an awful lot of time here. Your mother had her home in Whistler Village to go to after work. Where do you go?"

"Here." Cassandra's shoulders dropped.

The words Anita didn't speak were clear: *where is your life?*

"I do dream about having a home away from work. And about having a relationship with Rayce."

"Your mother would be happy to hear that." Anita took Cassandra's hand and gave it a squeeze. "Take a chance on him. He's a great guy."

Well. Rayce did have his reckless moments. And that would never change. Also he didn't trust his own heart. She hated that he called it stupid. A person should never use that word to describe any part of themselves. The body listened to those words. And if he couldn't get beyond not trusting his heart, that could present a problem should she decide to offer up her own.

But did *she* trust her heart?

"I do want to give him a chance," she said. "Or rather, I did. We had an argument. Oh, I wish my mom were here to talk to. But..." She inhaled and let it all out through her nose. *Let it go.* "I can't thank you enough for letting me talk to you like this. It means a lot."

"Anytime, Cassandra. And don't worry. People argue. It's what we do to learn about one another, yes? And then we realize it's not worth the anger. If you care about him, tell him."

Cassandra nodded as Anita left and closed the door behind her. She did care about Rayce. And she had come down from her anger enough to realize their argument had been hasty and not at all what her heart desired.

So much had happened since Rayce Ryan had set foot in the resort. Her heart had altered in many ways. She had conceded and turned on the tree lights without finding the ornament. Because it had made others happy. And in the process, it had brought a smile to her face. It had lightened her grief to know her mother would have approved.

This was supposed to be the happiest time of the year. A wonderful life! Yet one moment her heart swelled with joy, the next it sank into sadness.

Closing her eyes, she pictured her mom. Pale blond hair and tall lithe figure. Always elegantly dressed and, though Cassandra knew Cynthia Daniels's brain always spun one hundred kilometers an hour and never slowed down, she wore a smile for others and her kindness was always genuine.

"What do you think, Mom? About Rayce? He's special. He makes me laugh. I have fun with him. I forget about work and striving for perfection when I'm with him. I think I could love him."

Silent, she waited in quiet wonder for a vocal reply she knew would never come.

Did she need a sign? She liked hearing how Rayce thought of his grandparents as stars in the sky, always there, watching over him. Maybe her mom was up there, too. And if so…

"I have to follow my heart, with you as my guide."

With a nod she confirmed the conversation with Anita had been worthwhile. Her mom, who never took time to slow down and chat with anyone, had spent time in the mornings over tea with Anita. Another wonderful memory to store in that place in her heart designated for Cynthia Daniels..

Eyeing the tray, with the pot and upside-down teacup, her heart skipped. Would she find a surprise under the cup this morning?

Her heart sank. Probably not. She and Rayce had come to some sort of ending. Much as she regretted it. Was it too late to change things? It couldn't be. The man was good for her heart.

If she wanted Rayce, she had to fight for him.

With another determined nod, Cassandra got dressed. Sitting before the desk to check her emails before she started her rounds, she again eyed the upside-down cup. The suspense was killing her, and yet...

She shook her head and tapped at the keyboard to go through a short list of emails. The RSVPs for the employee Christmas party were pouring in. They always held the gathering a few days before Christmas Day itself, and brought in a celebrity chef and entertainment from Whistler. Secret Santa gifts were exchanged while photos were taken. No one ever missed it.

An email from Faith reminded her she had promised to go wedding dress shopping with her and her daughter after the New Year and gave her a few dates as options. The idea of gaining not one but three new family members had initially shocked her. Then she'd decided it was good for her dad. He needed the companionship, love and attention. And why not? Love did things for a person's heart.

And she was beginning to recognize that change in her own heart.

Typing a reply to Faith to say that any of the dates would work, Cassandra then absently reached for the teacup and turned it over, completely expecting the saucer beneath to be bare—

Cassandra let out a surprised chirp. Sitting on the plate was a small silver star that she knew had come from one of the wreathes in the lobby. Made of resin, it glittered when she tilted it. She recalled again how Rayce thought of his grandparents as stars in the sky.

With a tearful smile she tapped the star. "I haven't given up on you, either, Rayce."

CHAPTER EIGHTEEN

RAYCE SPIED THE white cat scampering over a snowbank and toward the equipment sheds. He took chase. Angling toward the employee cabins, he swung around a tall birch tree only to collide with Cassandra. He caught her by the forearms and steadied her from taking a fall.

"Are you okay?"

"Yes. Thanks for catching me. But what are you doing out here?"

He had not planned to literally run into her after their breakup. They'd both said terrible things. Had put their hearts out there. And it hadn't ended well. He owed her an apology. More than that, he wanted to talk until they moved beyond the argument and back into the trust and empathy they'd created.

Look at him, feeling all, well…the feelings!

"I'm on the trail of a wayward cat," he said. "You?"

"Same. I think it went that way." She pointed toward one of the vehicle sheds.

He bent to study the snow. "You are correct. Tracks!" He grabbed her hand and led her quickly across the snow. To talk now or wait until the moment was right? The moment might never be right. But what if he made the wrong move? Again!

A *crash* from inside the shed averted his attention. "Let's get that cat! I'm sure it went into the shed."

"I don't know how it could get inside. The building should be locked and…"

As they neared the shed, both were shocked to see one of the windowpanes was broken. Nearby on the ground lay a broken pine branch. Evidence that it hadn't been a purposeful break-in.

"That's a very crafty cat." Rayce inspected the tracks that leaped from the ground and landed on the windowsill to disappear inside. He peered through the broken window. "Here, kitty, kitty!"

"Let's check inside." Cassandra led him around the corner to the front door where she entered the digital code.

Inside the open-beam structure sat a fleet of the resort's vehicles. A Jeep and a four-wheeler were parked on one side, as well as some of the facility equipment. There was no need to flick on a light switch because daylight beamed through the half-dozen glass ceiling panels.

Rayce scanned around the room filled with assorted vehicles and his gaze landed on the scatter of broken glass. "You got a broom in here?"

"Don't worry about it." Cassandra inspected the glass that had fallen inside. "I'll send the groundskeeper out to clean it up and repair the window. We'll use the fallen branch in the fireplace tonight."

"You've always got everything under control. I adore that about you."

"Hmm, well, I do fall apart on occasion."

He opened his arms and gestured with his fingers. "Come here. Fall into me."

In her moment of reluctance, he watched as caution played over Cassandra's face, only to quickly wriggle into something familiar and much more welcome: trust. Cassandra plunged into his embrace and the two kissed in the dim quiet. Broken in different ways, they had learned to understand themselves through one another.

"You make the world kinder," she said to him.

"I don't know about that. We need to talk, Cassandra. I'm sorry."

"I am, too."

"Yeah? Well, hear me out." He exhaled a cloud of breath. "I'm willing to risk rejection for the prize. The crowd can boo all they like. If I feel what I'm doing is good, that's all that matters."

"What does that mean?"

"I like it here at the resort, Cassandra. I'm going to talk to your dad about staying on through the summer."

"Rayce, that's wonderful. We'd love to have you for as long as you're willing. I know my dad would agree. But what prompted your change of heart? I thought you had intended to train...?"

"That was boasting, Cassandra. It'll never happen. And you know? I don't want that anymore. The competition and relentless training? That was the first part of my life. Retirement feels right."

"It does?"

"It does. So now? Here? It feels like a new beginning. One I want to follow to the end."

"I'm proud of you."

He studied her face, beaming at him beneath her pink pompom cap. In Cassandra's eyes he never felt like he had to prove himself. Yet hearing her say she was proud of him felt like a million sparklers had just been lit in his body. He absolutely hummed with a jittery excitement. "Really?"

"Yes. You're following your heart. A very smart heart that may make mistakes sometimes, and then other times makes some very good decisions. It's not stupid. It's real. We all get hurt, Rayce. I'm sad that you were so devastated by what you thought was your heart, but you know, maybe that was the way life intended your path to go."

"Those are profound thoughts. I'm not much for destiny and

all that fate jazz. I just…" He had to go for the gold if he wanted this to work. The anticipation of the moment felt as bright as his inner sparklers. Could she see his nervous excitement? NASA space satellites must be able to see it. "There's another reason I want to stay here. It's because of you."

"Oh, Rayce, I…"

"I know what you said about me being reckless. I promise to do a badge check every hour. To never be off your radar."

"Thank you, for that reassurance. I shouldn't have gotten so upset. I know you are a professional. You can take care of yourself. It's just…"

Just what? Some of the sparklers extinguished. She couldn't reject him. Please?

"Mother Nature doesn't care how skilled or smart we are," he said. "I get it, Cassandra. And I want to stay safe. Because you matter to me. And I'd hate to know something I did caused you any worry or pain."

He kissed her. First on her cheek, then on her lips. Her lashes fluttered against his nose as he tilted up to kiss her on the forehead. Marking her indelibly. Making a claim that could only be interpreted by his heart. He took her gloved hand and placed it on his chest. She probably couldn't feel his heartbeat through his jacket, but who knew? Every piece of him felt turned up to eleven. And he had to make her understand that feeling.

"This place feels like it could be a home to me," he confessed. "That's part of what I really want."

"It can be your home."

"I don't mean a little cabin behind the resort. I mean like moving back to Whistler, becoming a member of the community. Doing…life stuff."

"Life stuff?"

"Like owning a home and car and having a family. Making a career of teaching others how to ski."

"You have big plans."

"They are small compared to what I have with you right now. The other part of what I want is… It's you, Snow Princess. Do you think we can continue this relationship? I promise I won't break your heart."

"You don't need to make any such promise. I shouldn't have yelled at you like I did." Now she pressed both her palms to his chest and considered her words before finally saying, "I've been leery, too. Trying to relax my tight control on everything, including letting go of my grief. But I had a talk with my mom today."

"You did? I talked to my grandparents earlier."

"I know you were thinking about them."

She…knew? He gave her a wondering gape.

"I got the star under my teacup." She kissed him. "You were talking to your two stars up above, weren't you?"

"I was," he said in awe of her understanding. She got him. And knowing that made him feel even better than knowing she was proud of him.

"Mom would want me to enjoy life," she said. "To put my heart out there. For someone to catch."

He kissed her hard. Deeply. And in the process transferred those shimmering sparkles he experienced to her. Clutching her to him, Rayce whispered, "Caught you."

"Don't ever let me go."

"Promise I won't."

A sudden cloud of dust fluttered down from the rafters. "That's weird."

"Kitty!" Rayce called repeatedly.

She followed his sightline as he scanned overhead along the rafters.

"I think the critter is up there—watch out!" He grabbed her about the shoulders and tugged her aside.

A falling cat snarled through the air. A box crashed three feet from where they stood, tearing cardboard and scattering the contents in a tangle of Christmas tree lights, tinsel and plastic lighting clips.

Secure in Rayce's arms, Cassandra hugged him tightly. Her rescuing hero. Who simply wanted a home. A place for his heart to be happy.

The cat *meow*ed and wandered to the scatter of old Christmas supplies. Sniffed at it. Then looked up to Cassandra and Rayce. Its next *meow* sounded insistent.

"I think it's okay," Cassandra said. "Seems to be walking on all fours without trouble."

Rayce let out a heavy exhale and his embrace loosened. "Whew! I didn't want you to get hurt."

"I'm okay, Rayce." She kissed him. "You made sure of that. I always feel safe in your arms."

She laughed a little because speaking her emotions surprised her and at the same time felt better than right—it felt…marvelous.

Rayce took a deep breath, and said, "Cassandra. Would you be my girlfriend?"

"Yes." She smiled.

"Yes?"

She nodded. "You need more than that?"

Meow!

He looked over her shoulder. "That darn cat is getting into the fallen—Cassandra, look!"

He took her hand and plunged to the floor over the tangle of lights. Cassandra plucked up the star made from twigs. A twist of silver tinsel had been twined around the sticks and glued here and there. And in the center was the photo of her and her mom.

"I can't believe it." She pressed the ornament to her heart. Tears spilled down her cheeks. "It's almost as if the cat led us here."

The cat, seemingly proud of its accomplishment, *meow*ed happily.

Cassandra had just been given a hug from Heaven by her mother.

* * *

The next morning after Rayce left for an appointment with a guest, Cassandra ordered a few things from a local craft shop. Later in the afternoon, using the delivered supplies, she put the finishing paint touches to an ornament. It had been years since she'd felt the crafty urge, but this had been necessity.

"A little odd looking, but it's the thought that counts. Right?" she said to herself.

Tucking the ornament in a box, she then picked up the star made of twigs and studied the photo of her and her mom. "Thanks for leading me to this, Mom. You've made this a perfect Christmas. And I think I can do the same for someone whose one wish is to have a home."

That evening the staff met in the lobby for Christmas carols and a festive Christmas cookie exchange with the guests. Heading toward the party, Cassandra could already hear the carols jingling down the hallway. The scent of cinnamon and pine enticed her further, and the jingle of bells brightened her smile.

She saw Rayce leaning against the reception desk, wearing a sweater emblazoned with the face of the kid who had been left home alone, palms to his cheeks as he realized his situation. She gestured and got his attention. He beamed at the sight of her. As did her heart.

He strolled over and she tugged him around the corner away from the crowd.

"What's up, Snow Princess? I figured you'd get into all the singing and merrymaking."

"I do. Does that comment mean you don't?"

He shrugged. "It looks like fun, but I don't have any cookies for the exchange. Feels wrong to participate."

"Oh, please, Anita brings enough for everyone. Besides, you're the little drummer boy. You bring your charm and kindness to the event. It's your talent."

"Really?" He shrugged sheepishly. "I can work with that."

"I love the sweater. You never did tell me where you found that figurine."

"Eh. It's sort of a good luck charm I've carried with me through the years. Along with the drummer boy."

"I know you claimed the drummer boy after you gave it to me. You can have Kevin back, too, if you want him."

"How about we share them?"

"I like that. I seem to recall Kevin got a happily-ever-after ending?"

"He did. His family returned and he was once again safe in his home." Rayce sighed. "Corny, but it gets me every time."

"You'll find your home one of these days," she encouraged.

"I know I will. Did you bring the ornament to hang on the tree?"

"Of course." She showed him the star. "But first." She handed him the small box. "I have an ornament for you. You can hang it on the tree or keep it for your own tree."

"I've never had a tree…" He accepted the box.

"Someday you will."

He kissed her. "I love you, Snow Princess."

The announcement landed in her heart like the warmest winter kiss. True words, spoken clearly and with meaning. They echoed her own heartfelt beliefs. Cassandra nodded eagerly. "I love you, too."

For a moment the two held each other's gazes, their smiles growing. Love zinged back and forth between their eyes, their smiling mouths, their beating hearts. A kiss was necessary. Slow, soft and sweet. Didn't matter if the crowd witnessed this wondrous sign of affection. This was their marvelous kiss. No mistletoe required.

After a sigh and a bow of his forehead to hers, Rayce jiggled the box she'd given him. "So what do we have here?" He pulled out the tiny resin model of the Cobalt Lake Resort that they sold in the gift shop.

Before his smile dropped, Cassandra rushed to point out the

detail she'd added. "It's our resort, but look there. The little man standing in the front?"

He studied it curiously. "Oh, yeah. He's wearing a green jacket."

"That's you! I painted the figure. Rayce, the resort is your home now."

He looked to her, his eyes going watery.

"You are always welcome here, in Whistler and…in my heart."

"I don't know what to say." He clutched the ornament against his chest. "It feels like a home. Especially when I'm with you. Thank you. This is the nicest gift I've ever been given."

She kissed him and then tapped his lips. "Oh, I've got a better one for you later. When we're in bed."

A single eyebrow zipped upward.

With dramatic flair, Cassandra pulled something out of her pants pocket and brandished it between them.

"Are you kidding me?" He studied the crumbled plastic mistletoe. "That thing has certainly gotten a lot of good use."

"Are you going to kiss me again or marvel over a silly piece of plastic?"

He didn't need any more motivation than her flutter of lashes.

"You've changed my life," he said after the kiss. "I love you."

"I'm so glad you came to Cobalt Lake Resort. You helped me to find a place in my heart for my mom's memory. And I have another place right here." She patted her chest.

"What's that for?"

"For you of course. You can stay there as long as you like."

"In that case me and my figurines are moving in."

"You'll all fit. My heart is your home." She tapped the ornament she'd made for him. "Shall we hang these on the tree?"

"Definitely."

They snuck in behind the guests who were singing in harmony to a Christmas song that Kathy played on her portable keyboard. Cookies were munched and hot chocolate sipped. Her dad, clad in an outrageous Christmas sweater decorated with tinsel and real flashing lights, stood across the room with an arm around Faith, who wore a matching sweater. He winked at her and nodded.

Lured by the twinkling lights on the Christmas tree, Cassandra led Rayce around to the front of it. He studied the pine boughs filled with tinsel and ornaments, and then hung his ornament in the front. "How's that?"

"I'll notice that little green jacket every time I walk by."

"You did get my charming good looks right." He tapped the tiny man. "Your turn," he said.

With a squeeze of his hand and a reassuring nod from him, Cassandra placed the star ornament front and center. Then she stepped back and into Rayce's arms. The place she felt most comfortable. And loved.

The memories she held of her mother were now safe in her heart. And this new memory of love and acceptance was exactly where it belonged. Now everything was...

"Marvelous," she announced.

EPILOGUE

ON BOXING DAY Cassandra glided slowly down the slope with Rayce by her side. She'd chosen a gentle run for her first time on skis in almost two years. But after a pep talk and a kiss from her boyfriend, confidence had flooded her system. And she felt sure her mom was watching her from above. Another star in the sky twinkling next to Rayce's grandparents.

Rayce skied closer and reached for her hand. "You're doing it, Snow Princess!"

"I am! I missed this so much!"

"Let's ski together every day," he said.

"Works for me!"

They neared the bottom of the slope and with a twist of her hips Cassandra came to a stop, followed by Rayce. He tugged off his gloves and leaned over to kiss her. His wink sparkled brighter than her heart. Oh, she'd been captured by his eyes. And his incredibly smart heart.

"I have a crazy idea," he said.

"Does it involve more cat-wrangling?"

"Hey, Caspar adopted me after the incident in the shed. He won't leave my cabin. I know it's because of my handsome good looks."

"Naturally. It couldn't be anything but." How she adored his self-effacing slips into ego. It was who he was, and she wouldn't wish him to change.

"But taking in a stray cat is not the crazy idea."

"Do tell?"

He took her hand and bowed his forehead to hers. Standing there for a moment, they shared the quiet stillness of the crisp winter day. And when Cassandra started to ask about his idea, he suddenly kissed her forehead and asked, "Do you want to look for a house together in Whistler?"

The question didn't even startle her. In fact it felt like the perfect next step in her dream that had come true.

"You mean a *home*?" she asked.

His smile beamed. "Most definitely. A home."

* * * * *